Protector of the
REFUGEE
PLANET

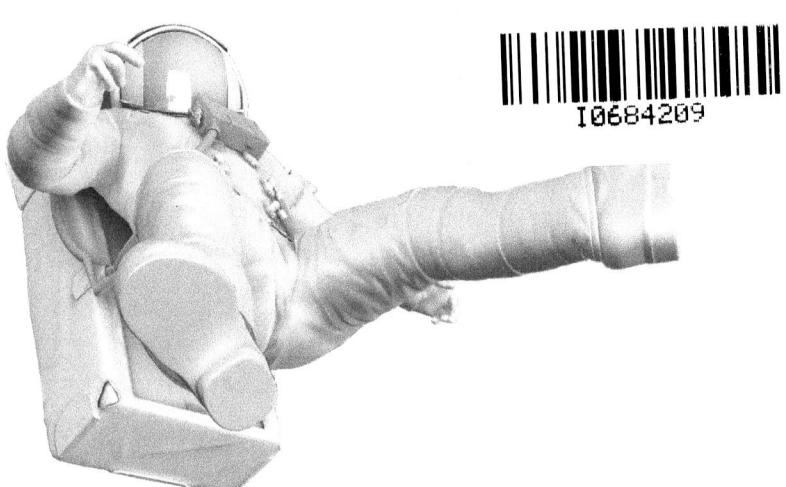

Dennis Mahoney

Stonehenge
Circle Press

Published by Stonehenge Circle Press

Printed in the United States of America

First Edition: August 2017

10 9 8 7 6 5 4 3 2 1

ISBN 978-1-68012-741-6

Cover and book design by Andrew Benzie

I dedicate this book to my wife, Diane,
in gratitude for years of love and support.

CHAPTER ONE

EIGHT AGAINST TWO, AND WHY
IT WASN'T FAIR TO THE EIGHT

"The Community of Protectors shall be divided into two branches, rangers and scholars, both of which shall serve humanity wherever it may spread in the Galaxy."
—D.F. Nathaniel

Steven loitered beneath a street lamp in a neighborhood decent people avoided. They avoided the entire planet if they had a choice. Volcanoes pocked its surface, and the air stank of sulfur.

Men and women with money enough to get roaring drunk, but without funds to abandon Medusa-Four for a better world, trickled by on their way to the saloons. Steven spoke to none of them, other than to refuse the frequent request for a hand-out. He waited for a street dealer to happen along and peddle him a narcotic that would turn his brain to jelly.

Steven's cheek felt a stab. That'll raise a red bump, he thought, as he squished the tuba fly munching on his skin. The flies represented the pinnacle of Medusa-Four's native life. After a billion years of nothing to eat but weaker insects, they'd taken to human flesh like kids to candy.

"Hey, big guy," a voice called. "Looking to score a kilo of delirium dust?"

Steven perspired beneath the coat that covered him from his shoulders to his ankles. He hated the temperature on Medusa-Four, sweltering like the deserts of Earth. But he needed to wear the coat while he bargained with the dealer. "Maybe I'll buy. If it's top quality. I'm tired of you lowlifes playing me for a sucker."

The dealer stepped into the light, and Steven detected a crooked body hunched on the wood planks of the sidewalk. His new acquaintance must have spent years digging up the raw materials to manufacture delirium dust. The mines had a way of warping a person's skeleton. The dealer pried open a tin box, revealing a glob of black mush. The stuff might be mistaken for something a dog would leave behind on a patch of grass. But it couldn't be that. Medusa-Four had neither dogs nor grass.

The man's grin set Steven to wondering how human teeth could turn such a shade of green without falling out. "I'm partial to kids with spirit," the man said. "So, for you, I'll shave ten percent off the going rate. And it's highest grade. Within five minutes, no pains and no worries. Try a hit, if you don't believe me."

Steven took a pinch between his thumb and forefinger, sniffed, and gagged. He touched a single grain to his tongue. "I don't need to take a hit. How much?"

The dealer's eyes lit up with greed. "Per kilo? You got a choice, kid. We'll break it into packets, a gram each, for a thousand credits, or we'll give it to you in one lump for eight hun'erd."

Steven had heard enough. He slapped the box out of the dealer's hand. The contents spilled onto the sidewalk. He stomped with the heel of his boot, grinding the glob into the rotting planks until it was even more disgusting than before.

"Fool!" the dealer said. "My Warlord's gonna string you up by your big toes and harvest your body parts to get that thousand credits."

Steven shed the coat, letting it drop on top of the mess of delirium dust. Before, he had hidden his physique, for fear of scaring the drug peddler away. Now, he showed it off for purposes of intimidation. The muscles of his arms and chest threatened to burst through a shirt that squeezed him like a second skin. "Shut up," he said. "Now it's my turn to give a choice. You can fester in a prison off-world. Ten years, unless we forget you exist, in which case you'll rot there till you die. Or you can lead me to the Warlord snake who supplies you with the delirium dust."

"You're a Protector, ain't you," the dealer sputtered. Steven carried the title with pride, but from this man's lips, it came across like an insult. "I should've guessed from your height." He whipped a zeta-ray pistol from a side pocket and leveled it at Steven. "My pals told me you freaks have been harassin' us hard-workin' businessmen."

Steven wasn't twenty yet. He'd never before faced the barrel of a pistol that wasn't part of a training exercise. More experienced members of the Community of Protectors had warned him his first time would be scary. They were right, but he had to carry on. "Did they also tell you…"

"Yeowch!"

"… that a Protector gets cranky when some lowlife points a gun at his nose?" Steven's right hand squeezed his enemy's gun-wrist, while his left hand swept down in a blur to snatch the weapon. He crumbled the pistol inside his fist, watching the bits float to the ground in the feeble gravity, and mingle with the dirt of the road. Overcoming a deadly weapon wasn't so difficult after all, he thought. Easier than he'd imagined.

The dealer rubbed his gun hand with his other. "You broke my fingers."

Steven scratched the recording chip tacked to his ear, camouflaged as a freckle. Satisfied it was turned on, and would preserve an audio record of his performance, he continued with the sting.

"If I'd wanted to break your fingers, I would have. They're in one piece, for now. But fingers have been known to fall off from intense cold in the prison my Community operates. It's on a frozen dwarf planet called Mordred. So far out at the fringe of our system, you won't be able to tell your own sun from a lightning bug. I got orders to nail a scumbag we can ship there tonight. Any scumbag." He shrugged. "Nothing personal. It's sort of a quota. If I can't find a Warlord, I'll settle for a second-stringer like you."

The dealer stammered. "If I—if I rat out the chief, his boys—they'll hunt me like a rabbit."

"So that's my problem... how? But lucky for you, I have a warm heart. If you help us capture a Warlord, we'll grant passage to any planet of your choosing, within reason. If you don't cooperate, you get a one-way trip to Mordred."

Steven put his hand over his mouth. He pretended to cough, to disguise the way he couldn't keep from smiling at the sound of his bluff. He knew full well the Community never wasted Mordred's scarce cells on street thugs.

The dealer trembled. "Well—there's this dive where my boss has been known to hang out some nights. I can take you there, but I can't guarantee nothin'."

Steven dropped his hands to his sides and formed them into fists. "Now we're getting someplace. If you don't want to spend the next ten Earth-standard years tromping on frozen carbon dioxide, you'd better pray your boss is there tonight. We'll check this dump out, but first I need to notify my leader. She's meaner than a scorpion. When you meet her, you'll thank the Lord I found you before she did."

A purple jewel, the size of a grape, nestled on a golden band that circled Steven's left index finger. He raised his arm and twisted the bauble a half-turn to send a silent signal. "Jan?" he spoke into the jewel. "Meet me at the signal's source. We stand a good chance of bagging a Warlord within the hour."

The two men waited in silence for a minute. Then, an even-sided triangle dipped out of the sky, with a grim-faced woman at the controls. Steven curled his lip in distaste over the flyer's design. It was nothing but a gray slab with a niche carved in the middle for passengers. His own preference ran to sleek flyers with bright colors and racing stripes.

The pilot ordered the flyer's computer to set her down across the street, while the dealer eyed her from a distance. "Could be a looker if she'd fix herself up," he whispered.

Steven had to agree. He noticed Jan's faded hair, hanging in limp strands across her neck, and middle-aged skin, bare of make-up. The Community's warm-planet uniform, a T-shirt and matching brown dungaree pants, drooped two sizes too large. "She never stresses over her appearance," he said, keeping his voice low. "Says her natural looks don't get in the way of apprehending lowlifes."

Jan crossed the street and positioned herself between the two men, towering over the dealer's crooked body. She examined him from top to bottom, and then frowned, as if he was a piece of merchandise that disappointed her. "What's going on? We were bent on nailing a Warlord tonight. If this bozo is a Warlord, I'm a sugarplum fairy."

"I never said he was a Warlord. But he can lead us to a saloon where his boss hangs out. I promised him a ticket to another stellar system if he delivers."

"You did what?" Jan's eyes went wide. "Man, you're softer than a creampuff. Any creep who'd peddle narcotics to little kids doesn't deserve a ticket to anywhere but the lowest ring of hell. I would've told him he'd better trot out his boss, or we'll haul his butt into deep space and toss him out an airlock, naked as a newborn."

"Yeah, I guess… I guess… um… um…" What was his next line? Steven had forgotten. In front of his supervisor! In his mind, he went over the script, and still he couldn't remember how he was supposed to respond after Jan accused him of being "soft." He froze, as the recording chip preserved the awkward silence for his superiors to judge him by.

He'd pulled off the bluff so well up to that point. He'd recited his lines exactly as he'd rehearsed them, and his threats, no matter how absurd, had appeared to strike terror into the dealer's heart. The man had even believed the nonsense about the Protectors having a quota. But now, the person Steven most needed to impress was observing, and he'd stumbled. He pictured the word "UNSATISFACTORY" plastered in bold red letters on Jan's next report to Headquarters.

After a lull that lasted an eternity to Steven, or about twelve seconds in real time, Jan rescued him with a prompt. "On the other hand, you did make a promise."

The word "promise" triggered his memory. He recited with fresh confidence. "I guess you're right, but see, I made a promise. It'd be wrong to break it." There. He'd recited the line.

Jan glared at the dealer, and went on with the charade. "Oh, fine, lead us to your Warlord, and we'll fix it so you can live out your sorry existence on some other world, safe from your ilk's retribution. Only because my partner promised. Now, get in that flyer and direct us to the saloon, before I come to my senses and handle this my way. I hear exposure to the vacuum of space is a grisly way to die."

Steven stifled his laughter. Jan talked a convincing bluff about exterminating her opponents, but he knew she would do nothing of the sort. In the first place, the Community of Protectors had rules against taking human life. In the second place, she was too soft-hearted. He had witnessed her put up with insect feet dancing on her breakfast sooner than squish a tuba fly.

"We won't need your flyer," the dealer said. "My Warlord's a few blocks that way." He pointed to his left.

Jan gave the dealer a shove. The two Protectors and their prisoner clomped along the sidewalk planks. The street lamps grew brighter as they crossed into the town's more populous sector. Steven saw, by their light, that the man's eyes had a glassy stare.

"You're hooked on delirium dust yourself, aren't you?"

"Ain't everybody hooked who lives on this sewer of a world?"

"You exaggerate," Steven said, though, he had to admit, not by much. "Why do you do this to yourself, man? You gotta know that garbage'll kill you."

"You wanna preach, kid? Find a church. You think I was always a successful businessman?"

"I don't think you're one now."

"So that's your opinion." The dealer turned away and talked into the empty air. "You grew up on that giant Protector home world, where they treat you like some kinda royalty. Me? Before I got promoted to sales, I worked forty feet below ground, diggin' up those clumps of clay they use to make the dust. You try sloggin' through muck in those mines for eighteen hours a day. See if you wouldn't swallow somethin' to make your stinkin' life more tolerable."

*   *   *

The dealer halted before a shack that looked like every other saloon in a cluster of establishments that served no purpose other than to intoxicate their customers. Most worlds would have been banned them within a kilometer of a school The outside walls, cobbled from rotting boards, made Steven wonder if their owners had ever heard of paint. Jan stepped over four men who appeared to be passed out on the sidewalk, and pushed open the door.

Music blared through the stench of alcohol. Two dozen customers, at various stages of drunkenness, lounged at tables in groups of two and three and four. One man had a table to himself. Rolls of flab lapped over the edges of his belt, as he toyed with a stein of rust-colored liquid. He wore the latest fashion imported by freighter from Paris, a blue jacket woven from the fibers of seven planets, with coolants built into the threads.

The dealer broke into a satisfied grin and rushed over to the man in the blue jacket. "I brung 'em, Mr. Crumm," he said. "Two of 'em. Just like you told me."

Steven looked to Jan for direction. His instructions said nothing about what they were supposed to do next if they discovered that, all along, the Warlord had wanted them to find him.

Mr. Crumm nodded. "Fine work, Maxwell. You'll receive your reward, with a bonus." He turned to Jan, flashing a smirk Steven longed to slam a fist through. "I'm beginning to think you Protectors aren't as smart as everyone says you are. If you were, my man Maxwell couldn't have tricked you into following him onto my turf." He folded his hands on the table. "Did you think I didn't expect you to try to frighten one of my people into betraying me? Or that I wouldn't stay a step ahead of you, and turn your clumsy attempt at a sting to my advantage? Don't try to escape. Those four derelicts you stepped over outside are awake and sober, and they are hiding zeta-ray rifles where they can grab them. They'll discharge the rifles on my command."

The sight of Mr. Crumm triggered a wave of revulsion that drove Steven almost to nausea. He'd detested the Warlords since the first time he saw a nine-year-old girl in a stupor from chewing delirium dust. The Warlords grew rich by exporting their drug to other worlds, but, to Steven, what they did to their own people was worse. What kind of a man would harvest the raw material for his drug empire with the labor of slaves, exterminating them like tuba flies if they tried to escape? Could such vermin be considered a man at all?

Steven whispered to Jan. "Is that creep even human?"

Mr. Crumm snatched a pellet from behind his ear, and held it between his thumb and forefinger. "This device conveyed your entire conversation with my man out on the street." He dropped the pellet on the table and called in a loud voice. "It's time for you to come in."

The four men they'd seen outside lumbered into the saloon, toting zeta-ray rifles. Four more like them joined from another room. All were in their thirties with massive builds and stupid grins. To a man, they had the same glassy stare Steven had seen on Maxwell. Good, he thought. Their addiction to delirium dust would slow their reflexes when the confrontation turned physical. Stay calm, he told himself, and don't be unnerved by a little thing like a lethal weapon pointed in your face. The music stopped in the middle of a tune. The customers, the bartender, and Maxwell edged out the door.

The Warlord drained half his stein in one gulp, and let out a belch that could be heard on the street. "You're going to show me to your base," he demanded. "Take me there, you live. Refuse, you die. Simple as that."

"Take you to our base?" Jan mimicked the raspy voice. She faced Mr. Crumm, but focused her eyes on the rifles. "So you can rain down zeta bombs on the other members of our Protector team?"

Mister Crumm's lower lip twisted. "Your call. Their lives or yours."

"I'm astonished," Jan said.

The Warlord chuckled. "You're surprised because you thought we'd be too scared by your reputation to fight back?"

"No—that isn't it. We knew you wouldn't let your empire crumble without a struggle." She gave Steven a wink, which he took as a signal she was about to bring the discussion to a close. "I meant, I'm astonished a man of your achievements would be so dumb as to believe eight rifle-toting morons would be any match for two unarmed Protectors."

The Warlord drummed his fingers on the table and sighed. "I can see that I'm going to have to demonstrate I'm serious." He nodded to one of the gunmen. "Take out her sandy-haired sidekick."

It would take a second for the rifles to build up enough charge to spit out a decent blast of energy, and another second for the gunmen to squeeze the triggers. Experienced Protectors often advised younger ones that two seconds could be as useful as an hour, if you knew how to use them. Steven was about to find out if they had told the truth. If not, his career would be over before it had started. He dove.

Jan screamed, "Now!" He was already in mid-leap. He slammed into one gunman's kneecaps at the same moment the rifle unleashed a burst of zeta-radiation. The blast sliced through the ribs of another assassin who chanced to be in the wrong place.

Steven felt a stab of pity for the injured men, then shoved his sympathies aside until he'd have time for them. He could arrange for medical attention after the brawl was over. Until then, he'd reduced by two the number of enemies who could threaten them further. Two down and six to go. The man who fired the shot writhed on the floor, clutching his left knee, no more of a danger than the stooge he'd accidentally hit.

Steven looked to see if Jan needed help. She dashed between two attackers who were taking aim. Her hand chopped down on one man's wrist, sending his rifle clattering to the floor. She paused for the blink of an eye, and her boot rose up and kicked the weapon from the other man's grip. Impressive, Steven thought. Two at once, and she hadn't so much as glanced at either opponent. Later, he'd ask her how she did that.

He hoisted an enemy over his head and body-slammed him into another attacker, and then ducked to dodge a zeta-ray burst passing over his head. He punched his fist into the face of the attacker who'd fired the most recent shot, and the man buckled over backwards. Two more rifles littered the floor, dropped by the men he'd just taken down. He crunched the heel of his boot onto their firing mechanisms, mashing them until each weapon was no more dangerous than a pair of popsicle sticks glued into the shape of a gun.

The man who'd been body-slammed rose and swung his fist. Steven could have blocked, but saw no point in defending against an assault he'd barely notice. The blow glanced off his chest. He picked up the man and threw him to the floor a second time, a little harder than before.

He twisted and saw Jan slam two more gunmen to the floor. She ripped the radiation cartridges from their rifles, and warned, "Stay down or we start fracturing limbs." Steven knew she would never have the heart to follow through on the threat, leaving him to wonder if there were any limit to how preposterous her bluffing could get. "Nice work" she said as she surveyed the men Steven had brought down, high praise from a woman who was stingy with compliments. He smiled, imagining the five-star rating he would get on her report to Headquarters.

Jan tossed him three grappling ropes from her shoulder bag. "Here—these'll finish the job. I count at least two who already have no hope of walking under their own power, so we'll divide the other six between us for trussing."

The cables were hard as steel and flexible as yarn. Steven coiled them around the arms and legs of a man on the floor, while Jan did the same. The material tightened under its own power, a handy invention that did away with the need to fashion knots. Too bad, Steven thought. He'd led his class in knot-tying, and would have loved to show off his talent.

The number of thugs with the ability to move had dwindled to four. They scrambled to their feet and bolted towards Steven. He braced for what he assumed would be a mass attack. Only four, all weaponless. Not much of a challenge. But they sped past him. They reached the saloon's exit at the same moment, where they proved the truth of Newton's theorem that multiple solid objects cannot occupy the same space at the same moment. Steven cringed as he watched the collision.

He ambled over to make sure their injuries from the fight hadn't gotten worse from the collision. They had tried to kill him, but that was no reason not to do the gentlemanly thing. At the sight of his outstretched hand, they untangled their limbs and dashed outside.

"A cheetah with its tail on fire couldn't catch 'em," Jan said. "Let 'em go. They aren't who we came for."

The Warlord drained the final drops from his stein. Jan dangled a grappling rope from the far end of the room. "Now it's your turn, Crumm. We've reserved a cell on the planet Mordred with your name engraved over the door."

Steven wondered if that could be true. He'd never been to Mordred.

Crumm snickered. "I'll grant you the first round, but the second belongs to me." He pulled back his sleeve to uncover a band around his pudgy wrist, and tapped a green button. Three more buttons circled the band, making a row of green, blue, red, and yellow. The buttons could seem pretty, like baubles on a bracelet, but only to someone who didn't know their purpose.

Steven had seen a deactivated sample of the same product during a classroom demonstration of weapons favored by cowards. Press the first button, as Crumm had already done, and a shield of energy would envelope the wearer. Press the next three, one after another, and ripples of radiation would flow in every direction, like circles from a stone hitting water. The ripples would incinerate anything in range with a pulse, with the exception of the weasel who'd pressed the buttons. That person would be free to view the carnage, untouched, from the safety of the energy field.

The Warlord tapped the blue button. Two more taps would turn the radiation deadly. Jan, further away, would never be able to reach the bracelet in time. Steven lunged, and crashed onto a table that smashed under his weight. He swept aside the wreckage, and lunged again, closing the gap in one leap, aided by the puniness of the gravity. He drew back his arm as the Warlord's fingers moved in a blur, tapping the red button. Steven thrust his fist at the same time the Warlord grazed the final button, the yellow one. His fist touched flesh just below the Warlord's rib cage, smashing blubber against whatever vital organs happened to be on the other side.

The chair toppled and spilled the Warlord onto the floor. Blood pooled in the spot where Steven's fist had made contact. Jan rushed over to examine the damage. Steven, from behind her, looked over the body for breathing or movement. He would have settled for a twitch, but saw nothing to convince him he hadn't just killed a man.

"Crumm's got to be alive," he insisted, as if saying the thing would somehow make it true. "Protectors don't kill people in brawls."

Jan looked up from the body. "Not usually. But one Protector just did."

Steven had no idea what he was supposed to do next. His teachers and mentors had taught him many lessons, but they'd never told him how to behave after he took a life. Why should they? He wasn't supposed to kill, according to their highest Precept.

"I guess this means poor Maxwell won't get paid," Jan said. She popped open the bracelet and deactivated the insides, wire by wire, then pulled an audio-link communicator from the Warlord's pocket. "I'd better notify the police. It's time for them to do something more useful than shooing drunks off the street, for a change."

"Hey, you, big guy," called the thug who had first tried to shoot Steven. He was sprawled on the floor, his right leg useless and smeared with blood. "Crumm would've murdered us all, with no more remorse than if he'd swatted a cluster of tuba flies. I know you didn't stop him for my sake, but thanks just the same. It wouldn't hurt you to thank him too, ma'am. He was a hero."

Jan finished her call to the police. "Wrong twice," she replied. "He did stop Crumm for your sake. And in our branch of the Protectors, we never thank our brothers and sisters for doing what any of us would do for the others. However, we accept your gratitude."

Two police officers in matching orange uniforms arrived at the scene. "Who's responsible?" one of them asked as he took in the aftermath.

Jan answered. "The two guys who are hogtied and the two who are crippled—they work for Crumm, or did until a few minutes ago. My partner and I took them down. Arrest them for assault with a deadly weapon, and later I'll fill in the blanks on your forms. This man here..." She pointed to Steven. "He killed the Warlord, bare-handed."

Steven looked at the floor to avoid meeting the eyes of the two officers. Wasn't she going to mention that he'd saved the life of everyone in the room? It seemed logical to claim self-defense when admitting to police officers that you'd killed a man. But apparently, that detail was of little consequence to the authorities on Medusa-Four. Both officers pumped his hand and praised him for ridding the Galaxy of such a villain. He feared the Guidance Committee, back at Headquarters, wouldn't be so congratulatory, after they found out he'd violated the Community's highest Precept.

One officer turned his attention to the disabled gunmen. "Two of those guys aren't capable of walking to the jail," he said. "Trouble is, one of our wagons is out scraping delirium dust addicts from the gutter, and the other's in the shop."

Jan volunteered. "We'll carry 'em."

Steven hoisted the gunman who'd been shot in the ribs. He slung the man onto his shoulder, grateful for something to do that didn't involve listening to everyone call him a hero. He jogged the five blocks to the jailhouse, where he dumped his burden. Blood drizzled down the man's shirt.

The officer-on-duty greeted Steven with a smile and a handshake. "You the fellow who killed the slimy toad who controlled the delirium dust operation?"

"Yeah, that'd be me. Word travels fast. Better call a medic to see about that guy's wounds."

He stepped back onto the sidewalk, where he came eye-to-eye with D.F. Nathaniel, the founder of the Protectors. Steven would have recognized the face anywhere. From childhood, he'd seen the founder's image staring down from portraits and looking up from textbooks. But he shouldn't have encountered Nathaniel on the streets of Medusa-Four.

Nathaniel had been dead for centuries.

CHAPTER TWO

A YOUNG WOMAN RECEIVES AN UNWELCOME ASSIGNMENT

"Protectors, ordered to undertake new missions, shall not refuse."
—D.F. Nathaniel

Sheera raced down the hospital corridor to catch up to the veteran psychiatrist making his rounds. She sucked in gulps of Earth's air, richer in oxygen than the atmosphere of her previous world. "Doctor, please help me. You're the only hope I have left."

"It can't be as bad as all that," the psychiatrist said, slowing to let her pull even. "What's the trouble?"

Sheera caught her breath. Dr. Aloysius amazed her every time she encountered him. How could a body so frail in appearance move at such a rapid clip? "Headquarters won't let me work under your supervision any longer," she said. "It assigned me to escort the seven-and-eight-year-old recruits on their journey through space, then help them adjust to serving with our Community."

The old man stopped, his thumb poised to touch the keypad on the door to a patient's room. "Yes, I saw the memo. I'll be sorry to lose you from the hospital staff, my dear, but is your new posting so terrible? I thought you liked children."

"I adore children. That isn't the point. A psychiatrist is all I ever wanted to be, ever since I was a little girl and found out the

Community operates a mental health foundation. A dream came true for me when Headquarters assigned me to work for the Galaxy's greatest psychiatrist…"

Aloysius smiled. "Don't flatter me, please."

"I never flatter. I speak the truth and you know it. I don't understand why I've been pulled away. Was something wrong with my performance?"

"Your performance has been exemplary. I surmise Headquarters thought your background would be helpful in consoling newcomers who are lonely or homesick. Will you work with children from the Community's intellectual branch, or from its warrior branch?"

"Both. They want me to be a counselor during Orientation on Merlin, before they separate the scholars from the rangers for separate training."

The psychiatrist narrowed his eyes. Sheera saw a glint of worry in his face, something she had observed only a couple of times before in the months she had apprenticed under him.

"I see," he said. "Be sure to apply a firm hand in dealing with urchins from the other branch. You'll find they're not so gentle and eager-to-please as the classmates you grew up with. Their natural aggressiveness serves them well after they mature and venture off to battle the criminal element, but it gets in the way of discipline at an early age."

"I'll keep that in mind, Doctor, but I didn't come to you for advice. I hear you exercise influence over postings. I need you to make Headquarters reconsider my assignment. It'll listen to you."

"I'm afraid it won't," the psychiatrist countered. "I have sway over posting decisions only when medical issues are a factor. I can arrange for one of our Community to be stationed at a particular location for reasons of health, but I can't interfere with a striker's posting merely because she doesn't like her new job."

His words were like a death blow to her dream. "Suppose you tell them I'll go berserk if I'm forced to leave London?" she said. "Would that qualify as a medical reason?"

"Going berserk, as you put it, would indeed be medical grounds for a different posting, if there was any danger that would actually happen," the psychiatrist said. "But we both know such a diagnosis would be a lie. My considered opinion is that you will do a marvelous job as a counselor."

Sheera wiped at her eyes with the back of her hand. "Then you can do nothing for me?"

"I said I cannot change your assignment to Merlin. I didn't say I can do nothing for you." Aloysius pressed his thumb against the keypad. A microchip read his DNA, authorized his entry, and slid open the door. He entered the patient's room, leaving Sheera standing alone, puzzling at his words.

CHAPTER THREE

THE MAN WHO WASN'T THERE

*"Protectors shall not take the lives of their enemies unless there
is no other way to prevent death or serious injury to themselves or
to other innocent persons."*
—D.F. Nathaniel

Steven looked over the emaciated cheeks and scruffy beard of the man who could have passed for a twin of the Community's founder. The stranger completed the illusion by wearing a shirt and matching brown trousers that looked coarse as burlap and hung loosely over his scrawny frame. Once, Steven had asked a teacher whether those clothes had been the fashion back in Nathaniel's day. He'd been told, no, that Nathaniel was a fashion designer's nightmare even for his own era.

"Good costume," he complimented the stranger. "You look exactly like D.F. Nathaniel."

"A resemblance that is no coincidence, for that is my name."

Joking or crazy, take your pick. Steven, having just killed a man, was in no mood to deal with either. "Sure it is, pal. And my name is Napoleon Bonaparte. Nice chatting with you, but I need to get back to work."

He tried to step around, but the intruder maneuvered to stay in front of him. "I should think you would wish to tarry, my son. How often does your Community's founder grant you an audience?"

Steven scratched his chin. "Considering that D.F. Nathaniel died centuries before I was born, I'd say he speaks to me… roughly… never. And I'm not your son." He longed to slap the pest aside. But this weirdo had done no harm. Such a misuse of his power would have violated the Precepts he was sworn to live by. "Okay, I'll play along with the gag. If you're a ghost, prove it. Do something… you know… ghosty."

"Do they no longer teach grammar at the novitiates I established? There is no such word as 'ghosty.' And don't think of me as a ghost." He shuddered. "Refer to me as an apparition. An apparition passes on to a better state, then returns for a visit. A ghost never really leaves. As to your request, I gather you wish to witness a paranormal activity of some kind—a feat that would be impossible for a person of flesh and blood to accomplish. If you insist…"

He vanished. An identical voice spoke from behind. "You'll find me over here, my son."

Steven turned around. He faced the same image of D.F. Nathaniel that he'd seen disappear before his eyes. "What are you? I'll bet you're a hologram. Some jackass thinks it's a joke to project an image of our founder, right? Or are you a hallucination? That's it, isn't it? I sniffed one fume too many from Maxwell's delirium dust, and now I'm hallucinating up a storm."

Nathaniel's image closed its eyes half-way, completing the resemblance to a portrait in the parlor of Medusa-Four's Protector base. "I told you. I am an apparition. Why do you doubt my existence? Joan of Arc conversed with spirits, so why should you not do the same?"

It was a fair question, but to Steven the difference was obvious. "She was a saint, and one of the greatest military commanders of all time. That's why this whole thing makes no sense. Why me? I'm so far out of Joan's league, I'm not even playing in the same ballgame."

"True. You are no Maid of Orleans," the image agreed, sounding wistful, as if Steven had done something wrong merely by not being Joan of Arc. "What a magnificent Protector that French girl would be. Never would she have broken a code of honor, as you have done." The image frowned. "Did I not teach you to respect all human life, including the life of thine enemy?"

Hallucination or hologram, the stranger put on a convincing impersonation. Nobody but the real D.F. Nathaniel would use a word as archaic as *thine*. "I had... I had no choice about killing that Warlord tonight," Steven stammered. "Even you allowed an exception for self-defense. Wait—why should I justify myself to someone who isn't real?"

"Your teachers drilled you in every form of martial art that is physically possible for the human species. Do you expect me to believe you had no defense in your arsenal but to slay a man bare-fisted?"

"Steven!" The young man looked away from the apparition. Jan stared at him. He hated it when she got that look on her face. It was the same face his mother had gotten when she had worried about him as a little boy.

"Who are you talking to?" she asked. "There's nobody there."

He blinked, and saw only empty planks of sidewalk where Nathaniel's image had stood. "Do you believe in ghosts?"

That look on her face grew more bothersome, as he told her all that had transpired since he left the saloon.

"It's normal to feel depression and guilt from taking a life," she said, after he finished. "But those emotions shouldn't cause you to see and talk to imaginary people." She wagged a finger. "You realize, don't you, that I have an obligation to report anyone under my command who shows signs of mental instability?"

Mental instability? That couldn't be good. He'd heard tales of the Community expelling strikers for less.

She paused, lost in contemplation, then added, "However..."

His sigh of relief lasted long and sounded loud. That one word—*however*—gave him hope.

"However," she repeated. "This has been a stressful evening. I'll overlook your disturbing behavior this time. But if it happens again, we'll need to ship you off-world for professional help. You'll need better treatment than Medusa-Four can offer."

"There won't be a second time," he said, unsure whether he could keep his promise. He didn't know what she meant by "professional help," but it sounded dreadful.

"Good. The police can finish cleaning up the mess. You and I should go home."

"You're pulling me off duty, aren't you?" He was scheduled to have another six Earth-standard hours on his shift.

She shot him her "worried mother" look again. "Don't take it personally. It's just for the night. Besides, I need to get you ointment for the swelling where the tuba fly bit you. You look like you have a grapefruit wedged in your cheek."

They boarded the flyer. Jan switched on the force shield to guard them from dust and wind chill. "Take us home," she commanded a panel of blinking lights, the face of the vehicle's computer. They rose and flew over the surface, ten meters high, except when they lifted higher to stay above the sulfur whiffs that leached from the planet's underbelly. Wind pushed against their skin. The company that manufactured the force shield had advertised it as ninety-eight percent effective in sheltering passengers from rushing air. Either the shield needed a tune-up, or the company had lied.

Steven kept silent during the first part of the journey, even when Jan reminded him she'd have to file a report on the Warlord's death with the Guidance Committee.

"Standard procedure when a Protector kills an adversary in the line of duty," she said. "My judgment is, you had no choice. I'll recommend the Guidance Committee clear you of any Precept violation."

"Thanks," he said, barely listening. "Jan... are you sure I was hallucinating back there?"

"Of course you were hallucinating. If it'd been a hologram, I'd have seen it too. What else besides a hallucination could have caused you to see a dead man that nobody else could see?" When he squirmed in silence, she said, "C'mon, you can't think he actually might've been... No. Not a chance."

Her voice sounded so confident. "Is it possible for a dead person to haunt a guy who's minding his own business?" he asked.

"I don't know whether it's possible. I only know it didn't happen to you, not tonight. If the real D.F. Nathaniel ever did cross back from the other side, he'd have better things to do than reprimand a striker who only wanted to save lives. That thing you saw back there—it was your conscience. Hey, I know how it is. The Novitiate drills it into our heads that we have a duty to preserve life. That makes it hard for us to come to terms with killing a man, even a worthless piece of trash like Crumm."

"I guess you're right," he said, trying to sound like he believed her, even as he doubted. If the Community's founder had looked down from wherever he was and decided the situation merited his personal attention, the killing of the Warlord must have been a screw-up of mammoth proportions.

They circled above the cabin that doubled as their office and barracks. They couldn't see it, though the sky was clear. They saw instead a volcano belching wisps of sulfur, a sight so humdrum on Medusa-Four that no passer-by would give it a second glance. They landed beside the "volcano," and Jan ordered, "Computer: switch off the holographic projection."

The sides of the volcano melted into walls, doors, and windows. Jan walked the short distance to the cabin, and touched her thumb to the keypad by the main entry. Steven waited a step behind. "Access denied," the cabin declared.

"Strange," Jan mumbled. "Oh, I see the problem." She examined her finger tips, smudged with red. "My DNA is contaminated with somebody else's. This blood must be from the bozo I carted off to jail."

D.F. Nathaniel winked into existence, arms folded. "Have you no regret over the life you took?" he asked.

"Steven—what are you staring at? You're seeing that thing again, aren't you?"

Steven weighed his options for answering. He could deny everything, but she'd see through the lie. Then she'd judge him dishonest and therefore unworthy to serve in the Protectors. He could tell the truth, but then she'd lecture him about mental instability again, and come to the same conclusion about his unfitness. As a last resort, he kept his mouth shut. Silence didn't appear to satisfy her, either.

"This proves the visions are all in your mind," Jan said. "Think. You saw blood back in town, just before the thing materialized the first time. You saw blood again, seconds ago, smeared on the keypad. That can't be a coincidence. The thing pops up whenever you see blood. Does that sound like something the real Nathaniel would do?"

Nathaniel's image laughed. Steven recognized the sound from clips about the life of their founder, who was known for a sense of humor that made him laugh at the oddest times.

"Your provincial is astute to observe how the presence of blood preceded both my appearances, but the coincidence is hardly remarkable. In the aftermath of a fatal blow, you can expect to discover blood spattered in more than one location."

Jan's voice broke in. "If it's in your head, you control it. Tell it to go away."

Steven had turned to listen as she talked. When he turned back, he saw nothing out of the ordinary. "Thanks. Maybe I do control it. It's gone now."

'Good. Now let's get out of the heat." She wiped the bloody spot from her thumb and tapped the keypad again. The door slid open.

She insisted he sit across from her at the table where they took their meals. "I can't ignore a hallucination a second time," she said. "When the freighter leaves Medusa-Four tomorrow, you'll be on board. It'll dock with a space station. You can catch a rocket to London from there."

"London? That's on Earth. Why Earth?"

"Because that's where an outstanding psychiatrist works. A doctor by the name of Aloysius."

CHAPTER FOUR

A THERAPY SESSION

"Protectors shall be subject to the authority of a Guidance Committee that shall investigate and pass judgment on suspected violations of these Precepts."
—D.F. Nathaniel

Steven stood two hundred and three stories above the River Thames. His hospital suite gave him a view that stretched for kilometers across the city of London.

His gaze fell on an office complex in the shape of a five-pointed star. He recognized it from news reports and travel brochures as the command center for the Galactic Treaty Organization. The star-shape had been some architect's idea of symbolism, a reflection of the G.T.O.'s importance to the flow of interstellar travel. Somebody had to regulate trade among human-occupied worlds and set rules for colonizing new ones, and most of that oversight happened inside the G.T.O.'s Main Office on the opposite bank of the Thames. The Community of Protectors complied with the G.T.O.'s regulations, most of the time, but had never signed the treaty to become a member. Protectors answered to no one but themselves.

Steven was more interested in the sites that had been part of London for ages, not for the mere century the G.T.O. headquarters had existed. He clapped a magnifying visor across his eyes. The micro-chip inside the plastic strip expanded

London's vista by a factor of ten. He looked beyond the clusters of skyscrapers, and searched for landmarks that made London a jewel among cities. Even with the visor, Buckingham Palace resembled a toy fort. The great Ferris wheel known as the London Eye, the seventh structure to bear that name, seemed smaller than a dinner plate. The needle near the Palace must have been the clock tower Big Ben. He dawdled, taking in the scenery, to distract his mind from the transmission staring at him from the desktop monitor. But he could keep from dwelling on the message for only so long. He stripped off the visor and read the monitor for the seventh time that day.

"Guidance Committee finds available information inconclusive whether Striker was justified in taking human life. Further investigation will take place to determine whether his conduct on Medusa-Four warrants expulsion from the Community. Reports of psychotic visions also troublesome. Psychiatric examination of his mental stability will proceed simultaneously with inquiry into the charge of misconduct."

Why couldn't the bureaucrats on Merlin make up their minds? The way they judged his case, he was either a murderer or a lunatic. Or both. Or neither. The cobblestone streets tempted, but he held back from jumping. The message had sapped his desire to live, yet he wasn't prepared to die. It seemed unwise to face Eternal Judgment so soon after killing a man. He'd have to figure out a way to wipe his soul clean before he approached the Pearly Gates.

The door to Steven's private quarters opened, and he turned away from the monitor. He looked past the bed and couch, into the hallway, where a man stood with a satchel in his hand.

The man bowed. "I am Doctor Aloysius, at your service," he announced in a voice that seemed too firm to come out of such a frail body. He entered the room without waiting for an invitation

Steven pondered what to do in reply. Was he supposed to bow also? The visitor was dressed exactly the same way as Steven, in the Community's cold-climate uniform. It was brown from collar to boots, in memory of the only clothing color whose existence J.D. Nathaniel had seemed aware of. Jan hadn't told him his therapist would be a member of the Community's scholar branch.

"Nice to meet you," Steven mumbled. "I didn't know the Community has scholars who are psychiatrists."

The doctor's tone switched from gentle to scolding. "Then you should have studied more. By the time a novice advances to striker, he should be familiar with every type of service we Protectors provide, whether it's done by scholars or rangers. Now, it's time for us to proceed with your treatment, wouldn't you say?"

Steven was agreeable to moving on with his treatment. It had to be better than getting chewed out for not studying hard enough. "Can you fix my head, sir?"

The doctor smiled with his lips tightly closed. "That's what we're here to find out. This device will help us." He snapped the satchel open, exposing vials of liquid, a towel, and a peanut butter and jelly sandwich. A helmet squished the sandwich, causing it to ooze a gob of purple jelly. The helmet, round and smooth as glass on the outside, sprouted wires and barbs on the inside, giving it the look of an instrument of medieval torture. Steven backed away.

"Be seated," Aloysius said. He pointed to a table with two chairs at the room's center, then grasped the helmet with both hands.

Steven wanted to flee, but he wanted to be cured even more, so he sat. He expected, at any moment, to feel a hundred barbs gouging into his scalp.

The doctor brought the helmet closer. "Relax. This won't hurt a bit."

Those words failed to provide comfort. Doctors usually uttered them moments before they inflicted pain.

"We will conduct this test before we proceed with the therapy," Aloysius went on. "It will determine whether you're schizophrenic."

"Is that what you think I've got?" He hoped not. He didn't know what the word meant, but any disease with that many syllables had to be horrible. "It's not contagious, is it?"

"Contagious? My heavens, no!" His mouth turned up into a hint of a smile. "Schizophrenia is as respectable as any other illness, and quite treatable nowadays. But I doubt that's where your issues lie. I merely want to eliminate the possibility. This device will allow me to search for a chemical imbalance by extracting part of your brain."

"Extracting what?" Steven drew back. "If it's all the same to you, sir, I'd like to hang onto my entire brain. We rangers have less to spare in that department than you scholars."

The psychiatrist chuckled. "Oh, don't worry, I'll only borrow a few molecules. You'll never miss them."

Easy for him to laugh. They weren't his molecules. "Well... as long as you're sure it's safe. When does the test start?" He braced for the barbs to burrow into his flesh.

"It's over."

Aloysius removed the helmet and took his place in the chair at the opposite side of the table. He peered at tiny lights that flashed among the wires. Steven assumed the lights revealed all sorts of memories, hopes, and fears that were none of this man's business.

"Congratulations," Aloysius said. "Your brain chemicals interact with perfect harmony. Ah, why do you appear so despondent? I assumed I was relaying good news."

Steven could have picked from a smorgasbord of reasons why he was "despondent," as the doctor put it. He chose the problem that seemed most pressing. "It's about those molecules, sir. Are you sure losing them won't make me dumber?"

"Quite sure. In the time we've been talking, brain cells containing a hundred times the matter I extracted have died a natural death."

Did his brain cells really perish that easily? The doctor's assurance somehow disturbed him and consoled him at the same time. "I guess I can live without the molecules, then," he conceded. "But something else bothers me. If I'm not mentally sick, then the apparition must have really been there. How would you like to have one of your heroes travel clear from the Other Side to scold you for messing up?"

"I wouldn't like it at all, I'm sure. But I'll need to learn more about your experience before we can concede you've seen something supernatural. Your records tell me you were part of the Protectors' mission to… what was the name of that world?"

"Medusa-Four."

"Please, call it by its given name, not by order of distance from its sun. You wouldn't call Mars 'Sol-Four' or Jupiter 'Sol-Five,' would you?"

Dozens of psychiatrists at the hospital, Steven thought, and he had to draw one who was easily offended. "Begging your pardon, sir, it doesn't have another name. I was posted there for over a month, and never heard it called anything else. Even the people who live there call it Medusa-Four."

Aloysius frowned. "It's no wonder their civilization declined into chaos, if they take so little pride in their world. Very well. Please describe the events on this Medusa-Four that preceded the apparition's appearances."

"Yes, sir." Steven had told the same story three times since checking in for psychiatric observation. It never became easier. He explained that the Protectors stationed a team on Medusa-Four to battle the flow of delirium dust to other worlds. He then skipped to his meeting with the street dealer, then told about his clash with the Warlord, and concluded at the point Jan caught him talking to their long-dead founder. All the time, Aloysius listened without speaking a word or twitching a muscle. At the end of the account, Steven pleaded. "Can you tell me what's wrong with me?"

"In due time, my boy. First, a question. Your vision invoked the name of Joan of Arc. Does she have any significance for you?"

"I did a paper on Joan for my Earth history class. Since then, she's been a role model to me. Almost like what Arthur Pendragon meant to Nathaniel."

Aloysius scratched notes on his electric pad, then set aside his pen. "Doesn't that strike you as remarkable? Out of thousands of historical figures to choose from, the apparition happened to compare you to someone you admire. Most likely, the image sprang from your subconscious, reprimanding you for not living up to the standards of two people whose approval you would crave if they were alive, Nathaniel and Joan." He leaned back in his chair, his arms folded. "In layman's terms, my boy, your conscience is troubling you."

So he was back to being mentally unstable rather than haunted. Not much of an improvement, if true. But the doctor's diagnosis seemed out of sync with his earlier finding. "How do you explain why your test turned up nothing wrong with me? A guy's conscience doesn't walk and talk, unless his brain is missing a few circuits."

"I said you're not schizophrenic. I didn't say there was nothing wrong with you. In fact, there is... or was... something very wrong. Atmospheric deprivation." He uttered those two words and leaned back, as if nothing further needed to be said.

Steven had no idea what he was talking about. "Huh?"

"Atmospheric deprivation. Your case is more severe than most, but I've seen it before in strikers on their first posting to a small planet. You arrived at the Novitiate at the age of... eight, was it? That's a long time to live under Pendragon's crushing gravity. It transformed you into the behemoth I see today, but all that pressure came with side effects."

Side effects? Nobody warned Steven about side effects from growing up on Pendragon. He felt betrayed by the Community. "Our instructors told us, whenever we complained about the pressure, that high gravity makes us stronger. Are you telling me they lied? That it did bad things to my body?"

"Not to your body. To your brain."

That sounded no better. Steven gulped. "My brain?"

"Your lobes acquired a dependency on heavy atmosphere. They couldn't absorb enough oxygen after you relocated to a planet where the air was thin. I've run across strikers who encountered spinning teacups, dancing cows, and so forth. Usually the visions don't appear at random. They follow a pattern, some kind of trigger that allows us to predict when they will occur. In your case, I believe Jan was correct that blood triggers your visions, and I also believe your feelings of guilt contribute to the problem. I'd like to perform an experiment. Do you mind?"

Did he have a choice? "It doesn't involve ripping more molecules out of my skull, does it?"

"I won't touch you. Watch carefully." Aloysius reopened his satchel and pulled out a vial of red liquid and a towel. He spilled the contents of one onto the other. "Well?" he said. "Do you notice anything out of the ordinary?"

"A psychiatrist spilling a vial of what looks like blood. That's a sight a guy doesn't run into every day. But I don't see dead people, if that's what you're driving at."

"Excellent. In rare cases, the hallucinations persist under Earth-standard conditions. But so far, you've only had your visions in sub-Earth gravity. That's promising."

Steven began to think professional help was not so bad after all. "Then, if that's the only thing wrong with me—a shortfall of oxygen to my noodle—there's no reason you can't certify me as fit for duty, as long as I get posted on a world with standard gravity or better. Right?"

"Oh, I'll certify you for duty. I have a proposal for your next assignment. It's only a recommendation at this point, but I'm confident Headquarters will agree as soon as it reads my diagnosis. In the meantime, enjoy your stay on Earth. You have time to catch today's tour of the G.T.O.'s Main Office on the other side of the Thames."

"I will, sir, but there's one other problem. Some people on the Guidance Committee say I might've violated the highest Precept when I killed the Warlord."

"I know all about the Committee's finding. I can't control the final verdict, but I can recommend that, for medical reasons, you return to duty pending the outcome of the investigation."

Steven leaped from his seat and pumped the psychiatrist's hand. "Really? Thank you. What planet will I be posted on?"

"You are going home, my boy. Back to the novitiate."

"Back to...?" Steven's voice trailed off. He remembered, too clearly, how novices spoke with scorn and pity about ranger strikers who were forced to serve their postings at the novitiate, instead of on worlds where genuine threats to humanity existed. Headquarters typically doled out novitiate postings to strikers whose performance hadn't been bad enough to justify expulsion, but hadn't been good enough to merit responsibility. He couldn't expect Aloysius to understand. Among scholar strikers, a posting at their novitiate was considered as honorable as any other.

"Does that mean I'll work with the novices on Pendragon?" He pouted, hoping to communicate his disappointment. He didn't expect Aloysius to change his recommendation, but sympathy would have been appreciated. He received none.

"Yes, and not only Pendragon. You'll also spend time at the novitiate for scholars on Merlin, so you can acquire exposure to reduced gravity. Your brain needs to build up a tolerance."

Merlin! That would be some consolation for his humiliation. He'd grown up seeing Pendragon's largest moon at night, longing to set foot on its soil, knowing it was forbidden to rangers until they advanced to the status of striker. He'd camped on Merlin for two weeks of orientation at the age of eight, like every other Protector, but that was so long ago it hardly counted.

Aloysius went on. "Your healing process will proceed faster if you realize you have no reason to feel guilty about the man's death on Medusa-Four. Had I been on the Guidance Committee, I would have reached a different conclusion. That Warlord was pond scum."

"I understand. It's just that... well..." He fumbled for words. "It's not that easy to shut out the guilt. I get rid of it for a while, then it comes back."

"You'll need someone at your new posting to help you sort through the feelings that contribute to your hallucinations. A Protector by the name of Sheera recently transferred from this hospital to Merlin. I intend to assign her to your case."

Steven pictured a female version of Aloysius, grey-headed and wrinkled, with decades of experience in psychotherapy. An old woman's wisdom might be what he needed.

Aloysius stuffed the helmet, the towel, and the vial back into his satchel, mashing what was left of the sandwich. He was clipping the satchel shut when Steven asked, "Did you say my hallucinations won't happen on a world with Earth-standard gravity?

"It is possible you could hallucinate on Earth, if your illness is severe, but unlikely. Why do you ask?"

"Because D.F. Nathaniel is standing to the left of you, and he doesn't look happy."

CHAPTER FIVE

INCIDENT ON THE PLAYGROUND

*"Protectors shall be trained from childhood in one of two novitiates.
One novitiate shall educate scholars to the highest possible level of
intellectual and spiritual development. The other shall educate rangers
to the highest possible level of strength and agility."*
—D.F. Nathaniel

The first passenger emerged from the starship at the summit of a rolling hill, where the shrubs had been cleared and the ground leveled to fashion a landing pad. The site overlooked Merlin's camp for recruits. Steven, watching from the park below, sat cross-legged in the grass. All he could tell about the first passenger, from a distance, was that she was too tall and shapely to be one of the children. Her voice carried down the hill through the thin atmosphere, as she commanded her seven-and-eight-year-old charges to disembark. Two straight lines, please, no punching, pushing, or lallygagging. You there, from now on don't spit out your chewing gum, except into a trash container. The voice was soft and appealing to male ears, even when snapping orders.

Ten Earth-standard years earlier, Steven had lined up like those children, eager to begin his training, yet terrified of the unknown. The Community gave him, and all the recruits, two weeks of play to ease the tension before they began their lessons. Now this new crop of youngsters carried on the tradition.

The park seemed smaller than he remembered it, though nothing was missing. Swings and climbing bars crowded the playground, but the Community had also made concessions to technology. The most popular toy, if these children had the same taste as Steven's class, would be the miniature flyers, with all the speed of a tortoise and the ability to rise about a meter. This posting could have been fun, if not for the shame of being a ranger striker assigned to non-combat duty.

The recruits filed out of the starship, sorted into two groups of thirty each. Steven distinguished one group from the other at a glance. The kids who would train at the Scholar Novitiate looked like typical children of their age, their massive intellects concealed inside run-of-the-mill bodies. The kids who would train at the Ranger Novitiate stood a head taller, on average, with thicker bodies to match.

The female voice carried down the hill again. "Welcome to Merlin. Feel free to play on the equipment until supper time. You're dismissed. Have a…"

The children gave a cheer and broke ranks. They descended on the park in a swarm.

"… good time." The voice trailed after them, causing Steven to grin. More figures, too tall to be children, exited the starship, and began the trek down the hill. He judged them to be the other counselors.

Girls and boys of assorted complexions surrounded Steven. Their common trait was humanity. They paused, eyes wide with awe, to ask Steven how many monsters he'd conquered, to which his standard fib was "only five so far, but I'm still a beginner."

Thump! Something that felt like a sack of potatoes smacked against his hip. He looked down and saw a boy sprawled on his back. A girl towered over the fallen child. She knelt beside her companion and pressed her palm against his forehead. Next she wrapped her fingers around his wrist and checked his pulse, or pretended to. She tilted her head upward and stuck out her tongue.

"You knocked over my friend Danny, you big gorilla." She unleashed a string of obscenities that Steven thought little girls weren't supposed to know the meaning of.

"I didn't knock over anybody, you gutter-mouth. Your pal didn't watch where he was going and crashed into me. Now, if you're done making believe you're a medic, I'll hoist him back onto his feet." Steven got to one knee and lifted the fallen child to a standing position.

Judging by his spindly arms and legs, the boy had traveled to Merlin to join the scholar. branch "Excuse me for bumping into you, sir," he said. "Is there a zero-gravity chamber on this playground? Bobbi promised to show me how to play weightless billiards."

Freckles stood out on Bobbi's pudgy cheeks. They twisted into a scowl. "Yeah, I'm gonna teach him, unless you broke his leg or something."

"Nobody asked you," Steven said to the girl. "There's a chamber over there," he added, pointing. He looked into the boy's eyes. "Are you sure you're not hurt?"

"Yes, sir, I'm fine. Thank you for inquiring."

Danny took a few steps in the direction Steven had directed, but Bobbi stood rooted to her spot, hands on her hips. "So where are the aliens?"

"Huh?" Steven said. "What are you talking about? The Community of Protectors is strictly a human organization."

"Well, that's rotten. What's the fun of going to another planet if you don't get to meet aliens? And I don't see why you don't let other species join. That's discrimination."

Steven had no fondness for aliens, but he would have preferred an extraterrestrial over the human he was talking to. "I don't make the rules, kid."

The boy tugged her shoulder. "I told you we wouldn't find non-human species here. I apologize for my friend's disrespect, sir. Let's go play weightless billiards."

"Okay," she said. "But I could've done that at home. I wanted to see aliens."

The two children dashed off, and crawled into a cube. They floated to its ceiling, and began doing flips in mid-air. Steven had memories of playing in the same zero-gravity chamber as a recruit. He knew now what he didn't know then, that the chamber was not so weightless as its name implied. Traces of gravity filtered through its walls, enough to allow its occupants to tell the difference between up and down. The boy and girl began their sport of knocking balls into pockets carved into all six surfaces.

"You must be Steven."

The voice spoke to him from behind. He recognized the speaker as the person he'd heard giving orders on the landing pad. He turned, and saw how she looked from close-up. The scholar branch had no prohibition against make-up or jewelry, but she hadn't bothered with it that day, aside from the stone on the ring that all Protectors wore. Her hair hung in dark, uneven waves over her ears and neck, as if she had hacked at it herself with a carving knife. She reminded him of Jan in her indifference to grooming, but younger, closer to his own age. Still, her natural good looks, and haunting green eyes, more than made up for her lack of attention to her appearance. The Protectors' temperate-world uniform, nearly sleeveless, clung to her frame and showcased her curves as plainly as Steven's uniform exposed his muscles.

"Yeah, that's me."

She said, "I'm Sheera. Dr. Aloysius sent me here to work with you on your problem."

This was Sheera? He blushed at the thought that another striker, especially an attractive one, knew the sordid details of his condition. "Did he... uh... tell you why I was transferred to Merlin?"

"He told me you've been hallucinating images of D.F. Nathaniel."

Faces nearby turned to look their direction. Steven cringed. "Say it louder. Every last pair of ears on Merlin might not have heard you."

"Sorry," she said, dropping to a whisper. "Your illness is nothing to be ashamed of, but we can talk in a more private setting if you prefer. I've arranged for the other counselors to watch over the kids while we tend to your medical issue. Accompany me to the infirmary, please. Doctor Aloysius reserved a private room for just the two of us."

How could he object to spending time with her in a private room? Just the two of them.

*   *   *

Steven walked at Sheera's side, wrapping his mind around the idea that she wasn't the old lady he'd been expecting. Not that he was complaining, but he wanted his visions to go away, and an old lady with decades of experience might have had a better chance of making that happen. "You don't look any older than I am," he said.

She flushed. "I'm not. I'm in my first year of striker training, same as you."

He sealed his lips until they'd passed beyond range of everyone else's hearing, then said, "Meaning no disrespect, are you sure you're qualified to treat my condition? I always thought talking to people who don't exist is a sign of a pretty serious illness. The kind of problem that needs the attention of a doctor who's spent years tending patients on psych wards."

He endured a cold stare from Sheera's eyes, and found them lovely even when she was annoyed with him. After several seconds she answered. "Did you know that scholar novices must complete a thesis on some aspect of Protector lore before we advance to striker status?"

"Yeah, I heard someplace that you're supposed to write a paper." If he had given the thesis any thought before, it was only to be grateful that ranger novices didn't have the same requirement. "What does that have to do with...?"

"I did mine on the establishment of mental health treatment as a Protector ministry. Not only that, I worked for three months at the psychiatric ward in London, directly under Dr. Aloysius. Well, not quite directly under, but he knows me by name. I suggest you follow my directions if you want to get cleared for duty. Duty as a warrior who battles oppression, I mean, not as a nanny who babysits new arrivals."

"Hmmm. One school paper and three months of emptying bedpans on a psychiatric ward. Wow, practically as impressive as earning a medical degree. All right, lead the way, Sigmund Freud." He chuckled at his own wit, but stopped when he realized he was the only one laughing.

"I'll have you know I didn't empty a single bedpan. On Earth, that's done by robots. Oh, what's the use of trying to reason with you? Just do what I tell you, and we'll get results."

She refused to speak another word, or look him in the eye, for the rest of their path. Steven paused before the entrance to the infirmary. "Is this where you scholar novices get doctored? It can't have more than a few rooms. We ranger novices had an entire hospital. But I guess our physical training causes us to suffer more injuries down on Pendragon."

Sheera softened. "It sounds funny to hear you speak of your world as down. I've spent most of my life orbiting Pendragon, so I think of it as up. I guess your perspective depends on what you see in your night sky." She spoke the word "open," and the door obeyed. She went on. "We have a hospital on Merlin, too. This place we're entering now is just an infirmary, mainly for treating emergencies at the orientation camp, but it's also a good place for us to conduct experiments." She ushered him into a room that stank like the saloon on Medusa-Four. "Don't mind the aroma. When you put all the serums in this room together, they give off a stench like whiskey."

"You know what whiskey smells like?"

"From simulations. We're trained to recognize all addictive substances by sight and odor." She reached into a drawer and pulled out a primitive needle, the type that might come in handy for sewing on buttons if you couldn't locate a machine to do it for you. She sterilized the needle with purple gel, raised it high with one hand, and plunged it downward to the palm of her other hand.

Steven's fingers darted out and grappled Sheera's wrist, a second before the needle could pierce her flesh.

"Let go of me and don't interfere." She glowered. "That's an order."

"Then write me up for insubordination. I'm not going to let you mutilate your beau... your skin." He'd caught himself before he'd said "beautiful skin."

She took a deep breath and explained. "We need to test whether Nathaniel's image is still lurking in your subconscious. Your record indicates the sight of blood preceded each appearance. We'll need a fresh supply if we're going to induce a hallucination and move forward with this experiment."

"So that means you have to slash your hand to ribbons? If you've had all this training you say you've had, you'd know how to draw blood with some kind of doohickey that's designed for that purpose." He narrowed his eyes. "Or maybe you don't know how to use real medical equipment."

"They're called syringes, not doohickeys, and I could use one in my sleep. But something tidy and medicinal might not have the effect we're hoping for. To increase our odds of calling up the apparition, the blood should ooze from an injury, the way it did when you saw it on that horrible drug boss."

"Need I remind you that a spill from a vial of blood caused me to hallucinate on Earth?"

"Yes, I read about that, and need I remind *you* that the apparition flickered out after a few seconds? Doctor Aloysius believes you might have sustained your vision longer if you'd seen blood in connection with an injury. Now release my hand immediately, or I'll add abuse of your strength to the other charges I'm compiling against you."

He squeezed tighter. Her hand was so slender and perfect, he preferred to hallucinate for the rest of his life rather than see her put a gash through it.

"In a way, it's sweet that you don't want me to get hurt," she admitted. "Moronic, but sweet." She smiled. "My hand is going numb. If you won't let go, will you at least relax your grip before you choke off my circulation?"

He loosened his grasp. She tugged, and her wrist slipped through his fingers. He realized too late she had tricked him. The needle plunged into her waiting palm.

"This should give us what we need," she said. "If our theory is correct, my injury will trigger a subconscious association with the blood you saw on that beast in the saloon. And don't worry about me. I can block pain with the mental discipline all us scholars learn during our training."

Steven marveled that Sheera never grimaced or cried out. That mental discipline must have been working wonders. His admiration for her bravery nearly overcame his annoyance at the way she'd outfoxed him. Trickles of blood oozed across her hand, and a droplet spilled onto to the floor. He shifted his gaze.

"Don't look away. It's imperative you observe this." She poised her hand in front of his face, leaving him little chance to avoid seeing the injury short of covering his eyes.

D.F. Nathaniel winked into existence. "Ah," the apparition said. "You believed you could get rid of me by traveling through space to this moon. Do not attempt to escape my judgment again. I will remain with you until you make amends for violating my highest Precept."

Sheera broke in. "Are you having a vision yet?" She pressed a sterile rag against her bloody palm.

"Oh, yeah. He seems so real, I almost forget you can't see or hear him." He struggled to keep his tone casual, so as not to show fear in front of her.

"We can get to work, then. But first, I must find out whether he can hear me."

The apparition spoke. "You may inform this attractive young lady that I hear every word she says."

Odd, Steven thought, that D.F. Nathaniel would describe Sheera as "attractive." History recalled the Community's founder as someone who never spoke of noticing such qualities in the opposite gender. Aloysius would undoubtedly have seen the compliment as evidence the apparition lived only inside Steven's head.

"He said to tell you he hears every word," Steven answered. "Uh, that was all."

"I figured as much. The human mind is like an iceberg, eighty percent below the surface. That's where your apparition lives, in your mind, below the surface. He hears what you hear, no more and no less, so he hears me. Where is he? Wait, scratch that question. He's not really there, so I mean, where do your sight and hearing perceive the image to be?"

He pointed to a spot on the floor a meter to Sheera's left. She twisted to face the spot where he had placed the apparition, and asked, "Why do you persist in haunting your follower?"

Nathaniel's eyes took on the sadness of one man wallowing in pity for another. "Because of the disappointment he causes me. My disciples in your era bestowed enormous power on him. He used his power in the service of death, in violation of his oath to use it only for the preservation of life."

That sounded more like something the real Nathaniel would say. Steven reflected that his subconscious had produced a convincing imitation of the genuine article. He repeated the message, word for word.

Sheera spoke again to what, from her point-of-view, must have been empty air. "Hear me, apparition—I'm talking directly to you—tell me what this man must do to make you leave him alone."

"I will not cease making my appearances until he…"

The walls swayed as an explosion rocked the infirmary.

*　　　　　*　　　　　*

The stench of smoke followed the blast, drifting in from the playground. "The kids," Steven said, his own problem seeming trivial all of a sudden. He dashed outside, with Sheera a few paces behind. Two medics, a man and a woman, rushed from the infirmary at the same time. A pile of rubble covered the space where the zero-gravity chamber had stood minutes earlier. The children who weren't running away shrieking gathered around the debris.

Steven remembered the boy and the girl in the chamber. Were they still inside when the thing exploded? He charged into the circle of children, and found the girl who'd accused him of knocking down her friend. She stood motionless in the midst of the crowd, drenched in grime. Three other counselors raced to the scene, edging children aside as they ran.

Tears tumbled across Bobbi's freckles, mingling with the soot from the explosion. "Danny!" she screamed. "Somebody do something!"

"We'll help your friend," Sheera promised. "Where is he?"

"He's... he's... he's..." A series of sobs stymied the girl's attempt to form a coherent sentence. She pointed at the rubble.

Half a shoe stuck out from under a chunk of the chamber wall. A counselor strained to raise the fallen piece. Steven rushed in to take the smaller man's place. He gripped the rim of the chunk, and pulled upward. It refused to budge. For the first time in his life, he had a reason to ponder what zero gravity chambers were made of. Solid lead? Sheera stood beside him. "Perhaps if all us counselors slide our hands underneath, and hoist at the same time."

That idea struck Steven as common sense. The other counselors, all scholars, lacked anything resembling his immense power, but four of them, pulling together, might supply the edge he needed. It was worth a try.

Bobbi snuffled. "I knew the big phony couldn't do it by himself."

Steven glanced around. Every eye, big and small, focused on him. He imagined his status shriveling in the hearts of the children who had worshipped him only minutes earlier. And not just the children. What would Sheera think of him if he failed? "Stay back," he commanded.

Sheera motioned with upturned palms for the crowd to back away. "All right, if he thinks he can do it, give him room."

Steven again gripped the sides of the slab. A child's voice made a remark about purple veins popping out on his arms. The chunk rose a few centimeters. He nudged it sideways until it cleared the boy's broken body. When he dropped it to the side, the onlookers erupted in cheers.

The cheering stopped as quickly as it had begun. Danny's body was sprawled on the ground, his arms and legs twisted. Blood drenched his flesh and his clothes. His head raised off the debris, and his eyelids flickered open. Then his neck jerked back, slamming his skull. Both eyes closed. The kids shouldn't have to witness such a gruesome sight at their age, Steven thought. He shouldn't have to witness it at his age, either.

A medic hustled to the boy's side, guiding a coffin-shaped stasis vault he'd snatched from the infirmary. He had activated the vault's low-yield flyer mechanism, causing it to glide a meter above the surface. It coasted to a stop above Danny, and lowered over him until its sides touched the ground. A panel slid underneath the boy, encasing him inside the device. Steven saw the boy's entire frame through the transparent material on the lid.

The vault hummed as it did its work, dulling the pain. Danny opened his eyes half-way. "I'm sorry," he moaned. "I didn't mean to light the flame."

"Never mind that now," Steven said. "Don't talk." Not if you know what's good for you, he added silently.

"I only wanted to find out how fire behaves in zero-gravity. It was an experiment. I didn't know a flame would make everything blow up."

Steven could hoist double his weight, but he was powerless to stop one small boy from blabbing about things better left unsaid. He raised a finger to his lips in the universal sign that meant "shut up." Somebody needed to teach that kid how to keep quiet before his big mouth got him kicked out of the Community.

A sign lay in the midst of the rubble. Smoke smudged the bold letters, but the message was plain. "NO EATING, DRINKING, ROUGH-HOUSING, OR LIGHTING FLAMES IN ZERO GRAVITY." If someone wanted to entice the children into setting fires, Steven thought, how better to succeed than by ordering them not to? Still, Danny's confession had the ring of a lie. During their encounter, he'd been so polite, so deferential. Some boys would ignore a safety precaution just to see what would happen. But not this boy.

"I know it's tight in there, buddy," Steven said. "Do you know what this container is for?"

"Yes, sir. I know what a stasis vault does. It will freeze my cells at a molecular level, which will have the duel effect of numbing the pain and minimizing further physical deterioration until I can receive proper medical attention."

"Uh, yeah, that's what I was going to say." Actually, Steven had intended to say the box would make the boo-boos stop hurting. The boy would fit in well with the Community's intellectual branch.

The medics guided the vault to the infirmary, and the crowd broke up, leaving Steven and Sheera to survey the wreckage. "Will the kid be all right?" he asked.

"If he is, it will be because of you. You were terrific."

Under ordinary circumstances, he would have delighted in her praise. But somehow, the admiration of his peers, even young female peers, didn't seem important. "But do you think he'll recover? Well enough to enter the Scholar Novitiate and go to his classes?"

She waited several seconds before she spoke. "Undoubtedly, his bones and tissues are crushed, but we have good medics on Merlin, and the latest technology for regenerating damaged organs."

That made twice in a row she hadn't answered his question. The children drifted back to their games, less merry than before the accident. Bobbi slunk away from the crowd, her shoulders slumped and her head down.

"It's so unfair," Steven said. "He didn't light the flame."

"Of course he didn't," Sheera agreed, as if he'd uttered the most obvious truth in the Galaxy. "However, I doubt if he'll tattle on the girl. What I can't figure out is, how did she smuggle a fire wand aboard the starship in the first place?"

Steven rubbed his shoulder where it ached from lifting the slab. "What should we do if he won't change his story, and she won't confess to causing the explosion? The Guidance Committee's going to demand an investigation. They know a zero-gravity chamber doesn't blow up for no reason."

"You're worried he'll be in deep trouble, aren't you?" Her mouth turned up slightly into something that was almost a smile. "Look, I've reviewed all these kids' records. I guarantee that if Danny gets better, nobody is going to expel him from the Community of Protectors, not with his qualifications. Can you believe he read Plato in the original Greek at seven? I didn't start doing that until I was ten. And another thing we look for in recruits is empathy."

"Empathy? Yeah, I can see that's important for the charity work you do."

"The boy's capacity for empathy is off the charts. How else would you explain his compulsion to protect his friend by confessing to an infraction he didn't commit? I predict he'll stick with his story. He might worry that he's sinning by telling a lie, the way Huckleberry Finn feared he would suffer eternal damnation for liberating the slave, Jim. But, like Huck, Danny will follow his heart."

The kid reminded her of a fictional character from a book over a thousand years old? Steven had been forewarned that scholars sprinkled their conversation with metaphors from history, literature, and Scripture, and now he'd heard a sample. It was just their way of talking, and seemed like a harmless quirk. "What about the mouthy brat?" he asked. "Are we going to let her walk away with no punishment?"

He pointed to Bobbi, who was engaging a male counselor in a heated argument. The counselor was insisting she shower, change her clothes, and get checked for burns. The girl, in return, demanded the right to accompany her friend to the infirmary in her present condition, drenched with grime.

"She can't afford to get into trouble. Her psychological profile is a mess. She makes up her own rules, instead of following the ones her authority figures set for her. On the other hand, her physical profile is first-rate. She'll adapt rapidly to Pendragon's harsh environment. The Admissions Panel approved her application on a split vote, on condition her behavior improves. She's out of here quicker than you can do a one-armed pull-up if the truth about the explosion leaks out."

He shrugged. "I don't like her much."

"That's as obvious as your biceps. But you don't want her to get expelled, do you?"

Steven had to think about it before he conceded. "I guess not. But it doesn't seem right that she gets away with causing so much damage, while the kid who probably did nothing wrong is lying in the infirmary, crippled and bleeding and…"

Sheera interrupted. "Bleeding, did you say? I saw it, too. He had trickles of blood all over him. Doesn't that mean anything to you?"

He guessed what she was driving at. Why hadn't the sight of the boy's broken body triggered another apparition?

CHAPTER SIX

THE JOURNEY HOME

"Rangers shall train in a harsh environment to develop their physical prowess to its maximum potential."
—D.F. Nathaniel

The thirty scholar novices gathered at the edge of Merlin's space port, waving good-bye to the friends they'd made over the previous two weeks. The other thirty campers, all ranger novices, drew near to the cigar-shaped rocket at the center, chattering about the fun they'd have after they launched to their new school on Pendragon. They wouldn't be so excited, Steven thought, if they knew how the g-force on gigantic worlds had a way of squashing skin against bones and paralyzing bodies.

Steven searched for Danny among the scholar novices, remaining on Merlin to train in gravity more hospitable to their punier physiques. He found the boy at the rear of the crowd. Orange trousers squeezed around Danny's legs, generating a force shield that would knit his bones together until they finished regenerating. His eyes were bloodshot from crying.

Steven stepped back and laid his arm on the boy's shoulder. "Still feeling the pain, buddy?"

Danny looked up. "No, sir. Thank you for inquiring. The force shield itches a little, but the medic tells me I won't need it much longer."

"Then what's the trouble? Is it your pal Bobbi?" What did he see in that little delinquent, anyway?

"Yes, sir. The whole time I was at the hospital, she visited me every day. We watched holographic videos and played games. She's the best friend I've ever had, and from now on we'll need to live on separate planets. I've read about why the Community needs two novitiates. Pendragon's high gravity would cripple me, and Merlin's low gravity would retard her muscular development."

Steven floundered, trying to think of words of comfort. "I wouldn't exactly say you can never again be on the same planet. After she gets older, her physical transformation will be complete, and she'll be allowed to visit small worlds. And you'll be able to take drugs to help you withstand Pendragon's environment."

"By that time, we'll be really old. Like, eighteen or nineteen."

Steven couldn't figure any other way to console the boy, and it was time to go. "Bye, kid. You'll make a great Protector some day."

Danny dropped his voice. His next words were to be for Steven's ears only. "Sir, I know you believe Bobbi caused the explosion. The lady named Sheera came to visit me at the hospital, and she told me about your suspicion. Promise me you won't tell anybody else that you think she was responsible. It's better if everyone goes on blaming me for lighting the flame."

"It'll be our secret," Steven promised. He would have broken that pledge in a minute, if necessary to spare Danny from disciplinary action or worse. But, so far, it was looking like the Guidance Committee intended to let the matter drop without any punishment.

Steven caught up to the ranger novices filing on board the shuttle. He made sure nobody squabbled, broke ranks, or engaged in other mischief. He knew what sort of misbehavior he needed to watch out for. It would be the same misbehavior he would have engaged in at that age, had he been able to get away with it.

Sheera dashed up. "Move along, kids," she called to the line of children who weren't yet on board. "Don't dawdle and don't stray out of line." She turned to Steven, smiling, and declared, "Sorry I'm late—but guess what?"

He hated it when people said "guess what." Whatever it was, why couldn't she just tell him? "Your scars are gone?" he asked hopefully.

She held her hands up, palms forward. Three brown lines, nearly faded, marked the times she'd stabbed herself to see if bloody skin would conjure Nathaniel's image. The first stabbing, minutes before the explosion, had generated the apparition, but the second two had failed to give rise to anything out of the ordinary. So far, the best theory was that, by saving Danny's life, he had mollified his conscience enough to make it stop harassing him. It seemed too easy, yet neither he nor Sheera could come up with any better explanation. They had even consulted Doctor Aloysius in a video link to Earth, and he had agreed it was quite possible.

Sheera held out her palms just long enough to guarantee Steven knew the scars were still there, then dropped them to her sides. "You've got to get over your obsession with my scars. The skin growth stimulant will take a few more days to complete the healing process. No, I'm talking about something lots more important than getting rid of a few measly scratches. The medic just confirmed that it's safe for me to visit Pendragon, so I got my assignment switched. I'm getting on board the shuttle with you."

Steven's heart rate doubled. He clasped his hands behind his back and stood, rigid as a totem pole. Must not let her suspect how excited she'd made him. "Well, as long as you're sure the environment won't be too intense for you," he said.

"I'll survive. It's all about bone density, blood pressure, muscle mass, and other physical stuff. Mine all check out healthy enough to let me remain on Pendragon for a week or so."

"That's swell, but… uh, did you know you're bouncing up and down?"

"Oops. Didn't mean to." She seemed giddy with joy. "It's just that the medic pumped my arteries full of drugs. They're supposed to alleviate most of the discomfort of living on Pendragon, but here on Merlin they make it an ordeal to stand still. They're moderately habit-forming, but I'll return to a more compatible environment before any addiction sets in."

"Why're you so happy about going to Pendragon?"

It would have been expecting too much, Steven knew, to suppose she'd answer that she wanted to spend more time with him. A Precept prohibited scholars from forming romantic entanglements with rangers, and she didn't impress him as the rebellious type where the Precepts were concerned.

She hopped back and forth from one foot to the other. "From our earliest days at the Merlin Novitiate, we hear tales about Pendragon. To us, the planet we orbit becomes a realm of mystery, where the kids from the Community's other branch get to live, but never us. Every night, we see it looming in the sky, appearing so grand. Any one of us can pick out the location of your campus among the swirls of yellow and green. Can you blame me for being happy? I'm going to be the first of my class to set foot there."

It was a superb reason, Steven had to admit. "When we get to my novitiate, I'll give you a tour," he offered.

"That would be nice," she accepted without hesitation. Hardly evidence she carried a crush for him, Steven thought, but better than a rejection.

Steven and Sheera followed the line of recruits through the shuttle's main hatch. They patrolled the aisle that ran between rows where the children sat, two to a row, and strapped in the recruits still fumbling with the locks on their safety belts. After they'd tended to the children, they latched their own belts, a ritual Steven complied with only because he felt compelled to set a good example.

A few minutes later, heaviness crept over every centimeter of Steven's body, signifying that the shuttle had achieved lift-off. The children whined in protest against the g-force that crushed them, growing worse as the shuttle accelerated. Sheera, seated beside him, turned pale. "Are the g's bothering you?" he asked.

"A little. The drugs are helping me, I'm sure. I don't want to think about the discomfort now. I want to watch for Merlin to appear on the video link to the outside." Her eyes grew wide, and Steven turned to see what she was gazing at. A green and white circle flashed onto a screen on the forward bulkhead. The circle filled the screen at first, then grew smaller with each passing second.

Sheera whispered. "I feel homesick when I see Merlin from space. I haven't been back to my birth-world since the day I left it to join the Community. I think of that round hunk of rock out there as home."

"Really? I thought the kids from your branch made regular visits to see your families, same as the kids from mine."

"We do." Her voice became flat. "The others did, but not me."

Steven couldn't imagine spending an entire decade at either novitiate without ever going home. Before he could ask why she'd been singled out for such a misfortune, the excess weight lifted, provoking a round of cheers throughout the cabin.

Steven punched a button in the bulkhead to establish a voice link with the shuttle's bridge. "You feeling the loss of Merlin's grip up there?"

The pilot answered. "My lunchbox just floated to the ceiling. How about you? Ready for me to shut off the artificial gravity?"

'These kids've been ready since we launched. Make us weightless, Captain."

Every gram of weight dissolved, catapulting the passengers into a bizarre dimension with no up or down. "Attention," Steven said. "You have permission to unstrap."

Unlocking the belts was easier than locking them. No one had trouble. The children floated from their seats and bounced off the walls, giggling and squealing in a paradise of disorientation. Most of them had frolicked in zero-gravity chambers, but in those, enough gravity leaked in to keep them aware of the difference between the top and the bottom. Between worlds, in contrast, *down* became a flexible concept that shifted about, and usually settled wherever the individual's feet happened to be. One person's *up* could be the next person's *down*.

"I hope nobody throws up," Sheera said, looking anxious.

"They can't. There is no up."

"You know what I mean."

Steven pushed away from his chair. Still in a seated posture, he hovered. "Space sickness won't be a problem. We ordered them to take a pill that prevents it."

"Look out!"

Steven dodged the remnants of the pancakes one child had eaten for breakfast. "On the other hand," he said, "ranger recruits don't always obey orders. Lucky I brought extra pills. You look a little green yourself. Open up." He popped a pill into her mouth.

The children spent the rest of the day drifting about the cabin, with no further incidents of space sickness. Steven got into the spirit and entertained his charges with mid-air summersaults. He planted his feet on the cabin's overhead after each round of twirls, like a spider on the ceiling, stuck to the metal alloy by magnets in the soles of his boots.

Sheera watched him from her seat. "You look funny, upside down like that," she said with a laugh.

"From where I stand, you're the one who's upside down. Come down… up… well, whatever direction it is, join me."

Steven stretched out his hands. Sheera took them, and let him guide her from her seat. The children howled as their counselors struggled to waltz in mid-air, drifting apart and clumsily pulling together. Some of the bolder children paired up with partners and tried to imitate the dance, with comical results. Amusing the kids was probably the only way he'd ever get her to dance with him, Steven thought.

∗   ∗   ∗

The morning and afternoon slipped away too quickly. The pilot called through an audio-link. "Approaching touch-down on Pendragon."

Steven eased from the ceiling back to his seat and called for the recruits to do the same. They met his command, first with a chorus of whining, and then with cooperation by all but three. He snatched the three rebels out of the air by their ankles, and then belted them into their seats. "Don't unstrap until I tell you to," he warned. "Yeah, Bobbi, I'm talking to you. Keep your paws away from that buckle."

"I hope those three learn to follow directions better after they start their training," Sheera whispered as she fastened her own strap.

"They will," Steven said. "I did. Ten years ago, I was one of the kids who had to be plucked from the air. Do you feel heavy again?"

"Yes." She moaned. "Too heavy."

The shuttle bumped to a landing on the planet. "Unstrap your belts," Steven directed.

Nobody obeyed. He hadn't expected them to. A few children made half-hearted attempts to lift their hands far enough to reach the buckles, then gave up. The cabin echoed with groans.

Sheera stayed in her seat. She grimaced as she raised her arm and offered it to Steven. "Help me onto the deck, will you? Even with the injections, I feel like sixteen bull elephants just piled on top of me. Thanks. How do you stand this?"

"Feels normal to me," he said. He braced her elbow with his arm. "Can you walk?"

"I think so. The medic promised the drugs would stimulate my muscles enough to keep me mobile. The more important question is: what about those kids? Will they be able to walk?"

"Depends on how you define 'walk.'" He sauntered about the cabin, unbuckled belts, and then took up his station against the forward bulkhead, facing the children. He looked into a sea of eyes squeezed into slits and faces squashed flat, as their skin pushed against their skulls. The kids would despise him for what he was about to do to them, but that couldn't be helped.

"Welcome to Pendragon, boys and girls," Steven said, pretending not to notice the misery surrounding him. "Congratulations. You are now novices, officially members of the Community of Protectors. It's time for you to leave the shuttle and get to know the place you'll call home from this day forward. It's an opportunity we give to less than one kid in a thousand who applies, so don't mess it up. It'd be a shame if we had to send you back to your birth-world, but we will if you don't obey orders and comply with the Precepts." He looked directly at Bobbi.

The recruits-turned-novices twitched their hands and feet, and one boy scratched his ear. But the moment they tried to rise, an invisible force slammed them down. Steven made his voice fierce to be heard over the moans. "Get your rears out of those chairs. We Protectors don't want slackers on our team."

There would be no punishment for remaining in their seats, but Steven had no intention of revealing that. The whole point was to terrify them into obedience. The children heaved their bodies onto the deck, and then scuffled off the shuttle onto a field of freshly-mowed clover surrounding the rocket port. The sleek, one-story dormitories and classrooms of their new home stretched over the flat terrain like silver snakes, a few hundred meters distant. They might as well have been in the opposite hemisphere, for all the hope the new arrivals had of narrowing the gap on foot. The children edged forward until they collapsed, one by one, littering the clover like a bunch of slugs. Steven stood tall and whispered to Sheera. "I carried my part off without a hitch." Surely she would be impressed.

She tilted her head upward to meet his eyes. "This is cruel. Shame on you for taking that harsh tone. I had no idea you put your novices through this ordeal."

"Cruel?" he repeated. She acted like he was some kind of an ogre, just for doing his job. "It's a period of adjustment. My classmates and me, we all went through the same struggle, and we've got no hard feelings." Maybe a few hard feelings lingered, but he wasn't going to admit to them in front of her. He resorted to the justification he'd heard from more senior rangers. "They'll forgive me eventually. Until they do, it builds up their camaraderie. They'll bond with each other over their common hatred of me."

"Make any excuse you choose. I still say it's cruel. I know they have to adapt to the gravity, but why can't you start them on drugs like the ones I'm on, and gradually wean them off?"

Steven threw up his hands. "Why does everybody talk like I make the rules? There's some medical reason, I think, why they're not supposed to have the drugs at this age. Take it up with Headquarters."

She squeezed his hand. A tingle passed through his body that, he was sure, she hadn't intended for him to feel. "Sorry, I didn't mean to blame you. What happens to them next? You can't just leave them helpless and practically paralyzed."

He pointed to a squad of novices a few years older than the newcomers, heading their direction, oblivious to the crushing pressure. "That's what those other kids are for." He noticed Sheera gawking. "Guess you think they're funny-looking. It's like those heads ought to be stuck onto different bodies, right?"

"That's it," Sheera said. "They have the faces of twelve-year-olds, but bodies that are bigger and more muscled than most adults." She looked Steven up and down. "But I can see they'll grow out of it. You must have gone through the same stage, and you turned out nice-looking."

It was the first time she'd complimented his looks. "Um... um..."

One boy jogged ahead of the others and spared Steven the need to respond to Sheera's flattery. "They didn't tell us you'd be in charge of this latest batch of newbies." the boy said. "How come you're back so soon? I thought strikers didn't get posted on Pendragon unless they'd screwed up."

Steven stifled an urge to hit the boy. "The reason I'm here— it's complicated. I'll explain later." Maybe he could invent an explanation by then.

The boy looked doe-eyed at Sheera. "You're a scholar, aren't you? Can you come talk to us later? We'd like to learn what your training is like." He pointed skyward. "Up there."

"We'll see," Steven said, grateful that Sheera had distracted the boy's attention. "You'd all better see to the newcomers. They're hurting."

Every member of the squad knew what to do. They scooped the fallen children into their arms, and carted them away.

"The older kids'll carry the younger ones to their dorm," Steven explained. "We always get plenty of volunteers. Gets them out of physical training for a day. They'll drop the new kids off at their bunks and stay with them for a while. In a few days, a week at the outside, the recruits will adapt enough to walk. In a month, they'll be running marathons."

She appeared deep into her own thoughts. "I'm trying to show you we're not cruel," he went on. "Did you hear a word I just said?".

"You didn't tell him."

So? All he'd done, Steven thought, was neglect to mention that he'd been recalled to Pendragon for psychiatric problems and a possible Precept breach. Did she have to make it sound like he'd pilfered from the poor box?

She went on. "When are you going to get it through your thick head that your assignment here is nothing to be ashamed of? I'll bet if these kids knew the full story of your posting on Medusa-Four, they'd hail you as a…"

"Don't call me a hero. Not for killing a man."

"As you wish. At least, you may not have to deal with awkward questions from novices much longer. I wanted to wait until we were alone before I told you some news I heard this morning. I called in a few favors, and I may have secured a posting for you on a planet called Pitcairn, way out on an arm of the galactic spiral."

A posting on another world? That was such fabulous news, it hardly mattered that it was on a planet he'd never heard of. But how could it be true, considering the Guidance Committee's inability to reach a verdict on whether he'd violated a Precept?

"Thanks," Steven said. "But I don't see how…"

"Welcome home, my friend." A middle-aged man was striding towards them. Steven recognized him as a Vice-Dean. And when a Vice-Dean interrupts your discussion, you stop to listen to him, no matter how annoyed you are by his timing.

The Vice-Dean, like every fully-grown ranger, towered over Sheera. "I got word you'd be on board." He coughed and seemed uneasy. "You're welcome here, of course. It's just that we don't often see scholar strikers on Pendragon. How are you bearing up under our environment?"

Steven surmised it was this man's job to make sure the gravity didn't paralyze their guest. If she suffered injury, he'd shoulder the blame.

"I can move about, sir," Sheera said. "The drugs appear to be doing their job. I suggest you focus on making sure the pressure doesn't injure the new arrivals."

"The little ones? They've already undergone rigorous testing to make sure they have body-types that won't suffer permanent damage."

In other words, Steven thought, it's not your responsibility.

The Vice-Dean went on. "It's you we need to look after, young lady. Sometimes I fear we put too much faith in those drugs. We have a wheelchair standing by in case you need it, and special quarters with the gravity adjusted lower. And now that you've experienced our conditions, our medic will look you over." He coughed again. "Just a precaution. Please follow me."

Sheera said nothing, but looked at Steven. Her eyes pleaded with him to step in, either to get her out of the exam, or to go with her. But he knew his duty. He had to stay with the children while they settled into their dorms. And even if he could have found a way to cancel the exam, he wouldn't have tried. He agreed with the Vice-Dean. The less risk to her health, the better.

"You'd better go," he said. "We can talk about my new posting later. Join me for dinner?"

She let out a deep breath. "I'll go, but I don't need any stupid wheelchair." She trudged off with the Vice-Dean, her footsteps falling in thuds.

* * *

Steven, left alone, set out for the dorm reserved for newcomers. Along the way, he passed a squad of fourteen-year-olds doing push-ups to the instructor's count of two hundred. Another cluster of novices, having a more enjoyable time, blasted zeta-ray pistols at paper targets.

The recruits' dorm was beyond the firing range. Its outer walls glinted like silver in the sun, and stretched across the grass for two hundred meters. With an entire world to construct their campus on, the Protectors had little need to build upwards. Steven followed the last of the volunteers, who were settling the children into their bunks.

He wandered from one bunk to another in the boys' quarters, to see if anyone needed help. Satisfied that all the boys were safe and miserable, he did the same rounds in the girls' quarters across the hall, and made the same finding. The volunteers appeared to be handling complaints without his help, so he proceeded to the computers, shiny round plates fixed to a wall on the boys' side. He pressed his thumb against one plate. After all these months away from the planet, it still recognized his DNA and granted him access. "Tell me about Pitcairn," he said.

The computer hummed and answered in a business-like female voice. "Pitcairn is an island on Earth, settled by mutineers from the H.M.S. Bounty."

That couldn't be right. Sheera had called it a planet on an arm of the Galaxy, not an island on Earth. "Is there also a world by that name?"

"There is no record of a world named Pitcairn in the available data base."

"Impossible," Steven said. Even a fleabite like Medusa-Four was registered with the Data Base of Worlds. Maybe Sheera had mispronounced the name. New arrivals sometimes garbled their speech, due to the pressure against their jaw muscles.

Funny thing, though. She hadn't mispronounced any other words.

CHAPTER SEVEN

WHO WILL GUARD THE GUARDIANS?

"A ranger and a scholar shall neither marry one another nor engage in any relationship of a romantic nature with each other."
—D.F. Nathaniel

Steven grabbed a tray and got in line at the Dining Commons, the cavernous room where he'd taken nearly every meal for ten years of his life. A teen-aged novice hurried over to him and talked over the surrounding chatter.

"I didn't expect to see you back on Pendragon so soon. A bunch of us are over at that table." He pointed. "Come sit with us and tell us about your adventures."

Steven mumbled "Mmm-hmm," as he piled his plate with hamburgers—the good kind he'd grown up with, fashioned from synthetic proteins, much tastier than the genuine beef he'd eaten on Medusa-Four. The boy's invitation offered a distraction. Talking about his "adventures" might keep him from obsessing over Sheera's failure to rejoin him.

The novices at the table peppered him with questions about the planet where he'd served. He regaled them with stories about the Community's battle against Medusa-Four's delirium dust industry. Maybe Sheera would be impressed if she walked in and saw how they treated him like a celebrity. They would show the same awe towards any returning striker, but she didn't need to know that. Where was she, anyway? He'd resigned himself to not seeing her again that day, when he noticed her loading her plate at the salad bar.

He called, and she took the seat next to him with a hasty apology for her lateness. "Sorry. I thought that medical exam was going to go on forever. But in the end, the doc cleared me for a week on Pendragon."

Sheera's small stature and plodding gait marked her as an outsider. "I've never met a scholar so close to my own age before," said the girl sitting across from her. "How do you know Steven? Did you serve on Medusa-Four together?"

A chunk of synthetic beef caught in Steven's throat. The wrong words from Sheera could shatter his reputation beyond repair. She smiled sweetly and said, "No. We met after he'd finished his assignment on Medusa-Four, and I'd finished mine in London."

So far, so good. She hadn't told them she was treating him for mental instability.

"Yeah, I wondered about that," a boy said, shoveling asparagus into his mouth. "Why did you get re-posted so soon?"

Steven had been bracing for that question all day, but he'd yet to figure out a reply that would cover up his disgrace. The entire table fell silent, poised to receive the answer he didn't have.

Sheera dove into the conversation. "Headquarters decided he was ready for greater responsibility. He volunteered to help with the new recruits during the brief interval he's between postings on other worlds. Hey, did he tell you how the warlords on Medusa-Four treat their miners like slaves?"

Steven exhaled. Their companions must have been satisfied with her explanation, vague as it was. They didn't raise the topic again.

*   *   *

Merlin ruled the night sky by the time Steven and Sheera slipped away from the dining commons. He had in mind to propose a stroll beneath Merlin's light. There was the taboo against scholar-ranger romance to consider, but, strictly speaking, the Precept didn't forbid a male from one branch from merely taking a walk with a female of the other. It was possible Sheera wouldn't laugh in his face. He'd confronted armed assassins without blinking, but now he struggled to find his courage. "I promised you a tour," he said.

"Yes, you did."

Here goes, he thought. "I don't suppose you'd want to start with the gardens?"

"The medic said I'm bearing up well under your gravity, so a walk through the gardens sounds like fun. But first, I'd like to check out the dorm and see how the children are acclimating."

Steven had already spent the entire afternoon watching the children acclimate. By now, it seemed roughly as exciting to him as watching the clover grow. He looked into her eyes, bright with sincerity and compassion, and mustered as much enthusiasm as he could fake. "Great idea."

Together they entered the boys' dorm. The children read, slept, played games, or watched videos in their bunks. They moved their arms and twitched their fingers more easily than they had when they first arrived on Pendragon, and they opened their eyes wider. The scene on the girls' wing was the same. Steven waved to the teen-ager who had taken over his shift, a novice in his final year at the novitiate.

"They're adapting on schedule," Steven said, as he steered Sheera out the door.

They left the cluster of classrooms and barracks behind, and set out along a path that meandered among rows of daisies, roses, and tulips, transplanted from Earth and genetically engineered to withstand Pendragon's environment. Dewdrops on the blooms sparkled in the moonlight from Merlin and its sister-moon, Guinevere. Climate-control technology kept the air at room temperature, and the technician who managed the weather station had filtered in a faint breeze. The scent of the flowers wafted in their direction.

"Why, those are bees," Sheera said, as she pointed to a cluster blanketing the flowers. "They're wonderful. Their wingspan makes them resemble hummingbirds."

Steven walked on and didn't bother to look. He'd seen the giant bees, and in his experience knew of no other variety. "Sometimes, you can hear 'em buzzing at night before you fall asleep. In the early days, some gardener ordered a bunch of hives from Earth. Ninety-five percent of the bees couldn't get off the ground and died the first week, but a few queens survived, and their descendants evolved powerful wings. Don't be afraid of 'em. They're genetically engineered to not sting humans."

They didn't speak of the Precept that barred them from romantic entanglements. But it rattled constantly in Steven's thoughts, as he snatched glances at Sheera. Would they be touching by now, if they didn't have that Precept to hold them back, and if they touched, what would her skin feel like against his?

"You were lucky to grow up with such a magnificent garden in your backyard," Sheera said. "Is all Pendragon like this?"

"Most of it is barren and dusty. Only the area around the novitiate has been terraformed with greenery and wildlife transplanted from Earth. Outside of the Protectors, the only sign of human presence is mining operations, and those function almost entirely with robots and machines."

Sheera appeared not to have heard. "This is how I'd picture Eden," she said.

Of course you would, Steven thought, because you couldn't let the evening pass without drawing at least one analogy from history or literature or the Bible. "It turns into a forest up ahead," he said. "Would you like to walk into the woods? It's safe. The landscape architects who designed the place were careful not to import any dangerous animals."

"Safety is the furthest concern from my mind when I'm with you. Something tells me it wouldn't matter if we stumbled onto a mama grizzly protecting her cubs. You'd handle it."

After high praise like that, the time was ripe for him to respond with something clever and charming. "Um. Oh. Well…"

Sheera's smile lit up her entire face. "Lead on."

Flowers gave way to trees, and a canopy of oaks and pines replaced the garden. "Pendragon didn't have enough carbon dioxide to evolve much in the way of native greenery," Steven explained. "These trees and plants are descended from seeds and pine cones shipped from Earth. They can only grow because the engineers who terraformed the planet injected carbon dioxide into its atmosphere." For a guy who had nearly flunked botany, he was doing fairly well at sounding like he knew what he was talking about. "You know, plants take in…"

She nodded. "I know. Plants take in carbon dioxide in almost the same way we take in oxygen. Our terraformers had to do the same thing on Merlin."

He supposed there was no point in trying to impress her with his knowledge of… well… pretty much anything aside from sports or combat. There was probably no other subject she didn't understand better than he did.

Sheera began to breathe in heavy gasps. "Picking up my feet is a chore," she said. "The drugs help, but only to a point."

They paused for a rest beneath a pine tree, on the first bench they encountered. They took care to allow a respectable gap between them. Merlin floated high in the heavens, swirls of green and white covering its surface, with Guinevere rising, a silver disc in the sky. Both satellites had moved into their full phase, a showcase the heavens provided less than twice in a month.

Hooting sounds pierced the silence. "Owls, too? Your terraformers thought of everything." Her face beamed. "Now I can finish telling you my good news, without anybody to interrupt."

"Is this about that planet you mentioned? Pitcairn, was it?"

"Pitcairn is part of the total picture. This morning, just before I met you at the launch site, I persuaded the medics to clear you for regular duty. You're free to lend a hand any place in the cosmos where people are in trouble, and Pitcairn is the next available posting."

"Oh. That's... um... swell." Steven had spent most of his waking hours, since leaving Medusa-Four, longing to hear the words she had just spoken. Now that he had heard them, he was not sure they were welcome. A new posting would carry him light-years from the person he most wanted to be near. "How can I be eligible for a job outside the Excalibur star system? " he asked. "Nathaniel has stopped haunting me, for now, but I have a bigger problem. The Guidance Committee hasn't cleared me of a Precept violation in the death of the Warlord."

She scrunched her face, and seemed as perplexed as he was. "I don't know," she admitted. "But an administrator named Harold granted you a pre-posting interview, so the charge against you must have been dropped somehow. Our contact on the planet says the assignment has something to do with fighting a harpy. Oh, stop looking at me like my head is missing a few cogs. I'm sure she doesn't mean a harpy in the literal sense of the Greek myth about women who looked like birds. Most likely, it's some alien that reminds people of the legend."

"Are you sure Pitcairn is the correct name? The computer at the barracks never heard of it."

"Then we'll just have to fix the computer. The planet's diameter is barely half Earth-normal. According to Doctor Aloysius, that's exactly what your brain needs. If you never cope with the lighter atmosphere of a puny world, your lobes will never be forced to adapt to a low gravity environment."

"Yeah, back on Earth, he told me the same thing, that I should get posted on a small planet." He looked at her across the space that separated them. "Would Merlin qualify?"

"I'm sure it would, but why do you want to know? I thought Merlin was the last place you wanted to be posted." She smiled at a squirrel scampering up a tree. "You keep telling me you feel disgraced, having to work at the novitiates, though heaven only knows why. And you seem so impatient with the small ones."

"Yeah, I know I'm short with them sometimes, but that doesn't mean I don't like the little brats." He took a deep breath, daring to hope she'd be pleased by what he was about to suggest. "Maybe I should stick around Merlin for a while. I'll have plenty of time later to rebuild my reputation with off-world assignments."

She stared at him, and he glanced away, embarrassed to meet her eyes. "You want to work at the Scholar Novitiate? Well, that's a shocker. Until now, all I heard from you was that you wanted to jump back into action on the Galaxy's frontier. Hmmm. I'll be posted on Merlin, too, after I finish my work here and get back from a long overdue visit to my birth-world."

He squirmed. "That's a coincidence. Maybe we'll see each other around." After an agonizing pause, he gave up the lie. "Oh, who'm I kidding? You know the real reason I'd like to transfer to Merlin."

"I think I do."

The gap between them on the bench evaporated. Her body grazed his. He draped an arm around her. She didn't protest when he pulled her closer. Her skin felt soft compared to the rippled flesh of the girls from the ranger branch, and he relished the way her tiny arms and shoulder muscles yielded against his fingers.

His lips settled against hers, and, to his amazement, even then she didn't pull away. They kissed again and again, and then after a while paused to take a breath. She drew back. "We're violating a Precept," she said.

He closed the space between them. "Does it matter?"

"I suppose not," she said, and tightened her arms around him. *I suppose not*—that was the last answer he'd expected to hear from her. In his experience, a scholar would rather get stranded on a frozen dwarf planet than breach one of Nathaniel's rules. They continued to violate the Precept, with mounting passion and little concern for the consequences, until a little voice squealed in disgust.

"Eewwh! Stop that, you two!"

They ripped apart, like they'd each learned the other carried a contagious disease. Bobbi was standing about three meters away, her eyes fixated on them.

"How long have you been there?" Sheera asked.

"I dunno. Pretty long. It was like you two were never gonna stop… doing that… if I didn't say something."

Sheera turned the shade of a ripe tomato. "But, you're out of bed. I didn't think that was possible so soon after arriving."

"Rare, but it happens," Steven said, beginning to sweat. "Every once in a while, a new novice will adapt quickly enough to walk before the first night is out. You did say her physical qualifications were exceptional."

Sheera stiffened. "Why did you follow us?"

The girl gazed at her feet and whimpered. "After I saw you leave our dorm together, I guess I wanted to thank you for not telling on me. You know, about that explosion. Danny told me you figured out I was the one who lit the flame that made the chamber blow up. I thought for sure you'd tell, and then they wouldn't let me be a Pr'tector like the other kids." She sneezed.

Steven thought back to his visit to Danny the day after the explosion. "I told him we had an inkling you'd done it, but the truth is, we were sure. We won't tell on you, but that doesn't mean we approve of your conduct." His voice grew stern. "That sign told you not to light a fire. We put up signs like that for good reasons. If you expect to fit in with our Community, you're going to have to follow every rule from now on. You understand, don't you?"

"Uh huh." She wiped away a tear.

"Good. And you shouldn't be wandering around yet. Just because you can crawl out of bed doesn't mean your body is ready to withstand the gravity for long distances. Go on back to your bunk until your receive a medic's permission to leave."

"Is that a rule, too?"

"Yes," he lied.

Bobbi didn't budge from her spot. "That mushy stuff you two were doing. Isn't there a rule against that?"

Steven groaned, and Sheera said, "Yes, honey, there is. It's one of the Nathanielian Precepts, and around these parts, that's the highest kind of rule you'll find. Sometimes, we big kids don't do what we're supposed to do either. We were wrong, and we'll never break that rule again."

"We won't?" Steven said, then, realizing his words had spilled out sounding like a question, he amended. "Right. We won't. It would be better if you don't talk to anybody about what you saw tonight."

The girl, apparently satisfied, mumbled "Okay," and turned back in the direction of the barracks.

"I'm an idiot," Steven declared when they were alone.

"I concur, but for the brand of idiocy we engaged in tonight, it takes two."

"Just so there's no misunderstanding, I meant I... we... were idiots for getting caught, not for what we were doing. Do you expect she'll tell anyone?" He left unspoken the truth they both knew. A few words of gossip from the girl, uttered when the wrong ears were listening, could land them in a heap of trouble. And he was already on probation.

"Whether she tells anyone or not is beside the point. Getting caught, as we did—it's a wake-up call. Perhaps a warning from God."

Uh-oh. He knew he was in for a rough time when she dragged the Almighty into the mix. "God's too busy running a universe."

"I'm serious. There are sound reasons for the Precept that forbids romantic entanglements between scholars and rangers."

"Really?" Steven cringed. He didn't like the direction the conversation was heading. "I know most of the Precepts make sense, but I never thought the one that keeps rangers and scholars apart had much of a reason behind it. I always assumed it was just one of those customs we carry on because Nathaniel told us to do it hundreds of years ago, even if it's out-dated now."

Sheera's face could not have registered greater horror had he insulted motherhood itself. "Don't speak of our founder in such a disrespectful tone. When he set up a system to develop your kind into the most powerful fighting force in the Galaxy, he set up a parallel system to train my kind to function as your superiors. That's why we can never be your lovers. Placing you under our authority, and requiring us to keep an emotional distance between us, is the only way to prevent your kind from abusing your abilities."

He wasn't sure which was worse: her stubborn loyalty to an outmoded Precept, or her scornful opinion of his comrades. "You make it sound like we rangers would be nothing but a gang of bullies without you scholars to rein us in. I was taught, from my first week on Pendragon, that I'm to use my abilities only in the service of the powerless. I'd never betray that teaching."

"I understand," she said, but she didn't sound as if she understood at all. "I didn't mean you personally. I'll grant that you, as an individual, wouldn't harm anyone without good reason. But other members of your branch might spin out of control if they aren't subject to our command. That's why the ban on romance between us is so vital. A relationship that gets too close in... in certain ways... it interferes with our objectivity, and jeopardizes the position of superior to subordinate. Don't expect me to ignore the Precept again." She softened her voice. "But I'm delighted you're now willing to accept a posting on Merlin. My closest companions are away on missions to other worlds. I could use a new friend."

A new friend? Was friendship the most she wanted from him? Why didn't she just take a dagger and plunge it into his heart? That morning, on Merlin, he might have been willing to settle for her offer, since there had never appeared much chance their relationship could ever progress any further. But after their minutes of closeness, he could no longer set his sights so low. "Are you afraid of getting caught?" he asked, with a touch of desperation. "Is that it? We were careless tonight, but we could be more cautious in the future."

He realized from her expression, even before she responded, that he'd said the wrong thing. He had a habit of doing that, especially around her.

"Sneaking around would be worse," she said. "This isn't an issue of getting caught. Well, perhaps it is, partly. But mostly, it's a matter of trust. Of integrity. We both took a vow to live or die by the Precepts for as long as we swear allegiance to the Community. I don't go back on a vow. Never."

"Are you kidding? You just did. We both did."

"I know. I never set out to. Honestly, I thought we were just going to take a stroll in the gardens. It was like I was under a spell, all of a sudden. It must have been the effect of Merlin and Guinevere floating in the night sky, so shiny and romantic. And of finding out you were willing to suffer the ridicule of your peers, just to be with me a little longer."

He thought over her proposal of friendship—when had that once-beautiful word become so painful?—and saw it as offering him nothing more than a constant reminder that she could never give him what he needed. And what if she found someone new, someone from her own branch? Could he bear watching her lavish on another guy the affection she couldn't give to him? "Once I could have been satisfied, being just your friend," he said. "Not after what we did tonight."

"Fine. But don't expect me to give in." She crossed her arms, pouted, and looked away.

Something had changed. Steven could no longer abide sharing the same stellar system with Sheera, not if they had to live there under Nathaniel's restriction. The restriction was beyond his power to change, but he had an opportunity to quit the stellar system.

"That little girl's not the only one who needs to take it easy in this environment," he said. "We should get you back to the dorm."

CHAPTER EIGHT

AN INTERVIEW THAT TURNS INTO
A BIOLOGY QUIZ

"Protectors must become strong in order to defend the weak."
—D.F. Nathaniel

Steven's posting interview would either salvage his career, or send it careening down the toilet, depending on whether he gave the correct answers. And he had no idea what those answers should be. He fidgeted, waiting for old Harold to arrive, in what was supposed to be an office. It had the feel of a cell, with no windows, no decorations, and no furnishings except the chair he was sitting on, and a wall clock that flashed the time in purple numerals every five seconds. Twenty minutes slipped by, if he could believe the clock, but the clock had to be wrong. It seemed more like he'd been sitting there somewhere between an hour and eternity.

He dozed. Sheera came to him in a dream. He stroked her cheek, then draped his arms around her shoulders and drew her body near. The real Sheera never wore perfume, but the dream Sheera must have spilled a bottle over herself. He inhaled a fragrance that suggested the flowers they had strolled past the previous night. She brought her mouth close to his, as if to kiss him, but paused and parted her lips to talk. The real Sheera spoke in tones that made him yearn to listen forever. Her dream counterpart snarled in a male voice.

"Striker! I need you awake!"

His head jerked and his eyes snapped open. A wall appeared to have melted away, leaving him staring into another office that flowed into the space he was sitting in. He'd seen other rooms at the novitiate with the same technology. Usually, they served as video links between Pendragon and Merlin, a way to communicate from one world to the other with the illusion of conversing in the same room. A vase of flowers in a corner of the far-distant office matched the scent of dream-Sheera's perfume. The rumor was true, then. New technology could transfer smells across space.

A man behind a desk sat with hands folded directly across from him, so seemingly near that Steven's impulse was to offer a polite handshake. He spared himself that embarrassment by remembering, in time, that an invisible void, thousands of kilometers across, loomed between them. The man's eyes peered from under thick brows the color of coal. Gray streaked his hair and creases lined his face, completing his look of someone who took charge of any situation. So this was Harold, the scholar who would decide Steven's fate. So much for a favorable first impression.

Steven sank low in his seat. "I'm sorry, sir."

"See that it never happens again." The man tapped on a writing tablet, then looked up as if noticing Steven's presence for the first time. "I would have preferred to shuttle over to meet you in person. But the pesky medics won't clear me to make the crossing. Those quacks say my heart can no longer handle your world's gravity."

Steven was sorry the old man had medical issues, truly he was, but he didn't know what he was supposed to say or do about them. "It's nice to meet you, sir," he mumbled.

"No, it's not, and we both know it. If you found out you could get your posting without having to endure this grilling, you'd turn handsprings. But as it is, you have to go through me before you get to Pitcairn." Harold pointed a boney finger. "Tell me what you expect to accomplish on that obscure little world."

If the first question was any indication, Steven was in for an uncomfortable interrogation. What exactly had he already learned about this posting? Not enough to impress anyone with his research skills. "I'm told my opponent will be a monster that some natives call a harpy. Not that I believe in genuine harpies." What was it Sheera had said? He couldn't go wrong by quoting her. "It's probably some alien that reminds people of the mythical creature."

Harold nodded. "You're correct."

Steven sighed with relief. He wasn't sure what he'd been correct about. Maybe everything. The important thing was, he hadn't blurted out anything stupid. Yet.

Harold continued. "My source is a physician who's been stationed on Pitcairn for years. She says the creature has characteristics of both humans and birds. In this, he resembles the harpies of Greek mythology."

Steven had been ten when he'd heard the tale of the Argonauts rescuing the King of some ancient Greek city from a flock of disagreeable harpies. "I understand, sir, but begging your pardon. You called it *he*. I thought harpies were female."

Harold scowled. "An irrelevant quibble. I'll explain more about this creature later, but first I need to test your knowledge of another subject. Tell me about the Carthoris Phenomenon."

Steven welcomed the change of topic, since he had nothing more to contribute concerning Greek mythology. And he might be able to give an acceptable answer, provided Harold would be satisfied with basic facts he remembered from his class in interplanetary genetics. He coughed. "The Phenomenon takes its name from a science fictional character created by the twenty-first century American author, Burroughs."

"Twentieth."

"Oh. Sorry. I get those two centuries mixed up." Now who was raising an irrelevant quibble? "Carthoris was half-human and half-Martian, the son of John Carter and Dejah Thoris. There's no such thing as a Martian, but people didn't know that back in the twenty-first... I mean, twentieth... century. Cross-breeding of species from different worlds is named for him."

"Yes, cross-breeding of species from different worlds." Harold leaned back in his chair. "Is it possible?"

Steven's hands trembled. He hadn't come prepared for a biology quiz. "It happens, but only in rare cases, sir. Do you want to hear more?"

"Proceed."

"Thank you." For what, he wasn't sure, but expressing gratitude at that point seemed like the proper thing to do. "Mainly, Carthoris occurs in plants. There are flower species that can pollinate with flowers from other worlds. And once, the Phenomenon cropped up in bugs. Scientists found a kind of insect that can mate with an insect from half the Galaxy away. The queens can lay eggs that hatch into little half-breeds. Shall I go on?"

Steven tried to read Harold's expression. Was the old man pleased by the response so far? He detected no reaction, and guessed that Harold was rating his performance as less than stellar but better than complete failure.

"I didn't tell you to stop."

"I guess you didn't. About nine years ago, reptiles from different planets mated in a laboratory experiment. The eggs never hatched, but the embryos were definitely hybrid. That's the highest life form so far that's interbred between worlds. Oh, there's one more thing that's kind of important. Carthoris has never worked for any species of Earth origin." He would have rattled on if he could have, but he'd exhausted everything he knew about the Carthoris Phenomenon. He'd be sunk if Harold demanded more details.

The old man nodded, without smiling. "Your answers have been adequate. Not exemplary, but adequate, so far. Do you believe cross-breeding between worlds could account for a mix between a human and an alien?"

The question struck Steven as ludicrous, the answer, obvious. "Well... I don't think so. There's never been a hybrid mammal.

I guess some humans have… you know… gotten together with intelligent aliens, but nobody's ever come up with offspring that way, not even an embryo. Something about incompatible chromosomes." He held his breath, hoping Harold wouldn't ask him to define a chromosome.

"The prevailing belief is that it is impossible for cross-breeding to occur between humans and aliens," Harold said, tapping his fingers on his desk. "But I will show you evidence to the contrary."

Harold's image vanished, along with his office on Merlin. A split screen flashed in its place, plastering the entire wall. Steven gazed at three-dimensional images of two species he never before knew existed, one above and the other below. A four-legged bird peered at him from the upper screen, through black marble eyes, as plainly as if it was really there. Its beak curved forward like the edge of a saber. Every leg ended with talons in place of feet. The creature's torso would have resembled a deer, if the deer happened to be sprouting green feathers from every pore. Its wings, of the same shade, had to be mainly decorative, maybe some evolutionary tool for attracting a mate. They certainly wouldn't be of any use for flying. It was a matter of aerodynamics. A wingspan that small—no more than two meters from one wingtip to the other—couldn't give the power of flight to a body that bulky. On the whole, the creature was no more remarkable than any of the thousands of other alien bird species cataloged by the scientists who cared about that sort of thing.

The lower image, however, made no sense at all. Could Harold be testing him to see if he had wits enough to detect a hoax? The creature resembled the species in the upper picture from the neck up, with the same beady eyes, but with flatter features, like those of a human face. It had two human-looking arms and balanced on two legs in a homo-sapiens posture. The legs, blanketed by feathers, would have fastened neatly into the hip sockets of a human frame. The wings copied the wings on the creature in the top picture, except the green was paler, more of an olive. Hands, instead of talons, stuck out from the feathers on its wrists. The creature might possess the ability to manipulate tools, if it had brains enough to know what to do with its opposable thumbs.

The images disappeared in a burst of light, and Harold reappeared on the screen. All this talk about the Carthoris Phenomenon, and now, a creature who was neither fully man nor fully alien. There seemed only one reason why Harold would have steered the interview in that direction, but it couldn't be. It would be lunacy. Steven proceeded slowly, uneasy over how ridiculous his words must sound. "You can't be saying this thing—the one on the bottom—is half human and half alien?"

Harold folded his arms, and after giving Steven a long stare, said, "What do you think?"

Steven didn't know what to think, but he couldn't reveal his ignorance, so he groped for an answer. "I think... I think it can't be a half-breed. Carthoris has never happened with any kind of mammal species. And if it did happen, it wouldn't produce a monstrosity like... like that. Whenever it's happened in the lower species, there's been perpendicular evolution first."

"Parallel."

"Right. The kind of evolution that churns out species with different ancestors, but who still look a lot alike. The real-life examples of interplanetary cross-breeding match a flower with a flower, a bug with a bug, and a reptile with... well, with something that sort of looks like another reptile. If humans ever produce offspring with aliens... and I'm not saying it'll ever happen, but if somehow it does... it won't be with a species that scoots around with feathers and wings."

Harold grew thoughtful. "Until recently, I would have agreed, as would any sane biologist. Yet—if the creature in the picture is not a hybrid, I'm at a loss as to what it is."

"A hoax, maybe? A man in a bird costume?"

"I might suspect the same, except the plea for help comes from one of our Community's most trusted physicians, someone too smart to be deceived by a trick so crude as a man wearing a costume. Whatever it is, it preys on the human settlers, and the local military is powerless to stop it. I thought by now you would have remarked on the fangs. It uses them to rip into its victim's jugular and deposit a deadly venom." Harold's lips curved into a sideways smile, the first indication he had a sense of humor, even a perverted one. "Does that frighten you?"

Steven's mind raced. If he answered yes, Harold might take him for a coward. But if answered no, Harold might assume he was reckless. For the moment, the monster's fangs didn't frighten him, but the prospect of giving the wrong answer did.

"It doesn't matter whether I'm scared," he said with careful thought. "If that creature is terrorizing innocent people, it's my duty as a Protector to overcome my fears and bring it down, even at a risk to my own life." There, that ought to please him.

Harold nodded, apparently satisfied, and held up an electronic tablet that displayed an image of the hybrid creature. "This so-called harpy has strength beyond that of a normal human. Whoever undertakes this assignment should be prepared for a likelihood of hand-to-hand combat. I've reviewed your qualifications. Your victory in the martial arts competition was impressive. The rest of your record is satisfactory. With one exception."

Steven gulped. Had the little girl blabbed about the Precept violation she'd witnessed? No, it was too soon for a child's gossip to leap the chasm of space and filter up to the Community's top management. But there was another possibility. "If you mean my visions of D.F. Nathaniel, I'm cured of those." He considered himself to be on reasonably safe ground in saying that. After all, he hadn't had an apparition since the day he saved Danny, in spite of having seen blood twice.

"The visions aren't the problem. Maybe you really did see Nathaniel. Even if you didn't, Doctor Aloysius recommends testing you in actual combat." He cleared his throat. "There is that other matter. The Guidance Committee remains unconvinced you had justifiable cause to slay the drug lord. It agreed to give you a second chance, but with some dissension. The vote to return you to combat duty was three to two."

"With due respect, the two people who voted against me weren't in the saloon that night."

"You may as well know, I was one of the two dissenters."

Steven stared at the floor, searching for a hole he could crawl into.

"You are still on probation, striker," Harold went on. "Your provincial on Pitcairn will be under orders to suspend you from duty at the slightest indication of a Precept violation. If you fail the citizens of that world, your remaining time with our Community will be brief. Do you accept your posting under these conditions?"

It wasn't like he had a choice. Not unless he was willing to throw away everything he had trained for and dreamed of. "Yes, sir, I accept. All I ask is a chance to prove myself."

"You have it. Effective immediately, you are relieved of your duties overseeing the newcomers. Report to the medical center, where you'll spend the rest of today receiving inoculations to protect you against native viruses."

"I understand, sir. I went through the same preparation before I was posted on Medusa-Four."

"No, you don't understand. Medusa-Four is such a barren hell-hole, even the germs don't want to live there. Human settlers are in very little danger from disease. Pitcairn is different. It teems with microbes, including one that causes a fatal illness called helium rejection syndrome. It renders atmospheric helium poisonous to the human system, and we have no vaccination or cure."

Steven hoped that, with the slight color distortion of a video link transmitted through vacuum, Harold wouldn't notice he'd turned pale. He was trained to fight monsters, not microbes.

Harold spoke rapidly, as if there was someplace more important he had to get to. "Tomorrow, you'll launch in a shuttle that will carry you to the space port that orbits the planet Morgana, where you'll transfer to a galactic freighter. Later, you'll leave the freighter to pass through a portal that will carry you into Pitcairn's system. Do you understand everything I've told you?"

"Uh…"

"Good. There is one more thing. I have instructions directly from Doctor Aloysius." Harold's fingers grazed over the button on his desk that would shut off the video link. "If at any time you observe a person or object you suspect has no physical reality, you are to immediately report the problem to your provincial."

The video link flashed off, ending the interview before Steven had a chance to ask why the computer in the dorm had no record of Pitcairn's existence.

CHAPTER NINE

THE ONE LEFT BEHIND

"A Protector, as a citizen of the Galaxy, shall not have allegiance to any government, or to any world, but only to the Community. Nothing in this Precept shall discourage a Protector from complying with the just laws of any country or world where he or she is stationed."
—D.F. Nathaniel.

Sheera trudged across the lawn from her dorm to the rocket port. She noticed, for the first time, that on Pendragon even the sprouts of clover were thicker. The injections were wearing off, impairing her ability to walk, in roughly the same way as donning lead-weighted boots would have done. If she remained on Pitcairn one more day, her system would become totally injection-free, and she would not be able to pick up her feet at all.

"I'm supposed to be so smart," she thought as she struggled to cross the distance. "How could I have been so stupid?"

She hadn't seen Steven since that evening in the woods, when she'd broken first her oath and then his heart. The next morning, when he didn't join her for breakfast, she became convinced he was avoiding her. Since then, she'd combed every centimeter of the campus in search of him, determined to talk with him at least one more time before they moved on to their new postings. But her quest had hit a dead end when his friends told her he'd already launched for some planet they'd never heard of.

"Where are you going?"

A cheerful voice called from behind. Her again. Bobbi, for the previous three days, had seemed to be lurking around every corner. Sheera would sometimes stay clear of open spaces, unless she knew her one-girl fan club would be occupied elsewhere with a lesson. But on this occasion, Sheera was pleased to see her. It wouldn't have felt right to exit Pendragon without saying farewell… and thank you.

Sheera slowed until the girl caught up. "I'm traveling to my home world to visit my family."

"Then you're comin' back to Pendragon, right?"

Bobbi's face lit up with so much hope, Sheera couldn't bear to reveal the truth. Telling a lie would have been worse, though. "I can't return to your world for quite some time," she said. "I have medicine in my body that helps me walk about, but it's nearly worn off, and it will hurt me if I take it again too soon. Besides, I have another job lined up for after I finish my trip home. The kids on Merlin need me to watch over them." When the girl's face fell, Sheera added, "Hey, perhaps I'll see your pal, Danny. Would you like me to carry a message to him?"

The girl pondered long and hard, then replied, "I dunno."

Sheera glanced about. This was her first opportunity to speak with Bobbi with no one else in hearing range.

"I need you to tell me the truth," she said. "You remember, when the big guy kissed me…."

"He did more than that. So did you."

"Right." Sheera blushed. "You know there's a rule against what we did. Why haven't you reported us?"

The girl cast her eyes down. "You didn't tell on me. So I didn't tell on you."

Sheera hugged the little girl. "Thank you. And good-bye." She staggered onto the shuttle for the first leg of her journey.

CHAPTER TEN

A DISTURBING METHOD OF TRAVEL

"A Protector's territory shall be any place within reach of humankind where there is suffering or injustice."
—D.F. Nathaniel

Steven had traveled over twenty thousand light years on the freighter *Moons of Neptune*, bound for the hinter-most reaches of the Galaxy. His mode of transportation, like everything else in the physical universe, was bound by nature's ironclad prohibition against outpacing light. Yet there he was, less than a week out of Pendragon, so far from his starting point that empires could rise and fall while light was just beginning the same journey.

Steven sank into the middle cushion of a couch in the freighter's observation lounge, surrounded by other passengers reading or snoozing under a cavalcade of stars. The dome over his head shut out the cold and the vacuum, but allowed in a view of the heavens more spectacular than he could have seen from the highest peak of Pluto.

The view prompted him to remember, with quiet smugness, the day his interstellar physics teacher gave him the highest possible score on an exam. All he'd had to do was repeat the official explanation of how humankind had bridged the gap to the stars.

The universe is a sphere, he'd written on the exam. Our five senses can only perceive the portion of the universe that stretches across the sphere's surface, like the hide of a soccer ball. He'd gone on to explain that the asteroids, comets, planets, stars, and galaxies are sprinkled on the surface, like glitter. Slice through the sphere's interior, and you can zip from one star to another in no time. Literally no time, because, inside the universe, time does not exist.

Parroting the correct response hadn't been the same thing as understanding it. It seemed to Steven there had to be something inside the universe. But that would have been deemed the wrong answer, and cost him points on the exam, because scientists insisted there was nothing inside. Zilch. Nada. They didn't mean the sphere was hollow. Hollowness would have possessed height, width, breadth, and time, all in measurable amounts. They meant the inside of the universe had none of those pesky dimensions, so impossible to avoid on its outside. With no time or distance to slow you down, you could slip through a gap in the sphere's skin, and pop out thousands of light years away in less than an eye blink. Humankind's ability to leapfrog the stars was limited only by the number of portals nature had carved into surface space.

Steven glanced about the lounge, and saw no evidence he was living on the skin of nothingness. Yet he had to agree something fantastic came into play every time a spaceship slipped into a portal. How could he deny it? He was out among the stars, wasn't he? Men and women had crisscrossed their own galaxy because scientists had discovered over five thousand such portals. Someday, they might find a passage to Andromeda or some other distant galaxy, but if that existed, it awaited discovery.

The portals had worked well enough, so far, to carry *Moons of Neptune* from the ringed planet Morgana, in Pendragon's stellar system, to within four trillion kilometers of Pitcairn's sun. Right next-door by standards of interstellar distance. But Steven would still have to face months more of traveling, unless he could narrow the gap by passing through one final portal.

*   *   *

A passenger stepped into the lounge. *Please don't sit next to me,* Steven thought, moments before the newcomer's rear end occupied the place next to him on the couch. He was probably a perfectly nice man—if he could be defined as a man—but Steven cringed when he saw the third eye where a nose should have been.

Steven sprang from the couch. Then, fearful his sudden departure would offend his seat-mate, he smiled politely.

Except for the eye peculiarity and silver skin, the face that looked back at him had the characteristics of a human. "Does my appearance disturb you?" the alien said. The sound emitted, not from vocal cords, but from a bronze collar that muffled the speaker's voice and translated his words into human tones and language.

"It's not that." Actually, it was that, but to admit it seemed rude. "Just a little surprised. I didn't know we had non-human passengers on board."

"As far as I'm aware, I'm the only one. My world has few starships heading to my destination, so I booked passage on your Earth-vessel. Your species and mine are both oxygen-breathers, so there's no problem."

Steven felt the third eye gawking at him, and tried not to gawk back. But maybe that species always gawked, so it didn't matter. "Right. No problem. Nice talking to you. 'Scuse me. I have business in another part of the ship." That much was true.

*   *   *

Steven paced through the ship's passageways, hunting for the Chief Steward. He brushed against the bulkheads to allow other passengers to squeeze by. He never chanced upon the Chief

Steward, but settled for a man he recognized, from the launch-day introductions, as the Junior Assistant to the Chief Steward's Associate. Joe? Bo? What was his name again? He was a skinny man, a few years older than Steven. The stewards tended to the needs of the two hundred passengers, who were an afterthought to *Moons of Neptune's* main function of transporting cargo.

He tapped the man's shoulder lightly. "Can you tell me how soon the shuttle to Pitcairn will be leaving?"

The Junior Assistant appeared surprised. "The shuttle to...? Oh, are you the Protector?"

Word that a Protector was on board had spread, and he'd grown weary of answering the same question over and over. "No. I'm this size because my mother was frightened by a bull-ape while she was pregnant with me."

The Junior Assistant appeared to take the sarcasm with good humor. "My! They certainly do ship you fellows out to the boonies of the Galaxy, don't they? Call me Moe. I've been making this same run for two years, and you're the first passenger I've met who wanted to transfer to Cherry Pit."

"Pitcairn, not Cherry Pit. You can get me there, can't you, Moe? The space liner company signed a contract that promised you would."

"Oh, we'll keep that promise, but there won't be any shuttle. Not enough demand, for one thing. And we couldn't commission a shuttle to launch through the nearest portal even if half our passengers were clamoring to go along for the ride. The portal can't accommodate a vessel the size of a shuttle. You know, don't you, that over seventy percent of known portals are too small..."

"Yeah, too small for a ship to pass through. I heard that. So what good will this portal do us? I thought dwarf portals were only useful for communication links, or sometimes for transferring cargo between sectors of the Galaxy."

"Mostly, but on occasion we use them for passengers. You know where the launch bay is, right? Be there at sixteen hundred hours, and you'll find out how we'll transport you to… what was the name of that planet?"

"Pitcairn." He braced his hands on his hips. "It shows up on your ship's computer, doesn't it?"

Moe shrugged. "Beats me. But it must have shown up on somebody's computer, or we wouldn't have been able to locate the coordinates to send you there. Don't be late. We'll be in position for only a few minutes. Leave your luggage behind. No room for it."

Steven turned and strolled back down the passageway. He wouldn't miss his luggage. Protectors always traveled light, and other members of the Community gave them what they needed after they reached their destinations. But he wondered what form of transportation would be so cramped it couldn't accommodate a backpack or a satchel.

Looking for something to do until the appointed hour, Steven wandered into the library. He planned to download information about Pitcairn. But the library's internal data base had never heard of the planet, and sending a link through portals to a distant data base would have taken days. He gave up and devoted the duration of the waiting period to playing checkers against a computer.

$$* \qquad * \qquad *$$

Two stewards, including the ever-smiling Moe, waited for Steven in the launch bay. The cube-shaped compartment barely had room for its three occupants. A spacesuit hung from brackets, crowding the room further. The arms, legs, chest, and gloves were fitted for a man his size, but the boots were double what he needed to accommodate his feet. The oxygen tank stretched from the shoulders to below the waist. A tank with so much capacity meant the designer had intended the wearer to survive for more than a day outside the shelter of a breathable atmosphere. There should have been no reason for such massive storage, unless…

"Don't tell me I'm supposed to travel through space in that flimsy contraption."

Moe wagged his head up and down. "It's either that, or bypass the dwarf portal and spend months hitching a ride to Pitcairn on some ship crossing surface space. That's if you can find one traveling there, which isn't likely."

"If the world is that obscure, how can you be sure you have the right coordinates? I'll bet I'd bypass the entire planet if your calculations are off by a thousandth of a decimal."

"The suit is programmed to make course corrections if necessary. We rarely miss the target."

Steven looked toward the launch bay door, fighting the urge to dash back to the safety of the library. "Rarely? What happens if I'm one of the rare ones?"

Moe hesitated, as if he had never been asked the question before. Finally he said, "I assume you'd get swallowed up by the sun. But the odds of that happening are so remote, I wouldn't give it a second thought."

Steven fingered the suit's fabric. It was no thicker than the cloth of the shirt he was wearing. "I wouldn't give it a second thought, either, if I wasn't the one who might get fried. Besides, a guy could starve to death in that suit."

Moe patted the suit with such pride that a casual observer might suppose he'd invented it. "You won't starve. This baby comes equipped with two tubes you can suck on. One slurps up water. The other feeds you some kind of goop that tastes like a chocolate milkshake, and supplies your minimum daily requirement of vitamins and fiber. And if the tubes malfunction, you won't be in space long enough to die of anything. A mere twenty-six hours."

"Twenty six hours! What if I have to... you know. I can't unzip the suit when I'm billions of kilometers from the nearest source of heat and air."

"I was wondering when you were going to ask that. It's usually the first question. When you feel the urge, relax and let nature take its course. The suit is designed to accommodate personal needs."

The other steward, an older man who seemed impatient to get the whole affair over with, joined the discussion. "Of course, if you are scared to leave the ship, we can't force you. It's a matter of Galactic Treaty Organization regulations. We can't compel any passenger to travel by spacesuit."

"Who said anything about being scared to leave the ship?" He had hoped it wouldn't show. He strode over to the space suit. "How do I get into this thing? And will it itch?"

"You'll need help," the older steward explained. "As for itching—I certainly hope not. You won't be able to scratch until you touch ground."

The two stewards held the bottom half of the suit while Steven stepped into the trousers. Next they set the top half over him as he raised his arms. They zipped the two parts together, leaving an invisible seam. He could bend enough to walk, but he wouldn't be much good at running, fighting, or picking up a knife and fork.

"Hold still," Moe commanded, and secured the helmet. "See that box hooked onto the chest? Click on the switch in the upper left corner if you want to listen to music."

Steven looked at the two crew members through a visor that would soon be the only thing standing between his nose and temperatures near absolute zero. From outside the suit, he hadn't been able to see inside the helmet. But now that it covered his head, he could see through the visor as plainly as through any window. "I hope I don't freeze to death before I get a chance to appreciate the scenery."

"You won't. Climb into this tube, please," Moe urged.

The two stewards slid open a hatch in the bulkhead, and gestured for him to scramble into a cylinder that was five times his height from one end to the other. He peered inside. In the light streaming from the launch bay, he saw the interior was gray, smooth, and wide enough around to accommodate a normal-sized man in comfort. It would be a tight squeeze for Steven.

"I feel like I'm going to get crammed down the barrel of a rifle. The old-fashioned kind that works on gunpowder."

"Good comparison," Moe answered. "The system operates on the same principle as shooting a bullet from a gun, but without the powder burns."

Steven crawled through the hatch. It clanged shut behind him, blocking every ray of light. "Well?" he called. His voice echoed in the chamber. "When do I...? Whoa!"

He never felt the blast. One moment, he was in blackness, his arms and legs pinioned by his surroundings. The next moment, the cylinder had vanished, and the entire ship with it. He drifted in a pool of space, more alone than he'd ever been in his life. He saw only sky, speckled with stars above and below, two directions that had ceased to have any logical meaning. What he perceived as above could as easily be classified as below.

Moons of Neptune was nowhere in sight, dashing his hope of watching it fade into the background. Thinking it over, he felt a little foolish for ever expecting he would witness the freighter soaring through space. He was speeding in the opposite direction at a pace of hundreds of kilometers per second. At that rate, *Moons of Neptune* hadn't stuck around long enough to register its image on his retinas. He must already be separated from it by a distance greater than the diameter of Jupiter.

The stars, no matter how madly they rampaged through space, appeared motionless to his sense of sight. With no wind to push against him, and no objects to pass him by, he had no sensation of his body traveling anywhere. He understood the stillness to be an illusion, but as the minutes ticked away, his certainty cracked. He realized, in a moment of panic, that *Moons of Neptune* might have left him frozen to one spot in space. He had no way to tell the difference between standing still and moving.

As if to settle his doubts, all space shifted in a flicker. The stars still engulfed him, but in different locations and constellations. He'd plunged through the nothingness at the heart of the universe, and come out the other side.

One star shined brighter than the others. That must be the nearest, Pitcairn's sun, he thought. He counted on that star to serve as a beacon, growing brighter as he approached his destination, proving he wasn't hurtling in the wrong direction. But if it swelled larger than it should appear from a world cool enough to support life, it would no longer be a welcome sight. Getting too close to the sun would be a sign he'd missed Pitcairn, and would keep on going until... he didn't want to think about it. He resolved to trust the stewards' calculations, and not be afraid. But his resolution only made his thoughts dwell all the more on everything that could go wrong.

The canopy of stars jogged a recollection of an old nursery rhyme. *Twinkle, twinkle, little star. How I wonder what you are.* There was something profound in that nursery rhyme. In its own way, it was a practically a prayer. He looked at the stars and wondered what they were.

He clicked the switch to set music to playing. He had a long journey in store, through the most gorgeous emptiness imaginable. He hoped the trip would culminate with a soft landing on a livable world.

CHAPTER ELEVEN

NO LONGER ALONE

"Protectors may cooperate with the lawful civil authority of any planet, but shall not commit an evil act at the behest of the civil authority."
—D.F. Nathaniel

The brightest dot in the heavens, by and by, melted into a blazing yellow circle. A different dot took its place as the most brilliant point of light, apart from the sun. Steven judged it to be Pitcairn.

Another kind of gorgeous wonder had entered the surrounding sky. Steven counted six orbs, like giant pinheads, trailing tails of silver and gold. He yearned to reach out, grab one of the tails, and swing the entire comet around his head like a lariat. What were the chances of witnessing even one comet by happenstance from a random location in a typical stellar system? He didn't know the odds, but they had to be long. Every system had its peculiarities, and this one's must have been an overpopulation of comets. But it was a pleasant peculiarity.

Hours slipped away. Pitcairn swelled to the size of a dinner plate. The swirls of white and blue, separated by patches of darkness, showed it to be a world with a mix of continents and seas and a generous cloud cover. Steven rediscovered the meaning of "down," and plummeted that direction. As a traveller entering an atmosphere without the usual security of a spacecraft, he dived at a pace too swift for his comfort. His speed accelerated, and he faced the prospect of incineration from air friction, or, if he survived the descent, of smashing into bits against the surface. Didn't the spacesuit have any brakes?

Steven plunged into a fog that he took for cloud cover. He emerged on the other side seconds later, to the sight of ground hurtling upwards. Could he be dead already, cremated by friction? The temperature inside the suit grew chilly, as it should after the refrigeration had clicked on, but the cold didn't prove he was still alive. Maybe the descent had charred him to a crisp, and the frosty tingles meant only that he wasn't heading to the Place Where It's Always Too Hot. And if he wasn't dead, he would become that way soon enough if he continued to accelerate towards the ground.

It wasn't fair. Death as a striker, before getting the chance to leave his mark on the Galaxy, was disturbing enough. It was worse to suffer the humiliation of perishing from a silly spacesuit malfunction, rather than flaming out as a hero in the heat of battle.

The ground drew closer, and still his speed surged. He'd given up hope of survival when the soles of his boots kicked upwards at his heels. He began to drift like some helpless bubble caught in a breeze. So that was why the designers of the spacesuit tacked on gargantuan boots. They housed the equipment for slowing his descent.

The terrain surrounding the landing area was sprinkled with hills that sprang from the surface like giant thorns. Vegetation was sparse, with occasional gray shrubs, but nothing that resembled a tree. His boots touched the rust-colored soil in the flat space between two hills. He wobbled at the impact, but caught his balance and stayed on his feet.

He removed his helmet and scratched his nose, a blessed relief. He thrust the helmet to the ground and gulped the air. Not bad. Icy to the lungs, but breathable, and didn't stink the way the air stank on Medusa-Four.

Human civilization, if it had made its way to that portion of Pitcairn, had left no trace. Steven unlatched the segments of his suit, and, one-by-one, cast them aside. He welcomed the chance to toss his gloves away, in part because his fingers had cramps, but mainly so he could twist the jewel on his communication ring. He trusted that an unknown Protector, who could be anywhere on the planet, would react to his signal. With nothing else to do while he waited, he leaped several times to test how far he could travel in one bound. Gravity was about equal to Mars, he judged.

Ten minutes went by too slowly, and then a flyer with fins attached to its sides skimmed across the desert floor. He recognized the fins as a fad from fifteen years earlier that seemed quaint in the current day. Nobody flew that model anymore, except, apparently, on Pitcairn. The top was folded back, giving him a view of the three passengers.

The driver, a woman about forty, had dark hair that matched her brown Protector's uniform. A man in military garb sat beside her. He was a generation older than the woman, or maybe the scowl pasted between his drooping jowls just made him appear that way. The passenger in the rear, about the driver's age, slouched against the seat cushion. He wore the same uniform as the older soldier, except the patch on his arm had fewer stripes. He grinned when he saw Steven and waved. He had smooth skin and a rumpled uniform. For the older man, who stared straight ahead and didn't acknowledge Steven's existence in any way, it was the reverse.

The flyer skidded onto the plain between the hills. "We've been expecting you," the woman greeted. "I'm Taryn, and I'll be your provincial. The soldier sitting next to me is General Halfbald, and that's Major Davis behind us."

"You're more than six kilometers from where you're supposed to be," General Halfbald snarled.

Steven stiffened. He refused to accept responsibility for a blunder that wasn't his fault, no matter how lofty his accuser's rank might be. "Well, don't blame me, sir. That'd be like blaming the arrow for missing the bull's eye."

Halfbald grimaced. It was plain he didn't like to be contradicted when he was dishing out blame.

"The error was probably the fault of the comets," Taryn suggested. "They crisscross this stellar system, and their gravitational pull, slight though it is, can throw calculations off. The important thing is, we found you, thanks to your communication jewel."

No, Steven thought, the important thing was, he hadn't missed the world entirely.

Taryn stepped from the vehicle and cupped Steven's hand in both of hers. "General Halfbald is Presiding General of this world. Since Pitcairn has a military form of government, his position is similar to president or prime minister on most worlds."

Or maybe dictator or fuhrer, Steven suspected, but again kept his opinion to himself. He returned Halfbald's stare.

Major Davis stood beside Taryn. She touched his elbow lightly. "The major is a biologist who has studied the avians. They're the native bird species that most resembles the alien you're going to do battle with. He knows more about both types of creature—the avians and the harpy—than any other living person."

"Which isn't saying much," Davis admitted. "Considering we know little about the avians and practically nothing about the harpy. Come on, take the seat next to me."

Once all four passengers had boarded, Taryn gave her order to the flyer's computer. "Take us to Fort Wilkerson."

The flyer rose, not high enough to clear the tops of the hills. It zigzagged its way above the terrain, avoiding collisions with hillsides by margins too small for Steven's comfort. "Welcome to Pitcairn," Major Davis said.

"Thank you, sir. Where does that name come from? Pitcairn—was he some kind of a lesser Roman god, or something?"

Halfbald let out a belly laugh, plainly enjoying Steven's display of ignorance.

Davis remained serious. "Our founders named our world after Pitcairn's Island on Earth. Near the end of the eighteenth century, a band of mutineers settled the island after they revolted against the Captain of a ship called the Bounty. They couldn't sail around on the high seas forever, but just as surely, they couldn't dock at a civilized port where the British Navy would nab them. They took refuge on a remote island."

"That's a good story," Steven said, confused but trying to be polite. "But what does it have to do with your planet? What possessed your ancestors to think an island on Earth would make a good namesake for a newly-discovered world?"

"I was getting to that. Our ancestors were the officers and crew of a spaceship, and they also mutinied against their Captain." He hesitated, then added a little sheepishly, "In fact, they killed him."

Halfbald turned around and gave Davis an angry look. "The Mutineers had to kill him. It was a matter of self-defense."

Steven suspected they had stumbled onto a sensitive topic over which Davis and Halfbald disagreed. He didn't have all the facts, so who was he to judge which of them was right? "I'm sure your ancestors did what they thought they had to do. What happened after they mutinied?'

Davis seemed to warm to the task of telling the story. His hands became animated, and he went on. "They couldn't go home, or even pass through a portal. Space around the portals was crawling with security ships from the Galactic Treaty Organization. Our ancestors sailed through uncharted space, pretty much aimlessly, with no plan except to hope they'd blunder into a life-sustaining world before they ran out of food and air. As luck would have it, they discovered a planet with an oxygen atmosphere and a mild climate. They became refugees on this world, and we—their descendants—have been here ever since."

Steven inhaled the air, rich in oxygen. "Then you're telling me this planet wasn't terraformed before humans settled here?"

"Not before, and not since," Taryn said. "You're looking at a world in its natural condition. Why do you seem surprised?"

"I thought small worlds hardly ever have enough oxygen to support life, unless the atmosphere is seeded by terra-formers the way it is on Medusa-Four and Merlin. Lighter gases are supposed to leech into space." Or something like that, he added silently.

"The oxygen does leech into space," Major Davis explained. "But slowly. Luckily for us, at the time the planet was formed, a reserve of oxygen was trapped in pockets below the planet's crust. It seeps up to replace what we lose to outer space. The same thing accounts for the over-supply of helium in our atmosphere. Helium was also trapped below ground."

Steven shrugged. The atmosphere plainly had plenty of oxygen, and Davis's explanation seemed as good as any. They were breathing, and that was all that mattered.

They flew low as evidence of human society emerged, giving Steven a chance to observe what sort of society the mutineers and their offspring had constructed. He wasn't impressed. They passed over a town of crumbling houses, crammed together in clusters separated by dusty roads. The inhabitants went about on foot, or on the backs of six-legged creatures with pink hides. The beasts resembled starving cows with two extra limbs. Further on, he saw animals of the same species, appearing no healthier, pulling carts and wagons. He saw nothing mechanical that moved under it's own power, aside from the vehicle he was sitting in. "Its like I stepped back in time when I slipped through the portal," he said.

"You can't literally go back in time," Taryn said. "Too many paradoxes. But you're right that a visit to this world creates a sensation of having time traveled. You'll get used to the rustic surroundings, like I did. As for the natives, this is the only life they've ever known."

Halfbald ignored her, but Davis nodded. "Only one person born on Pitcairn has ever traveled off-world," he said. "We lack the technology for space travel, and no starship bothers with this sector of the Galaxy except the occasional research vessel. You don't find many companies eager to peddle modern wares to us, not when it takes months at near light speed to reach us, and we have nothing to pay them with anyway. Our lack of space travel must seem primitive to you."

Something about the major's words made Steven uneasy. He couldn't pinpoint the cause at first. Feeling sorry for the local population? That was part of it, but something deeper gnawed at him. Suddenly the implication became clear. He stammered. "But—but—if you don't have space travel—how'm I ever gonna go home?"

"You just got here," Taryn said. "Why focus so soon on leaving?" Then she laughed. "Don't worry. A research vessel will be in the vicinity for a few more weeks. I've arranged for it to carry you back to the dwarf portal and launch you by spacesuit through to the other side, where a freighter will be waiting to scoop you out of space."

Halfbald turned to glower at Steven. "I suggest you stop worrying about how you're going to get away from Pitcairn, and concentrate instead on what you're going to do for us while you're here. We'll set down inside Fort Wilkerson, where you'll get a briefing about this harpy-thing you're going to fight."

The flyer dropped into a yard surrounded on its four sides by walls of brick and wood. Steven reflected that George Armstrong Custer would have felt at home inside the Fort. It even had stables, though they were occupied by six-legged beasts instead of cavalry horses. Men and women in blue, faded military uniforms hustled between buildings and went about their business or, if they had no business, gawked at the flyer and its four passengers. The soldiers near the landing site snapped to attention and saluted at the appearance of General Halfbald.

"Major Davis will show you to your quarters," Taryn said as the four passengers stepped from the vehicle.

"My quarters? Aren't I going to bunk at the Protectors' Base?"

Steven could have sworn he saw amusement in Taryn's eyes. "We have no base," she said. "Only the Clinic, where I care for helium rejection syndrome patients. The general insisted you lodge at the Fort."

"You'll be workin' for the Army from now on," Halfbald said, his voice laced with satisfaction. "You'll follow orders. You can start by snapping to attention and saluting me like the rest of the troops under my command."

"I can't, sir."

"What do you mean, you can't?" Halfbald thundered. "Don't sass me, kid." The soldiers in his line of vision had stoney faces. Behind his back, his troops grinned, or cupped their hands over their mouths to suppress snickers.

"He's right, General." Taryn said. "He can't. We Protectors would look upon a salute as recognition that you're his superior officer, and our Precepts forbid us from subjecting ourselves to anyone's authority but our own. He can cooperate with you, but he can't serve under your command."

Halbald turned crimson and his eyes bulged. "We'll see about that." He paced away, taking huge strides, as uniformed men and women darted out of his path.

CHAPTER TWELVE

MILITARY POLICY

"All Precepts relating to treatment of humans apply with equal force to treatment of alien species with comparable intelligence to humans."
—D.F. Nathaniel

Steven scooped a spoonful of scrambled eggs into his mouth at the Fort commissary, as Major Davis tapped his foot. "We need to be on our way," the major said before Steven could swallow. "It'll go badly for us if we're late for our appointment with the Ruling Council."

"Badly for you, maybe, but what can they do to me?" Steven answered with his mouth full. "But don't worry, I won't make you get in trouble on my account." He didn't know what the Ruling Council was, but if its members were friends of General Halfbald, he expected to dislike them.

The major escorted him through the grounds of Fort Wilkerson. A squadron of recruits practiced rifle movements under the watchful tyranny of a drill instructor. Other soldiers went about their morning errands, rushing from one building to another, sometimes on foot, and sometimes on the backs of the six-legged beasts. One of the beasts, riderless, trotted over and sniffed Steven's hands.

"She likes you," the major said. "Our ancestors were lucky to find herds of hrows, native to the planet. I doubt we could have built our towns without their help."

Steven petted the hrow and walked on. "Why commission just one person to go after this creature?" he said. "Why not send in a whole company of your best fighters, armed to the teeth?"

Davis seemed surprised by the question. "Do you think we haven't tried that? It was a waste of time. The harpy won't go near a human if there's more than one, or two at the most, and we haven't got a clue where to find his lair. The only way to flush him out of hiding is to set up a lone person as bait."

"Why me?" He looked at the soldiers who were all around him. "Plenty of your own guys look like they're in top shape. Why not sic one of them on this harpy of yours?"

"Six tried," Davis said. casting his eyes down on the black asphalt. "At least four died. The other two vanished from the face of the planet, presumed dead, maybe eaten. We only agreed to let Taryn summon you because… well, the Ruling Council won't admit to this, but our finest soldiers proved themselves inept against this threat. Halfbald initially opposed asking the Protectors for aid, but eventually came around."

"What changed his mind?"

"I haven't the foggiest idea. One morning, he issued a press release. He announced he was going to ask Taryn to summon a member of the Protectors' ranger branch, without explaining why his opinion that day should be different from what it had been every day before. To hear him talk now, you'd think he'd been of the same mind all along."

The major stopped before a building with a sign nailed to its outer wall that said "COMMAND CENTER" in crimson letters. He flashed his military identification to a bored-looking soldier who slumped against the doorframe. "Hi Tony. Request permission to enter." He spoke at a rapid clip in a mechanical tone, making it obvious his request was a military formality rather than a serious plea for entry.

The soldier swung the edge of his palm to his eyebrow in a half-hearted salute. "Hi, Major. Yeah, come in. Watch out for generals. The joint is crawling with them. Some kind of meeting."

"The Ruling Council of Generals is the highest authority on all Pitcairn," Davis cautioned as he and Steven strolled along a corridor. "Stay respectful, whatever you might think of them." He pushed, and a door opened with the squeak of hinges badly in need of oil.

General Halfbald was hunched over the head of a conference table, clutching a gavel in his left fist. Six other soldiers, three male and three female, sat around the table, their eyes focused on Halfbald. Ribbons of every color plastered their chests. Taryn was the only civilian among the group, and the only friendly face. Wallpaper, in a pattern of daisies, covered the walls except in the places it was peeling off in strips.

A face peered from a portrait nailed against the wallpaper. The man in the picture had a mop of hair that gave him the look of having a silver possum perched on his head. The style had been popular among males in a bygone era, but to Steven, a man with such a haircut appeared ridiculous.

The people at the table, absorbed in some noisy debate, ignored the two newcomers. Steven judged it safe to ask the major a question. "Who's the goofy-looking weirdo in the picture?" he asked, then realized a hush had fallen over the room a second before he'd opened his mouth. Everyone had heard the question, and all eyes focused on him.

"That's Captain Wilkerson," Davis said. "He organized the Great Mutiny and led his followers across space to Pitcairn. He means as much to us as D.F. Nathaniel does to you." He turned and faced the stone-silent assembly. "Generals, this is the young man who is going to finally capture the creature."

"Kill," Halfbald corrected.

The other generals, except one, nodded to Steven in greeting. A woman at Halfbald's elbow refused to engage in even that much of a courtesy. "What is he doing here?" she asked. "He'll just be following orders. Our low-ranking soldiers don't get to sit in on our deliberations. Why should he?"

Steven regretted that he was on probation and that his provincial was present. If he didn't need to stay on his politest behavior, he would have told the general what he thought of her and her deliberations.

Taryn raised her voice. "He's here because I choose for him to be here. If you're offended by his presence, General Carstens, he'll leave. But if he goes, I go with him."

"Then go," Carstens said. "I never thought you belong in our meetings either. You're not part of the Ruling Council. You're not even a citizen of Pitcairn."

Taryn sighed. "It's like this, General. When I say we'll both go, I don't mean out of this room. I mean, away from this planet, forever. How you abuse your own troops is something I have no control over. But you're dealing with the Community of Protectors now. This man and I will both sit in on every strategy session that has anything to do with battling the harpy. If you don't like it, defeat your monster on your own."

Carstens crossed her arms and sank into her leather chair, wearing one of the deepest frowns Steven had ever seen. Nobody else brought up the subject of whether he had the right to attend the meeting.

The generals went on with their business. The issue on the table was whether to increase the appropriation for Army-issued underwear. They discussed the matter, voted to raise the underwear allotment by twelve percent, and then moved on to other equally burning issues. Steven counted the daisies on the wallpaper.

He was approaching a count of four hundred by the time Halfbald declared, "The next item on our agenda is the winged alien." Steven's eyes darted away from the daisies and back to the table.

Halfbald continued. "We're here to resolve a matter of policy. Do we kill the monster? Or do we merely capture him? Personally, I think the right choice is obvious, but some fool stuck this item on the agenda, so we need to waste our time debating the issue before we vote to kill."

"'Scuse me, sir," Steven said, raising his hand. "Considering that I'm the one who's going to fight this thing, can I say something?" He figured he ought to tell them he was already in trouble for slaying one adversary. He couldn't afford to slay another. They would have to settle for disabling, at worst.

Halfbald slammed his gavel onto the table. "You're outta order. You've got no voice in this deliberation. It's for us to establish the policy and for you to carry it out."

Steven looked to Taryn to see if she would come to his defense again. She spoke up, but not with the words he wanted to hear. "Their protocol requires us to wait until after opening arguments before we comment," she said.

Halfbald went on. "None of the Ruling Council members was fool enough to state the case against killing the harpy. But never let it be said that we ain't open to all sides of an issue. We invited Major Davis to present the argument for letting that monster live, because he might be the only person at this fort crazy enough to feel that way. Major, proceed."

Davis glanced over a sheaf of notes, and then stood, facing his audience. Three generals began to peruse reading material, and a fourth yawned. "Thank you, sir. I made a formal petition to have this topic placed on your agenda, because we face one of the most burning questions ever to confront our colony on Pitcairn. Will we destroy the only known specimen of a hitherto undiscovered species, probably a species of high, maybe even human-like, intelligence?"

Groans echoed through the room. One general looked up from his reading and called out, "That ain't no species. It's a freak." Another general shouted, "It murdered four of our best troops, and dozens of civilians."

Davis raised his voice until he could be heard over the groans and shouts. "The facts lead to only one logical inference. This hostile alien represents an entirely new species. What else could he be? I know you've all heard the rumors his heritage is half-human and half-avian."

Taryn whispered into Steven's ear. "The avians are an indigenous bird species."

The species he'd seen on the top half of Harold's split screen, he assumed.

Davis went on. "I can testify, as a biologist, that the rumors are nonsense. The Carthoris Phenomenon is extremely rare, even between simple life forms. Between mammals, it is impossible, and between a mammal and a non-mammal, it is ludicrous. When all explanations but one have been eliminated, the one that remains must be true. The creature must be a separate species, native to some unexplored region of our world, probably cousin to the avian in the way the human is cousin to the chimpanzee."

"Ain't no chimps in my family," Halfbald said.

Another general remarked, "Well, that would explain my brother-in-law."

Steven saw nothing funny, but Davis joined in the round of laughter. "I've met your brother-in-law, General Philips, and you might be on to something. But to proceed with my presentation, we can infer the creature is more intelligent than it's distant relative, the avian, perhaps a being of human or near-human intellect. It could be at a primitive stage of social evolution, comparable to our ancestors during the Cro-Magnon era."

The room filled with murmurs, and someone yelled, "What makes you think it's anywhere near as smart as me? You have no proof."

The major persisted. "We can look to the creature's physical form for evidence. Nearly all intelligent alien species have at least three characteristics in common with humans. First, they have close-set eyes for depth perception. Second, they are bipedal, to free up the hands for holding tools. And third, they have thumbs, which is convenient if you want to manipulate those tools."

"Gorillas have all those traits," Philips remarked, but Taryn said, "No, gorillas aren't bipedal."

"Those three characteristics are markers of human-level intelligence. The creature exhibits all three markers, so it's probable we're dealing with an alien with the ability to reason. And if he has the ability to reason, killing him is nothing short of murder. But you ask: can we be certain the creature is intelligent?"

The major paused before answering his own question. During the silence, he seemed to transform from a dispassionate scientist into a fiery preacher.

"No. And do you know why we can't be certain the creature is intelligent?"

A general who had not previously spoken muttered, "We don't care."

Davis ignored the interjection, and continued. "Because we have no specimen to study. It would be criminal for us to destroy our only means of discovering whether our world contains a new alien race, capable of communication and commerce with humans. Incapacitate him, if you must, but take him alive, so that I may solve one of the most monumental mysteries in the history of galactic exploration."

Steven clapped his palms together twice before he noticed nobody else in the room was applauding. He guessed the generals had never heard the major talk before with such passion, judging from the shock registered on their faces.

"Get off your high horse," Halfbald said with a weariness. "One more talking alien ain't all that monumental. If you ask me, the Galaxy's got too many as it is. You done?"

Davis sat down in response.

"I'll state the case for the other side," Halfbald announced, pushing off from the table to a standing position. "Unlike the good major here, I don't know much about biology. Don't know much about aliens, neither. I do know something about soldiering. I know that if some jackass is fixing to kill you, and you've got the sense the Good Lord gave a guppy, you'll kill him first. I don't know what that thing out there is. I don't much care. I know that, if it was a human, attacking people who never done him no harm, it'd be my duty as a soldier to make sure he never hurts nobody again. The only way to do that would be to make him pay for his crimes with his life. And if that's what I'd do to a member of my own species, there ain't no way I'll give a pardon to some funny-looking alien who, Major Davis admits, might be no better than a bird."

He plopped into his chair. "That's all I got to say. Let's take our vote."

"Not yet," Taryn said. "Your rules allow for discussion."

General Carstens glared. "We agreed to let you observe our deliberation—against my advice—but don't assume you have permission to state your opinion."

"General, you don't have a choice. The population of this planet holds me in high regard for the medical care I've given to their family members, while you're about as popular as a case of Centaurian flu. You won't dare make your subjects furious at you by refusing me a voice at this table. I'd tell them what you did, and you know they'd believe me."

Carstens turned scarlet and began to sputter. Halfbald grunted. "You can speak, Doctor. But be quick about it."

"You forgot this young man's allegiance is to the Community of Protectors, not to your military government, which makes him bound by our Precepts. One of these Precepts forbids him from taking a life except in defense of himself or others. Aliens are to be treated as an intelligent species until proven otherwise. And that, my dear generals, is why you needn't waste your time taking a vote. He won't kill the harpy unless there is no less drastic means to protect himself." She looked around the room at the angry faces staring back at her. "Don't worry that the creature will get away. Members of his branch learn more ways to cripple an enemy than you knew existed."

"How dare you?" General Carstens snapped. "If you think you can dictate to the Ruling Council what to do…"

"Actually, in this case, she can," General Halfbald said with a sigh. "She's forced our hand. This meeting is adjourned. Major, escort our visitor to our Indigenous Species Protection Unit. They'll brief him on our plan of action."

Halfbald's capitulation produced a roomful of gaping mouths. He banged his gavel a final time, rose, and darted into the hallway, muttering that he was late for his golf tournament.

Taryn hugged Steven, wished him luck, and then sauntered out the door without uttering a word to any of the officers. Her exit left him the only civilian among military uniforms. He knew it was rude to gloat, but the opportunity came too easily to resist. "Well, Major Davis, I guess we won that round."

"You would have lost the round if your boss hadn't butted in where she had no business," Carstens said. "She won't be there to help you when you battle the harpy. If you lose then, the thing's fangs will rip your neck to shreds."

He kept his voice steady, refusing to give her the satisfaction of letting her know her words troubled him. "I won't lose. I've trained all my life for battles like this."

Carstens stood, so that she was looking down at him. "Oh? You think you've prepared for this type of situation? Have you trained to wait, alone in darkness, until a killer with fangs and wings selects you to be its next meal? We'll provide you with a lethal weapon. I recommend you use it, regardless of what your Precept says. We'll have a squad of soldiers standing by, but we can't guarantee they'll be near enough to save you if the monster slices your throat. We've learned how it operates from accounts of the few survivors. It won't attack unless you are by yourself, and the hour is late."

Steven wished he could borrow some of the mental discipline Sheera claimed to possess. If he could, maybe he'd find it easier to hide his doubts from General Carstens. He rose and stood directly in front of her, taller than her by a head. "Alone or with help, day or night, I'll capture the enemy without killing it. But are you sure all the attacks follow the same pattern of going after victims who are alone? After the first few tragedies, why would any of your people go outside after nightfall without a companion?"

Carstens sneered. "You'd be amazed how stupid some people can be."

Steven couldn't argue with that.

CHAPTER THIRTEEN

A DIFFERENT KIND OF ENEMY

"Protectors shall not harm any animal, whether of Earth or alien origin, except to procure food, or unless there is no other way to prevent death or serious injury to innocent humans or aliens."
—D.F. Nathaniel.

Loitering at midnight on a dangerous street was nothing new for Steven. He had done that on Medusa-Four, while waiting for the delirium dust dealer to happen along. It hadn't bothered him then. The streets of Medusa-Four had stars and lamps to cut the blackness. But Pitcairn was a moonless world, with a generous cloud cover to filter the starlight. He'd seen primitive bulbs providing electrical light at Fort Wilkerson, but nobody had bothered to install one in the alley where he lingered. He held his hand in front of his face, and couldn't see his fingers.

Steven heard a noise that sounded like feet padding along the road. Probably not something with designs to eat him. Any self-respecting predator would stalk in silence. It might have been some panhandler, foolish enough to ply his trade after dark. He clicked on a light attached to his belt. In the narrow beam, he saw only the blank wall of a diner, closed for the night. "Step out of the shadow and show yourself," he demanded.

A clucking sound rose from the vicinity of his knees. He cast his eyes lower, and noticed a creature of a species he didn't recognize, nuzzling his legs with a protrusion that resembled the bill of a duck. It backed away, walking upright on webbed feet, with a waddle that Steven found adorable. Yellow feathers smothered its penguin-shaped body.

Steven grinned for the first time that evening. "Hey, little fella. You're not the harpy, are you? No, I don't suppose you could be. Your wings are too small, and so is everything else about you. Maybe you'd better move along. It could get nasty around here when the fighting starts." He reached out and patted the feathered skull.

More footsteps approached from behind. "You guys must travel in flocks," he said to the animal.

A stench filled the air that reminded him of the time the cooling circuits failed in the novitiate kitchen and the raw chicken spoiled. He whirled, and the beam shined on something that had the face of a bird with a body that was more or less human. It must have been so confident of victory that it didn't bother to muffle its presence.

Steven had seen its image in sketches based on the descriptions of survivors. The attacker's body, larger than that of most men, had arms as muscled as any ranger, and seemed even bigger with its wings stretched to their full width. Fangs curved across the edges of its beak, longer and sharper than he remembered from the sketches.

Steven raised his hands in a defensive posture. Every muscle in his body urged him forward, but he backed away, taking half-steps. He had to keep his neck clear of the harpy's beak at any cost. Major Davis had warned him not to let the fangs pierce a vein. They would leave behind a venom that would cause death to any being with Earth ancestry.

The creature lunged. Steven felt a grip snare his shoulders. Pain from the force of his enemy's fingers seared across his skin. He was battling an opponent as powerful as any Protector.

He shoved his hand back against his attacker's throat, feeling the bone, like an iron plate under the padding of feathers. The birdlike head bent backwards. Steven considered that, by keeping up the pressure, he might snap the neck and end the battle. But he couldn't do that yet. He had a Precept to obey, a Guidance Committee to impress, and a committee of generals to prove wrong. He needed to keep his opponent alive for the time being. He intended to disable the creature—fracture a bone or two—and slap on the Army-issue handcuffs that dangled from his belt. If he started to lose the battle, there would be time enough then for deadly force. In that event, he could only hope the Guidance Committee would understand and General Carstens would resist the urge to say "I told you so."

The harpy's wings beat against the air. Seconds later, Steven's feet were braced against... absolutely nothing. So, his enemy had never planned to plunge those fangs into his neck while they were both on the ground. The goal all along had been to spirit him away alive, probably to devour him. He broke into a sweat, contemplating—in the instant he could spare for the luxury of terror—what it would be like to be the main course on a monster's supper table.

He needed to break free before the harpy hoisted him so high a fall would destroy him just as surely as the fangs. His enemy probably assumed the ability to fly gave him the edge, if his brain could think that deeply, but Steven saw an advantage of his own. The harpy, his hands preoccupied with the task of holding up his prey, had no way to punch or defend. Steven twisted and landed a blow to his enemy's mid-section that would have splintered an oak plank.

Steven crashed to the street. He sprawled on his back and watched the harpy circle the air for what looked like another charge. He tried to leap to his feet, but his knee buckled.

The harpy, reflected in the glow from the belt light, landed and crouched like a tiger, ready to spring. Steven hated to admit it, but Carstens had been right. He needed to kill the thing, and worry about the repercussions later.

He pulled an Army revolver from his belt. It was the old-fashioned kind of gun, powered by explosions that expelled tiny pellets with death-dealing power. He fired point-blank at the creature's chest. The archaic weapon, with its recoil, was harder to manage than a zeta-ray pistol, but that shouldn't have mattered. A monster pierced by a bullet ought to be every bit as dead as one struck by an energy burst. So why wasn't he? The harpy refused to do the logical thing, which would have been to collapse in a bloody heap. He leaped into the air instead.

Steven watched helplessly as his enemy jumped and landed behind him. Steven tried again to rise and defend himself, but his leg crumpled. The harpy leaped again, came down on top of him, and scraped two fang punctures into his neck. Steven screamed and jabbed at the repulsive face. The creature fell back and cawed wildly with what Steven hoped were yelps of pain, and feared were shrieks of triumph. Steven pointed the gun and emptied the chamber with five shots, at a close range that made missing impossible. The last thing he saw, before his eyes closed, was the harpy soaring into the sky.

Why hadn't his opponent killed him when he had the chance? Or maybe the harpy was satisfied that he had indeed killed him.

Steven forced his eyes to open from a stupor. He wiped his neck over the spots where pain burned at his skin, and, in the light from his belt, saw red smears on his hand. At the rate blood trickled from his body, he would soon bleed to death, if the venom didn't complete the job first. He was grateful for the pain, the only thing keeping him awake long enough to cry for help. He pulled from his pocket a radio, archaic like every other piece of equipment issued by Army Supply. The silver slab in his hand was a blur to his failing vision, but he picked out the button that would contact reinforcements, and poked at it.

"Needsum help," he murmured into the transmitter. "Bloody. Can't move."

The receiver was silent as a chunk of brick. He would have shouted, but his strength had ebbed below any possibility of raising his voice or even talking in a coherent fashion. He could only mumble. "Hey. Anybody dere? Um in bad shape."

Steven tossed aside the radio like a piece of trash. He twisted the jewel on his communication ring. Taryn would receive his SOS call. She would rescue him in her flyer, and patch him together before the bleeding or the venom finished him off. He would survive, thanks to the way Protectors always watched each others' backs.

The jewel was supposed to light up to a deep purple when the person at the other end received the message. He twisted the stone until it rubbed his fingers raw. It responded like any ordinary hunk of rock, by doing nothing.

He passed out. He couldn't tell how long he slept before something slimy stroked his face, waking him. He forced his eyes half open, and stared into a green tongue sticking out from razor-sharp teeth inside a duck-like bill. The little alien licked his cheek. Was it a scavenger sampling the taste of its next meal? It had no arms to be seen, but tiny wings spouted from its shoulders and hung at its sides.

"You wanna bite me?" Steven said. "Yer too late. See, dis demon beatcha to it. I t'ink it killed me." He closed his eyes to the rhythm of the little alien clucking, and then opened them. D.F. Nathaniel's image had returned. He would have told the apparition to go away and leave him to die in peace, but he lacked the strength.

CHAPTER FOURTEEN

AN OLD FRIEND REAPPEARS

*"Rangers shall have primary responsibility for physical combat.
Scholars shall not incur unnecessary risk by engaging in combat
maneuvers outside the scope of their training."*
—D.F.Nathaniel.

"Y ou'd better come take a look at this."

Taryn, jarred by the urgent tone of the summons, crossed to the corner of the office where her assistant stared at a circular screen. The images told the story of a conflict taking place elsewhere. Black shadows, set against a white background, signified streets, buildings, and vegetation. A yellow point of light represented Steven. She asked, "How's he doing?"

"Not so well." the assistant answered. "For no apparent reason, he rose straight up to about this level…" She pointed to a spot on the screen.

Taryn hesitated, as if in disbelief, and then said, "Even a ranger can't jump that high."

"He dropped all of a sudden, and he's barely budged ever since. He doesn't respond when I contact his communication jewel. He must be hurt or unconscious or even… I can't say it."

"Dead?"

The assistant nodded. "If anything has happened to him, it's my fault. I request permission to take the flyer and go after him."

"Your fault? Sheera, how can anything that's happened to that boy be your fault? You've just arrived on Pitcairn."

"Because of something I didn't tell you. Back on Pendragon, I... I sort of encouraged him to go after this particular posting. I maneuvered to get him stationed on my home world."

Taryn turned from the screen and looked intently at the girl. "Why was it so important to you that he serve his next posting on your home world?"

Sheera glanced away, her cheeks burning. She had already revealed too much.

"I understand," Taryn said. "You've acted on romantic yearnings, in violation of a Precept, but in view of the emergency, we'll postpone that discussion. I'm glad I took the precaution of injecting tracers into his bloodstream before we parted. Have you ever tracked a tracer signal to its source?"

"Never in a real-life situation," Sheera said, relieved to have a question she could answer without further embarrassment. "But I performed well on simulators."

"Good." Taryn tapped her thumb against a panel built into the wall. It took a DNA reading and opened. She removed two items and presented them to Sheera, who went wide-eyed at the sight of them.

"I thought zeta-ray pistols and force-shield blades were illegal on Pitcairn."

"They are. We Protectors have sources the Army doesn't know about. Pilot the flyer, find Steven, and bring him back. Carry these for protection. The blade's force shield is only half as long as your finger." She demonstrated, twisting a dial that caused a shaft of green energy to light up one end of the small blade. "But don't let its size make you underestimate its value as a weapon. It will slice through rock if necessary."

Sheera snatched the pistol and the blade. She rushed outside into the Clinic's courtyard, surrounded by a collection of one-story medical wards, scattered across the plain in a haphazard fashion. At less urgent times, she seldom passed through the area without veering into one of the wards to help tend the victims of helium rejection syndrome. This day she hardly noticed the wards. She focused only on the flyer parked in front of Taryn's office. She boarded, and commanded the computer tucked behind the control panel. "Locate bloodstream signal."

"Code?" the computer demanded in the deep tones Taryn had programmed into it.

It was funny, Sheera thought, how women tended to give their computers male voices and men tended to give them female voices. "I don't need a code," she scolded. "Nobody else within half a light year has blood tracer technology, so there's no chance you'll hone in on the wrong individual. Follow the only signal you detect."

"Southwest minus eight degrees," the computer chimed.

"Thank you," Sheera said, according to her habit of expressing gratitude to talking machines, even though they had no feelings. "Activate flyer."

The machinery hummed and the control panel flashed blue. The computer lifted the flyer into the air, and it soared above the plains. It made automatic course corrections along the way, focusing on the signal from the nano-circuits in Steven's blood. After a few minutes, it circled above the streets of the planet's largest city.

"We are directly over the target," the mechanical voice intoned.

"Thank you," she said again, knowing the computer was less than completely truthful when it uttered the words "directly above." The tracing agent was accurate only to a hundred-meter radius, at best.

She landed the flyer along a row of shops and diners that had long-since closed for the night, and stepped onto the deserted sidewalk in front of a pawn shop. She pressed forward, taking a last glance over her shoulder at the safety of the flyer. Steven could be somewhere on the darkened streets, alone and dying.

Sheera clutched the force-shield blade in one fist and the zeta-ray pistol in the other. By setting the blade's glow on maximum power, she had furnished enough light to see where she was going, more or less. Would she have the skill to use the pistol against a harpy lurking in the shadows? She regretted skipping the novitiate's optional class in marksmanship. She wasn't even certain the weapon was turned on. At least, she was fairly sure it was pointed the right direction.

She heard a clucking noise from behind. She whirled around, her pistol aimed, though her hand shook too much for her to get off a decent shot. A pudgy creature, about knee-high, waddled out from an alley. It gazed at her with pathetic eyes set deep into the tangle of yellow feathers that covered its face. It was the same expression dogs used to guilt humans into giving them treats. She lowered the pistol and gave whatever-it-was a quick pat on the head. Her fingers sank into the softness of the feathers. She pulled back her hand and edged forward along the sidewalk.

The animal spun around, waddled towards an alley between two storefronts, and halted just short of it. He (for some reason she thought of her new acquaintance as male) whistled as his eyes grew larger and sadder.

"No sane person would venture into a dark alley at night," she said to the fluffy alien, glad for his company even if he couldn't talk back. Then she added, "But whoever said I'm sane? Do you want me to follow you, sweetie? Very well, lead the way. Your direction is as good as any. I hope you're not a baby harpy searching for his papa."

She stepped into the alley, trying not to be distracted by the pounding of her heart. From the light of her blade she saw heaps of hrow manure on the ground, but the alley seemed otherwise bare, good for nothing but a shortcut between city streets. She rested her finger on the switch of the pistol. Her mind raced over the directions for setting the firing mechanism. Had she had remembered them correctly?

The light from the end of her blade fell across her little friend standing over the body of a human. Steven! She holstered her weapon and ran forward. "Please be alive," she pleaded.

She reminded herself she wasn't supposed to have special feelings for him. She was there to do what she would have done for any other fallen comrade, nothing more, nothing less. She pressed her fingers against his wrist, and sensed a faint tick where a pulse should have been. "Thank God," she whispered. She removed her fingers from his skin, and her joy fizzled. He was alive, but he wouldn't stay that way much longer unless she could prod him awake and get him moving.

She shook the muscular body with all her strength, then slapped both cheeks. Next she tried mouth-to-mouth resuscitation, without sparking any sign of life.

She sighed. It was practically the same thing as kissing him, but she supposed that only worked for Snow White. "Hey!" she cried. "What are those marks on your neck?"

Two punctures trickled blood from each opening. Had the wounds been a hair closer to his jugular, she'd have been kneeling over a corpse. She ran the blade across the fabric of her uniform near her shoulder, slicing off one loose-fitting sleeve. She pressed the makeshift bandage against the wounds. Blood smeared the material.

"Keep breathing until I get you back to the Clinic," she begged. "Taryn's a medic. She'll patch you up. All I have to do is figure out how to get you into the flyer." She looked back at the entrance to the alley, too narrow for the flyer to squeeze through. "Open your eyes. We don't have time for me to fly off and bring back help. You won't last. Our only chance is for you to stand up and walk to the flyer under your own power."

She knelt in the alley, sobbing. Steven hadn't responded to a word she'd said to him. Her alien companion bowed until the feathers on his face scraped Steven's nose. His tongue lashed and lapped at Steven's face, reminding her of a puppy showing friendliness or sympathy.

Could she be certain the gesture conveyed either of the same emotions for this alien's species? He might be sampling the taste of a prospective meal. Razor-sharp teeth grazed Steven's cheek. She aimed her pistol at the creature's ample rear end, but couldn't bring herself to fire.

"I guess if you intended to harm him, you had plenty of opportunity before I arrived on the scene." She holstered her weapon. "I'll trust you're not going to bite."

The alien chomped on Steven's shoulder.

"None of that!" She sank her fingers into the feathers covering the animal's midsection, and yanked him away. Only after she'd grabbed at the creature did it dawn on her that she was exposing her own flesh to his teeth.

"Hey! Dat hurt." It wasn't much of a voice, but it proved the nip had jarred him into consciousness. His upper and lower eyelids squeezed nearly into slits.

"Sheera? Wudder you doin' here?"

"I'll explain later. Can you stand up? Come on. You've got to."

"Stannup? Lemme tink. Uh, no. I can't."

"Don't be stubborn. I can't carry you, so you've got to get on your feet. Come on, just a few steps. That's an order, mister."

Steven rose, fell, and rose again. "Leg hurts."

"Yeah, well, it'll hurt a lot more if I don't get you back to the Clinic. Put your arm over my shoulder."

He did, and they collapsed together in a tangle.

"Okay, putting your arm around my shoulder was a bad idea. You'll have to make this trek on your own power. You rose to your feet once. Do it again."

His eyelids dropped, prompting her to shout. "Don't go to sleep on me now, or I'll have our pal take another gobble out of you!" Only next time, she thought, he might not wake up. Ever.

Steven pushed himself to a standing position and shuffled forward. He balanced his weight on the one leg that was steady, and dragged the other, wincing every time he scraped his bad leg along the pavement in the alley. Sheera saw the struggle as a race against time, to lure him into the flyer before his knee buckled. Time appeared to be winning.

She backed up. "Keep following me. It's not far."

He staggered a few paces, gained momentum, and eked out fourteen steps. She knew the number was precisely fourteen, because she kept count. "C'mon. Pick it up and put it down. Pick it up and put it down. A few more steps."

The flyer was in sight when he collapsed forward. She dashed to catch him. He toppled like a domino, bringing her down with him and sprawling on top of her.

This could be romantic, she reflected, if she weren't sworn not to feel that way about him, and if he weren't about to die unless he got up. "Uh, Steven? I can't move. Well, all right, I'll try." She squirmed, trying to wriggle away. "Nope. It can't be done. You're going to have to boost yourself up, one more time."

"Dun tink I can."

"Then don't get all the way up. Crawl. You can do that much, can't you? See how near the flyer is? Crawl over to it. Oof!"

She grunted as his elbows, then his knees, mashed against her face. He scooted across the ground, pausing beside the flyer.

She wiped away a spot of blood where her nose had been on the losing end of an encounter with his kneecap. "Brace a little and boost your body through the door. That's it. A little more."

He stopped moving with two-thirds of his body flopped over the vehicle's edge. She swung his big feet until they were entirely inside, and then said "Close" before he could slide out. The door slid shut at her command.

She squeezed into whatever space she could find that wasn't already occupied by some part of Steven's body. In the headlights, she saw the little alien. He stared straight ahead with the same pitiful expression he'd used to goad her into following him into the alley. She had no defense against the manipulative power of sad eyes.

"Yes, you can come with us, sweetie. We owe you that much."

She got out of the flyer, scooped up the animal, and tucked him into the rear compartment, between Steven's left foot and the door. He appeared content to remain there, as docile as a stuffed toy. She returned to her seat and ordered the computer to plot a route back to the Clinic.

CHAPTER FIFTEEN

REUNION

"A scholar may command a ranger only for the purpose of accomplishing the Community's mission, and never for reasons of personal advantage or comfort."
—D.F. Nathaniel

Steven had no clue how he'd ended up in a bed, but he was sure he hadn't stumbled there under his own power. Two spots seared his neck like hot pokers, and under a thin blanket his right leg felt like a hrow had stomped it. He remembered a feathered alien poised to bite, D.F. Nathaniel looming over him, and finally Sheera, speaking in a voice laced with panic. He sat up in bed, rubbed his leg, and tried to make sense of what he had witnessed. The alien might have been real, but the two humans were another matter. Since neither Nathaniel nor Sheera could possibly be on Pitcairn, his hallucinations must have come roaring back. His own blood, trickling onto the street, could have triggered them, more serious than before. This time, his mind had conjured up apparitions of two different people, only minutes apart.

He looked around the room and saw scattered chairs, a desk, and one person. The room's other occupant, a slender female, had strings of dark hair drooping across the back of her neck. He could see her only from behind.

"Excuse me, Miss," he called. He was surprised to have a voice at all, since by all logic he ought to be dead. "Can you tell me where I am and how the Devil I got here?"

Sheera turned and smiled. "I'm so glad you're awake. You're in a room at the Clinic where we Protectors treat helium rejection syndrome. And the Devil had nothing to do with getting you here. I carried you in our flyer."

"You saved my life?" His shock gave way to suspicion. "Say, you're not another hallucination, are you?"

Her face softened. "Is that what you believe I am?"

He watched as she walked over to to his bedside. If this was all in his mind, his imagination had done an amazing job of replicating the real Sheera's voice and image. Entranced by her closeness, he began to think hallucinating had its benefits.

She bent slightly, folded his right hand in her left, and squeezed, firmly but not hard enough to hurt. "When you had your encounters with D.F. Nathaniel, you saw him and you heard him, but you never felt him, right? He never touched you. Well, I'm touching you now. That ought to prove I'm more than some silly old figment of your imagination."

"I'm not so sure of that. What are you doing on this planet?" He rested his hand under hers. His imagination, if that's where she sprang from, had also done a superb job at duplicating the softness and warmth of her skin.

"I live here," she said. She pulled her hand away, and he struggled against the urge to grab it back. "Pitcairn is my home world. I'd been looking forward to seeing my family, but after I got here... well... don't get me wrong." She seemed ashamed for what she was about to say. "I've loved spending time with my parents, and meeting my little sister for the first time, but I found I needed the company of Protectors. Nobody else goes through what we do. Nobody else understands."

Steven nodded. He'd experienced the same yearning every time he visited his home world, and he'd felt it again while he'd boarded at Fort Wilkerson. That didn't prove Sheera was physically with him. He could have been projecting his own feelings onto his hallucination.

She went on. "I tried to look you up, but the officers at Fort Wilkerson stonewalled. They kept insisting you weren't allowed to have visitors. Meanwhile, I was afraid I'd go out of my mind if I didn't get back to doing Protectors work, so I volunteered at the Clinic. I didn't know that, once I was there, Taryn would assign me to monitor you through the tracing agents in your blood."

"Tracing agents?"

"Yes. Do you remember how she hugged you just before she left you alone with those stuffy generals? Maybe you felt a pinch? She was injecting you with nano-circuits that signaled your location. That's how I was able to trace you to that alley and bring you here. Nurse Gretchen closed off your wounds and gave you an antidote to the venom."

"No, your story isn't believable," Steven insisted, shaking his head. "Major Davis told me only one Pitcairn native has gone off-world in something like two centuries. Frankly, I don't know why I'm having a conversation with a hallucination." He shut his eyes to see if she would be gone when he opened them.

"How many times do I have to tell you? I'm every bit as flesh-and-blood as you. Your major was correct. Only one Pitcairn native has journeyed off-world." She pointed her thumb at her chest. "You're looking at her. Or you will be, when you open your eyes."

"You're telling me the only person ever to leave Pitcairn was a little girl of... what... seven?" he said, eyes open wide. "Doesn't seem likely, does it?"

She grabbed the edge of her chair, scooted it over to his bedside, and sat so near that her knees scraped his blanket. For a hallucination, she had a knack for making him tingle all over just by her closeness.

"I can see I'll have to clear up a few matters before you'll accept me as genuine. To begin with, I met Taryn at the age of six. I arrived at the Clinic, suffering from helium rejection syndrome. I nearly died that winter, but some patients develop an immunity to helium molecules, including me. Once I recovered enough to walk about, I begged her to let me nurse the other patients. My attitude must have impressed her, because she suspected I was scholar material."

"I can guess what happened next," Steven said. "She gave you a bunch of tests to see if you qualified for novitiate training, right? The same thing happened to me when a scout noticed I was bigger and stronger than other kids my age."

"We all went through something similar," Sheera said. "But the difference, in my case, was that I couldn't just hop on the next available starship to Merlin. Taryn had to use her influence with the Ruling Council to get a variance from the law that prohibits starships from docking..."

"Wait a minute! There's a law against docking on Pitcairn? Why would any planet put such a ridiculous rule on the books? I figured starships never visit here because the planet is so far from the nearest full-size portal."

"Oh, we're off the beaten track, sure," she said with a nod. "But there will always be a few intrepid explorers who will travel as long as it takes to reach a backwater world. Look at the early days of sea travel between Europe and the Americas, when entire crews wouldn't see their families for years at a time. Or the beginnings of planetary colonization, when a round trip between Earth and the moons of Saturn took..."

Another time, Steven would have been amused by her habit of comparing current events to happenings of the distant past. But now he was impatient to understand. How, out of billions of star systems, had the two of them happened to end up in the same one? He needed to put a stop to her rambling before she digressed into the entire early history of space exploration. "I get the picture," he said. "You're saying that, once Taryn got the variance, she found a freighter willing to give you passage out of here. Did the same freighter deliver our flyer?"

"Yes, and I'm told it dropped off several other items before it departed with me on board. I spent nearly an Earth-standard year in space. Factoring in time-contraction from periods at near-light speed, I only experienced about three months, but that was still a long time. That's why I could never go home again, until now. I had to wait until I reached the minimum age the Galactic Treaty Organization requires for launching through a dwarf portal in a spacesuit."

She'd convinced him she was genuine, but another mystery troubled him even more. "Back on Pendragon, when we talked over the Pitcairn assignment, how come you forgot to mention it was on your home world?"

She squirmed. "I couldn't sleep last night, worrying that you were going to ask me that very question. I guess I have no way out except to tell you the truth. I..." She hesitated, then spoke rapidly. "I didn't want you to know I was deliberately setting up an opportunity for us to spend time together. It was for pretty much the same reason you lied about why you were willing to serve your next hitch on Merlin."

"Maybe I wasn't honest at first, but then I told you the truth, that I wanted to go to Merlin because I expected you to be there. How long did you intend to keep me in the dark? Didn't it occur to you I'd start asking questions the second I noticed we happened to be cohabiting the same world?"

"I was going to tell you before you launched," Sheera said. "I probably would have told you that very night, if that little ranger girl hadn't interrupted us. I tried to find you later to tell you, but you were never around." She lowered her head.. "I'm sorry I hurt you that night."

He wished she hadn't apologized, because her remorse made it only decent for him to admit the truth he had long-since come to recognize: that she had nothing to apologize for.

"Do you know what the most grating part is? I realized later—when we weren't sitting beneath the two most gorgeous moons in the Galaxy—that you were right. The Guidance Committee has it in for me as it is. I don't dare give it an excuse to punish me. That's why it's a mistake for us to be on the same world. As long as I'm within shouting distance of you, I'll be tempted to violate the Precept that keeps us apart."

He didn't tell her the rest of the truth—that he longed to hold her at that very moment. It might be easier to remain strong, he thought, if she wouldn't perch so close to the edge of his bed.

She fell deep into thought for several seconds. Finally she said, "You're going to have to get over your reluctance to be around me, because Taryn has a plan that will require us to see a great deal of each other. It has to do with fighting this bird-creature together. She wants us in her office tomorrow, ten a.m. sharp, to give us our orders. That makes us officially a team." She smiled and offered a handshake. "Partners, then?"

He took her hand for only a second, fearful that if he held it any longer he'd never let go. "Yeah, okay. Partners. But I'm not sure this is a good idea."

She stood up to leave. "It doesn't matter whether it's a good idea We have no choice. Besides, we're in no danger of violating the Precept. I still think you're cute, but a few wayward hormones are no match for the mental discipline I learned on Merlin. I let that discipline lapse during our evening together in the woods. Never again. Now I have my emotions under control."

She left the room too soon to hear him murmur. "I'm glad one of us has this thing under control."

CHAPTER SIXTEEN

A SESSION OF STRATEGIC PLANNING

"A Protector's promise shall be unbreakable."
—D.F. Nathaniel

S teven hoisted a cast-iron bunk above his head with one
hand and trotted across the length of the Clinic's juvenile
ward. The bunk's occupant, a boy of about five, squealed
with joy. The nineteen other children laughed and applauded.
He set the boy down, giving silent thanks to the orderly who'd
arranged for him to entertain sick children with stories and feats
of strength. It was the first fun he'd had since arriving on
Pitcairn. Not enough fun to distract him from obsessing over
what it would be like to work with Sheera, but close. He'd
already bent an iron bar, balanced a case filled with videos in the
palm of his hand, and pumped a hundred one-armed push-ups
in under two minutes.

"I'll bet you can lift anything," a girl said in an awestruck
tone.

"Not anything," Steven said with fake modesty. "I can lift
awfully heavy weights, though."

"Can you lift a hrow?" a tiny voice called from the back of
the room.

"Easily," Steven answered. He had no idea how much the
six-legged beasts weighed. What did it matter? The children
could never put his boast to the test.

Or could they? "There's a hrow," called a boy, kneeling on his bunk and pointing out the window. A ward full of excited voices chimed in. "Yeah, there's a hrow."

"Oh. So there is," Steven said, peering outside, hands folded behind him. Sure enough, a hrow munched on scraggly weeds in the open pasture beyond the juvenile ward.

Steven tried to think of a way to evade the challenge. There wasn't one. He could make up an excuse—maybe a shoulder strain—but the children weren't dumb. They'd see through a lie. He faked a confident smile and then trudged out of the ward. He paused in a parlor-type room to shut the heavy door to the ward behind him, sealing off the parlor, and then opened the door to the outside. The nurse had warned him never to let the ward come into direct contact with the atmosphere. Something about filtering out helium molecules.

He took care to pass through the hrow's line of vision and clear his throat noisily as he walked onto the pasture. There was a chance it would see or hear him approaching and scurry away. That way, he could avoid the test of strength and pretend to be disappointed. The children crowded at the window's edge to watch.

The animal mooed as Steven came near, but it didn't try to escape. He wrapped his arms as far as they would reach around its torso, just above the middle set of legs. He found it surprisingly light. Soon he was triumphantly balancing the hrow above his head. The children cheered as the beast flailed all six legs and bellowed in protest.

"Put that poor creature down, young man," chided an elderly woman's voice from behind. "You're liable to get arrested for mistreating an animal."

Steven set down the hrow, which galloped away. He turned around and saw a small woman with fading hair, hands on her hips, muttering "Tsk, tsk."

"Hi, Nurse Gretchen. Do you really have a law like that on this world?"

"Well, if we don't, we should. Shame on you." She looked as if she'd been born to cuddle babies and bake cookies.

"Aw, Nurse, I was just having a little fun with the kids."

"Well, have your fun later. Taryn sent me to fetch you. You're supposed to be in her office."

His eyes went wide. Was it that time already? "It's not my fault I lost track of the hour. It gets confusing when you keep switching planets, and they all have different lengths to the day." He waved to the children, still watching through the window. "Sorry, kids, I have to go now." They groaned.

The old woman walked beside Steven. "How is your leg?" she asked. Her scolding tone had vanished, and an angelic smile spread across her face.

"Feels like it was never sprained. Thanks for handling the regeneration yesterday. The effects of the venom are gone, too."

"Don't be sure of that, young man. Just because you feel chipper, that doesn't mean we've neutralized all the poison in your system. I'll need to give you at least two more dosages of antidote."

"Do I have to?" Each injection felt like five seconds of contact with the scalding end of a branding iron.

"Only if you want to live. Some hero you are, terrified of a pinprick. Now I suggest you apologize to the Clinic Director for your tardiness."

$$*\qquad*\qquad*$$

Steven and Nurse Gretchen entered Taryn's office together. Monitors and screens covered the wall at one end of the room, with a round table at the other. Taryn and Sheera gestured to Steven and Gretchen to join them around the table. "Sorry I'm late," he mumbled as he sat. "I was at a kids ward. Just putting on a show for them."

"I've worked on the children's wards," Sheera said. Her voice choked. "It's so… so sad."

"Sad? Huh? I had loads of fun."

Sheera and Taryn exchanged glances.

"He doesn't know," Nurse Gretchen said. "He was in the ward for the most recently infected children. They had few visible symptoms of the disease."

"Those kids," Taryn explained. "Seventy percent will be dead within six months."

Steven's mouth gaped open, but his voice failed him.

"I should have told you," Sheera said. "When I was on that same ward years ago, I was one of the fortunate ones. I got better, but the majority won't."

"For adults, the survival rate for helium rejection syndrome is even lower," Taryn said. "We're not even sure what causes it. All we know is that people with the disease become allergic to the helium that occurs naturally in the atmosphere. During the early stages, we isolate them in special units—like the ward you were in—that filter the helium out of the air. But as the disease progresses, the sensitivity to helium grows beyond our ability to screen it out. A few molecules becomes enough to kill the patient."

Steven was only half-listening. He kept thinking of the children he'd been entertaining. Seventy percent? "There must be some kind of treatment."

"I've been searching for the cure ever since I got to this planet, without getting any closer to finding one. The body appears to develop a natural immunity, though. The most we can do for our patients is keep them alive as long as we can through the filtering process. There is a chance the immunity will kick in before the disease progresses too far. If that happens, and only if that happens, the patient recovers."

"The immunity is permanent," Sheera said. "That's why I'm in no danger. Neither are you. Everyone who contracts H-R-S carries a certain gene. The medics on Pendragon checked your blood to make sure you don't have it. Hey, look who's decided to join us."

Steven welcomed the sound of clucking from beside his knees. Any distraction was better than dwelling over the eventual fate of the children he'd been entertaining. Another living being had waddled into the room, a non-human. Steven recognized it in a vague way, like he might remember someone he'd encountered in a dream.

"This little critter—he's not intelligent, is he?"

Taryn smiled slightly. "If you're asking whether our little friend can process information in a humanlike manner, the answer is no. We call these guys fluff-bellied polliwumpers. They mostly live in the wild, but a few have migrated to the towns, where they attach themselves to humans for food and companionship."

Steven eyed the polliwumper's teeth, nestled ominously against Sheera's left hip. "Is it safe to pet him?"

"Oh, Pengy loves to be petted," Sheera said. "We named him that after the terrestrial animal he most reminds us of. If not for him, you wouldn't be standing here. He pointed me to the location where the harpy left you for dead."

Reminded of the aftermath of his struggle, Steven also remembered his hopelessness, on his knees in the alley, dripping blood, convinced he had no way to call for help. He turned to Taryn. "Thanks for injecting me with the tracer nano-circuits, but you could have spared me a lot of grief it you'd told me what you were doing."

"I didn't dare mention the tracer while the generals were listening," Taryn said. "If Halfbald had found out I could track you at will, he would have jammed the tracer's signal. I couldn't take a chance on losing my connection with you. I feared the Army might fail to save you, and that I'd need to step in. Only, I believed the Army's failure would be due to its incompetence. I never expected one of its members would deliberately sabotage your rescue."

"You believe there was sabotage?" He was relieved to hear the word coming from somebody's lips other than his own. He had come to the same conclusion, but had hesitated to speak his suspicion for fear of being laughed at.

"What else could it have been? The jewel on your finger was hollow. Somebody substituted a fake, probably while you were asleep. And consider something else. Fort Wilkerson's Supply Department could have issued you a defective gun by mistake, or a defective radio by mistake, but not even Army Supply could have issued you two separate pieces of defective equipment out of sheer ineptitude. It could only have happened on purpose. Someone at Fort Wilkerson schemed for you to fail, and either planned for you to die or didn't care if you did."

"Halfbald," Steven said with disgust, as if the name itself was an obscenity.

Taryn shook her head. "He has stooges at the Fort who would tamper with your equipment at his whim, and he's depraved enough to order them to do just that. But before we accuse him, we need to demonstrate more than opportunity and moral degeneracy. We also need motive. Where was Halfbald's? He wanted you to defeat the harpy."

Steven had already pondered the matter, and was swift with an answer. "Maybe he thought it would be an embarrassment for a Protector to succeed where his own troops had failed. That qualifies as a motive."

Taryn reflected for a moment, then said, "No, he had too much at stake. He's convinced the people—the gullible ones, anyway—that your presence here was his idea from the beginning. It would have made him look good if you'd won the battle."

His number one suspect having been eliminated, Steven turned to number two. "How about that witch, Carstens? She hates me."

"I wouldn't leap to any conclusion about General Carstens, either. There's a big difference between hating a person and plotting to murder him. All we know is, there's a saboteur on the loose. We don't know who, or for what reason. That's why, until your next battle is over, you're going to stay clear of all Pitcairn natives who so much as smell like they have anything to do with the Army."

An urge to cheer came over Steven. The boost to his spirits infected Pengy, who stomped up and down in what looked like a waddle of joy, as if he'd understood what Taryn had said.

Taryn snatched a trio of objects from a compartment in her desk, and went on. "If we're going to save this planet on our own, we'll need the proper tools. These are the first three. The fourth is outside."

Steven recognized the first item as a zeta-ray pistol. He accepted it from Taryn's hand, running his fingers along the cold metal of its barrel and across the smooth curve to its grip. He shifted his attention to the second item, a grappling rope, the type he'd used on Medusa-Four to immobilize the thugs in the saloon. He imagined how delightful the rope would look, coiled around the harpy's arms and wings, constricting on its own power as its prisoner struggled. Finally, he examined a knife that gave a green glow at its tip when he squeezed a button. A force shield blade could slice solid rock. It ought to be able to stab through harpy flesh and bone, he thought.

"How can weapons this up-to-date exist on Pitcairn?" he asked. "I know that a freighter delivered your flyer ten years ago, but it couldn't have delivered the gun and rope. They're the latest models. Less than a year old."

"They're new additions to our arsenal," Taryn said. "I sent a message to Harold back on Merlin, asking him to find a way to ship these items to us. Bless that man, he arranged for a freighter to launch a packet of small articles through the same dwarf portal that carried you into this stellar system. If you're impressed by the pistol, the rope, and the blade, wait till you see the invention I'm going to share with you next." She faced a rear door and commanded, "Open."

The door obeyed. It led into a courtyard, walled off from the eyes of patients and visitors by a fence of wood stakes. The three Protectors and Nurse Gretchen stepped outside. Steven stared, awestruck, at the object that waited for them. "Wow!"

Taryn regarded the final item and opened her arms wide. "I'll bet you've never seen a flying bicycle before. It came to me years ago, carried as freight by the only ship ever to dock on this world. I've kept it in storage, unused, because there was never anyone on this planet with the strength to make it function, until now. She's a beauty, isn't she?"

The bicycle sported a pair of wings attached to the spokes by a maze of cables. Technically, it wasn't a beauty. It could even have been described as ugly. But Steven understood her meaning. He couldn't wait to try it.

"My, my," Nurse Gretchen said. "It looks dangerous."

Sheera touched it with one finger. "This thing can't really fly, can it? Where's the engine?"

"There's no need for an engine. It runs on muscle power, just like a regular bicycle."

"But… people have attempted to fly under their own power since the dawn of history. Nobody has succeeded. The dream of human-powered flight dates at least back to the wax wings that Daedalus fashioned thousands of years ago, but that was only a myth."

Steven suppressed a snicker. The moment he saw the aerobike, he'd assumed it would be only a matter of time before one of the two scholars dredged up the obvious precedent from Greek folklore.

"We make it work through a combination of factors," Taryn said. "First, we find a low-gravity world. Then, we build the bicycle of extremely light-weight materials. Finally, we use a design that makes maximum use of the muscle power available. This machine is over 99 percent efficient at converting the body's energy to the purpose of operating the aerobike."

Sheera wasn't ready to concede the reality of human-powered flight. "Still, we're talking about lifting a person's weight into the sky. Even with all those elements you listed, muscle power alone shouldn't be enough." She stared at the bike. "Not unless somebody's altered the laws of physics."

"Altering the laws of physics is beyond our ability," Taryn said with a laugh. "But we can tinker with our own physiology, and the Community of Protectors has done that. It's a rare person who has the ratio of muscle mass to body weight needed to make this bike airborne, but it so happens the Community has engineered a breed of humans who possess that characteristic. We're standing next to one of them now."

"I don't much care much about the science of how the bike works," Steven said. "As long as it works. Can I take 'er for a spin?"

"Not yet," Taryn said. "First, you must understand the aerobike's purpose."

Steven shifted his weight from one foot to the other and back again. "To chase the harpy if he flies away. I figured out that much. So now we've got that out of the way, can I...?"

"Yes, to chase the harpy through the sky," Taryn rattled on, oblivious to Steven's mounting impatience. "But I'm hoping that won't become necessary. I think you can defeat him on the ground, this time. You'll have a better idea of what to expect than you did before, and if you need to use weapons, you'll have two that haven't been tampered with." She ducked back into her office, and returned with the zeta-ray pistol and force shield blade in her hand. "You can probably disable him with the blade. If that isn't enough, set the pistol on low power for your first shot. If that doesn't work..." She hesitated. "In that case, I'll just have to explain to the Guidance Committee why you had no choice but to fire at full power."

"I'd suggest one change," Sheera said. She jerked a finger at her own chest. "If somebody has to serve as bait, let it be me."

Steven's mouth fell open in the silence that followed. "That's crazy," he said. "Do you think you're qualified for combat-to-the-possible-death against a monster with fangs and poisonous venom?"

Sheera's eyes twinkled. "Of course not, silly. Listen, I've figured out why some victims were murdered while others were kidnapped. I say, the creature was never as brave as we all assumed he was. He gets scared whenever someone resists, and defends himself the only way he knows how: by sinking his fangs into his victim's neck. He only carries away people who are too terrified to put up a fight."

"Assume, for the sake of discussion, that I buy into your theory," Taryn said. "That doesn't tell us why I should allow you to go one-on-one against a killer. There's only one person in this yard who's trained for a battle of this intensity."

"Don't you see? The harpy is scared of Steven now. He'll recognize the guy who came closer than anyone else to defeating him, and will keep his distance. But if he spies me standing on a lonely street, looking all weak and helpless, he'll pounce like a hawk on a field mouse, and spirit me off to wherever he hides his captives."

"Your analogy doesn't help your case," Steven said, rolling his eyes. "Hawks eat field mice."

"Wait. There's more. Once he traps me in his lair, I'll signal you on my communication jewel. You'll trace the signal, rescue me, and overpower the harpy." She paused, and then added, "Or shoot him, if there's no other way. to keep yourself safe."

Nurse Gretchen shuddered. "Oh, my!"

Taryn shook her head back and forth, her eyes cold and unsympathetic. "There's not an icicle's chance on Mercury I'll approve. that crazy plan. I'm sorry, Sheera. I know you want to help. But you lack the training and prowess necessary to confront a hostile alien. Your role will be to retrieve Steven and the harpy with the flyer, once the battle is over. Do I make myself understood?"

Sheera sulked. "Yes."

"Good. Now, Steven, would you like to take the aerobike for a spin? Squeeze the handlebars as tightly as you can. They divert additional muscle power to the wings."

At last. He climbed aboard the saddle.

"Wait."

"But you said I could…"

"I know what I said. I just want you to be safe. Put this on." She handed him a bundle that resembled a backpack. "If you should tumble off, or the bike should malfunction, this portable thruster pack will cushion your landing enough to keep you from fracturing any body part you can't spare. It works on the same technology as the thrusters that guided you from Pitcairn's stratosphere to a safe landing on the plains."

Steven didn't see why he needed to take precautions. The bike looked sturdy and he didn't intend to fall off. But it was easier to agree than to argue, and, besides, the admonition to wear the pack sounded suspiciously close to an order. He looped the pack over his shoulders. Next he pushed as hard as he could against the pedals and squeezed the handlebars. The bike bolted into the sky.

"Yahoo!" he cried. He circled through the clouds above the Clinic, feeling the bitter wind against his face and not minding it a bit. The device was a snap to control. He found he could bounce higher by squeezing the handlebars tighter, and drop lower by relaxing his grip. He almost hoped that, the next time he encountered the harpy on the ground, the creature would escape and fly away. He'd welcome the excuse to give chase.

CHAPTER SEVENTEEN

INSUBORDINATION AND ITS CONSEQUENCES

"Protectors shall obey the commands of the provincial of the sector to which they are attached."
—D.F. Nathaniel

Sheera latched the Clinic's rear gate behind her, slowly so as to make no noise. Satisfied nobody had seen her sneaking out, she hurried to the nearest bus stop. She was violating a direct order, but justified her transgression on grounds she had no choice. They had tried Taryn's way of going after the harpy for twelve nights. Twelve nights of Steven setting himself up on street corners to become the harpy's next target. All they had to show for their effort, so far, was twelve failures, plus a collection of disturbing news reports. Two boys had stumbled onto a dead woman with punctures in her neck. An eyewitness had seen a man carried off by the harpy. A couple pleaded for help to find their daughter after she had disappeared. How much longer would those happenings go on?

To Sheera, the problem was obvious. The harpy was terrified to go near Steven, the only human who had come close to conquering him. And the attacks would continue until the Protectors used someone for bait that the harpy had no reason to be afraid of. Why couldn't her companions understand those things?

Her violation came with potential consequences. She had heard that a soldier who refused to obey orders could receive either a court-martial or a commendation, depending on whether the disobedience led to defeat or to victory. As a Protector, she was in almost the same position. She couldn't be tried under a court-martial, because the Community had no such thing. But she could end up on the wrong side of something equally ominous, called a "disciplinary hearing." And there was another way her scheme could backfire. She could die before the night was over. Well, that would be one way to avoid a disciplinary hearing.

What the natives of Pitcairn called a "bus" was actually a carriage pulled by a pair of hrows. She boarded the first one that happened along. She rode, paying no attention to where she was going, until there were no other passengers. The driver hesitated before he opened the door for her.

"Are you sure you want to get off here, Miss? There's nobody else out on the streets this late, and last night that flying monster was sighted lurking around."

"I'll be all right," Sheera answered. "I don't have very far to walk." That was true. The nearest deserted alley would do.

She left the bus and found a suitably dangerous spot to wait. Three hours slipped away. She would get no second chance. By morning, Taryn would figure out where she'd gone, and make her a virtual prisoner of the Clinic from then on.

Two more hours dragged by. The night had no sounds except the occasional wails of some nocturnal bird species, and the rhythm of her own breathing, too heavy. This time of year, the darkness lasted only six hours. If the harpy was going to make his move, he'd better make it fast. She thought of Steven, who was lurking on some other street, perhaps nearby. He had tried to discourage her by telling her the harpy might swallow her whole before help could arrive. The discipline she had learned on Merlin couldn't banish every trace of fear that he was right, but so far it had given her the strength to hold her ground.

Dawn peeked over the horizon. The nurses on the early shift at the Clinic were doubtlessly wondering where she was by now. Gretchen might fret so much, she'd swoon.

Wings flapped above her head. The sound told her that her opportunity to become the kidnapper's next victim had finally arrived. For a moment she considered that it was also her last chance to come to her senses and flee before the creature nabbed her. She thought about the picture she'd seen of the girl who had recently vanished, a child named Patricia. The image strengthened her resolve to stay still, no matter what, and not to resist. If her plan worked, no more girls would disappear in that manner, or boys either. If it failed… she didn't want to think about that.

She grabbed for her communication jewel to summon Steven. But her reflexes lacked his years of conditioning. The stench of rotting chicken permeated the air, as human-like fingers grasped her arms in a grip that made her cry out. Her palm swiped past the jewel without reaching near enough to make contact. She squirmed, but not to fight back. Resistance might only encourage the harpy to kill her. Rather, she squirmed only to free her arms long enough to slide her right hand across to the bauble she wore on her left. If she could do that, she could contact Steven. He'd be incensed at her, but he'd rescue her all the same.

The harpy swept her away from the pavement. She stretched to touch the ground with the toes of her boots, but fell short, then gave up her effort to summon help. She wouldn't be able to tap the jewel unless she loosened her captor's grip, and if that happened she would plummet to her death. She sucked in her breath to suppress a scream. A sudden noise could startle the beast into dropping her.

Dangling in mid-air, Sheera left the city behind. Her skin itched and burned beneath the creature's fingers, probably from welts swelling on her skin. But the creature hadn't harmed her yet in any other way. She waited, and stayed alert for an opportunity to signal Steven before her captor worked up an appetite.

A hill beyond the edge of town blocked their path. It sprouted straight up from surrounding land that was flat as a pancake, as most hills in that region of Pitcairn did. The higher the hill rose, the narrower it became, giving it the look of a giant stalagmite. The peak appeared from a distance to come to a point, but Sheera perceived, as they came closer, a smooth top with room enough for one or two people or aliens to perch. The harpy soared over the peak, and let go.

Sheera dropped to the level spot at the peak, and dug her fingernails into the rocky soil. She momentarily considered climbing down, but a glance below changed her mind. Not even a spider would have been able to cling to the slope without tumbling.

The harpy circled above her like a vulture, and then landed and squatted beside her, not touching, but staring into her face with round, black eyes. She knelt, rigid, squeezed into the tiny space he had left for her. A hand with three fingers and a thumb darted out and grabbed her left wrist. Why hadn't she listened to Steven's warnings?

The harpy thrust forward his other hand and pawed at Sheera's knuckles. She realized he meant to pilfer her ring, her only way to call for help. She grabbed at the bauble with her free hand. The harpy might object to her putting up a struggle, but what difference would it make now? Without the ring, she might as well be dead anyway.

They engaged in a tug-of-war over the ring for a second, then the harpy's stronger grip won the day. He held the communication jewel between them, then tossed it over the side of the hill. Could he have somehow known that he was throwing away her lifeline to the rest of the Protector team? She held her breath, until he jumped over the edge and fluttered to the ground. Sheera exhaled. Her captor had stopped only for a rest, not for a snack.

Sheera called down. It was a long shot, but according to D.F. Nathaniel, it never hurt to open communication with the enemy. "I… I don't suppose you can talk, can you?"

The creature squawked.

"I didn't think so. Or maybe that noise you keep making is talking in its own fashion. Are you trying to tell me something?"

The creature lay down, wings folded behind his back, as if preparing to sleep. She couldn't tell whether he had the wits of a human or the wits of a bird, but either way, he had wits enough to be aware she could not escape under her own power.

CHAPTER EIGHTEEN

A CHASE THAT WAS NEVER SUPPOSED TO HAPPEN

*"If a Protector believes a command from a provincial is destructive
or unjust, he or she may appeal to the next highest level of authority,
but if the appeal is unsuccessful, the alternative to obeying
the command is to resign from the Community."*
—D.F. Nathaniel

S teven had spent twelve lonely nights on the streets. Over that time, he'd come closer to catching pneumonia than the harpy. He would have preferred to swallow a bowl of locusts than admit Sheera was right. But he was beginning to suspect her theory might not be totally bogus. Maybe his enemy really was terrified to go near him. It was flattering, in a way. But even if Sheera had been right about the harpy keeping his distance, he wouldn't have been able to go along with the part of her scheme that put her in danger. The notion of pitting an untrained girl against a deadly beast violated everything the Protectors stood for. Not to mention common sense.

His communication jewel blinked green. That was odd. He hailed Taryn by the jewel's audio link.

"A weird thing just happened," he said. "I'm receiving what looks like a call for help from Sheera. Isn't she back at the Clinic with you?"

Taryn's voice spoke through the ring on his finger. "I just received the same message. She never reported to her station this morning. It's no mystery where that little menace went."

"Do you have voice contact with her?"

"No. Her SOS comes through, but she doesn't respond when I call her audio link."

A knot formed in Steven's stomach. The most probable explanation was that she had triggered a continuous alarm moments before the harpy had done something to make it impossible for her to communicate further. "I'll go after her," he said.

"Good. You trace her signal on the aerobike, while I do the same in the flyer. Whoever reaches her first will assess the situation and take appropriate action."

Steven paused, paralyzed by the awkwardness of the moment. How did he enlighten his middle-aged provincial that she sounded as reckless as her teenaged protégé? "Meaning no offense, but are you sure you don't want to leave this rescue business to me? You're no more trained to fight monsters than she is."

"Don't argue. Just trace that signal."

She was right, Steven conceded. Not about her intention to join the rescue effort. That was insanity. Rather, she was right that he shouldn't argue. He'd never change her mind. He'd only waste precious seconds he could be using to search for Sheera, hopefully finding her and vanquishing the enemy before Taryn arrived on the scene. He broke off communication, then scrambled onto the aerobike's saddle. He shoved his feet against its pedals with every gram of his strength, and squeezed the handlebars so tightly his knuckles ached. The bike absorbed a surge of muscle power, and bolted skyward.

"Trace signal," he commanded the computer embedded in his ring. Moments later, a yellow arrow materialized on the jewel, pointing to what he assumed was the correct direction. He soared over a cluster of buildings, beyond the town's borders into the desolate hill country.

He was aware, for a moment, that wind pelted like shards of ice against his body, and then he lost all sense of both the discomforts and thrills of aerobike travel. His mind had no room for any purposes beyond keeping the aerobike in the sky, going wherever the tiny arrow told him to go, and praying he would find Sheera alive.

He glided through the obstacle course of giant stalagmites. Each skinny hill looked the same as any other, but only one had something moving at its peak. He shifted course to investigate the clue. A human waved at him. Long before he could make out the person's features, he had no doubt of her identity. The signal emanated from her direction, and besides, who but Sheera would get herself into such a predicament? His anger gave way to a slow smile, then to giddiness, after he recognized her face. The harpy hadn't yet sat down to supper. And he couldn't have harmed her much, if she could stand and swing her arms back and forth.

He swooped down for the rescue, but Sheera shook her head and waved him away. "Down there!" she screamed. "The harpy is down below. Never mind about me. Capture the harpy before he gets away."

The arrow pointed straight down, where Sheera's communication jewel beamed its SOS, automatic and continuous. He saw the harpy, but couldn't go after him yet. He circled the peak. "First, I'll get you away from here. To somewhere safe."

"Don't you dare. He'll see you and fly away." She pointed. "Hurry—he's spotted you already."

The creature stared upwards, then took to the air at the sight of his nemesis.

"Go after him, you dim-bulb! For the children. Forget about me!"

He refused to leave her stranded with no way down, no matter what insults she hurled his direction. Taryn, tracing the signal in the flyer, would be along by and by, but he didn't see how she could pluck Sheera from her perch. The flyer couldn't hover, and there wouldn't be space enough for it to land.

"Don't just circle aimlessly over my head like you have nothing better to do. The harpy's getting away."

The creature became a speck on the horizon. Steven snatched the thruster pack from his shoulders and lobbed it to her. "This'll get you down. Bye!"

He thought he heard her yelling at him to avoid unnecessary risks, as if she were in any position to get preachy about too much risk-taking. He pedaled off in the direction of the speck. His left leg throbbed with pain. His right leg, still recovering from his previous encounter with the harpy, felt as if it would detach from the rest of him at any moment. He ignored his body's demand that he rest, and pushed harder to boost his speed. He needed to narrow the gap between the harpy and himself before he could put his plan into action.

Plan?

What plan? He didn't have one. He was like a dog, chasing a cat, with no idea what he'd do if he caught it. He'd rehearsed the battle many times in his mind, but usually he'd envisioned a contest on the ground. He knew exactly how he would sidestep the fangs, how he would attack with his arsenal of martial arts, and how he would subdue his opponent long enough to slap on the grappling rope. Unfortunately, none of his preparation was of any use at two hundred meters in the air.

He'd also foreseen the possibility the harpy would escape to the sky before they concluded their battle. He'd intended, in that event, to pursue until the creature landed, as it would need to do sooner or later. But pain radiated through one leg. Even pain was preferable to the other leg's lack of all sensation whatsoever. The muscles and nerves from his thigh to his ankle felt like they were no longer part of him. The creature would still be airborne long after his own stamina had deserted him.

Steven squeezed the handlebars until they bit into his palms, and the aerobike picked up its pace. Hand-to-hand combat in the sky, never the most desirable option, had dropped entirely out of consideration the moment he lost all hope of surviving a tumble. Maybe tossing his thruster pack to Sheera hadn't been the smartest idea.

The speck on the horizon swelled until it sprouted a pair of wings. At the pace they traveled, he would pull even, assuming his legs didn't refuse to continue moving. He removed five fingers from a handlebar and braced them against the smooth hilt of his radiation pistol. His gesture reassured him that he could pull it from its holster and still apply enough pressure with the other hand to keep the bike in the air. If he could close the gap a little more, the pistol would be all the plan he required.

Taryn had ordered him to fire with reduced power to spare the creature's life, but in the sky, it wouldn't much matter whether he used full or partial power. Either setting would do enough damage to send the harpy careening downward. If he didn't die before he struck the ground, he would just as surely die with the impact.

Steven preferred to bring back his quarry alive, if only to prove a point to Generals Halfbald and Carstens. But bringing him in dead would be better than not bringing him in at all. The harpy had killed, and would kill again if nobody stopped him, putting all those future deaths on Steven's conscience if his quarry got away. The Guidance Committee would frown upon a striker who was two-for-two in killing during his postings, but he could make the excuse that he was following Taryn's orders. And the harpy was probably an animal anyway.

He soared near enough to see the tail feathers sticking out of the creature's rear end. He slid his finger across the cold metal of his pistol, rested it on the firing button, but hesitated to shoot. The Guidance Committee, while it might exonerate him in the end, would demand to hear all the details leading up to the killing. Sheera's name would be dragged into the investigation, and the bureaucrats would become aware of her insubordination. He pictured Harold sitting in judgment behind a desk, glowering at Sheera, holding her responsible for the creature's death. It would look as if her disobedience had put Steven in a position where he had no choice but to take his opponent's life.

He holstered his pistol. There had to be a non-deadly alternative. His eyes fell on the rope he carried. He remembered a trick he'd seen in videos set in the American West, about an era so long past that people in the videos relied on horses for transportation.

He removed both hands from the handle bars. His speed slowed, but that couldn't be helped, as he needed all ten fingers for what he intended to do next. He fashioned the sort of knot that would create a noose, soared above his enemy, and sent the noose tumbling through the air. The trick was harder than it looked in the cowboy videos, but he didn't need perfect aim. All he had to do was snag one of the creature's body parts. Any body part would do—a wrist, a leg, a wing, it didn't matter. The rope was programmed to tighten on its own.

He flung the noose fourteen times, missing his target. On the fifteenth attempt, the loop, aided by a gust of wind, caught the harpy's left ankle, just above the claw. The circle of coil constricted around the harpy's flesh. Steven secured his end of the rope around the handlebars, then relaxed the pressure on the foot pedals. The vehicle shifted into a downward trajectory. He dropped below the harpy and continued his journey towards the ground, dragging his enemy like a fish snagged at the end of a line. The harpy squawked, flailed his arms, and pounded his wings against the air. Steven watched the struggle from beneath, with smug satisfaction at the thought that resistance would only tighten the noose.

His captive couldn't understand, but he called out anyway. "Terrified, are you? Maybe now you know how your victims felt."

Steven crashed onto the plains, tangling his arms and legs in the spokes of the aerobike. Chains snapped and sprockets bent. "No way this contraption will fly again," he muttered. It seemed a shame, but he had more pressing concerns.

His ribs ached as he stumbled away, with the rope tied to the wreckage. With one hand, he rummaged in his pocket, pulled out his force shield blade, and squeezed it to call up the green glow at its tip. It was designed for slicing through barriers, not for fights that were supposed to be to something less than the death. It would be too easy to slip, and slice off one of your opponent's body parts, or even one of your own if you got careless. Still he found it reassuring to stash it away for emergency use. He smiled. With all the tools Taryn had given him—the rope, the pistol, and the blade—he was prepared for the rematch.

He shut off the glow and looked up at the creature trapped above, like some living kite, straining against the line that tethered him to the ground. Wings pounded the air in what looked like a pathetic effort to lurch forward and upward. Steven pulled on the rope and observed the bizarre dance going on above his head.

"Take your time," he called. "I'm in no rush. We're going to face off pretty soon, and the more you tire yourself out, the better for me."

The harpy turned and aimed for Steven in a kamikaze dive, jaws wide open.

Steven held his position until his enemy was nearly upon him, and then leaped aside. The harpy plunged into the rocky soil. "I'll bet that knocked the wind out of you," Steven said. The harpy leaped up, stood on his talons in a human-like posture, and bared his fangs. The two foes stood face-to-face. "So you like to go after skinny teenage girls," Steven taunted. "Now pick on somebody your own size."

The creature sprang forward, beak wide open, and snapped at Steven's neck, forcing him to dodge. He landed a kick to his enemy's chest. The harpy staggered back, then screeched and charged forward. Steven inhaled a whiff of stinking breath before leaping aside. The creature was powerful, and seemed able to recover instantly from any blow, no matter how crushing. But he was reckless, and either untrained in martial arts, or too much of a dumb animal to learn them.

Steven kicked again at the harpy's chest. The creature screeched from what must have been pain. Steven was satisfied he had scored a hit, possibly broken a rib or two, if his opponent had ribs under that coating of feathers. But, mindful that an injured beast is more dangerous than a healthy one, he resolved to finish the contest. He grabbed the harpy by an arm and a leg, raised him overhead, and slammed him to the ground. Then he knelt, wedged a knee against the fallen creature's spine, and circled arms, legs, and wings with the grappling rope. The coil contracted and squeezed against the alien's flesh and feathers.

Steven relaxed for the first time since receiving Sheera's cry for help. He crumpled beside the harpy. Once down, he couldn't stand up again. A surge of adrenalin must have been the only thing keeping his legs functional throughout the chase and the fight, he realized. He rethought the wisdom of lying so near to those fangs, still exposed, and crawled beyond his enemy's reach. He set his communication jewel on rescue mode.

"I guess neither one of us is in shape to go anyplace," he said to his captive. "Battles sometimes reach a point where neither side can fight any longer. When that happens, the victory goes to the side that can summon reinforcements." He grinned. "Luckily for me, I can and you can't." He knew his musings sounded like gibberish to the harpy. He figured his taunt was no sillier than the one-sided conversations pet-lovers sometimes have with their dogs.

Some of his swagger vanished, as he thought things over and realized he might be wrong. He went on. "You can't summon reinforcements. Or can you? For all I know, you might be telepathic. Or maybe you're one of those critters who can beam messages at frequencies too high to register on human eardrums. Right now, you could be contacting a nest crammed with brutes like you, telling them to swoop down and save your sorry butt."

Steven fell flat against the ground, waiting for a response to his signal, and watching out for fresh monsters. Something that resembled a cross between a bunny and an armadillo scurried across his stomach, and a wild polliwumper observed him from a distance, but nothing appeared that showed any inclination to aid the harpy.

The Protectors' flyer dropped out of the clouds, with Taryn at the controls while Sheera traced the signal. They cheered as they set down the flyer beside the harpy's helpless body.

"You're safe!" Sheera squealed. She stood over the harpy's body, trussed from wings to wrists. "My idea worked."

"Lucky for you it did," Taryn said. "Your insubordination happened to pay off this time, but it could just as easily have gotten you eaten. Don't try it again. Ever!" She turned her head and nodded. "Steven—well done. It appears you've just saved an entire planet, as well as the life of one reckless female striker."

"Thanks," he said. "That ought to satisfy the Guidance Committee that I'm not a killer. And General Carstens will be so disappointed that I've proven her wrong. There's just one problem." He rubbed the leg that had no feeling. "I can't walk."

He doubted Sheera had listened to a word he'd said. She had fixed her eyes on the harpy, who was keeping up a steady flow of squawks.

"Nurse Gretchen will regenerate any part of you that's suffered damage," Taryn said. "I'm not surprised your legs have gone useless. I ran calculations on the way here. No matter how often I recheck my figures, they always come out that it's physically impossible for human muscles to keep the aerobike in the sky for the speed and distance you traveled."

Steven threw back his head and laughed. "I'm glad nobody told me I was doing the impossible while I was doing it. Sheera, how did you get separated from your ring?"

The girl appeared to have ears only for the sounds spilling out of the harpy's beak.

"Hey, I asked how you got separated from your ring." He massaged his legs but still got no feeling in his nerves.

"Huh? Oh, sorry." She held her gaze on the harpy. "Um, the creature yanked it off my finger. Funny. It was like he knew what it was for. Luckily, I was able to set it on automatic SOS mode just before he pulled it away."

"He couldn't have known you use the ring for communication," Taryn said. "Most humans don't even know that. Let's get him out of here. We'll construct a cage to hold him while I conduct research to find out what manner of creature we're dealing with." She rubbed her hands together eagerly. "I can't wait to draw a blood sample. My analysis will lay to rest, once and for all, the myth that he's partially human."

"There is something you both ought to know," Sheera said. "I've been listening to those noises he keeps making. There's a pattern. He's talking to us."

CHAPTER NINETEEN

A DISPUTE OVER WHO GETS TO KEEP THE TROPHY

"Protectors shall not take advantage of positions of power to abuse prisoners under their custody, no matter how reprehensible were the prisoners' crimes. All reasonable efforts shall be made to duplicate the native environments of non-human prisoners."
—D.F. Nathaniel

"Meet Quirip," Taryn said to Major Davis. She pointed to the creature trapped inside a shelter that resembled a giant canary cage.

Steven looked beyond the cage to the flat rooftops of the Clinic buildings down the road. He detected pride in Taryn's voice, as if she was exhibiting a prize-winning stallion, rather than a monster. He didn't mind sharing the credit for the capture. There was enough glory to go around, just so long as the Guidance Committee understood who had defeated the creature in physical combat. Without killing or even injuring it.

Major Davis looked up and down the harpy's body, from the tuft of feathers at the crown of the skull to the talons at the end of the human-like legs. The cage, fashioned from the toughest alloy available on Pitcairn, stood tall enough for the creature to stand and spread his wings, with no room to spare.

Davis stretched out his hand to rub the scalp of the little alien that had waddled over to nuzzle his leg. "I'm glad your polliwumper has adjusted to living among humans." He nodded towards the harpy. "What will you do with your prisoner? Turn him over to the Army?"

"So Halfbald can tie him to a stake in front of a firing squad?" Taryn's eyes narrowed. "You must be joking, Major. Why do you suppose the General gave in so easily, that day before the Ruling Council, when I refused to pledge we'd kill the harpy? There could've been only one reason."

"I catch your meaning," Davis said. "Halfbald intended to let you take the harpy alive, then kill him anyway. Look, I want to preserve his life as much as you do, but you can't hide your secret for long. The Army has the right under our law to confiscate any wild animal held in captivity. What will you do if Halfbald's troops swarm in and nab him?"

Sheera gasped. Steven supposed, from her startled expression, that it had never before occurred to her that the Army would try to steal their prisoner. For his part, he wondered what was taking it so long.

"He wouldn't dare," Taryn said.

"He wouldn't?" Sheera repeated. "Um... why not?"

"What's he going to do? Commission a hit squad to snatch Quirip from me at gunpoint? Half this planet's population owes its life, or the life of a family member, to the care I provide at the H-R-S clinic. The people would rise up in arms at a show of force against me. Even dictators depend on some level of public approval. Besides, if Halfbald makes me too angry, I can pack up the Clinic and return to Merlin. I'd like to see him keep the disease under control without my skill and resources."

Davis grinned. "You've wheedled concessions out of the Army, over the years, by playing that trump card. But, eventually, you're going to threaten to abandon our world once too often, and Halfbald will call your bluff."

"What makes you think I'm bluffing?"

"Bluffing about what?" A gravelly voice snarled behind them. Steven groaned in recognition. Generals Halfbald and

Carstens tromped along the path that connected the Clinic to the harpy's cage.

The harpy squawked and flapped its wings. "Be quiet, Quirip," Sheera said, as she might talk to a yapping dog. The creature fell silent. Was he responding to tone of voice, or had he picked up the meaning of the word "quiet?"

"Generals, welcome," Taryn said. Steven had never heard a welcome sound more insincere. "How did you find this place, and why have you come?"

"You know why we're here," Carstens replied. "As to how we found you, we intercepted your communications with the major. I demand to know why you arranged for a low-ranking officer to view your catch, but no member of the Ruling Council."

Steven said with mock-sympathy, "Did you get your feelings hurt because nobody invited you to the party?"

"Shut up," Carstens snapped, wagging her finger. "When officers of our rank are present, you'll speak only when we grant you permission."

"Get this straight," Taryn said. "On my turf, we go by my rules. No member of our Community ever needs permission to speak, from the youngest recruit on up to the Provincial-General on Merlin."

Halfbald harrumphed. "You did a good job, boy. In capturing the monster, that is. Now, Doctor, explain why you sent word to one of my officers about the specimen, without informing me."

Taryn's voice was chilly. "Because I need his expertise, General, not yours. The major knows more than anyone else about this world's indigenous wildlife. He can advise us as to Quirip's diet and natural environment."

"Don't see what for," Halfbald countered. "You ain't going to be holding that thing long enough to fret over its quality of life. I'll dispatch a squad of my troops to take it off your hands before nightfall."

"Send an entire company, for all I care," Taryn answered. "Either way, we will refuse to turn him over."

Steven watched in amusement as a purple vein pulsed through Halfbald's thinning hair. But the General's voice stayed amiable. "My purpose is to keep you safe, Doctor. This place ain't no prison." He indicated, with a sweep of his arm, the empty plains surrounding the cage and the Clinic buildings in the distance. "What if the thing gets lose and goes after the sick kids at that hospital of yours? At Fort Wilkerson, we've got guards and maximum security cells. Resources to make sure this monster never hurts nobody else."

Taryn wore a tight smile. "You're correct, General, that Quirip will never harm anyone else once the Army assumes custody, but only because you will kill him within the hour."

"You mean you don't plan to execute your captive?" Carstens asked, startled or pretending to be. "That is the most selfish, irresponsible thing I've ever heard. As long as he remains alive, there will always be a chance he'll escape and terrorize innocent people. But then, you're not one of us, so our safety is of no concern to you."

"I guarantee he won't escape," Taryn replied. "We'll build a stronger enclosure, and post a guard to make sure he doesn't harm anyone as we conduct our research."

All eyes turned to Steven. He realized, with a sinking heart, to whom Taryn was referring when she spoke of posting a guard. "Wait," he protested. "You expect me to stay and watch over the harpy? I thought my work on Pitcairn was done once I captured him."

Halfbald chuckled. "What's the matter, boy? Are you so anxious to leave our world? Don't you like Pitcairn?"

Steven bristled. "A world oppressed by a dictator who can't provide his people with the most basic of modern conveniences? What's not to like about that? But whether I like this planet has nothing to do with why I want to leave. I have personal reasons why I'd rather be someplace else. Reasons that are none of your business."

"I'll interpret that as a request for a transfer," Taryn said. "As you wish, but I can't accommodate you right away. The research vessel that's in this sector of the Galaxy is due to launch for home next week, and I'll need you and Sheera both to stay beyond the departure date. I'm sorry to break the news to you this way. I was going to tell you both tonight."

Steven lost interest in the debate over the harpy's fate. It was cruel, in a way, making him work with Sheera, inflicting on him the constant reminder that they could never be together in the way he desired. He looked at her for some outward sign of how she was reacting to the news. But her expression was fixed, steady as a stone bust, as she listened to the arguments back and forth.

Steven followed her example, forcing his attention back to the matter at hand. He hadn't missed much. During his lapse, neither Taryn nor the generals had budged from their positions.

Carstens was pressing her case. "I've never understood why it's so important to you scientists that you study every alien species we humans meet up with. Seen one alien, seen 'em all, as far as I'm concerned. But if it's research you crave, we can accommodate you. We'll take a blood sample And you can have the whole stinking carcass to tinker with after the execution."

Tarym gave Carstens a cold stare. "I took a blood sample yesterday. As for the body, I already have a pretty good notion of how Quirip will behave after he's dead. If he's like every other biological organism in the universe, he'll be extremely quiet. My research needs to focus on his habits while he's alive."

"That's three or four times you've called the creature 'Quirip,' Davis said. "Why do you do that?"

"Because that's his name," Taryn said, in a matter-of-fact way.

Carstens burst into laughter, and Halfbald grunted, "You gave that thing a name? Sounds to me like you've gone and made a pet out of it."

"What? You misunderstand, General. We didn't... but I'll let my assistant explain."

Steven enjoyed a sense of smugness. Sheera was going to speak directly to the generals, in spite of her lack of rank. That would irritate Carstens to the depths of her heart, if she had one.

Sheera answered politely, oblivious to Carstens' withering glare. "Quirip is what the alien calls himself. Sort of. Pronouncing his name as 'Quirip' is like saying 'bow-wow' in a human voice to imitate the sound a dog makes. I've deciphered a few words of his language, but I can't imitate the sounds very well."

"Language?" Halfbald snorted. "It can't have language. It's an animal."

Steven found himself in surprising sympathy with Halfbald's opinion, for the first and maybe the last time ever.

Sheera persisted. "I used to think the same thing, but not anymore. Not after I listened to him. That's one reason we need him alive. If we execute him, we'll miss the chance to connect with a newly-discovered alien intelligence."

Halfbald scratched the day's growth of stubble on his chin. "Sure looks like an animal to me. But if you folks refuse to do the honorable thing and surrender this monstrosity, I might as well head back to Fort Wilkerson."

Carstens opened her mouth halfway, as if to voice an objection. She clapped her lips shut when her commanding officer scowled at her.

Halfbald grumbled words that were impossible to comprehend, and then turned, walking away. "Don't think this is over," Carstens warned, and followed.

Davis's gaze focused on the generals' retreat, until they passed beyond hearing range, and then he said, "He's up to something."

"Then let's get busy with our research," Taryn said. "If the Ruling Council has a secret plan to seize our prisoner, we'd better cram as much learning as we can into whatever time we have remaining."

"Agreed. I can give you information about the avians' food and other requirements. The avians are the most similar species we know of. We suspect our guest has been dining on human flesh, but we don't know that for sure, and either way we need to find a different menu for him. The avians' diet is as good a place as any to begin."

"Thanks. Before we work together, Major, I have a question. Did you sabotage our man's equipment the night he nearly died in a back alley?"

Steven felt an urge to clap a hand over Taryn's suddenly out-of-control mouth. But Davis appeared to take no more offense than if she had asked who trimmed his hair. "No," he answered. "But I understand why you would suspect me. My interest in keeping the harpy alive gave me a motive, and I had plenty of opportunity to damage the pistol and the radio. Does it matter?"

Taryn considered the question before she answered. "No, it doesn't matter anymore. If you betrayed Steven, you did it because you didn't want him to destroy the only available specimen of a new species. You no longer have a motive, now that you've got what you wanted. The harpy is yours to study to your heart's content."

"I'm glad that's settled," Davis said. "Before we get to work, tell me how much you've already learned about the creature. You mentioned a blood sample. Did it provide you with useful information?"

"Useful? You be the judge. I previously tried to test samples of his venom and saliva taken from his surviving victims, but with results that seemed so impossible I wrote them off to contaminated specimens. But now I've examined his blood under the purest laboratory conditions, and I get the same outcome. You and I and every other scientist might be wrong in our conviction that the Carthoris Phenomenon exists only in lower life forms."

Davis raised his eyebrows. "I can't believe what I'm hearing."

"Believe it, Major. We scientists laughed at the idiots who thought the harpy was half-human. Well, the idiots might get the final laugh. Quirip has human DNA."

CHAPTER TWENTY

DICTATING AN ALIEN'S STORY

"Protectors shall make every possible effort to achieve peaceful communication with their enemies, whether human or alien."
—D.F. Nathaniel

S teven sat cross-legged in the dirt and weeds. He carried a zeta-ray pistol on his belt, with a grappling rope slung over his shoulder, watching and listening, as Sheera deciphered their prisoner's squeaks and squawks.

The cage had long-since been dismantled. A dome towered in its place, popping up from the soil like a gray bubble, with dozens of windows too tiny for a harpy body to squeeze through. It sheltered Steven, Sheera, and their prisoner, with room to spare for the harpy to exercise by flying about. Rodents and flightless birds, native to Pitcairn, skittered across the ground beneath the dome. Watching the harpy pounce on the small animals, and then devour them, was one of Steven's few amusements. Sheera, for her part, looked away whenever the creature dined.

A week had gone by since Taryn had removed the harpy's shackles, to Sheera's delight and Steven's horror. He had kept his hand on his zeta-ray pistol every moment under the dome since then, ready to blast their prisoner if he turned menacing. But the harpy never gave any cause for a fight. His docility was almost disappointing.

Sheera, during their weeks together, had seemed barely aware Steven existed when the harpy was around. She kept busy typing notes on her slate, interrupted from time to time by visits from Major Davis, as she focused on deciphering the noises that came from their prisoner. At the end of each day, when they walked back to the Clinic, Steven listened to her chatter about all the new phrases she had translated. He found it hard to believe she could pick out words within the torrent of what to him was gibberish.

Watching their captive devour rodents reminded Steven that the dinner hour had long since come and gone. It didn't seem fair that he starved while a criminal got to eat his fill of vermin. He tapped Sheera's shoulder.

"It's getting late," he said, competing for attention with a string of squawks.

She knelt on the ground and pecked at the holographic letter keys from her slate, as she did for hours every day. "Say that again, Quirip," she said. "I didn't quite get the middle part. Ah, that's better. I understand."

He tapped her shoulder harder and spoke louder. "I said, it's getting late. We should wrap this up for the night, and grab some dinner."

"Huh? Oh, in a few minutes. I've made breakthroughs today in learning his language. If I you don't disturb me, I'll have exciting new details to share with Taryn."

He got her message. She wanted him to shut up. The "few minutes" stretched into an hour, and still he waited. He grew hungrier and grouchier.

"Quirip told me quite a story today," she said at last, standing. Her voice drowned out the rumbling in his stomach. "Communicating with a newly-discovered species is so rewarding. Oh—thanks for protecting me. Though I'm certain Quirip is gentle now."

The two strikers hiked the kilometer to Taryn's private quarters, Steven in silence, Sheera gushing about the day's accomplishments. How could she be so oblivious that he wasn't listening? They burst into Taryn's kitchen.

Taryn finished her supper with her right hand, while she rubbed Pengy's scalp with her left. "I thought you two would never show up. There's plenty left. Would you like to see what I taught Pengy today?"

She produced a yellow rubber ball from her pocket, and tossed it across the room. saying "Fetch." The polliwumper waddled over to the object, grabbed it with his beak, and returned it to Taryn, who rewarded him with a spoonful of ice cream.

"Good trick," Steven said. He began to wolf down greasy poultry, prepared from the descendants of eggs brought to Pitcairn by the mutineers' starship. He noticed Sheera didn't touch her meal. Didn't that girl ever get hungry?

"You've got to hear this," she insisted. "I learned so much about Quirip and his species today. I've entered all the data into my slate, in his own words. The first thing you ought to know is, he said he's sorry."

A hunk of meat lodged halfway down Steven's throat, gagging him. He coughed it loose, and said, "Sorry? What exactly is he sorry for? For leaving me for dead in a deserted alley? Or for slaughtering over two dozen innocent victims?"

"'Um, yes, I think that's what he means. Both those things."

"He's not sorry for what he did," Steven said. "He's only sorry he got caught. So how'm I supposed to reply when a killer who tried to slash my jugular offers an apology? Should I smile and say, 'Hey, don't worry about it. We've all done things we're not proud of?' But then, he shouldn't apologize to me. At least I survived. He should apologize to all the moms and dads who, thanks to him, will never again see…"

"Enough!" Taryn said. "If you can stifle your sarcasm, I'd like to hear the report."

Sheera began to read. "*I am sorry. I did not believe my actions were wrong, until I spent time among humans. Now that the human female Sheera is my friend…*" She paused and looked up from her slate.

"Quirip can't really pronounce my name. That's just how I translate the sound he makes when he means me."

"He thinks of you as a friend?" Steven said. "You never told me that."

"You never asked. Where was I?" She continued. "*Now that the human female Sheera is my friend, she explains to me how much pain I caused to humans. I understand that what I did was wrong.*"

"Wow, he figured out that murder, kidnapping and maybe cannibalism are bad," Steven said. "Was that supposed to be a profound moral insight on his part?" Taryn glared, and Steven cast his eyes down. "Sorry—I won't interrupt again."

"*This may appear strange to you, but I believed I was doing a good thing, even though I knew my people intended to kill the humans I captured. I believed that, by attacking humans, I saved the lives of many of my people.*"

"He has people?" Steven asked.

"Well, that's probably not a very good translation," Sheera admitted. "I don't mean his people are... you know... people-people."

Taryn broke her own rule against interrupting. "How could these aliens save their own lives by taking ours?"

"I'll skip ahead to that part," Sheera said. "*The custom among my people, years ago, was to demonstrate our devotion to our gods by sacrificing one of our kind at a ceremony we conducted every twenty-first day...*"

"The equivalent of human sacrifice?" Steven's lips twisted. "The more I hear, the more I dislike them and their gods both."

Sheera acted like she hadn't heard him. "*... every twenty-first day, a practice that dates back to when our population was larger. Recently, our high priest announced that our gods had spoken to him. They gave him permission to spare our species and to offer humans in sacrifice from that day forward.*"

Taryn interjected. "Barbaric as that all sounds, it might mean they're merely a few thousand years behind us in social and religious evolution. Many ancient cultures on Earth engaged in human sacrifice, then progressed to animal sacrifice, and finally to ritual sacrifice. We might have stumbled onto a culture in transition to what, from its perspective, is comparable to animal sacrifice."

"No," Sheera said, shaking her head. "They don't consider us animals, exactly. It's more like, to them, we're demons. Evil. Their high priests tell them we oppose their gods, and for that reason, we deserve to be put to death. That explains why Quirip didn't think he was doing anything wrong when he killed the victims who resisted."

Taryn frowned. "This is bad. It won't be easy to establish friendly relations with a species that looks on us as demonic."

"Quirip doesn't believe such terrible things any longer," Sheera said. She lifted her slate and quoted from her notes. "*I now believe humans have good in them.*"

Steven glanced up from his potatoes. "I'm flattered. It's a real morale boost to learn that someone who murders and kidnaps thinks humans aren't such bad folks after all."

He felt a nudge against his arm. Pengy was offering him the yellow ball. "Oh, yeah, buddy, do your new trick." He tossed the ball, said, "Fetch," and watched as their little friend waddled after it.

"Wait. I'll keep reading." She went on. "*The male human could have killed me, but he captured me instead, hurting me as little as possible. The female human takes care of my needs. I do not fault them for fearing I will hurt others of their kind if they release me. My friend tells me the other female cares for members of her species who are sick with disease. I believe they suffer from the same illness that sometimes afflicts my people, although we have a cure while they do not. The good works I see, and learn about, convince me that my people are wrong to see all humans as evil.*"

Steven slammed his fist onto the table so hard the dishes shook. "I can't take any more of this rubbish. What business does a serial killer have passing moral judgments about the three of us? Or about anybody else, for that matter? It's like getting lectured on quantum physics by the village idiot."

Sheera set down the tablet. "You miss the point. What's important is, if he can change his mind, so can others of his species. Taryn, is something wrong?"

The senior Protector stared into space. Her eyes were vacant, and she wore a Mona Lisa smile on her lips. "Wrong?" she repeated. "It might be that something finally went right on this crazy planet. Didn't you hear what Quirip said? His people, whoever they are, have discovered a cure for helium rejection syndrome."

"He's probably confusing H-R-S with some other disease, " Sheera said. "Something that's not so resistant to a medical solution. You've been searching for a cure for nearly twenty Earth-standard years. If a scientist like you can't conquer the disease with modern medicine, how can witch doctors succeed with herbs and incantations?"

"Maybe I've been looking in all the wrong places. The virus is indigenous to Pitcairn, so the answer might lie in some herb that's also indigenous. As to why witch doctors, as you call them, can succeed where I've failed, that's simple. They've had a head start by thousands of years. We can't be certain what cures an alien will cure a human, but whatever Quirip's tribe uses, it contains a substance that attacks the virus. At a minimum, it would point me in the right direction. But something still puzzles me. Exactly who are his people? Is there an undiscovered species that exhibits the same mix of human and alien traits?"

"No, Quirip was clear about that. He's one-of-a-kind. The other members of his species don't resemble humans the way he does. They selected him to seek out victims for the sacrifice because his body is better suited for the job. His human characteristics give him superior strength and agility."

Steven started to ask. "Does he know…?

"No, he doesn't know why he is different. I didn't ask about the human DNA. He hasn't progressed far enough in understanding our language to enable me to explain that concept." She pondered a moment. "Besides, I doubt he comprehends enough biology to fathom a concept like DNA."

"Then the avians must be his people," Taryn concluded. "All these years, a race of primitive but intelligent aliens has been functioning on this world, keeping mostly to themselves, and we've mistaken them for a flock of birds. Now this race of aliens might hold the secret to curing H-R-S."

Steven recalled the children who had been so enthralled by his feats of strength, "Nobody wants to save those kids more than I do." He reached for the ice cream. "But I don't see how we'll get the native aliens to help us. You heard what he said. His people look at a human and they see a monster. What's even scarier is, they believe killing us is a moral good. We can't just rap on their door and ask if we can borrow a few grams of anti-H-R-S serum."

"Why not?" Sheera asked. She looked down at the table and noticed her dinner for the first time. She stabbed her fork at a vegetable and smiled. "That's exactly what I propose we do."

CHAPTER TWENTY-ONE

SEEING NEW PLACES AND MEETING NEW ALIENS

"Scholars should place themselves in dangerous situations only if the end to be achieved justifies the risk and the circumstances require their skills. "
—D.F. Nathaniel

"This scheme is insane. So are you for suggesting it, and so am I for cooperating." For an instant, Steven considered smashing the flyer's controls with his fist. There seemed no other way to prevent Sheera from getting herself killed.

The flyer rested just outside the black dome that, until that morning, had served as the harpy's prison. Now it was empty except for whatever rodents had yet to burrow their ways out. Sheera leaned against the flyer's hood and made a sour face. "Stay home if you prefer," she said. "I never ordered you to come along, and, the last I checked, neither did Taryn."

"I'm not going to let you travel into the Valley of the Winged Aliens with no company except that feathered freak. Without me for protection, you'll have zero chance of getting home in one piece. The mission will be dangerous even if I'm with you, but then you'll have... maybe... twice the chance."

Sheera looked perplexed. "Twice zero is still..."

Steven tried to hold his temper in check. "So I never claimed to be any good at math. Taryn should never have bought into your idea in the first place. Scholars should stay clear of life-threatening situations. Nathaniel said so."

"He said nothing of the sort. He forbade us from barging into combat scenarios that we never trained for, but he also commanded us to accept dangerous assignments when the work calls for our skills. Establishing first contact with a new species is a diplomatic mission, not a military one. There's no limit to what each of our two species could learn from the other, starting with a cure for H-R-S." Her tone switched from argumentative to self-righteous, which was even worse. "Don't you want those kids on the ward to get better?"

That was a low blow. "I don't believe those buzzards really have a magic elixir that'll cure the disease, but if they do, there's a better way to go after it. The Galactic Treaty Organization requires that planetary authorities be the ones to establish first contact. They should journey into the valley, not us. They'd have the firepower to defend themselves, just in case the other side doesn't share your warm and fuzzy inclinations. You're the smartest person of my age I know, but face it. You're out of your league confronting aliens who look down on you as some kind of a demon."

"Pitcairn isn't part of the Galactic Treaty Organization," Sheera reminded. "Which is a good thing, because on this world the planetary authorities would be the worst people to handle a first contact." She laughed in a mocking tone. "Halfbald and Carstens would misuse all that firepower. They'd dredge up some excuse to unleash it onto the avians. And you can bet they'd refuse to work side-by-side with Quirip."

"With good reason. I can't believe you've decided to trust him. Speaking of your ugly boyfriend, look who's here on schedule." He jerked his thumb in the direction of the pair that was approaching.

The harpy fluttered above the desert floor, keeping pace beside Taryn. No ropes or chains confined him. He could have bolted into the sky at will. The creature had pledged not to make a break for freedom, but a killer's word carried no weight with Steven. He tensed for the possibility of hot pursuit, consoling himself with the knowledge that, this time around, tracking the harpy would be easy. A double-dosage of tracing agent, injected by Taryn, flowed through the creature's veins.

"We have no choice but to work with Quirip," Sheera insisted. "I can't imitate those sounds he makes. What good is a diplomatic mission if you can't communicate with the other side?"

Taryn called to them as she grew near. "I don't deny the risk attached to this assignment," she said. "We'll have to take the chance. What sort of Protectors would we be, if we pass up an opportunity to explore a new alien culture at the same time we save countless human lives? We agreed to face danger when we took the oath. Not mindless danger, but danger that serves a higher purpose."

Steven sighed. He had no quarrel with jeopardizing his own life for a deserving cause. But nobody had warned him he might be called on to deliver a young girl—a girl he cared about—into the clutches of hostile aliens. He climbed into the flyer and sat behind the controls, wearing his deepest scowl in hopes the other two humans would get the message that he still didn't approve of the mission.

Sheera took her place beside him in the passenger compartment. Taryn reached into the flyer and squeezed Steven's hand. "You should know this before you leave for the valley. An hour ago, I finally heard back from the members of the Guidance Committee. They denied my petition to lift your probation. They demand to see more evidence that you can comply with the Precepts in a stressful situation."

No, thought Steven. He must have heard wrong. How could the Guidance Committee deny the petition, after all he had done to prove himself worthy? Didn't those aging scholars have a rational side to their brains?

"Oh, I'm so sorry," Sheera said in a voice that sounded distant, though she was sitting next to him.

He gripped the edge of the flyer so tightly it bit into his fingers. "I could have shot my enemy out of the sky with one clean blast of zeta-rays." He nodded towards the harpy. "Instead, I lassoed him and wrestled him hand-to-hand. If that wasn't loyalty to the highest Precept, what more could those bureaucrats want from me?"

"Calm down," Taryn said. "Harold and the other Guidance Committee members don't know the full story of how you captured Quirip. I told them only that he attacked you and that you prevailed in the struggle. I didn't dare tell them anything more. Had I gone into the details, they would have probed. They would have discovered how Sheera disobeyed orders."

Sheera cast her eyes down. "Oh... now I'm even sorrier. It's because of me the Guidance Committee doesn't understand how courageous you were that morning. Taryn, don't shield me from the consequence of my action. Tell the full story."

"No—don't tell the Committee anything more," Steven said. He looked at Sheera. "It wasn't your fault. I'll find a different way to impress the Committee."

"You've already found one," Taryn said. "Few strikers have borne the responsibility you will carry on your current assignment. Bring back the antidote. Better yet, open the door a crack for diplomatic relations with the avians. The Guidance Committee will do more than lift your probation. It will accelerate your advancement to Full Membership in the Community."

Undoubtedly, the mission would advance his standing with the Community, as she predicted—but only if it succeeded. Steven wished he could share her confidence in the likely outcome, or even in their chance of getting back alive. "Let's get this over with."

"Quirip, you can ride in the rear compartment," Taryn invited.

The harpy hesitated, refusing to move his legs or wings. Steven understood. Their prisoner had probably never before ridden in a moving vehicle, aside from his one journey bound as a captive, a flight that would have discouraged him from wanting another.

Sheera beckoned with her hands. "Get in. Nothing in the flyer will hurt you."

Quirip twisted, turned, and tucked into the available space. The engineer who designed the flyer had obviously never expected it would someday need to accommodate a pair of wings.

"Wait, this isn't right," Steven said. "Sheera, you take over as pilot."

"But, what difference does it make who drives?"

Steven rolled his eyes. "If a rabid wolf darted up to you, growling and foaming at the mouth, I'll bet you'd pat it on the head and say, 'nice doggy.' Somebody has to guard the prisoner, and you're not qualified. Trade places."

Sheera frowned, but exchanged seats in silence. Steven sat sideways, able to see where they were going, while from the same place he could watch over their passenger in the rear. A streak of what appeared to be haze stretched across the horizon. Sheera waved to Taryn and commanded the flyer to rise, then circled back and called down. "Are you sure we're programmed to head in the right direction?"

Taryn cupped her hands around her mouth and called up. "Yes, but if you don't trust the programming, go east until you see a mountain range. Major Davis tells me you'll find a colony of avians on the other side."

"Then… here we go," Sheera said, and set off for the Valley of the Winged Aliens.

* * *

Steven rode with his hand against the hilt of his zeta-ray pistol. Sheera and Quirip kept up a stream of jabber throughout the journey. They talked in their own languages, each able to understand the other, but neither with the right sort of larynx to mimic what the other said. Steven gathered they didn't much care what they talked about. The main idea appeared to be to improve their vocabularies. Sometimes, Steven could decipher a word from the garble that flowed from the alien's beak. But he could never string together enough recognizable sounds to keep pace with the conversation.

They flew over terrain that changed every few minutes. Steven saw lakes that covered the surface as far as he could see in every direction. Between the lakes, they passed over rolling grasslands, forests with trees greater than redwoods, and jungles of snarling vegetation. He also saw hrows thundering along the plains, in groups so large it must have taken hours for the entire herd to pass a single point of land. Great reptilian beasts lumbered across some regions, or poked their heads above the treetops in the rain forests, proving that on Pitcairn the dinosaur had never gone extinct.

After they had left behind an especially majestic river and woodland, Steven remarked, "I had no idea your world was so beautiful."

"I never knew that either," Sheera said. "And there's more natural beauty up ahead. Look—snow-covered peaks."

Mountains loomed before them, covered at their summits by a dusting of snow, probably frozen water, as the temperature wasn't cold enough for carbon dioxide to solidify. As they got closer, they admired the green vines and shrubs that covered the rocky mountainside. Sheera fidgeted and kept her eyes straight ahead. "Computer, increase altitude enough to clear the peaks," she said, and turned to Steven. "If Major Davis gave us the right coordinates, we're within minutes of the Valley of the Winged Aliens. We'll be the first humans ever to set foot there."

Steven glanced back and forth between the harpy and the scenery ahead. "If nobody's been there, how do we know it exists? I thought Pitcairn doesn't have the resources to launch surveillance satellites."

Sheera considered. "For one thing, Quirip told us it exists. Before that, I'm not sure. I guess military pilots flew over the valley one day, and recorded sightings of what they believed was an indigenous bird species. They never got low enough to detect signs of a civilization. Just as well. I'm sure a cultural exchange under those circumstances would have concluded badly."

Steven wondered what made her think their present efforts would end any better.

The flyer soared over the summit of the mountain range, then shifted to a downward trajectory. Steven surmised they were inside the crater of what, millions of years ago, had been an active volcano. The peaks circled the valley, forming a natural fortress that shielded the valley's occupants from any outside influence that couldn't fly.

"Computer, give us a gradual forward descent that will take us to an altitude of twenty meters in exactly three minutes," Sheera instructed.

As they drew lower, they detected structures of brick, stone, wood, and combinations of all three, scattered around the valley's floor. The highest buildings, about four stories by human standards, clustered at the middle of the village, possibly an alien version of downtown. The rooftops curved down to their centers, like saucers.

"Wouldn't water pool on top of the houses when it rains?" Steven wondered.

"They must have some method of draining the rainwater," Sheera said. "I'd expect a species that flies to make use of its rooftops for living space. It's as if each house has its own nest on top."

The flyer skirted a flock of creatures covered in green feathers, creatures who resembled animals from the neck down, with heads that placed them in the harpy's species from the neck up. The flock scattered at the sight of the flyer.

"I recognize those critters from the picture that old Harold showed me on Pendragon," Steven said after the flock had skittered away. "They look different, somehow." He snapped his fingers. "Hey, I've got it. Hands! They have hands, and— and—" He looked closely at the limbs of an avian who nearly collided with them. "Their hands have fingers. Three of 'em. Plus, what I'm sure is an opposable thumb."

They skimmed above the highest rooftops. "Of course they have thumbs, silly," Sheera said. "That's one of the traits aliens with human-like intelligence have in common. Those hovels down there won't win any prizes for architecture, but you can bet the carpenters who built them had hammers, saws, screwdrivers—all sorts of primitive tools they manipulated by using their thumbs."

"But these aliens should be different. The one in the picture had claws instead of hands."

"That's odd." Sheera seemed mystified, but not concerned. "Maybe there's more than one variety of winged alien on this world. We'll ask Major Davis when we get home. First, let's go make new friends."

She coasted the flyer barely above the dirt, traveling no faster than they could have strolled. The avians on the ground split into two roughly equal groups. Half the flock galloped or flew away, while the other half paraded after the flyer, chirping furiously. They reminded Steven of an old horror movie he'd seen of peasants with pitchforks, harassing an ogre.

"I have a feeling this isn't a welcoming committee," Steven said. "What are they saying?"

"It's better if you don't know. Defend us with martial arts if they attack, but don't harm them. They're probably more scared of us than we are of them."

"That's no comfort. A scared animal is the most dangerous." He counted six avians brandishing weapons of stone, chiseled into blades.

"They're not animals," Sheera said. "Quirip, point us to the palace of your king."

"They have a king?" Steven asked. He pictured an avian wearing a crown and holding a scepter. The image would have made him laugh, if he hadn't been distracted by pursuers who might be plotting to tear them to pieces.

"I don't know. I mean, I don't know whether they're governed by a hereditary monarchy. But they have a leader who calls the shots around here. Until we learn more about their political system, 'king' is as good a translation as any."

The harpy uttered one of the few sounds Steven understood. It meant "stop." Sheera ordered the computer to halt the vehicle in front of the nearest thing to a mansion that existed in the village. The place, crafted entirely of orange brick, towered above the surrounding structures. Steven was first to climb out. A trio of avians circled him, clutching knives.

"If this king or president or prime minister lives here, he probably has guards," Steven said. "I'll bet that's who these three uglies are." He raised his right palm, ready to slap the weapons out of their hands if they leveled them in a threatening fashion. "I'm no good at deciphering their facial expressions, but I've got a hunch they're not pleased to see us."

The harpy "spoke" a few words with the guards, who stepped away from the door. Steven hesitated before approaching the entry. "Shouldn't we knock or ring a bell or something? We don't want them to mistake us for burglars. That would make a lousy first impression."

"No, Quirip tells me we can barge right in. It seems pushy to us, even hostile, but different species have different customs. For all we know, privacy could be an unknown concept in this society." She pushed lightly on the door, which gave way. The ease of their entry raised Steven's suspicions. Were they stepping into a trap? They entered a hallway with walls set far apart to accommodate wings spread to their full width. They saw, by the light of torches strapped to the edges, a squadron of four avians at the opposite end.

Sheera looked at the harpy. "Tell them we come in peace."

Steven snickered. "Well, that's original."

"Quiet! And, tell them we want to be friends. That we need their help to overcome a sickness that afflicts our species."

Quirip translated the opening pleasantries. A creature who appeared to be the leader stepped forward and replied in the same language.

"What?" Sheera cried, turning pale. "No! You can't do that!"

"What'd he say?"

"He... he thanked Quirip for delivering two more humans to be sacrificed to their gods."

Steven made an about-face. "That's all I needed to hear. I'm getting you out of this madhouse, and don't even think of ordering me to get lovey-dovey with these freaks." He pushed her to the exit, without bothering to ask whether she wanted to go there.

The trio of guards stood between them and the way out. They stood on two legs, their wings fluttering up and down. Steven guessed they were the same three avians who had been brandishing knives outside the dwelling. They held up their weapons and squawked. Issuing a threat? Demanding surrender?

Steven slapped the weapons from their hands, and shoved their bodies aside, as if they were straw dummies. He injured them, or he didn't. He neither knew nor cared. He was willing to damage inter-species relations beyond all hope of repair, if that's what it took to spirit Sheera away to the safety of the flyer.

The door beckoned, a few steps away. He feared the avians had bolted the exit shut, but if so, he wouldn't let that stop his progress. He intended to smash the barrier to splinters with one well-aimed kick, if necessary. Fighting his way to the door, though, turned into a struggle against his own body. His legs stiffened and refused to cooperate. He felt as a sentient tree might feel, rooted to one spot. "What're you monsters doing to me?" he said, in a voice he didn't recognize. It came out thick and slow.

Steven tried, first to move, then to merely stay on his feet. Cold stone from the flat end of a guard's blade smashed against his temple.

He watched the guards close in. The throbbing from the blow was a small concern, compared to the horror of seeing the bird-like creatures lay their four-fingered hands on Sheera. He flailed his fist, but never connected. His arm sank into paralysis before he could land a blow. He thumped to the floor, crashing his skull against a stone surface. Sheera sprawled beside him, her eyes half-closed. He saw the harpy, straight and tall, wings outstretched, looking down at them and squawking. Steven blacked out, convinced his foe was laughing at them, for good reason.

CHAPTER TWENTY-TWO

A SURPRISINGLY COMFORTABLE PRISON

"A Protector, if captured, has a duty to escape if possible. It is permissible to injure or kill a captor, or to destroy the captor's property, if necessary to accomplish the escape."
—D.F. Nathaniel

Sheera opened her eyes in a bed designed for her species. The mattress was lumpy and smelled of perspiration, but humans had been known to sleep on worse. Her head rested on a pillow. And a blanket, tattered and filthy, covered her body. She lifted her arms and bent her legs to test her ability to move them again.

"You're finally awake."

She welcomed the sound of a human voice, even if it was female. Not the voice she yearned to hear. She ignored her queasiness and forced herself to sit up. Light streamed over her from a square gap in the ceiling, so far above that she felt like she was at the bottom of a well. A girl, five to six years her junior, perched at the edge of the room's other bed. The girl's soiled blouse and frayed pants fit in well with the dreariness of the room. A table and mismatched chairs completed the furnishings.

"Where am I?" Sheera asked. The question slipped out in a yawn.

"This looks like a bedroom," the girl answered. "But that's not what it is. We're trapped in some kind of jail that belongs to the Bird People."

Sheera struggled to keep her voice calm. So she was a prisoner, and the only person who might have the ability to break her free was nowhere to be seen. He could be injured, or worse. But she couldn't afford to shed a tear. She was still a Protector, and had to be strong—or pretend to be—as an example to her cell-mate. "The Bird People? Did they kidnap you?"

"That thing that's half-bird and half-man kidnapped me," the girl answered, dabbing at her eyes with a sleeve that was filthy to the point of disgusting. "It carried me to the Bird People, and they brought me here. Did it kidnap you, too?"

"I came to this valley by my own choosing," Sheera said. "Is your name Patricia?"

The girl gaped in surprise. "How did you know? Did my dad send you here to rescue me? If he did, I'm sorry you got trapped because of me."

"Please, will you quit wiping your lids with that filthy sleeve? I've nothing to treat an eye infection with. Now then, Patricia, your dad has nothing to do with why I'm here. I guessed at your name because I've kept track of the harpy's victims. He's kidnapped only one girl of your age. What were you doing outside all alone after dark?"

"I ran away from home. My parents weren't mean to me, or anything like that, but I wanted adventure. In a way, I guess I got it. I was never so scared as when the thing came after me. It's fangs have got to be at least ten centimeters long."

"Four centimeters, tops." Sheera chose not to say anything about the harpy's recent escape from captivity. That topic could lead to questions about who was at fault. She couldn't pin the blame on Steven this time. He had warned her, and now, because of her scheming, he was missing-in-action. "Have you seen a boy about my age around here?" she asked. "A big fellow, probably bigger than any other boy you've ever met?"

The girl wrinkled her brow. "No, nobody like that. Three guys have been here since the Bird People first stuck me in this room, but they were ordinary size. The guards took them away, one at a time. It's been lonely since they left." She added, brightening, "Do you suppose the Bird People sent them home?"

Patricia evidently didn't know about the grisly fate her captors had in store for their prisoners. Sheera looked into the girl's eyes, and couldn't bring herself to smother the hope she found there. She glanced about the place, searching for an excuse to change the subject. She settled on a door that was partway open. "What's that room over there?"

"That?" Patricia turned her head to the open door. "That's the bathroom. They built one almost like the bathrooms we have at home. You can't take a shower, but you can do anything else you'd need to do in there. Seems funny, doesn't it, that the Bird People designed a bathroom that fits humans?"

Sheera talked to keep her mind from dwelling on Steven's disappearance. Talking, she found, always helped when she was scared or anxious. "These human conveniences might not be as odd as they seem. Tell me, how have the Bird People treated you since they locked you in this..." She nearly said "cell," but her surroundings didn't square with her image of a prison. "Since they confined you to this room?"

"You could say they don't treat me any way at all. They bring me food three times a day, and every so often they bring in books and videos so I'll have something to do." She giggled. "Some of the books are about subjects I don't understand at all, like a textbook on quadratic equations. I think they can't read our language, so they have no idea what they're bringing me. I never see the Bird People otherwise."

Sheera nodded. "They're trying to re-create our natural habitat as much as possible, using objects they've gathered from people's homes."

"Listen," Patricia said. She darted her eyes in the direction of a scraping sound from the other side of a wall. "I hear some of them now."

A door on the opposite wall from the bathroom swung open. A flock of avians crammed the passageway beyond. They heaved a massive human figure into the cell, and then wasted no time slamming the door behind them. Sheera sprang to the floor and knelt over Steven's body. He inhaled great gulps of air and exhaled them smoothly, but showed no inclination to open his eyes.

Patricia eyed his muscles. "He's cute."

The girl's observation forced a smile to Sheera's lips, long enough to say, "I agree," and then the smile disappeared. "Bird People with knives attacked him while we were trying to make first contact with their species. We'd better check for injuries."

Together they tugged on his shirt and pulled it up, exposing his trim waist and barrel of a chest. Sheera said, "He looks all right on this side..."

"He sure does!"

"....but we'd better check further. Help me push him onto his side."

Patricia seemed eager to help. They turned him over and found bruises but no gashes.

Sheera sat on the edge of a bunk. "It appears the Bird People want him to survive. They could have stabbed him through the heart, but at worst they struck him with blunt objects. Still, I wish I could do a more thorough exam. If we were back at the Clinic, I'd have the equipment to check for internal injuries."

"The Clinic? Do you mean that place where people go when they're sick from H-R-S?" Recognition dawned over Patricia's face. "You're the two Protectors, aren't you? That's why he's got such humongous muscles."

"You've heard of us?"

The girl seemed startled, as if Sheera had asked her the stupidest of all possible questions. "All Pitcairn knows about you two. How he fought the monster that's half-bird and half-man. How he almost got killed. How you found him and saved his life with help from a polliwumper. How General Halfbald said the Army would continue its efforts to kill the creature, in spite of the Protectors' failure. The news didn't talk about anything else for a week."

"I don't listen to local news much." Sheera had never seen much point in listening to a state-run monopoly that spewed only its self-serving version of events. "You were kidnapped before you had a chance to hear about our second run-in with the harpy. We captured him that time. You should have seen the big guy. He was magnificent."

"Was I?" a male voice said. "At the time, you called me a dim-bulb."

Steven was rubbing the drowsiness from his eyes. Sheera sprang to the floor and hugged him.

"Hey—cut that out!" He grimaced, as Patricia snickered.

"I'm sorry," Sheera said, relaxing her hold and backing away. "I forgot your bruises would still be tender. I'm just... just so thrilled to see you alive."

She waited for him to utter some expression of joy over their reunion. But he only grunted. "Where are we, and where did all this junk come from?"

"We're trapped in an alien prison. And I have a theory about the furniture. Do you want to hear it?"

Steven got to his feet and stretched. "I might as well."

"I surmise that, for the past two hundred years, the avians have been observing us more than we imagined. More than we observed them, for certain. Sometimes they borrowed articles from our homes..."

"Plundered articles," Steven corrected. "If they gave them back, that would have been borrowing."

"Plundered, if you prefer, but for a reason that reveals a glimmer of decency. They want us to subsist in our own environment, the way the best zoos try to duplicate the natural habitat of the animals in their custody."

Steven's eyes glanced about the room. "Scattering a couple of pilfered beds and a few rundown chairs around a prison cell doesn't make them our friends. But it does look like we have one new friend." He broke into a smile for the first time since he'd entered the valley, and stretched out his hand to Patricia. "What's a sweet girl like you doing in a crummy joint like this?"

Patricia shook his hand, her fingers tiny against his, and beamed under his attention. She told him her name, then related her tale of how she had run away from home, only to be kidnapped by night. Steven's smile dissolved in anger when she described the part about the harpy swooping down and gripping her shoulders.

"There's no bottom to how low that monster will sink," Steven said. "It even goes after children. I swear to God, I'll recapture it."

"Recapture," the girl repeated. "Do you mean it escaped?"

"Yeah, but don't worry. As soon as we bust out of here, I'll go after it again."

His self-assured smirk gave Sheera her first ray of hope. "Bust out? Do you think we can?"

"We'll find out." Steven crossed the few paces to the door and kicked. "Ow! That barrier is more solid than it looks. Hey, don't look so downcast, you two. We're still Protectors, and if there's one thing our Community is good at, it's rushing to the aid of other Protectors." He rested a hand on Patricia's shoulder. "And we come to the aid of our friends, too. I'll contact our provincial and arrange for a first-class rescue." He grazed the fingers of his left hand with his right, and touched only bare skin. The smirk disappeared from his face.

"They removed my communication jewel, too," Sheera said, holding up her finger. She kept her voice calm, for Patricia's sake. Mustn't let the girl discover that Protectors experience fear, like everyone else. "There won't be any rescue. Neither of us has tracing agent in our bloodstreams. And even if Taryn knew where to find us, she couldn't cross into the valley without a flyer, and we took the only one she had. If we're going to break out of here, we'll have to do it on our own."

Steven looked up at the open space in the ceiling. "It's a long way to the top, but in such wimpy gravity, this'll be worth a try."

He pulled a chair across the floor, and positioned it directly beneath the gap. He climbed onto the chair, stretched his hands as far over his head as he could, and jumped. He fell short of the target by an arm's length.

"Maybe it's just as well you couldn't jump high enough to reach the way out," Patricia said. "The Bird People might kill you if they catch you outside this room."

Sheera's eyes met Steven's. She could tell they shared the same thought, one they wouldn't speak out loud in front of the girl. The Bird People intended to kill them anyway.

CHAPTER TWENTY-THREE

THE LOSS OF A NEW FRIEND AND A VISIT FROM AN OLD ENEMY

"Protectors shall respect the culture and traditions of alien species,
except when the culture and traditions would lead them to violate
another of these Precepts."
—D.F. Nathaniel

Weeks dragged by. The prisoners' dream of concocting an escape plan never came near to reality. Steven, his fists raw from pounding the walls, talked often about seizing a guard and holding him hostage until the enemy agreed to release every human prisoner. But the avians never gave him an opportunity to find out whether his plan would succeed. Through a grate in the wall, they shoved food, most of it edible by humans. Apparently, they had figured out the human diet, to a degree, from groceries stolen out of kitchens. They never approached any closer than the other side of the door. Patricia said they had been bolder about entering the cell before Steven became their captive.

The prisoners had a library of books they supposed had been pilfered along with the furniture. Sheera poured over one musty volume after another, all fashioned of paper and ink, as electronic reading devices were hard to come by on Pitcairn. Steven and Patricia had their own favorite activity. He entertained her with sagas about the life of a Protector-in-training. She would sit spellbound on her bunk or in a chair, hero-worship in her eyes, while he talked of faraway realms like Pendragon, Merlin, Medusa-Four, and London. To a girl who'd never been away from her own world, and had seen nothing worth mentioning of that, the places he spoke of seemed as exotic as Mount Olympus.

He also told her about his struggle against the drug trade on Medusa-Four, without mentioning his hallucinations. And he relayed every element of his two battles with the harpy. He set the record straight about the first encounter, supplying crucial information Halfbald had left out of the official version. She was shocked to learn someone in the Army was a saboteur, but never questioned a word of Steven's account.

One afternoon, Steven was standing, as he usually did when he was telling a story, while Patricia occupied one of the two stolen chairs and Sheera read on the floor with her back against the wall. He was recalling a memory about a martial arts victory on Pendragon, when Patricia said, "There's one thing I don't understand."

Always happy to expound on whatever Patricia wanted to learn, whether he knew anything about the subject or not, Steven waited for her to ask a question.

She went on. "You must be the toughest guy in this sector of the Galaxy. You even defeated the harpy."

Steven waited in silence for what he expected would be more flattery. Sheera looked up from her page and cocked an ear to listen.

"But the first day the two of you got to this valley, Bird People with knives attacked you and took you prisoner. Why couldn't you overcome them?"

Steven had already told her they were captured by guards while entering the king's residence, but had supplied few details of how it happened. "I could have beaten them in an honest fight," Steven said. "But they didn't play fair. They sprayed us with something. Some kind of gas, I guess. We couldn't see it or smell it, but it paralyzed us, then knocked us out." He exhaled. "Now do you understand?"

Patricia nodded. Sheera set aside her book and said, "She may understand, but I don't."

"What are you talking about?" Steven said. "You were there."

"I was referring to their ability to use what seems like advanced technology. On the whole, they're quite primitive, wouldn't you say? As we flew into this valley, I didn't notice a single non-living object that moved under its own power."

Steven sank onto the other chair, with barely enough room for him to squeeze between its arms. "They're primitive, all right, and their lack of machinery isn't the half of it. The Neanderthals brought down T-rexes with weapons more advanced than those cruddy knives they attacked me with."

Sheera smiled the way she usually did when Steven had made a show of his ignorance. "The Neanderthals lived millions of years after the tyrannosaurs," she said. "But you're correct about the rest. Our stone-age ancestors possessed armaments more sophisticated than what we've observed in this valley. So it's peculiar, wouldn't you say, that they overcame our resistance with what could only have been a colorless, odorless gas? It renders humans immobile and unconscious, but it has no effect on avians. That's quite an accomplishment for a tribe that has yet to invent the bow and arrow."

Steven said nothing at first, aside from the occasional "um" or "er," as he tried to concoct an explanation that wouldn't make him sound stupid in front of Patricia. At last he spoke. "If Taryn is right about how they came across an H-R-S treatment, they could've discovered the knock-out gas in the same way. Mixed it together from something that exists in nature. Maybe they have immunity, and we don't, because their bodies developed a resistance after millions of years of exposure."

Sheera looked back and forth between Steven and Patricia. "Perhaps. But even if they used a naturally-occurring substance, it was an impressive achievement. Somehow, they isolated an invisible gas, and found a way to target it against humans. Their H-R-S antidote might be some indigenous weed they feed to their sick in its original state, the way the British Navy fed limes to sailors to prevent scurvy. The knock-out gas is different. It can only serve its purpose with the intervention of a skilled chemist."

Only one explanation seemed possible. "Are you suggesting they had human help?" Steven asked. Possible, but disturbing.

"It wouldn't surprise me. Just as it wouldn't surprise me if the person who helped them develop knockout gas turns out to be the same individual who sabotaged your first encounter with Quirip."

Steven frowned. "Do you really think Halfbald is that determined to stop us from getting credit for defeating the harpy? He's a jerk, sure, but he wouldn't supply our enemy with a weapon. He's not that much of a fool. They might target the gas against his troops some day."

"I didn't say the traitor was Halfbald."

Patricia clapped her hands over her ears. "Stop it! You're scaring me. It's bad enough that the Bird People have a half-human monster who kidnaps our people. Now you're telling me they might have a weapon more powerful than anything the Army has? What if they attack our settlements? They could make slaves out of our families."

Sheera put a hand on Patricia's shoulder. "I wouldn't worry. If they wanted to use paralyzing gas against the Army, they would have done it already."

Patricia only pouted. Steven doubted Sheera's reasoning had brought her any comfort. It had brought him no comfort, either.

*   *   *

A few nights later, Steven slumbered on the bare wood floor, between the two bunks he'd turned over to the ladies in a gesture of chivalry. He heard the squeak of hinges, as if in a dream. The squeak faded, and then Patricia's scream woke him. In a stupor between sleep and consciousness, he dismissed the scream as a nightmare. Who could blame the girl for having nightmares, after all she'd suffered through?

The second scream caused him to jerk his head up and forward, in time to gaze into the darkness and see two shapes with wings dragging the form of a human through the cell door. A third shape, also with wings, held a torch that broke the night with just enough twilight to make the bodies visible. Steven jumped to his feet and rushed to the door, hand extended to grab the avian intruders and toss them across the room. They slammed the door shut, from the opposite side, before he could reach them.

He pulled at the door, then pounded and kicked it. Finally he sank back to the floor in the total blackness. "I let the kid down," he said. Then, without thinking, he added, "We've got to find a way to help her."

Sheera's voice reached him out of the dark, cold and logical. "How, when we can't help ourselves?"

*　　　　*　　　　*

It had been two days since Patricia had disappeared. Chirps and caws of avians talking among themselves filtered through the wall, and then the door burst open. Steven sensed an avenue of escape. He even indulged a fantasy of rescuing Patricia, though he had no idea how he would find her. For a fraction of a second, he pondered whether to attack his captors or try to flee past them with Sheera in his arms. Then a familiar enemy appeared in the doorway, and he decided to do neither until after he found out what was going on.

Steven clenched his fists and stood face-to-face with the harpy. Guards followed and flanked the creature beside each wing, under the apparent delusion their spears would intimidate their human prisoner.

"I know you can understand me," he said to the harpy. "Give me one good reason why I shouldn't kill you where you stand."

"I'll give you a reason," Sheera warned "The Precepts. On Medusa-Four, you had an argument for self-defense. That's not the case now."

Steven straightened to his full height. "So who's gonna tell the Guidance Committee? You? Even if you rat on me, it'll be worth it to guarantee this monster never hurts anybody again." He lowered his voice and glanced at Sheera. "But I'll do it your way. I'll negotiate." He stared the harpy in the eye. "Bring the human girl to me, unharmed, then arrange for the three of us to walk out of this prison, back to our flyer, and I'll let you live... for now."

The guards stood like statues, holding their spears, as Quirip produced a flurry of high-pitched sounds. Sheera translated. "He says it's not within his power either to help the child or to grant us freedom. There's one more thing." Sheera looked at the creature and said, "He asks you to forgive him."

The harpy extended his right hand, palm open, in a distinctly human custom. He suspended his hand in mid-gesture. He could dangle it there until Pitcairn's sun went nova before Steven would accept it.

"You think I'd take the hand of someone who betrayed me?" He shook his head and glared. "No—not some*one*. Some*thing*. You're less than a person, less even than one of those bird-freaks. You're nothing but some horrible mistake of nature. Destroying something like you isn't murder. It's... it's exterminating vermin."

He lunged, throwing the guards across the room like two canisters of hydrogen in a cold-fusion plant. He raised his fist, prepared to deliver a blow that would would end his feud with the harpy once and for all.

He flinched. Killing on purpose didn't come as naturally to him as he'd expected. It's not as if the harpy was a member of his own species, he reminded himself, and again found the will to carry out the deed. This one's for you, Patricia, he thought, and tried to chop he edge of his hand down against his adversary's throat.

The light from above disappeared, leaving Steven to fight on in darkness. He didn't need sight to achieve his goal. The harpy's distinctive odor could guide him to his target. But his arm dropped to his side, and his legs became like stumps. A thump told him Sheera had already dropped to the floor. He stood for as long as his legs would support him, and then fell and passed out

The next thing he knew, he was regaining his senses, not knowing if a minute, a day, or a week had passed. He lay face-down on one of the bunks. Sheera didn't possess the strength to lift him by herself, even in light gravity, so his captors must have stashed him there. He saw by the restored light that the Bird People were gone. But he and Sheera had company in their prison. D.F. Nathaniel stood at the foot of the bunk. The founder and patron of the Protectors laughed at him. Cruel laughter. Not at all the friendly chuckle Nathaniel was famous for.

CHAPTER TWENTY-FOUR

A PLAUSIBLE THEORY ABOUT THE SOURCE OF THE APPARITIONS

"Protectors shall strive for reconciliation with their enemies, whether human or alien."
—D.F. Nathaniel

Steven groaned. "What are you doing here?" he demanded of the apparition. It had the same gaunt cheeks and scraggly beard as in the pictures and statues, but the expression was haughty and the eyes were cold. "I thought you gave up haunting me back on Merlin."

"Who are you talking to?" Sheera asked, from the other bunk. "Your hallucination is back, isn't it?"

From the opposite direction, the apparition said, "You believed you left me behind on Merlin?" It laughed a second time. "Have you forgotten I came to you in the alley here on Pitcairn?"

"The night in the alley doesn't count," Steven argued, trying not to tremble. "I was delirious from venom and loss of blood. Anybody would have hallucinated."

"What?" Sheera said. "You had a hallucination you never told me about?"

Steven silently cursed his own big mouth. Before he could answer, the apparition snickered. "You were a fool if you thought you'd gotten rid of me on Merlin. You actually believed

209

you could be absolved of the sin of murder by helping a boy get out from under a toppled wall? It's time you learned the truth. Saving the child's life had nothing to do with my decision to leave you alone during the next few months."

Sheera sprang up, crossed to his side of the room, and leaned over him. "You control your vision. He exists in your mind. If you don't want him, tell him to go away."

"You heard her. Get out of my head." He blinked. The apparition continued to stare down at him. Steven closed his eyes and put his head into his hands. *I can do this. I can make him vanish.*

He looked up, and discovered he'd been wrong. Nathaniel mocked him with more laughter. "Do you think you can get rid of me that easily?"

The apparition appeared larger than before, a giant of a man. Or maybe, Steven thought, the growth was just his imagination. In fact, the whole thing was his imagination. Or was it? If the vision wasn't real, why couldn't he make it go away?

"He's still there, isn't he?" Sheera called.

Steven nodded.

"Mmm. All right," Sheera said. "Do you trust me?"

What kind of s silly questions was that? "Of course."

Nathaniel crossed his arms and stared, with no apparent intention of going back where he came from, wherever that was.

"Then stand up, turn away from the apparition, and take a few steps toward me."

Why not? Steven followed her directions. His right leg, numb from the paralyzing gas, scraped the floor. His left was only a little better, but he found the strength to stand and walk. At the same time Sheera moved closer. Unable to fully control his limbs yet, he bumped into her in the middle of the room. "Sorry," he said.

"Don't apologize. I wanted that to happen." She stood on her toes and wrapped her arms around him.

"What about Nathaniel?" In case the apparition was more than his imagination, it seemed like a bad idea to engage in a Precept violation in full view of the Community's founder, even dead.

"Never mind him. Concentrate on me. Only me. Concentrate. Look at my eyes."

He had no problem concentrating on her eyes. He would gladly have drowned in them.

"Tilt your head down a little," she said, and stood on her toes.

"Are you sure… mmph."

She was kissing him. He gave in—never mind the Precept—drew her closer, and kissed her back. Harpies, Bird People, generals, and even apparitions didn't matter. It was almost as if they no longer existed for him. For the moment, nothing in the Galaxy mattered. Except her.

She pulled back. "Look behind you."

He took a backward glance. "Nathaniel—he's gone."

She took another step away from him, wiped her lips with her grimy sleeve, and stretched her arm in front of her. The gesture told him the embrace was over.

"It worked," she said. "I remembered that, when the apparition appeared on Merlin, it disappeared when the explosion distracted your attention." Her eyes darted around the room. "I couldn't very well cause an explosion in here, so I did the next best thing. As I'd hoped, shifting your concentration got rid of your hallucination, for now. Under these circumstances, I wouldn't say we breached the Precept."

So it had all been in the line of duty? He went back to his bunk and slumped onto the lumpy mattress.

She touched his arm. "I didn't mean to hurt you just then."

"You didn't," he lied.

Maybe he could convince her it was the apparition's appearance, and not her dismissal of the kiss as some sort of therapy, that caused his downcast expression. Actually, he judged the two events produced about equal levels of misery.

But if he talked about the kiss, he'd probably end up saying something he would later regret. He filled in details about the apparition instead. "Nathaniel said something strange. He told me that saving Danny's life wasn't what caused him to stop haunting me."

Sheera sat beside him and rested her hand on his. "It wasn't really Nathaniel. It was your subconscious, and I think your mind was just pushing to the surface something you've known deep down for a long time."

He turned towards her. "Then I wish my conscious and my subconscious would get in sync for a change, because I'm more bewildered than ever. If saving Danny's life had no effect on my hallucinations, why was I free of them for so long? Don't tell me I had an apparition today because I carried a load of guilt over trying to kill the harpy. I'm not sorry I did it. My only regret is that I didn't succeed."

"It takes more than a guilty conscience to bring on the apparition. It also takes a trigger, the same one each time. After your final hallucination on Merlin, I listened to recordings of your encounters with the apparition, and detected something each appearance had in common, besides the sight of blood."

"There were recordings?" Nobody had said anything to Steven about recordings.

She nodded. "On Medusa-Four, in the confusion that followed the Warlord's death, you forgot to turn off the chip you'd been using to preserve an account of your sting operation. And Doctor Aloysius always records his therapy sessions. As long as your hallucinations seemed under control, I thought it would be better not to mention my suspicion—that blood was never the trigger, as we had all assumed. If I was wrong, talking openly about my theory might have done more harm than good. But now that Nathaniel has returned, we'd better re-open your case."

Steven folded his arms behind his head and leaned back against the wall. "Sure, Dr. Freud. Whatever that image is, spirit or guilty conscience, I'll try anything that might stop him from harassing me ."

"Good. Doctor Aloysius and I both believed that the sight of blood produced a flashback to the incident with the Warlord. We must have been wrong. There was no blood visible today, was there?" She exhaled a deep breath and went on. "You and I are going to piece together what happened just before you killed the Warlord, and just before each hallucination. I've already figured out the common thread, and now, so will you."

Steven's spirits sank even lower. "Offhand, I can think of nothing I'd rather do less than talk about the night I killed the Warlord. Look at me. I'm a prisoner of aliens who will kill me sooner or later. I've lost someone special, thanks to my failure to protect her. I'll probably lose you the same way. I've let down the people of this world who depended on me to protect them. My only consolation is that the Guidance Committee won't get a chance to rule against my petition, because I'll never get out of here alive. Do you really think this is a good time to dredge up memories of the worst experience of my life? Are you trying to rob me of the shred of sanity I have left?"

"If I'm correct, I might help you hang onto that sanity. We'll start with the night on Medusa-Four. Picture the scene. You and your provincial are in the saloon. The Warlord is seated. What do you say?"

He shrugged. "I didn't say much of anything. Jan was in charge of the sting, so I let her do the talking."

"No, you offered your point of view. Think. It's all in the report. You look at the Warlord. The very sight of him disgusts you. You turn to your provincial and you whisper."

She slid so close, their knees touched. Her nearness took away some of the pain that came with the memory of Medusa-Four. "I guess I did mumble something. Didn't amount to much. I just kind of wondered out loud whether such a creep could even be considered human."

"Exactly. You're doing great." Sheera squeezed his arm. "Now, it's moments before your first hallucination. You talk to a police officer who's impressed by what you've done. Do you remember what he compares the Warlord to?"

"Sure. He called him a frog."

"A slimy toad, actually, but your answer is near enough. We'll proceed to the second time you saw Nathaniel. Your provincial offers you words of assurance. What were they?"

Steven fidgeted. He could tell, from Sheera's persistence, that she was determined to see her line of questioning through to wherever it took them, no matter how painful. "Um, she said Nathaniel wouldn't scold me for disposing of trash."

"Correct," she declared, looking pleased. "Now, you're on Earth, near the end of your psychiatric exam. What does Doctor Aloysius say to you moments before you have your only hallucination that takes place in standard gravity?"

This was tougher. Aloysius had prattled on about all sorts of topics. Sheera's stare burrowed into him during his long silence, until she gave him a prompt.

"Think back," she said. "Dr. Aloysius tells you not to feel guilty, and calls the Warlord a disparaging name."

"Oh, yeah. He said the Warlord was pond scum."

"Good. We're almost finished. There was never a recording of the next incident, but I don't need one. I can rely on memory. It's our first day on Merlin, and we bicker over whether I should slash my hand to induce a vision. I refer to the drug pusher by an unflattering word. Do you remember the word?"

Steven rested his chin on his fist and said nothing, because nothing occurred to him.

"A beast," Sheera said, sounding exasperated. "Don't you remember? I call him a beast. Do you detect a pattern?"

He tried. He honestly tried. "Uh, no."

"We all used a disparaging term to insult the person you killed. Toad. Trash. Scum. Beast. The commonality to our insults was that we pictured him as less than a man. Your provincial, Doctor Aloysius, and I—we all did it, because we believed we would make you feel better and help you get over the burden of guilt that shackled you. Now I realize we only made you feel worse, by triggering your memory of the way you questioned the Warlord's humanity." She took a deep breath. "And... don't take this the wrong way... you... uh... you might have been justified in feeling guilty."

Steven remembered. Terms like trash, scum, and beast, when he heard them, had done nothing to relieve his guilt, so she was partly correct. But telling him he'd been right to feel guilty—that hurt, especially coming from the person whose respect he most craved. "Are you telling me the killing wasn't justifiable self-defense?" he asked.

"Oh, it was self-defense." she said quickly. "But we need to revisit how justifiable it was."

Her air of certainty irritated him. How could she be so sure? She was behaving like one of his teachers, peppering him with questions in class, rather than like a friend helping him sort through his confusion.

She went on. "Any ranger can perform feats of physical prowess that appear borderline supernatural to the rest of us. With that level of skill, couldn't you have found some means of disarming your enemy that didn't involve smashing his vital organs? If you'd really wanted to?"

He wiggled and slapped his legs, partly to coax back the feeling the gas had stolen from them, and partly to look busy while he figured out what to tell her. He'd asked himself the same question, and already knew the answer. He just hadn't wanted her to ask it, because now he had to admit the truth to her. "Maybe I could have fractured his wrist or his arm or something like that," he said. Still, he hoped she would understand why he could not be held to blame. "When a man tries to kill you, you don't stop to think through your options. I had about one heartbeat standing between me and incineration. I went with my first instinct."

Her eyes were sympathetic, but the words sounded cold, almost heartless. "And your first instinct was to kill rather than to disable? When you questioned the Warlord's humanity, you inferred his conduct was so despicable, it reduced him below some threshold that marks us as members-in-good-standing of the human race. I know this is hard for you to accept—hard for me to accept, too—but perhaps the Guidance Committee was right to put you on probation. Do you think the Warlord is the last truly evil person you'll encounter if you pursue a career in our Community? If our highest Precept is going to mean anything, we can't give in to our impulse to treat people—even vile people—as if they have no right to live."

Sheera pressed her knee against his. He could hardly feel her, for the stubborn numbness in his leg. Then she laid her arm across his shoulder, where his sense of touch had long-since returned to normal. It was the kind of contact she usually avoided, for fear of breaching the prohibition against romantic entanglements between scholars and rangers. He tried not to let her closeness distract him.

"Let's say you're right," he said. "Let's say I killed the Warlord because I looked down on him as sub-human. How can we connect that to my two most recent hallucinations? In the alley, I called the harpy a demon, and here in the cell, I said that killing him was no different from exterminating vermin. Are you saying I hallucinated because, each time, I called the harpy by a name that implied he wasn't as good as a human?"

"Not exactly. Name-calling can be a powerful weapon for hate, but I think the source of your hallucinations runs deeper than that. The names were a manifestation of what was going on inside you. I believe the apparition came to you on Pitcairn because you treated an alien's life as if it has less value than the life of a human. It's your prejudice, not just your words, that cause Nathaniel to haunt you. The words are only a reminder. A trigger."

"In the alley, I had no choice but to shoot the harpy in self-defense. Even the Guidance Committee probably would have agreed."

"I'll grant you that, but why did you wait until you were injured before you fired your gun? Was it because you placed value on alien life? Or was it because you wanted to impress the Guidance Committee and get off probation?"

"A little of both?" he said, realizing, only after he had spoken, that his answer had sounded more like a question. Seeing her eyes narrow with skepticism, he admitted, "Mainly for the second reason, I guess."

She pulled her arm from his shoulder, edged away, and turned to face him. She went on. "Why do you always call Quirip *the harpy*, instead of granting him the dignity of referring to him by his given name? If you're determined to kill him, at least recognize him as a person entitled to the same rights as us. Don't hide behind the excuse that you'd be exterminating vermin."

Steven stood and paced across the room, noticing some improvement in his legs. He turned his back to Sheera. He didn't want to look into her eyes while he reflected on what she'd told him. After a minute, he faced her. "Suppose I treat the har... ah, Quirip... more like he's a person, instead of... well... whatever it is that's not as good as person. Would the apparition leave me alone after that?"

"It's possible."

Steven came back and sat on his bunk, near to Sheera but not quite touching. "Maybe," he said. "But after the way I pounced on him, I'll never get that chance. He'd be crazy to show his face around this cell again."

Exactly one day later, as days are measured on Pitcairn, he found out how crazy his winged adversary could be.

CHAPTER TWENTY-FIVE

A PRECEPT IS A PRECEPT

"A Protector who is trapped with no apparent means of escape shall use all available means to communicate his or her situation to members of the Community who are outside the area of entrapment."
—D.F. Nathaniel

Sheera sat cross-legged on the floor, as she perused a novel from her favorite era of literature, the twenty-fourth century. She glanced up from a page, distracted by the sound of squawks, coming closer. Could the Bird People be planning to grab one of them as they had grabbed Patricia? Knowing they wouldn't dare to attack while Steven was conscious, she braced for the paralyzing gas to strike her. Perhaps if she covered her mouth and nose this time—would that screen out its effects?

She listened again. The walls muffled the sound, but this time she heard enough to be certain of who was squawking.

"Listen," she said. "He's back."

"Are you sure it's the harpy?" Steven asked, pausing his morning exercise routine at his two hundred and twelfth pushup. "I'd guess all Bird People sound alike to human ears."

She pressed her ear against the wall and listened. "It's him, all right. He wants to come in, but says that first you have to swear you won't assault him like you did the last time. Who else would say that?"

Steven dropped his voice until it was too low for a listener on the other side of the door to overhear. He had failed to consider that Bird People might have sharper hearing than humans, Sheera thought. She was willing to take that chance to hear what he had to say.

"I can't swear I won't hurt him," Steven whispered, edging close to her ear. "Even if what you say is true—that by treating him more like an equal I might cure my hallucinations—I owe it to Patricia to take him down."

Sheera understood. Patricia was like a little sister to him. And in fairness, he was after more than vengeance. He wanted to make sure no more children suffered the same fate. Her only chance of preventing violence was to persuade him that attacking Quirip would serve no useful purpose.

"It won't do you any good to attack him," she pointed out. "The Bird People will unleash the gas again. Instead, treat him as you would another human, one you don't have any grudge against. You won't get blasted by paralyzing gas then, and you might get rid of the apparition once and for all."

Steven grimaced, but called through the door. "I won't hurt you," He turned to Sheera. "There. Satisfied?"

The squeaking of rusty hinges grated on Sheera's ears. Quirip strode in with a guard on each side. Walking upright with the gait of a human, he towered over the guards, who crouched and padded on three limbs in the manner of their species. Steven faced his enemy, fists clenched but safely down by his side.

Sheera translated as Quirip squawked. "He says he still hopes you will forgive him... mmmm... mmmm... and asks you to accept his hand the way you would accept the hand of a member of your own species."

Steven stared in silence at the alien palm that reached out to him. Disgust swept over his features.

Sheera wondered why the harpy seemed obsessed with exchanging a handshake. She knew Steven would rather stick his fingers into a hornet's nest. "Go ahead and shake," she urged. "I doubt he has anything contagious. And Patricia would want you to."

He turned to her with a look of bewilderment. "She would?"

Her mind raced. She'd made the mistake of blurting a conclusion without giving any forethought as to whether it was true. Now she had to drum up a logical explanation, and drum it up quickly, as to why Patricia would want Steven to take the hand of someone she despised. "You bet she would. If treating Quirip as an equal cures your hallucinations, then I'll be able to certify that your brain is normal as apple pie. That way, if we ever get out of this trap, the Community will permit you to remain a Protector, and you can continue defending the weak. Patricia would like that." She held her breath, waiting to see if her argument, made up on the spot, would be convincing.

He looked at the bare floor, frowning, until he muttered, "I guess you're right."

"You're darn right I am. Get this over with. Your subconscious will thank you later."

He squeezed Quirip's open palm, with all the enthusiasm of a farmer scooping up pig dung in his bare hand. Quirip reached out his other arm and, for a moment, pressed with both hands, curling Steven's fingers together and smothering them in feathers.

"Ow! What was…?"

Quirip squawked at a pace so rapid that Sheera had to concentrate to understand. "He thanks you and says he needs to leave now," she said.

Quirip bolted from the room, with the guards following at his talons.

Sheera gazed at the closed door and tried to make sense of what she had just observed. "That was weird. It's almost as if his entire purpose in coming here was to join hands for a few seconds. And why would he clasp with both hands like that? Could that signify peaceable intentions in his species?"

Steven stared down at his open palm. "Peaceable intentions? That's not why he grabbed me the way he did. He wanted to slip something to me without the guards noticing, and that was his way of reducing the odds I'd drop it. He probably told the guards he was imitating a human gesture."

He held out his hand. Sheera looked into his massive palm and saw a communication ring nestled against his skin. The jewel sparkled with a glint of light from the opening over their heads. That ought to convince him Quirip is on our side, she thought.

"It's a trick," he said. He held the ring between his thumb and one finger and examined it. "I'll bet those freaks infected this ring with some virus they want us to come down with. Don't touch it. You might die in excruciating agony from some horrible disease. It's probably already too late for me."

Sheera snatched the ring. "If they want us to contract a disease, they can inject it into our food. Quirip slipped us the ring the only way he knew how, with guards lurking over his shoulder. He wants us to summon Taryn for aid."

"Strange that he insisted on sneaking it to me rather than you," Steven said. "He must have known you'd be more willing to accept his handshake. My guess is, he was afraid I'd clobber him if he touched you. He would've been right."

"Or, he wanted to make you a peace offering. Either way, he didn't realize Taryn has no means to rescue us. But that makes no difference to what we're obliged to do next. The Nathanielian Precepts are clear. If we discover ourselves in a dangerous situation with no avenue of escape, we must notify another Protector if the means are available."

She held her lips near to the bauble. "Contact T-A-R-Y-N," she ordered. A minute went by, and then she threw the ring onto the floor in exasperation. "It's just as I feared. The audio link is useless in this valley. Pitcairn doesn't have the resources for a satellite hookup, so the signals have to travel the air waves near the planet's surface. The mountains are blocking them."

Steven stooped, picked up the ring, and handed it back to her. "Then we won't be able to talk with Taryn. How about using the ring's SOS function instead? That would tell her we're alive, for now. Can we send her a tracking signal?"

Sheera shot him an angry look, that she realized a second later had been unfair to him. It was just that he annoyed her by remaining so calm in such a hopeless situation, and worse, by being so right. She didn't want to merely send an SOS signal, especially one that wouldn't accomplish anything. She wanted to chat with Taryn, to leave behind a record of what became of them in case they never escaped. Still, he had a point that any communication was better than none.

"The tracking signal has a chance of getting through," she admitted. "It's stronger than the audio link, and might punch its way beyond the valley. But don't expect anything to come of it. Even if Taryn traces our signal, she'll still have no way to rescue us. However..." She set the tracking signal in motion. "A Precept is a Precept. Nathaniel required us to relay the location of our captivity the best way we can. There—I obeyed our founder's command. For all the good it's likely to do us."

CHAPTER TWENTY-SIX

UNINVITED GUESTS AT A CEREMONY

"Protectors shall never interfere with the right to freely engage in religious practice, unless such practice would cause injury to another person or alien."
—D.F. Nathaniel.

D ays later, as the two prisoners were reading on their bunks to pass the afternoon, the walls began to vibrate, rocking the room and its occupants back and forth. Steven jumped to his feet and steadied himself. The room settled down after a few seconds. "Must've been a quake," he said.

Of course he would say that, Sheera thought. Growing up on a stable world like Pendragon, he probably never experienced a quake. "No," she said. "On Merlin, we deal with quakes so often, we think nothing of them. This felt different. It seemed to emanate from every fiber of the air, not just from below ground."

"Maybe quakes feel different on different worlds," Steven suggested. "Wow—look at the wall."

An emerald glow shined where the wall met the floor. The glow whittled its way up, slicing a trail through the brick. When it reached human height, it veered to the right, then worked its way down until it had carved an opening. A section of the wall, the width and roughly the shape of a human body, clattered to the floor. A feathered animal waddled through the empty space.

Sheera cried out. "Pengy! What are you doing here?" She waffled between delight and terror, fearing that the Bird People had kidnapped the Protectors' little mascot.

"He came with me."

A tall woman with muscled arms emerged through the gap in the wall. She held a force-shield blade in her right hand. Sheera recognized it as the one Steven had carried during his rematch with Quirip, or the identical model. The woman snapped off the green light at the blade's tip. "Always did want to use one of these tools for a prison-break," she said. "Sliced through brick like it was no more solid than a heavy mist."

"Who are you, and what's going on?" Sheera demanded.

"I'm bringing you home, if you don't mess up this rescue by wasting time with questions." She beckoned them to follow, but when she turned to flee, she froze. "Hey—how come I can't move my legs?"

No light seeped in from the passageway, and when the opening in the ceiling snapped shut, the darkness turned total. Sheera felt the creep of paralyzing gas make her arms and legs grow stiff. Didn't those Bird People know any other way to attack a human? She trusted Steven to protect her against any enemy he could kick or punch, but even he couldn't shield her from an invisible gas.

Or could he? A light blinked on, dim, but enough for her to see Steven standing beside her. He'd thought to switch on his communication ring, bathing the room with its glimmer. His features grew rigid as his facial muscles froze, and he collapsed. He called to the woman in a voice that was growing thick. "Quick. Did you bring any weapon that might let us carve a hole into the ceiling?"

The woman held up a sphere the size of a grapefruit.

"Toss me your solar applicator, while you still can."

She lobbed the device, clumsily, as if she had steel beams stuck to her shoulder sockets in place of arms. The sphere plopped to the floor, short of Steven's hand, and bounced away.

His legs crumpled, and he collapsed, too far from the sphere to retrieve it.

Steven crawled. A centimeter… two. At that rate, he'd be out cold before he could reach the sphere.

One occupant of the cell didn't appear to mind the paralyzing gas. He waddled about, licking the faces of the stricken humans. Sheera imagined the panic that must be going on inside that little brain, at the helplessness of his friends.

"Pengy," Steven called. "Help me out, buddy. C'mon, fetch!"

The little alien recoiled his tongue from Sheera's cheek. He scooped up the orb in his teeth, then spit it within easy reach of his human companion's fingers.

Steven's tongue barely moved. "G'boy." he congratulated. He grasped the orb with both hands.

Sheera had trouble telling the top of a solar applicator from its bottom. She prayed that Steven was holding the device right-side-up. If it was upside down, he'd sear a hole through his chest. He pointed the device at the ceiling, with no need to aim for a specific target. Any spot over his head would do.

A flash of light made the room bright as a sunny afternoon, but it wasn't ordinary light. It was an energy burst shooting upward. The room went dim as quickly as it had turned bright, then objects and faces came into better focus in the reflection from the energy burst's point-of-contact with the ceiling. A patch over their heads progressed from red to yellow to white, then melted. Fresh air gushed into the cell. The paralyzing gas swooped outside, and from there, Sheera presumed, it mingled with the atmosphere, where it would do them no more harm.

Their rescuer stumbled to a standing position, nearly tripping over her feet. "Explain to me later why we froze," she said. "Sheera—carry Pengy and follow me. Steven and I will fight off any avians who try to stop us."

"How do you know my name?"

Steven scooped up Pengy in one hand and thrust him into Sheera's arms. "Do what she says. Hold your questions."

Their first steps outside the cell, through the hole in the wall, led them to a sealed passageway. The woman paused before the closed door and muttered, "This was open when I came through here earlier. No matter." She sliced through the barrier with her blade, and the group stormed through.

Torches lined the sides of the corridor, none of them lit. A faint light, from up ahead, supplied them with enough vision to hurry forward with a minimum of bumping into walls or each other. Sheera felt her legs, stiff from the lingering effect of the gas, wobble as she ran, and she deduced from their awkward motions that the others were having the same trouble. They moved in silence, except when Steven murmured, "Why isn't anyone trying to stop us?"

The corridor grew brighter, until they came to the source of the light. Their rescuer had led them to a place where the wall had been reduced to rubble, and they could see through to the outside. A flyer straddled the gap, half inside and half out. The flyer was a boxy model plated with armor. Designed for combat rather than looks, it had survived the collision without a scratch.

"Get in," the woman commanded. "Sheera, ever pilot a battle flyer like this one?"

"Never in my life."

"Then you're going to learn quickly. Get behind the controls, turn this thing around, and take off. Steven and I will ride shotgun with the zeta-ray blasters." She patted the polliwumper's head. "But safety comes first. We'll secure Pengy into his seat." She strapped their feathered companion into the flyer with one hand, as she passed a weapon to Steven with the other.

The space in front of the pilot's line of vision was plated with the same armor as every other centimeter of the vehicle. Sheera supposed the lack of windows would be an advantage in a collision, but it came with a drawback. "How will I see where I'm going?"

"Same way you'd see outside a shuttle in outer space. With help from video."

Their rescuer tapped a switch, and the bulkheads lit up with a view of their surroundings. Sheera saw the landscape of scraggly trees and shoddy avian shacks, as plainly as if nothing at all stood between her and the open air. The stone of the prison passageway, where the flyer's front half still rested, filled her view of the other side.

She refused to be rushed. "My arms and legs feel like they're drenched in molten lead. It won't be safe for me to pilot a ship until the gas completely wears off. If I need to make a manual override of the computer, my reflexes will be too slow."

"Odds are slim you'll need to do that," the woman said. "And if you do smash into something, in this machine we'll come out the winners."

"I know what a battle flyer is capable of. I'm not worried about our own security. Just the opposite. I don't want to accidentally crash into some avian family's dwelling and leave them homeless at best, dead at worst. I suggest we stall until our reflexes get back to normal. It doesn't look as if we need to hurry off anyhow. Do you see anyone in hot pursuit?"

Steven holstered his pistol and sat back. "Now that you mention it, I'm baffled by the lack of resistance. Somebody must have been around to unleash the gas and seal the openings in the ceiling and the passageway, but now the vicinity seems deserted. Maybe there was only one avian on duty today, and now he's scared to face us. It's... it's kind of eerie. In a way, I'd feel more at ease with an enemy in sight. At least that'd be normal."

"Perhaps they panicked and flew away," Sheera said. "We'll be in no danger if we set aside a few minutes for questions." She pointed a finger at their rescuer. "Starting with... who are you and how did you get here? I thought the two of us and Taryn were the only Protectors within hundreds of light years."

The urgency faded from the woman's voice. "Not anymore. Taryn has told me so much about you, I almost forgot you and I have never been properly introduced. But you must have read about me in the file Doctor Aloysius gave you. I was the first person Steven spoke to about his apparitions."

"You were his provincial back on Medusa-Four? Steven— why didn't you tell me?"

He rolled his eyes. "I had more pressing matters to occupy my time, like getting you and Pengy out of jail in one piece. Jan, what are you doing on Pitcairn?"

"Taryn sent for me. Well, not for me specifically, but for a ranger with my qualifications. As soon as Taryn received a signal showing you were alive and probably captured, she contacted Headquarters for assistance. Luckily, I had business on Pendragon when the request arrived. As soon as I found out Steven was in trouble, I volunteered. I came through the dwarf portal, same as you did." She smiled. "I never stop caring about the strikers who serve under my command."

Sheera bent her arms and flexed her legs, and found the effects from the gas were nearly gone. "Isn't this flyer too big to fit through the portal?"

"In one piece, yes. It traveled in eight packets, and I assembled them at the Clinic."

Sheera cradled Pengy like a baby, as the little alien cooed. "Why did you bring along our polliwumper?"

"Two reasons." Jan answered. "One, because I like him. And two, because he has a schnozzle like a bloodhound."

Sheera studied the little alien's face for some hint of anything that resembled a nostril. "He does? I didn't know he even had a nose."

Jan reached out and scratched the back of Pengy's neck, and the polliwumper cooed. "He's got one, all right, under those feathers, and it's quite a sniffer. I traced the jewel's SOS only up to the point where I smashed into the prison. It was Pengy who caught your scent and led me the rest of the way to your cell."

Sheera hugged the polliwumper. "Then we have another reason why we owe our lives to our little guy." With her limbs back to normal, and her curiosity satisfied for the moment, her fantasies revolved around eating a decent meal and changing her underwear. "Thanks for filling me in. Now let's get back to the Clinic. The gas pretty much wore off while we were talking."

"Not yet." Jan pointed at the sky. "One of those creatures is heading our way. I say we hold our ground. If it's here to parley, we might learn something, and if it's here to pick a fight, the four of us should be more than a match for it." The alien took shape. "It's more human-like than the ones I observed as I was flying into the valley. That must be the infamous harpy I've heard so much about. Computer, slide the roof open."

The top of the flyer slipped away, exposing its passengers to Quirip's eyesight. He began to squawk, and kept up his pattern of alien speech after his talons touched the ground.

Sheera concentrated. "Slow down. I can't understand you when you yabber so fast. All right, that's better. Uh huh. Uh huh. Near as I can figure, he was attending this month's human sacrifice when a rumor buzzed around that another of our kind had invaded the valley. He guessed the new human had received our signal and come to help us escape, so he rushed over here to tell us... what? Really?" She listened to the squawks and caws, then translated. "Patricia is alive. But she won't be for much longer if we don't dash over to their arena."

"Patricia?" Jan repeated. "Who's she?"

"We'll explain along the way," Sheera said. "Quirip, can you lead us to the arena?"

The harpy nodded, his beak bobbing up and down. He folded his wings, and crammed into the passenger space alongside the humans, filling the flyer with his stench.

Pengy made a move to crunch his teeth into the new arrival's flesh, and would have succeeded if Steven hadn't held him back. "I know how you feel, buddy. But if I'm not allowed to do what comes naturally, neither are you."

Sheera ordered the computer to lift the vehicle. They flew low over the village, looking down on gravel streets as deserted as the skies. They soared beyond the dwellings, shifting course whenever the harpy chirped a new direction. They saw, ahead of them, a round coliseum, half constructed of stone and half carved into a hillside. Thousands of winged aliens nested there on stone blocks or tiers of soil.

"Is that their entire population?" Jan asked.

"Most of it," Sheera said. "Back when Quirip was teaching me his language, he mentioned that nearly all his people attend the ritual, except a few who can't be spared from their jobs. That's not a very big gene pool. I guess they're an endangered species."

"Yeah, well, I'll endanger them even more if they harm Patricia," Steven said. "Take us lower, so we can see if there's anything human down there."

The flyer dropped, as Jan peered over the side. "There's a human at the center of the arena," she said. "Looks naked and tied to some kind of a stake. And surrounded by a mob of those creatures."

Quirip clucked a sentence in his language, as Sheera translated. "After the ceremonies are over… oh, my God!...after the ceremonies are over, the king will set the sacrificial offering on fire."

Steven glowered. "Like hell he will."

"Guide us as near as you can to the person at the stake," Jan instructed. "To the ground, if possible. The two of us will do the rest, on my order."

As the flyer closed in on the arena, hundreds of spindly fingers pointed upward. A swarm of Bird People stormed from the arena, by land and by air. The speedier aliens knocked the slower ones to the ground in their haste to fly away. The clucking of thousands of throats rose into the air.

"Do you understand what they're saying?" Jan asked.

"No, not when they all squawk at once," Sheera said. "I'm not so sure those are words, anyway. I think that's the sound of terror. Hmmm… I can make out the victim's features now. She's Patricia, for sure."

The arena's seating area emptied, but one flock of aliens stood its ground in a tight circle around the stake. "They look like soldiers or police," Jan said. "I'll bet they're every bit as scared right now as the mob that fled at the sight of us. The difference is, they're more terrified of what their commander will do to 'em if they run or fly away than of what we'll to 'em if they don't."

Sheera listened to more chirps from Quirip. "We'd better hurry. He says, now that they expect us to interfere, they'll probably skip the opening rituals and proceed directly to the sacrifice. He says their gods will never miss a few incantations, but they'll get angry unless the Bird People present them with a dead human by the end of the day."

As if to prove the truth of her translation, one of the creatures approached the girl, holding a lighted torch.

"Bye!" Steven pushed open the door and jumped into empty air, plummeting the distance between the flyer and the ground. Sheera screamed as three aliens grabbed him. He shook them aside, and waded into the circle of feathers and flesh that surrounded Patricia, swinging like a mad man at anything with wings. The ranks of soldiers or police shrank by two thirds in a matter of seconds, as one Bird Person after another took to the air, squawking their sound that signified panic. They scattered in the way a crowd of humans would flee from a ravenous tiger.

Steven rampaged through the midst of the defenders who gamely stayed behind and stabbed him with their knives and spears. Sheera watched from above. One-at-a-time, she knew, no Bird Person could be a match for Steven. But when they descended on him as a knife-wielding mob, they shifted the odds too much for her comfort. The flyer set down in the arena, and Sheera snatched the zeta-ray pistol from Jan's holster. She couldn't hit the broad side of a starship, but maybe, with a lucky shot, she could score some kind of a hit that would improve Steven's chances. She would fire, if only her hands would stop shaking.

Jan slapped the pistol from her grip. "Don't even think about it."

Steven reached Patricia's side at the same moment the king touched his torch to the native brush around the stake. The girl shrieked. Flames licked her ankles and crept higher.

A maze of rope tangled Patricia, binding her to the stake. Steven wrenched at the rope until it snapped. He snatched the girl away from the fire and held her under one arm. He turned to face what was left of the mob and hesitated. Sheera, watching, saw no way he could shield the girl from the wave of knives. She picked the pistol off the deck and raised it again, then lowered it when she saw Jan was with them, toppling aliens like dominoes to clear a path. Steven carried the girl to safety, spilling guards in every direction with his free arm. The two Protectors muscled their way to the flyer, then squeezed into whatever space they could find.

Jan was first to speak. "Sheera, get us..."

"Computer, one hundred meters up, then due south, maximum speed."

"... out of here." Jan's voice trailed off. They were already sky bound as she was completing her command.

Sheera concentrated on putting as much distance as she could between her band of humans and their enemies. Somehow, their mission to the Valley of the Winged Aliens hadn't resulted in the diplomatic breakthrough she had hoped for.

*   *   *

Sheera wanted to hug Steven, but with avians scattered across the sky in every direction, she focused on the course ahead. She felt his arms and shoulders, rock solid, pressing against her as he squeezed beside her. She draped an arm across his back without looking at him. When she pulled her hand away, she discovered a smear of blood at the tips of her fingers.

He wiped a drop of blood from his ribcage. "A few scratches. Nothing to get alarmed about. Those stone blades of theirs couldn't slice butter." Patricia was behind him, still uncovered. He fixed his gaze elsewhere, ever the gentleman.

Patricia shivered in silence, her eyes dazed. Jan examined her for burns and injuries, a task the girl's nakedness made easy. Patricia found her voice. "It hurts where the fire touched me."

"We'll take care of that," Jan said. She dug out a first aid kit and a blanket from the supply compartment, and rubbed a salve on the girl's burns. "This will numb the pain until Nurse Gretchen can take a proper look at those scorch marks. Now let's cover you." She wrapped the blanket around the girl.

Patricia pointed at Quirip. Her voice and her finger both trembled. "What's that thing doing here?"

"He won't hurt you," Sheera assured her.

"And if he tries, I'll stop him," Steven added.

"You couldn't stop a turtle after the way those avians hacked you up," Jan said. "You have six wounds by my count, at least four of them deeper than scratches." She began to smear the pain-killing salve on the injuries. "I'm disgusted with both of you. Steven, you would've avoided most of this damage if you'd waited for my order so we could've attacked as a team. And as for you…" She gave Sheera an icy stare. "What were you thinking when you pulled that stunt with the pistol? The situation might have appeared deadly to you, but for me, it was nothing more than what I'm trained to deal with bare-handed. If I hadn't stopped you, we'd have a heap of dead birds down there, and one more striker facing a Guidance Committee investigation."

Jan's words told Sheera nothing she hadn't already figured out, but they stung all the same. "I'm sorry. All I could think at the time was that I would do whatever it took to drive away those guards. Thank you for preventing me from killing someone. And for saving Steven from more harm. He'll be all right, won't he?"

Jan finished applying the salve and pressed a blanket against Steven's wounds. At once red splotches dotted the material. "Not if we don't get help. I've taken the pain out of the gashes, but that doesn't eliminate the danger. We'd better find a hospital that's closer than the Protectors' Clinic. Which way is the nearest settlement? Hey—look out!"

Sheera grabbed the manual controls and swerved to avoid a flock of Bird People, probably a band of refugees from the deserted arena. She struggled to concentrate on her piloting. "There are no settlements between here and the Clinic," she answered. She would have given anything not to have had to say that.

Quirip chirped a string of words that slipped by too quickly for Sheera to comprehend.

"Can't you keep that buzzard quiet for a change?" Steven said.

Sheera looked at him with a mix of frustration and sadness. Steven sounded as bitter towards the harpy as he'd ever been, dashing her hope that the events of the last half-hour would soften his attitude. "Don't compare him to an animal. This would be a bad time to hallucinate again." Then, she said to Quirip, "Say that again, please. Okay, I've got it. He can lead us to a doctor of his species, and—this is hard to believe, but I swear it's a proper translation—this doctor is skilled at treating human patients."

Jan's eyes narrowed. "He's wrong, or lying outright. This tribe might have some sort of witch doctor, but I can't believe it would know the first thing about human physiology. Besides, how can we trust any of these creatures? From what I've observed, we're not the most popular species around these parts."

"You're right," Steven said. "I'd rather bleed to death than be treated with voodoo by a freak who believes I'm the Devil."

Sheera translated another flurry of chirps. "He agrees most doctors of his species haven't got the ability or the desire to aid a human, but says this one is different. He's treated humans before."

"How can he be so sure?" Jan asked.

"Quirip knows all about this particular doctor. The doctor is his father."

CHAPTER TWENTY-SEVEN

AN UNCOMFORTABLE HISTORY LESSON

"Protectors shall never close their ears to hearing the truth."
—D.F. Nathaniel

The flyer circled beside the face of a mountain where the terrain was steep, almost forming a cliff. Either a quake or the tools of an intelligent species had carved a niche into the mountain. An avian dwelling covered every centimeter of ground inside the niche, aside from a ledge barely wider than the flyer. Trees and shrubs dotted the mountainside, but the ledge's stark flatness made it a potential landing spot. The only landing spot.

"If that doctor lives here, he must not care much for the companionship of neighbors," Jan remarked. She rested her palm on Steven's forehead. "We'd better land. He has a fever already. The way he's leaking blood, he may not last until we reach the Clinic. We'll have to take a chance that the harpy is right about this alien doctor."

"No," Steven said. He felt drained of energy and his skin was clammy, but he didn't dare slouch or complain. Visible signs of weakness would only give the ladies more ammunition to delay their escape on his account. "I'd rather take my chances traveling at maximum speed back to the Clinic. If we set one foot inside that house, the owner might spray us with another dose of paralyzing gas." He looked at Patricia, huddled inside her blanket. "I didn't pull her away from a flaming pyre just so those Bird People could lash her to another."

"Quirip promised you'll get medical attention," Sheera retorted. "You can't seriously believe he'd lie to us after helping us twice. We're going to pay this doctor a visit. Don't argue, and stop pretending those gashes don't weaken you."

They set down on the ridge in front of the doctor's house or laboratory, whichever it was. Maybe both. The flyer balanced on the strip of ground between the front porch and a sheer drop, with room for a human to stand, very carefully, on either side of the vehicle. Jan was the first to exit, squeezing her feet onto the remnant of ground. She pulled Pengy from his seat and cradled him. "Polliwumpers aren't the most graceful walkers in the Galaxy," she said. "I'll hang onto him to make sure he doesn't waddle over the side."

Steven went next. "I guess a species with wings wouldn't bother to put up a guard rail," he said. He took Patricia's hand and helped her step out of the flyer, barefoot and clutching her blanket with her free hand. He would have offered his own shirt to provide her with a more modest covering, but it was in shreds.

They faced a door wide enough to accommodate wings stretched to their full span. Steven eyed it. He'd crashed his way through stronger-looking barriers. "Jan, what do you say we kick this thing down?"

"Step away, and I'll kick it," Jan said. "You're in no condition for martial arts right now."

Quirip clucked, and Sheera translated. "There's no need for either of you to break the door down. He says it's unlocked."

The door flung open. An avian squatted in the entry, balancing himself in the manner of his species on two legs and one arm, as he beckoned the visitors with his free hand. "I gladly share my home with humans," he said.

Their host was male, judging from the rainbow of colors in his feathered crown. Steven didn't know enough about the Bird People to determine whether he was young or old, large or small, handsome or ugly. But he knew something had just happened that wasn't supposed to be possible. "Wait. Did you just talk to us in our language?"

"I did." The voice came from their host's beak in a low-pitched croak, as a frog might sound if it mastered the art of speech. He shifted into the language of his own kind, and exchanged squawks with the harpy. Steven tensed, ready for a fight, leery of trusting any member of the winged species.

"How did you do that?" Sheera asked, as she crossed the threshold into the residence. "I thought your kind is incapable of imitating our speech."

"Correct. What I do is quite impossible," the avian agreed. "That man is injured. Do you wish to bring him into my laboratory?" His round black eyes peered at Steven. "He is what you would call a male, is he not? I can distinguish your genders through a medical examination, but I find it difficult to tell the difference with only a visual observation, especially when you conceal your forms with artificial coverings."

Jan nodded, following along. "He's male."

"Leave the door open," Steven said. "I want a steady flow of fresh air at all times."

The doctor faced him. "Are you concerned I will deploy the gas that immobilizes life forms from your planet? I never resort to that terrible weapon. Come along."

More craziness, Steven thought—subjecting his body to the whims of a doctor whose society despised humans. The friendly welcome could be part of the trap. But Jan, still cradling Pengy in her arms, would surely order him to accept treatment if he refused. The four humans and Quirip trooped into a room with a table in the center. Open cabinets jammed the walls from floor to ceiling. Bottles, holding liquids of every color, lined the shelves.

"Is this your laboratory?" Patricia asked.

The doctor stared at Patricia with his black eyes. "You're female, are you not, and young?" The girl nodded in silence, and the doctor answered. "This is one of my laboratories. I have another in the back of my home, where I treat patients of my own species. I reserve this room for your kind, but it has been many... in your measure of time, many months... since I have used it. You, the damaged human: remove your upper garment and lay down on your back on this table."

Steven thought: Why not? The doctor, if that's what he really was, could kill him as easily standing up as lying down. He peeled off his shirt, wincing over the spots where the dried blood had made his shirt stick to his skin. Patricia gasped. Was she reacting to the ugliness of his injuries, or to the massiveness of his physique? And did it matter?

The doctor stood on two of his four legs, fluttering his wings to help him balance, and grabbed a bottle of liquid that Steven hoped wasn't poisonous. "My name, as nearly as I can pronounce it in your language, is Quixl," the doctor said.

Steven gazed into the face of the creature. He searched for a family resemblance to their prisoner, but didn't find one. "All right, Doc. First question. Are you really this bird's father?"

Quixl reached for bandages and made a clucking sound. Laughter? "My friend does not speak of biology when he calls me 'father.' His parents both died while he was in the shell, and I cared for him when he was a chick. Next, you will, no doubt, ask whether he had one human parent."

Steven squirmed as the doctor's feathers brushed against a bloody spot beneath his left shoulder blade. "Did he?"

The doctor clucked again. "His mother and father were both of my species. I told you, he hatched from an egg. Would that have been possible if one of his parents was human?"

Sheera grabbed a clean towel from a stack in the corner, and wiped trickles of blood from Steven's back. "We're well aware, Doctor, that it would be impossible for any part of Quirip's parentage to be human."

"You call him Quirip? I congratulate you. That is a reasonable pronunciation of his name, for a human throat." As Quixl talked, he tipped the bottle and splashed its contents onto a sponge. The liquid looked and smelled like sour milk. Quixl touched the sponge to a bloody spot.

Pengy opened his beak and lurched, nearly leaping away from Jan's grip. She pulled him back, a moment before his teeth would have clenched onto Quixl's arm. "Naughty polliwumper," she said. "This bird man is helping Steven, not hurting him.

"The male human is fortunate," Quixl said, ignoring the near-attack and dabbing the sponge onto another scrape. "The cuts are not deep, and there is no damage to his vital organs. Still, he is in danger. He may have no immunity to the microbes transmitted by the knives that slashed him. This potion will treat for infection."

The humans exchanged startled glances. "I can't believe this," Jan said. "On Earth, nobody knew microbes existed until the seventeenth century, when they were discovered by Lee… lee… what was his name?"

Steven had confidence Sheera would blurt out the answer within three seconds. He counted to himself. One… two…

"Leeuwenhoek," she said. "And civilization was well into the Industrial Age before Koch and Pasteur proved microbes transmit disease. None of this adds up."

Steven shared their confusion. A tribe as primitive as the Bird People ought to believe fevers and infections were caused by evil spirits. Somehow, a race that had yet to invent the wheel had knowledge of microscopic organisms.

"Now that we know our patient will survive, it's time for explanations," Jan said. "How is it you speak our language? You said yourself, it's impossible."

"Impossible for my species as the Great Spirit created us, but sometimes a surgeon improves on the original design. I wanted to communicate with my human specimens, so I arranged for one of my colleagues to alter my throat, using a procedure I developed."

"You had human specimens?" Patricia asked. Her eyes went wide.

The doctor sponged Steven's skin. "I've had many specimens over the years. They are prisoners, and my job is to keep the injured ones alive long enough to be sacrificed to our gods."

Jan shuddered. "Do you approve of killing humans in the arena?"

"If I approved, would I be here, instead of joining the crowds at today's ceremony?" His black eyes darted up from his work. "Can you imagine what it is like for me, treating members of your species, sometimes forming friendships, knowing my kind intends to set them ablaze? I cooperate, but only because my patients will die even sooner if I refuse to treat them. And because my job gives me a chance to study human biology. We have others who share my opinion of the sacrifice, but our numbers are small compared to the whole of our population."

Sheera's eyes were on the harpy. "Doctor, if Quirip 's not half-human, then why does he resemble a cross between your species and ours?"

The doctor lapsed into silence, and went about his work as if he had not heard the question. He bandaged two more wounds before he looked up from his task. "Even Quirip does not know the answer. I never told him, because I did not want him to hate me. The few others who know the truth have concealed it from him also. But after all these years, it is time for him to learn about the terrible thing I did. If he hates me for it, that will be nothing worse than I deserve. I am responsible for his deformity."

Steven tried to gage the harpy's reaction to what, to him, must have been a shocking revelation. It was no use. Emotions were too hard to read on avian faces.

"What did you do to him?" Sheera asked.

"He was an experiment. Your kind has many physical advantages over mine. We have only one over you. That one..." He tapped his wings with the four digits of his right hand. "... is obvious. On the ground, our bodies are weak, clumsy and slow compared to yours. Quirip came to me as an egg, with very little chance of surviving. The accident that killed his parents also cracked his shell. He was barely more than a yolk, far from ready to live outside the egg. It occurred to me that I could accomplish something with an unhatched chick, still unformed in so many ways, that I could never do with someone older. I could manipulate his tissue so that, as he grew, he would develop characteristics of a human. I wanted to create a superior being, someone who combined the best features of my species with the best of yours."

"By the looks of him, I'd say you succeeded," Jan said. She stroked Pengy's feathers. "How did you interfere with Quirip's natural development?"

"By surgery. And through what you would call drugs. I also made changes to certain microscopic organisms that all living beings possess. I don't know the term in your language. They are the elements that control the transmission of hereditary characteristics."

Patricia had been clutching her blanket and staring at Steven's gashes as Quixl applied bandages. She faced the group. "Even I know what transmits hereditary characteristics. He's talking about genes."

"Genes?" Quixl paused, then went on with his work. "Thank you for adding to my store of human words. I extracted a substance from the bodies of my human specimens and fused it into his genes. With that, I engineered his human characteristics."

"That explains the human DNA we found in his blood," Sheera said. "You're telling us that, working like Doctor Jekyll in a laboratory, all by yourself, you achieved a level of genetic engineering that leaves human medicine in the dust."

"You have a doctor who has performed similar experiments? I would like to meet this Doctor Jekyll of yours."

"No, you wouldn't," Jan said. "Sheera, don't make analogies to fictional characters. They're too confusing when talking to an alien."

Steven concurred. Sometimes, Sheera's analogies were confusing even when she talked to a human.

Jan went on. "How can your amazing medical achievement have been possible, Doctor, when—don't take offense, sir, but compared to our technology, yours is so primitive."

"Primitive?" the doctor croaked, and again clucked the sound that passed for a laugh among the Bird People. "Our genes are more easily manipulated than yours, but even with that taken into account, you question our ability to create a marvel such as Quirip. You do not realize we were not always as you see us. Before your ancestors arrived on our world, we spread across the globe in communities with grand dwelling places. We had machines, powered by electricity—yes, we had electricity then—that did our most difficult labor or gave us entertainment. Our greatest accomplishments were in medicine and biology. Our weakest skills, compared to what I have observed among your kind, were in weaponry. The result was that your species overpowered mine in the Great Invasion."

Jan protested. "Do you expect us to believe your society was too peaceful to develop advanced weaponry?"

"Some would have you believe that, but I don't think we were peaceful." Quixl patted the bandage covering the last of Steven's wounds. "We would have built more destructive weapons if we could have. We just weren't very good at it. The humans circled the skies in a flying machine as big as one of our villages, dropping fireballs that left chaos wherever they touched."

Steven saw an uneasiness spread over Sheera's features. He almost expected her to run outside to avoid whatever had suddenly troubled her. "A flying machine as big as a village," she echoed. "That could describe the spaceship the Founding Mutineers brought to Pitcairn. And the fireballs sound like bursts from the zeta-ray cannons that military vessels carry."

The doctor smoothed the final bandage. "Sometimes, my ancestors encountered humans on the ground, outside the great machine of destruction. Our legends say those humans attacked them with deadly rays from bands that circled their fingers, but I don't see how that was possible."

"It was possible," Jan said. "In those days, many armies equipped their soldiers with rings that shot small bursts of zeta-radiation. They became obsolete because zeta-rays that near to the skin cause cellular damage at best, and blow off knuckles at worst. But they would have been in fashion around the time humans first settled Pitcairn."

Steven put on the shreds of what had been his shirt. "Is that why you threw away Sheera's ring when you trapped her at the top of the hill?" he said to the harpy. "Because you'd heard the legends and thought she would hurt you with it?"

The harpy chirped an answer.

Quixl scampered about the laboratory on three limbs, restoring bottles and bandages to their proper places. "He says you are correct. He feared the female would harm him with the band on her finger. And that is also why he could not allow the guards to see him returning your ring to you. They would have accused him of giving you a weapon."

"Did your species do nothing to fight back?" Jan asked.

"They tried. With death rays blasting down from the sky, and humans on the ground shooting at them, our ancestors counter-attacked the best way they knew how, with chemical tools. They developed a gas that paralyzes humans, but is harmless as plain air to any life form native to our world. "

"The gas works," Steven said. "I ought to know."

"It works, yes, but not well enough. The gas can overcome a small group in a confined space, but it turned out to be useless against such a huge army of invaders. The paralysis wears off too quickly, and it dissipates in open air to the point where it becomes harmless. We had no choice but to stand by and watch that great flying machine destroy our communities, one by one."

"You're lying!" Patricia said.

All eyes turned to the girl. Jan wagged a finger. "Don't speak in that tone when addressing your elders, young lady."

Steven thought, what difference did her tone make? An avian probably couldn't decipher a human's tone any more than a human could decipher an avian's. And he was proud of her for her spunkiness.

Patricia's brow furrowed. "In school, we learned that when the Founding Mutineers stumbled upon Pitcairn, they discovered a world with no higher life form than animals. I know you guys must have been here then. But I don't think you had any big cities. I think you were already hiding away in these mountains. If you refused to show your faces out in the open, it's not our fault if we thought there was no intelligent life here and claimed the world as our own."

"Your schools do not tell all that happened," Quirip said. His emotion—or lack of it—stayed the same. as far as a human could discern. "The survivors of the Great Invasion retreated to this valley to wait for the end, but the end never came. For unknown reasons, the humans stopped pursuing us. We have lived here ever since, hiding from the invaders. We venture outside the valley only to capture humans to sacrifice in the arena, or to steal from their homes, or to hunt for food. We left most of our technology behind, and we lack the resources to reconstruct it."

"My species would describe your condition as a dark age," Jan said. "But your medical skills appear to be of the highest order."

"Yes, equal to yours on the whole. Superior in some areas. Before the Great Invasion, this valley was the site of a hospital that included the building we are in now. The records, the equipment, and the medicine survived. Of course, after all this time, much of it has worn out or been exhausted. If nothing is done, in a couple of more generations we will sink into a dark age in medicine, just as we have in every other field of study."

Steven slid off the table. He assumed Quixl must have experienced some sense of despair as he predicted the coming collapse of medical science. How could he not? Still nothing changed in the doctor's face or croaking voice.

"Lucky for me, your medicine hasn't reached that dark age yet," Steven said. "Thanks for patching me up, Doc. Now, I strongly suggest we fly back to our own people. No offense, but I'd like to get checked over by a doctor whose typical patients don't have wings or lay eggs."

"Must you leave so soon? I hope you will return and visit me. I enjoy exchanging information with humans. But I warn you: my attitude differs from most members of my species. They cheer in the arena because they want to eliminate as many invaders as possible. Ridiculous, aren't they? I, for one, believe we have more to learn by talking with you than by slaughtering you. Unlike so many of my people, I don't hold you responsible for what your ancestors did."

"They weren't my ancestors," Jan said.

Steven agreed. "Not mine, either."

"But they were mine," Sheera admitted in a soft voice, breaking her long silence. "I never told you my last name."

"So?" Steven said, curious that Sheera would bring up a topic that had never seemed important before. "We don't use last names much in the Community. I don't know the last names of half the kids who advanced with me."

"My full name is Sheera Wilkerson," she said with disgust, as if her surname was shameful. "The Mutineers named the Fort after my great-great-great grandpa. He must have been the commander who gave the order to unleash the zeta-ray cannons on the indigenous population. And, to think, I've always been proud of my lineage."

In the silence that followed, Steven tried to think of some way to lift her spirits. "Maybe he wasn't all bad," he suggested. "The doc did say the attacks stopped for no apparent reason. Maybe your grandpappy had a change of heart."

"History records that Captain Wilkerson died as the Mutineers were laying the foundation for the first human city on this planet," Sheera said. "The attacks stopped because the command passed to his successor. Somebody who wasn't the monster my ancestor must have been."

Patricia raised her chin in defiance. "Wilkerson was no monster. It's all a lie. Wilkerson was a great man."

Steven could not bring himself to shatter Patricia's delusion further. From the awkward silence, the other humans must have felt the same.

"Maybe you're right, Patricia," Jan said at last. "Let's get you back home. Your parents must be worried sick, and I'm sure Sheera's family feels the same. Is everyone ready to board the flyer?"

Quirip backed away, chattering as he did. Everyone, except Quixl, looked to Sheera for a translation.

"He says he's not going with us. He wants to stay here with his father."

"Yeah, I'll bet he does," Steven said. "Well, there's not a popsicle's chance on Mercury of that happening. My assignment was to bring him in alive, and that hasn't changed." He shot a glance at Sheera. "This is nothing personal against his species. I'd say the same thing if he was human."

Quirip interrupted with a flood of chirps and squawks. "He's talking kind of fast," Sheera said. "As near as I can make out, he says there's no home for him, no matter where he goes. If he comes with us, our people will imprison or kill him for his crimes. If he returns to the village, the Bird People will do the same. They saw him helping us and will consider him a traitor. He wants to hide out in Quixl's home temporarily, until he figures out what to do next."

Steven pulled his zeta-ray pistol from his holster and leveled it at the harpy's chest. "You're getting in that flyer. How is it any concern of ours that you might get punished for your crimes? You should have thought of that before you murdered innocent humans."

"I have an idea…" Patricia ventured.

Quixl interjected. "He didn't have a choice. My species forced him to use his abilities to an evil end. He deserves a chance."

"We'll let a jury decide," Steven insisted, keeping the pistol raised.

Patricia's voice could barely be heard as everyone seemed to be talking at once. "Why don't you…?"

"Oh, sure," Sheera responded. "As if there's ever been any such thing as a jury on Pitcairn. How can you deny this request, after he returned your communication jewel, and helped us save Patricia's life?"

"WON'T SOMEBODY LISTEN TO ME!"

Patricia had grown red in the face. Jan laid a hand on her bare shoulder. "All right, honey. We're listening."

"Here's how I see it. Why don't you cut a deal? You came to this valley in the first place to get medicine that'll cure H-R-S, right? I'll bet this bird doctor has some. I say: we trade him the harpy for the medicine."

Sheera nodded her approval, but Steven held his pistol steady. "How can you suggest a deal that will set this creature free?" he said to Patricia. "Think of what he did to you."

"Yeah, I know, but we really need that medicine. Three of my friends died of H-R-S."

The harpy directed a series of chirps and squawks at Quixl. Sheera summarized for the human audience. "He's explaining the nature of the medicine we're after."

The doctor, balanced on three limbs, put another roll of bandages in its place along a shelf. "Yes, I have a serum in my other laboratory," he said as he continued to tidy up. "It cures the disease that makes our air poisonous to breathe. I can trade you a vial of serum in exchange for Quirip's freedom."

"Not so fast," Steven said. "The harp… Quirip… must have known all along that the doc has the serum. Why didn't he take us to this place in the beginning, instead of leading us into a trap?"

Quixl translated the harpy's answer. "He says he wanted to introduce you to our leaders. He hoped he could convince them you weren't the demons they took you for, and from there forge a new relationship between our species. He didn't expect them to attack you."

"I don't know or care whether he deliberately led you into a trap," Jan said. "All I know is, patients at the Clinic will die if Taryn doesn't get a chance to analyze that serum. We'll accept the deal. Now put away the gun."

Steven slammed his pistol back into its holster. Couldn't she have at least discussed the proposal before she made up her mind? They made the exchange, then the humans, and Pengy, left the dwelling. Steven boarded the flyer first, clutching a vial of liquid that resembled green catsup. He gripped it carefully, and a suspicion took hold of him. He could be holding a container of useless gunk, or worse. It occurred to him—as it didn't seem to occur to anyone else—that they were placing enormous trust in an alien they hardly knew. The doctor could have hoodwinked them into trading their prisoner for a vial of poison. But his companions were eager to get moving. It was too late to change their minds.

Jan had pulled rank and made the decision to release the harpy. He had to obey. If the harpy resumed his reign of killings and kidnappings, Steven wouldn't be the one to take the consequences before the Guidance Committee He took little comfort in that knowledge. The harpy's victims would be just as dead, regardless of where the Guidance Committee pointed the blame.

CHAPTER TWENTY-EIGHT

RETURN TO HUMAN TERRITORY

"Protectors, having no allegiance to the civil authorities of any planet, may resist the authorities when they engage in acts of injustice."
—D.F. Nathaniel

The battle flyer, swift even by military vehicle standards, crossed the distance to the Clinic in under an hour. Sheera said, "I can't wait to take a shower," as they touched ground in the courtyard where Steven had lifted the hrow, surrounded on all sides by H-R-S wards.

Steven gripped the vial. "Taryn will be happier than a high-jumper on Earth's moon to get this," he said. "Let's hope she'll discover a microbe inside that attacks the virus. I'd hate to find out we exchanged a mass murderer for two grams of worthless glop."

It was the first time he'd mentioned his suspicion to the others. "What makes you think Doctor Quixl would give us worthless glop?" Sheera asked. "He seemed sincere."

Steven was about to ask how somebody so smart could be so easily taken in by a huckster, when three figures rushed towards them.

Taryn reached the flyer's side first. Major Davis kept pace a step behind. Nurse Gretchen huffed and puffed a few paces down the path, toting a medical supply satchel. "Thank God you're here," Taryn said. "Is everyone all right?"

Sheera answered for the group. "We're dirty, smelly, and starving. And Steven has a bunch of ugly gashes that might be infected. Other than that, we're fine. Oh—and we brought you some serum. The winged aliens use it to cure their people of helium rejection syndrome."

Steven held up the vial. Something was wrong. Why were there no hugs and cheers over the announcement that they had retrieved the serum?

"A serum?" Taryn said with no show of interest. "I'll analyze it later."

Jan exited the flyer, her lips twisted. "What's the matter with you? We risk our lives to retrieve the Holy Grail of medical research, and all you have to say is that you'll look at it later?"

"Please don't think I'm not pleased," Taryn said. She accepted the vial and passed it along to Gretchen, without glancing at its contents. "It's just that, right now, there's more at stake even than curing H-R-S. We need to do something about Halfbald's latest insanity."

Steven moaned. "What's he done now?"

"He intends to wipe out the Valley of the Winged Aliens," Davis answered. "He vows he won't leave a single one of their kind alive."

Sheera, Steven, and Jan stared at one another in disbelief. Patricia broke the silence. "Wow! He'll need the entire Army to pull that off."

"No, just one flyer," Davis said. "Um, who are you?"

Jan replied, without giving Patricia a chance to speak for herself. "She's a young lady we rescued along the way. All in a day's work." She raised her eyebrows. "One flyer you say? Really? I wouldn't expect to find that level of technology on your world. When your ancestors first arrived in a spaceship designed for battle, sure, they could have done it then, but I'm told that spaceship has long since been cannibalized for materials."

"We've still got the technology," Davis said. "The spaceship carried a fleet of flyers with more than enough zeta-ray power to vaporize a city, and some of those flyers still function even after all these years. Are you with us in stopping Halfbald from blasting a species to extinction?"

Steven thought of how the Bird People tossed him in prison for no good reason. How they scorned humans. How they tied Patricia to a stake, and, if he hadn't interfered, would have cheered as she went up in flames. Halfbald had a point. Pitcairn would be a safer planet for humankind if the winged aliens went the way the dinosaurs had gone on Earth. And then he remembered the doctor's story. If even part of it were true, humans had already inflicted unspeakable damage on the planet's indigenous species. He nodded when Jan said, "We're in."

Sheera wiped the sweat from her forehead with a grimy sleeve. "The people won't stand for a mass extermination," she insisted. "They may not realize the avians have human-level intelligence, but they'll want to preserve an endangered species. Halfbald won't risk the public backlash."

Davis shook his head. "A lot happened while you were away. The General has the support of most of the population, and, in a way, you're responsible. He used your disappearance as a tool to manipulate public opinion. You Protectors are like demigods to most folks. They're convinced you're practically invincible in battle. When you failed to return from the valley, Halfbald claimed the avians must have killed you. At first there was general disbelief. That was followed by outrage when your absence dragged on. Finally, the outrage turned to fear, with demands for vengeance."

Sheera murmured. "So this is my fault." Her voice trailed off.

"Never mind that," Steven said. "What I want to know is: how did Halfbald find out we went to the Valley of the Winged Aliens?"

Davis answered. "The entire planet knows. Word leaked out. Somehow."

Taryn had been standing to the side, contemplating. "We can't appeal to Halfbald's sense of decency," she put in. "He hasn't got one. But maybe we can get to him another way. The people came over to his side because they believed the native aliens had killed two Protectors. They'll swing back the other direction once they learn those same two Protectors are still alive. If we convince Halfbald his scheme will make him about as beloved as foot fungus, he may back down. To sweeten the pot, we'll promise to let him hog the credit for halting the destruction."

Jan took a move back to the flyer. "Agreed. Nathaniel taught us to try persuasion before force, so let's see if you scholars can talk him out of it." She laid her hand on the grip of her pistol. "But I'll bring my weapon just in case..." In case of what? She didn't say, but only paused and suggested, "You'd better accompany us, Major. We'll never get past the sentries without you—not peacefully, anyway. How soon will Halfbald commence his attack?"

"Maybe next week," Taryn said. "Maybe tomorrow. Maybe thirty seconds from now. He didn't clue us in on his timetable. We need to act quickly, but there's one thing I'll need to do first. From the looks of that shirt, somebody took out his or her frustrations on Steven's chest and back. I'd better evaluate the extent of injury." She clutched the shreds of the blood-stained shirt, and tugged.

He backed away. He had no intention of becoming a reason for them to dither before taking action. "I feel fine."

"Yeah? Well, we don't care how you feel," Jan said. "What we do care about is whipping you into full fighting form in case we run into trouble. Taryn, can you repair the damage?"

"We'll find out." Taryn tore away Steven's shirt. Her eyes darted from Jan to Sheera and back again. "Whichever of you patched him, you couldn't have done better if you'd had a medical degree. No trace of infection. I'd still recommend a period of inactivity before returning to duty, but since that's not practical, we'll improvise. Gretchen, my medical bag, please."

The nurse passed the satchel to Taryn, who plucked out an orange pellet the size of a marble. She held it to Steven's lips. "Open wide."

He obeyed, and felt the pellet drop into his mouth. It dissolved, and a second later a surge of energy pulsed through his body.

Taryn returned the satchel. "That drug will keep you in one piece until I have time for genuine treatment. You'll be at full strength and stamina until the effects wear off." She turned to Gretchen. "Take this child, and get her a bath, some clothes, and… and…" She smiled at Patricia. "Are you hungry?"

"I'm not a child. Yeah, I'm starved, but I wanna go with Steven… I mean, with all of you… to see Gen'rl Halfbald."

"Sorry, too risky. Gretchen, get her some dinner, then find her parents. Speaking of parents, notify Sheera's family that she's returned. Give Pengy something to nibble while you're at it."

They discarded what was left of Steven's bloody shirt, and found him a replacement. Sheera took the controls of the flyer. The others boarded, and they soared in the direction of Fort Wilkerson.

* * *

The group crossed the plains between the Clinic and the Fort in minutes. Jan, Steven, and Sheera used the journey to tell the others what they had learned about the harpy's biological origins. They also supplied a summary of the massacre that took place soon after humans first arrived on Pitcairn, if Quixl was to be believed.

They landed, and approached Fort Wilkerson on foot. "I've always suspected the official version of Pitcairn's founding didn't tell the full story," Davis remarked as they neared the Entry Gate. "A government that suppresses historical research, as intensely as this one does, has something to hide. The avian's story explains why ninety-eight percent of Pitcairn is off-limits to exploration. The official version is that the ban exists for reasons of safety, but I think now the government doesn't want anyone to stumble across ruins of the ancient civilization."

"But why?" Jan pondered. "Why would Halfbald want to disguise the truth after two centuries? It's not like he's personally to blame."

Taryn looked grim. "If my guess is correct, every human on Pitcairn has reason to fear the truth getting out. Halfbald is terrified that..."

"Halt!" A sentry stood between them and the gate. He clutched a rifle with hands that shook.

"Put that toy away, Johnny," Davis said. "Do we look like terrorists to you?"

"Can't, sir. Halfbald's new orders. Sentries are s'posed to hold their piece at all times while on guard duty, loaded and ready to fire."

"Hmm. Well, all right. I don't want you to get into trouble. Just be careful." He flashed his military identification card. "These civilians are my guests."

"I can't let your friends come in," the sentry objected. He pointed at Jan's holster. "Not her, anyway. Civilians aren't allowed to carry weapons onto the base."

"But majors can," Davis said. "Better give me the holster and gun."

Jan glanced at Taryn, who conveyed her approval with a slight nod, and the transfer was made. Davis strapped the equipment around his own waste. Steven, who had begun to think of Fort Wilkerson as hostile territory, disliked the idea of venturing onto the base unarmed. How much, after all, could they rely on Major Davis for protection? But he saw no choice and followed the others.

The sentry stepped aside. A glint of recognition flashed onto his face when Steven and Sheera passed by. "You're s'posed to be dead," he said, as if the two Protector strikers had broken the rules by staying alive.

Sheera laughed from inside the Fort. "The rumors of our deaths have been greatly exaggerated."

How unoriginal, Steven thought, but how like the members of the scholar branch. Quoting Mark Twain.

Three more sentries blocked the way at various places between them and the Presiding General's headquarters. Major Davis displayed his card at every checkpoint, and they marched on. It came as no surprise that Pitcairn, unlike every other civilized world, had no bio-scan technology for confirming identity.

The final sentry stood guard with a rifle outside General Halfbald's office. "Major Davis and some civilians are here to see you, General," he called through the door.

They barged into the office without waiting for an invitation, nearly knocking the sentry to the deck.

Halfbald glanced up from his paperwork, scattered layers deep across his desk. Anyplace else, even on Medusa-Four, the data on all those pages would have been stored in the memory of an electronic device. The General grunted. "You're supposed to be dead."

Sheera snickered while Steven frowned. Maybe she found it amusing to be told she ought to be dead, he thought, but for his part, he was tired of it.

Major Davis snapped a salute, as Taryn marched up to the edge of the General's desk. "General, we've come to bring you the good news that my associates are alive."

Halfbald looked down at his papers and said, "That's unfortunate. As you can see, I'm busy. Make an appointment with my clerk, and I may squeeze you into my schedule later this week."

Davis dropped his salute and stepped forward. "You misunderstood, General. The winged aliens didn't kill them, as everyone believed. There's no need for retaliation." He raised his voice and moved quickly to the only argument that would have any chance of altering Halfbald's viewpoint. "The people won't support the annihilation of an alien species, not once they learn it's innocent of attacking humans."

Far from innocent, Steven thought. He remembered how close Patricia had been to becoming a human torch at the avians' four-fingered hands, but he held his tongue. Someday he would reveal the full story, but not then. It wouldn't help their case.

Halfbald scratched his signature on a piece of paper and snatched another from a pile. "Too late. Just because two annoying kids didn't turn up dead, that doesn't mean those monsters aren't dangerous. That harpy thing is one of 'em, and sooner or later a whole pack of critters just like it will devour us if we don't strike first." He looked up, and his eyes met Davis's. "Major, you're out of order. Go, and take these intruders with you, before I bust you to private and assign you to peeling 'taters. Like I said, I'm busy."

Sheera pleaded. "But the aliens are intelligent."

"So's m'dog, but I'd shoot'm if he went mad."

Sheera bit into her lower lip. Steven had known her long enough to recognize she was stifling the urge to tell Halfbald what she thought of him.

"I don't mean smart like dogs or dolphins or polliwumpers," Sheera clarified in a shaky voice. "I mean, they have I.Q.'s on the level of humans. We've been to their village. We've witnessed their architecture and medicine. And I've deciphered their language."

Halfbald returned to his papers, jabbering as he scribbled his signature on one page after another. "Intelligent, you say? I think you're lying, little lady, but if what you say is true, that's all the more reason for us to attack them before they attack us. Strictly a matter of self-defense, which, I believe, is permissible under those Precepts of yours." He yawned.

"We have no reason to fear an attack," Steven offered. "We could defeat them with our hands tied, even using the Army's old-fashioned weapons. They're primitive."

"So were the Huns when they sacked Rome." He raised his voice. "Why are you still bothering me? I've given my answer."

Jan stepped forward and leaned across the desk. "They weren't always backwards, General. The aliens in the valley are all that remain of an ancient race. The Founding Mutineers almost wiped them out, leaving only the remnant that exists today. I appeal to your compassion. Humans reduced them to their present level. Shouldn't humans allow them to retain what little civilization they have left?"

Halfbald gave her a cold stare. He was ignoring the pen and papers scattered on his desk. After a long silence, he said, "You made a mistake telling me that. Your knowledge is dangerous. So dangerous, it could spell the end of the human presence on this world if it leaks out. That's why I can't permit any of you to associate with another living soul for as long as you live."

Steven found it hard to believe he had heard correctly. Could the paralyzing gas have damaged his hearing? Even Halfbald would not utter such lunacy. But the shock on the faces of his companions convinced him he had understood perfectly. He was the first to speak. "You're babbling like a madman, General. You can't isolate us from the entire human race for the rest of our lives."

"I run this planet, kid. Don't tell me what I can't do." Halfbald tapped a box of dark metal that poked out from the clutter. "Send in two sentries. Immediately."

"General, this is ridiculous," Sheera said. "Are you arresting us for speaking the truth?" She stared into his eyes. "That's it, isn't it? You've known all along about the massacre. But why should you want to keep it hidden?"

Two uniformed soldiers rushed into the room, men built like gorillas, except they stood up straight and their arms were too short for their knuckles to scrape the floor. They toted rifles and stood at attention, like statues.

"Escort these trespassers to the brig," Halfbald directed. "All five of 'em, including the major. He has no more authority on this base. Treat him as you would any criminal."

The soldiers exchanged nervous glances. "Uh, Sir," one of them ventured. "Those are Protectors."

Halfbald nodded. "Yes, they are. All unarmed. As for our turncoat major, he's been far too absorbed with his nature studies to learn how to properly use that gun on his hip. You, on the other hand, are trained in the lethal weapons you carry. I gave you an order."

The two men shuffled forward a couple of meters.

"Sorry, boys," Jan apologized. "Nothing personal in this. Steven, take the taller one. Go!"

Steven thrust a hand in one sentry's direction, confident that Jan was beside him doing the same to the other. A heartbeat later, Jan and Steven each held a rifle. Jan cracked hers in two over her knee, and Steven followed her example. The major and Sheera shared a glance that seemed to ask: how do they do that?

Halfbald shook his head. "Pitiful. Get out of here, you morons. I can see you'll be useless to me."

No soldier had ever snapped to comply with an order more quickly than the two trembling sentries.

"It's a durn shame, what you're forcing me to do," the General said, once the two men were gone. He again tapped the box on his desk. "Halfbald here." he called.

"Good afternoon, General." Nurse Gretchen's voice, low and raspy, came from the box. "Did they arrive? I do so hope their flight was a safe one."

"Yes, the whole lot of them are trespassing in my office." Halfbald sounded weary. "Thanks for warning me they were on their way. What did you do with that urchin you told me about?"

"Such an adorable child. She finished her bath, then I treated her burns. Cook brought her supper a few minutes ago. She probably doesn't yet realize I locked her in her room."

"Wait fifteen minutes," Halfbald said. "Then implement the plan we discussed, unless I personally call you back within that time to countermand the order. Nobody can reverse it but me. Nobody."

There was a gasp at the other end of the line. "She's a little girl, Sir. Isn't there some other way?"

"Why does everybody question my orders? As a matter of fact, I'm working on another solution right now. If I succeed, I'll call you." He scanned his visitors' faces. "If I don't call you back, kill the brat."

"But, Sir…"

"Army Intelligence doesn't pay you to think about whether your orders are right or wrong, just to obey. Fifteen minutes, not one second more, not one second less. Halfbald out."

"Now we know who leaked the information that two Protectors had journeyed into the Valley of Winged Aliens," Taryn said. "How many more spies do you have on my payroll?" Steven had never before heard such a chill to her voice.

"Why should you care?" the General replied. "You'll never return to that hospital of yours. If your fannies aren't sitting in the brig by the deadline, the child dies."

Steven crossed the room in four paces and stood behind the desk. He grabbed hold of the General's left wrist and twisted his arm. "Call that traitor nurse back and cancel your order," he said. "Call her back, or I break your arm into so many pieces your troops will have to sweep it off the floor."

Steven's eyes shifted back and forth between Taryn and Sheera. If either told him to desist, he would disobey. Seconds ticked away, and they remained silent.

Halfbald wheezed. "This won't help you," he said between grunts of pain. "She's got instructions not to cancel the plan, even under my order, unless she hears a code word. I could speak a word to her, but you'll have no way of knowing whether it's the correct code or one that I made up on the spot." He glanced at a timepiece on the wall. "Thirteen minutes."

"He's telling the truth," Davis said. "Standard procedure."

Steven relaxed his grip. The general was right. Breaking an arm would not accomplish much if Patricia would die anyway.

It would give him satisfaction, maybe, but at a cost of a Precept violation that would probably get back to Headquarters..

"Why should we trust you not to kill her even if we do as you say?" Taryn asked.

"What do I look like—some kind of savage? Do you think I want to make war on a girl of her age? I take this action for the good of Pitcairn. Her death will be on your hands, not mine."

Jan braced both hands on the desk and brought her face within a few centimeters of the general's nose. "I'm going to raise the stakes. Call your spy right now. Rescind your order, and give her the correct code. Do you want to know why you're going to do all this? Because if I find out later that Gretchen harmed a hair on that girl's head, I'll return to break you in half, and the combined might of all your divisions won't be enough to stop me."

Beads of sweat stood out on Halfbald's forehead where his hairline receded. "Since that wouldn't bring your little friend back, it would be pure vengeance," he said. "Completely opposed to those Precepts you swear by. You'd never do that."

"Try me."

"No need. I rose from nothin' to become the most powerful man on this planet, and do you want to know how I did it?"

"We don't give a rat's rear end," Jan said. "But I have a feeling you're going to enlighten us anyhow."

Halfbald leaned back and set his feet on the desk. "I did it by always having a back-up plan, in case my first idea didn't work. I have another recourse, one I'd hoped I wouldn't have to use. It'll be messy, and set my troops to gossiping about matters that are none o' their business. However..." He sighed and tapped the box again. "Send Green Company to my office. Double-time."

The door burst open. In rushed three skinny teenagers with sweat trickling across their faces. Their rifles rattled in their hands.

Jan smiled. "Hi, fellas. Is this a joke, General? If two sentries couldn't force us into your silly brig, one more won't make a difference."

A fourth soldier joined the others. Then a fifth and a sixth, side-by-side. They came in twos and threes, until the office filled to its corners with men and women in uniforms, guns pointed and fingers on the triggers.

"There's twenty more just like 'em in the passageway," Halfbald said.

Steven struggled to maintain a grin. The time had come for serious bluffing. No matter how inept Halfbald's minions might be as individuals, their overwhelming numbers had turned them into a fighting force. "I'll grant, you General," he said. "If all those guns start blazing at once, a few stray bullets are bound to happen our way. But we can take down at least eight… maybe ten… before one of them gets in a lucky shot. I've killed bare-handed before, and my boss…" He waved at Jan. "… is even more dangerous than I am."

Fear showed in the eyes of the soldiers, and some shuffled backwards as they jockeyed for the rear.

"You're trying, boy, to unnerve my forces until they back down," Halfbald said. "Clever, but in this case your tactic won't work. First, because they're innocent kids, so you're bluffing. You wouldn't hurt 'em. Second, they're more scared of me than they are of you." He leaned forward and drummed on the desk with his fingers. "Unlike you, it won't bother me to give 'em the ultimate punishment."

"I think this game of chicken has spiraled out of control," Taryn said. "General, if we go voluntarily to your brig, will you let these troops go unpunished, and give the order to spare the life of the girl at the Clinic?"

"That's what I promised, and I'm a man o' my word. Of course, pretty soon it'll be too late to make a difference for the girl. I gave that nurse a deadline, and time's a-wastin'."

"Then I suggest we waste no more of it. General, show us the way to your brig."

CHAPTER TWENTY-NINE

A SECOND GENERAL MAKES AN APPEARANCE

*"Protectors shall not aid humans in conflicts with aliens if the
conflicts would cause unjust injury to the aliens' lives or property, or
impose human culture on aliens who do not accept it willingly."*
—D.F. Nathaniel

Steven bolted from his bunk, weary of sitting on a slab that
provided as much comfort as a chunk of granite. "A fine
thing," he grumbled. "When aliens give you a nicer prison
than your fellow humans." He perused walls of concrete in
three directions. Bars covered the cell's fourth side from floor
to ceiling.

Jan beckoned to him. Together they punched, kicked,
slashed, and pounded against the bars, with nothing to show for
their struggles but bruises on their feet and knuckles. Jan fell
back, panting. "You wouldn't expect a society like this one, that
can't seem to do anything else right, to build such a solid brig."

Taryn perched at the edge of her bunk, her eyes downcast.
"And I wouldn't expect someone of my experience to be taken
in by Halfbald's scheme as easily as I was. I intended to oppose
him at every turn. Now, I see that he manipulated me into
doing exactly as he wanted. He'll exterminate the remnant of a
great civilization, and I'll be to blame."

Steven sat beside her. His wounds itched under his
bandages, but now didn't seem like a good time to gripe.

"Looked to me like you were the only one with guts enough to stand up to that old tyrant," he said. "Like, back at that meeting of the Ruling Council, remember? He wanted me to kill the harpy, but you told him our Precepts allow us to take a life only in self-defense. You spoiled his strategy."

"So I believed at the time," Taryn said. Anger flashed in her eyes. "Now, I'm convinced the meeting ended exactly as he planned. He knew all along that I'd never authorize such a flagrant Precept violation. His argument in support of killing Quirip was a ruse to deceive the other generals into thinking he was on their side. Why do you suppose he backed down so quickly? His secret plan was for Quirip to survive and destroy you, and then go on to slay more humans."

"Think so?" Steven asked. He weighed the implications of Taryn's theory. "If he wanted me to die in my first battle against the harpy, that settles the identity of the double-crosser who…"

From the opposite corner of the cell, Sheera completed his sentence, like an eager school girl blurting out the correct answer. "Who tinkered with your gun to make it misfire, and substituted a fake for your communication jewel. Him, or somebody following his orders. Come to think of it, there was another time he backed down. Remember when we had Quirip confined to a cage? When Taryn refused to turn our prisoner over for execution? That other general, the cantankerous one—what's her name?"

"Carstens," Davis said.

"Yes, Carstens. She never got over being steamed about our lack of cooperation, but in the end Halfbald seemed resigned, as if he never really wanted to prevail in the argument. "

It all made sense, Steven thought. To a point. But something was still missing. "Where was Halfbald's motive? Why didn't he want to kill his enemy? Something tells me he didn't spare the harpy out of his deep respect for alien life."

Taryn replied without hesitation. "Because he wanted more humans to die by Quirip's hand, that's why. He intended to nurture the fear that was already brewing in the hearts of the masses—to convince the people that the winged aliens would produce more half-breeds, who would expand into a threat powerful enough to defeat even the Protectors. He knew Steven's death would rally public support for the goal he hoped to achieve all along—blasting the remnant of aliens from the face of the planet." She managed a weak smile. "The glitch in his plan was that Steven kept turning up alive."

"The Bird People aren't my cup of tea either," Steven said. He fidgeted, still feeling the energy burst from the pill he'd taken. "But genocide? Why should Halfbald hate them that much?"

Davis rested his chin in his palm and pondered. "I don't think he hates them. It's more that the creatures are an inconvenience, not because of anything they've done, but because of what humans did to them. Our ancestors' misdeeds threaten the continued existence of our settlement. Or they will, if word leaks out to the G.T.O."

Taryn nodded. "The Galactic Treaty Organization. That's what has him spooked about sharing our space with intelligent aliens. There's no higher crime in the G.T.O.'s eyes than displacing an alien population to make way for a human colony."

"If the G.T.O. found out, would it go so far as to evacuate Pitcairn's human population?" Sheera asked, with no hint as to whether she believed that would be a good thing or a bad thing.

"Hard to say," Taryn said. "This situation has no precedent. The G.T.O. has compelled at least five colonies to abandon their worlds for brutal treatment of the natives, but none of those colonies had existed for more than a few years. There's no statute of limitations, so it's possible the G.T.O would force humans to abandon Pitcairn, even after two centuries."

"Then the threat from the G.T.O. is genuine," Davis said. "Genuine enough to explain why Halfbald would rather put the five of us to death than risk us revealing the truth about the massacre. The only reason we're still alive is that he hasn't yet figured out how to make our deaths look like somebody else's fault. But he will."

Steven felt a chill. "He'll go after Patricia," he said. "As soon as it dawns on him that she probably knows everything we know about the Mutineers' crimes. I suggest we search for some way out of this hole."

*   *   *

Night arrived, followed by morning. The prisoners came no closer to finding a means of escape. About noon, a female voice berated a sentry on the other side of the wall.

"I know General Halfbald ordered you not to let anybody see the prisoners. I'm a general too, and I'm giving you another order, you worm. Open this door immediately, or I'll bust you down so far in rank, you'll be saluting cockroaches."

Taryn and Steven groaned in unison. Steven said, "I've heard that voice before. Lord, it's grating!"

"Does this planet have cockroaches?" Sheera mused.

The door from the outer room burst open. General Carstens stormed in, clutching a key in her right fist. Sweat dripped from her forehead beneath her frizzy bubble of silver hair. The sentry trudged behind her. Steven remembered the sentry as a man of average build. Now he seemed to have shrunk, an illusion caused by his nearness to Carstens' great bulk. She gave him an annoyed look. "Get out of here. I need to speak with the prisoners in private."

The sentry skulked away, and Carstens declared, "Halfbald's stark raving mad." She unlocked the cell. "He intends to exterminate the winged aliens, down to the last bird. I always knew he had a mean streak, but I never figured him to slaughter an entire species."

Steven refused to move at first, not ready to accept that freedom had arrived from such an unlikely source. But Sheera swung open the bars and took a step beyond the cell. "I take it,

General, you don't support the imminent attack. I was under the impression you weren't fond of the winged aliens yourself."

The general's lower lip contorted. Steven feared that, in a huff, she would shove Sheera back into the cell.

"What gave you that idea, girl?" Carstens demanded.

Steven noticed Sheera's eyes narrow with irritation, probably over being called "girl." But she recovered and spoke in a diplomatic fashion. "Sorry, Ma'am, I didn't mean to offend you. But after all, on two separate occasions, you insisted we kill the alien you call a harpy."

"Not the same thing. I wanted just retribution against a criminal. Halfbald's advocating murder. If I'm going to stop his craziness, I'll..." She paused, and twisted her face like the next few words would be painful for her to say. "I'll need your help." She gestured for the others to follow. They hesitated for an instant, and she added, "Don't worry. The troops won't re-arrest you as long as you're in my custody. They wouldn't dare."

They strolled out, as she had predicted, before the eyes of the sentries, who gave them quizzical looks but did nothing to interfere. Outside, they endured stares and frowns from the soldiers who saluted, but nobody challenged their right to pass. Steven absorbed the strangeness of fighting on the same side with the most aggravating woman he'd ever met. He silently questioned how far he could trust her.

"A warship took off for the valley minutes ago," Carstens explained as they walked. "I'll give you the code you'll need to track its path. Halfbald's on board. The sicko suffers from the delusion that this mission will bring glory to its crew, so he assumed command. You Protectors are the only living souls around these parts who refuse to lick his boots, which makes you the one hope those pitiful aliens have left. I'll lead you to your flyer."

"Our flyer?" Jan shook her head.. "I hate to disillusion you, General, but our flyer has no weapons. It's sturdy and it's fast. But it doesn't have a zeta-ray cannon to its name. If you expect us to dogfight with a fully-equipped warship, arrange for us to borrow one of the Army's flyers. One that has equal or better firepower compared to the ship that's now speeding to the valley."

"I can't do that," Carstens said, without giving the matter a moment's consideration. "We've been patching our flyers with tape, baling wire, and chewing gum ever since the Mutiny, but we can do only so much to keep those rust buckets ticking after two hundred years. We have four vehicles with any possibility of getting off the ground. Halfbald commandeered the sturdiest of the bunch, and the other three are in the shop for repairs. With luck, our mechanics might get one up in the air after a couple days of tinkering around the clock, but by then there will be nothing left of the winged aliens but ashes and dust."

Jan stared at the general. "Then kindly enlighten me: how are we supposed to engage in battle against troops who need only to press one button to vaporize us into atoms?"

"Well, if you'd had the foresight to come here with a better-equipped warship, you wouldn't have that problem."

That wasn't helpful. Now she was sounding more like the old battle-axe Steven detested.

Carstens went on. "We can stop over at the armory and get you zeta-ray rifles. We keep them under lock and key, but fortunately I'm in charge of the key."

"Hand-held rifles?" Steven said. "Against a battle flyer with cannons? Oh, that ought to work just swell. Should accomplish as much as lobbing popcorn against a charging rhino."

"We'll accept the rifles," Taryn said. "We can formulate a plan along the way."

Steven wondered who she meant by "we." Surely, she wasn't expecting to come along on a purely military expedition. She would only get in the way.

The group shifted direction and walked at a brisk pace to the armory. "Did you know, General, that the winged aliens have human-level intelligence?" Jan asked. "And that the Mutineers killed off all but a remnant of their species?"

"Is that all? Every member of the Ruling Council is aware of both those things. They're military secrets, but..." She shrugged. "I don't mind disclosing them. I've already dug my way into a court martial if Halfbald survives the day, so what's one more charge against me? That nonsense they teach little children—the business about how those creatures are dim-witted birds—it's a cover up." She repeated. "A cover-up. The more people who know the truth, the greater the probability the word will leak out to other worlds, and from there to the G.T.O.."

Sheera stepped briskly to keep pace. "But doesn't the Ruling Council realize it can't keep the secret forever, no matter how many pictures of avian hands you alter to look like talons? Sooner or later, some of your people will stumble onto the truth."

Carstens came to a halt so abruptly that Steven, directly behind, nearly collided with her sizable backside. "We're not stupid, little lady," she said. "We know we live in constant danger of the G.T.O. finding out what happened. That's why Halfbald is hell-bent on exterminating the winged aliens. He's convinced his crowning achievement as Presiding General will be the elimination of all physical evidence that Wilkerson's massacre ever took place. He hopes it will pave the way to improved communication with other human-occupied planets.

Steven drew back in amazement. "You mean, he wants to end Pitcairn's isolation from the rest of the Galaxy?" Until that moment, he'd assumed Halfbald harbored some irrational desire to keep his world mired in the technology of some long-gone era.

"Does that surprise you?" Carstens asked, shifting her hostile stare to Steven. "You never thought for one minute, did you, that we enjoy living in a backwater, while humans in other stellar systems enjoy inventions we can only dream of? We isolate ourselves out of fear that every visitor might be the one who finally discovers the truth. Worse, we're afraid to import any equipment that might make it easier for one of our people to discover the ruins that are surely out there. Flyers, especially, must be banned outside the military, except the two you Protectors pressured us into letting you import."

Steven remembered the forests, lakes, and landscapes they had flown over, traveling to and from the Valley of Winged Aliens. "So many gorgeous places on your world. But you build your towns on this dusty plain. That's to prevent your people from discovering ruins and artifacts, isn't it? Open spaces made it easy for the Mutineers to obliterate the remains of the old civilization, but you've been afraid traces if it might still be around in the jungles and forests."

Carstens' silence told Steven he had guessed correctly.

They continued walking, past a series of one-story barracks fashioned from logs. Taryn looked thoughtful. "General, if we survive this day, we'll have to include the information you just gave us in our report to Merlin. The rest of the Galaxy will know the Mutineers slaughtered most of the planet's native population."

"Suits me fine. If the G.T.O. chooses to boot us off our world, it can go ahead. Or it can let us stay. Either way, our isolation will be over. Our ancestors were refugees. If we also have to become refugees from the G.T.O.'s punishment, even that would be better than continuing to live as we do now."

They halted before the only structure in the fort, aside from the brig, that was cement rather than wood. "I'll take over," Carstens said to two soldiers who guarded a door that appeared to be of steel. "Take a thirty-minute break, starting now."

"But General, Ma'am," a sentry protested at the same time he saluted. "According to the rules, only one of us can leave our post at a time."

"The rules are whatever I say they are. Get out of my sight. I don't want to see you back until thirteen-hundred."

The sentries wandered off, murmuring to each other. Carstens unbolted the steel door, and swung it open to the sound of screeching. The stench of gunpowder surrounded them. Pistols and rifles, designed to fire bullets, dangled from racks along the walls of the vault. She passed over those as if they didn't exist, and headed directly for the zeta-ray rifles. Steven recognized them as models no longer in active use anywhere else, except for historical battle reenactments. He accepted a rifle, then cringed as Sheera took one also. She seemed determined, as usual, to dive into danger she wasn't prepared to handle.

"You won't need a weapon," he said. "Those of us with combat training will deal with Halfbald." His gaze settled on Sheera and Taryn at the same time. "We'll drop you two ladies off at the Clinic."

Sheera held tight to her rifle when he tried to snatch it. "Who says I can't be of any help, you big oaf? And furthermore…"

"Enough," Taryn said. "She'll come along. We're heading into the Valley of Winged Aliens, and she's the only human alive who understands their language."

"We have no choice about bringing the striker," Jan agreed, as Steven tried unsuccessfully to think up a suitable objection. "We may need her linguistic skill. But what about you, Taryn? You're too valuable to take risks with your life. I doubt there's another doctor on this planet with the skill to analyze Quixl's serum and isolate the ingredient that cures H-R-S. "

Taryn reached out to accept the rifle that Carstens offered her. "I appreciate your concern," she said, sounding as if she did not appreciate it in the slightest. "But I'm going with you."

Jan grabbed the rifle away from Carstens before Taryn could touch it. "If you insist on getting yourself killed, wait until after you discover the cure. Why do you want to come along? You have no business on a military mission."

Taryn stood toe to toe with her colleague. She tilted back her neck and glared up into a pair of eyes a head higher than hers. "Because I choose to. That's why."

"That's not an answer."

Carstens had been listening to the exchange with a deepening scowl. "Every minute you two bicker brings Halfbald a minute closer to the valley. Look, I'm not fond, myself, of dragging untrained baggage into a scrap, but as I understand the rules your bunch swears by, the brainy-types get the last word over the warrior-types. A proper subordinate follows orders."

"Fine advice from a soldier who is scheming to shoot down her boss," Jan muttered, as she handed over the rifle to Taryn.

They trooped over to their flyer, still parked outside the main gate, where they'd left it the day before. Everyone, except the general, climbed aboard and strapped in. Jan sat behind the controls, and directed the vehicle's computer to take it into the clouds over Fort Wilkerson.

CHAPTER THIRTY

LET'S ROLL

"Protectors shall place their own lives at risk if there is no other way to preserve the lives of others.
—D.F. Nathaniel

The four Protectors and Major Davis passed beyond the region dotted by stalagmite-shaped hills. A forest stretched below them. Were there ruins down there, hidden by foliage, the remains of a destroyed civilization?

For once, Sheera regretted the way the flyer's sound filter muffled outside noise. They had fallen into an unnerving silence, but she refused to be the first to speak. Steven might take her communication as a signal she was no longer peeved at him. After a few minutes, Major Davis broke the chill. He asked no one in particular, "We're not really going to use these rifles to trade zeta-ray blasts with cannons, are we?"

"Of course not," Jan said, as if he'd directed the question to her alone. "We'll warn the avians they need to evacuate."

So that was her entire plan, Sheera realized. Issue a warning? What made Jan think the avians would listen to humans? And even if they did, evacuation was hardly an ideal solution. She saw, from their skeptical expressions, that Steven and Davis had doubts as deep as her own. She looked at Taryn, who was staring at the hills below. If some strategy was percolating in that brilliant mind, she needed to reveal it soon.

"Evacuate?" Steven echoed. "They have one village on this whole stinking planet." He held up a lone index finger. "Where will they evacuate to? If Halfbald vaporizes their community, they'll be homeless. We could offer them shelter at the Clinic, but they'd trust the Devil himself sooner than us."

"Let's hear your better idea," Jan snapped.

"He's right," Sheera said. Finding herself on the same side of the argument as Steven, she nearly forgot she was angry with him. "Even if they had a place to go, which they don't, we have no means of warning them. I understand their speech, but I can't imitate the sounds I'd need to talk it." She sighed. "Believe me, I've tried."

"You forget," Jan said. "Two members of their species do okay with our language. That doctor-creature seemed downright fond of us. He'll listen, then he and that harpy-thing can spread our message."

"Well... maybe that will work," Sheera conceded. "So their job would be to fly through the village and sound the alarm? It'd be like Paul Revere's ride."

"Again with the metaphors," Steven muttered. "Paul Revere warned his neighbors so they could resist, not so they could scatter like terrified rabbits." Suddenly his voice turned gloomy. "But I gotta admit, I don't have a better idea."

Davis considered. "Encouraging them to evacuate, for all its flaws, beats going one-on-one against Halfbald's firepower. Taryn, you're in command. Is this plan satisfactory to you?"

Taryn murmured, "Do as you wish," without moving her eyes away from the hills.

Sheera, for the first time in her life, gave in to the urge to yell at an authority figure. "Is that all you have to say? If you don't trust me to be the only scholar on this mission, at least do what your job calls for. Make a decision."

Taryn slowly turned away from the hills. In a soft voice, more curious than offended, she asked, "What are you talking about? I never said I don't trust you to be the only scholar."

"Don't deny it. Anybody can see why you insisted on tagging along. You question my judgement. I can't blame you, after the mess I made of our previous job in the Bird People's territory."

Taryn turned away and went back to staring at the hills. "I'm satisfied with your performance in your previous assignment," she said. "I came along today for other reasons."

Sheera listened in disbelief. Could Taryn be ill? Had she been behaving like her normal self, she would have ordered Sheera to undergo at least three hours of therapy as treatment for such a burst of anger.

*   *   *

Another flyer materialized on the horizon within the hour. Sheera considered it funny-looking, but supposed it hadn't seemed that way to people living two centuries ago, when the ship had been state-of-the-art. The people back then had never seen a modern warship, with zeta-ray cannons that retracted until they vanished into a hull as sleek as a dolphin's back. They would have considered it normal for a warship, like this one, to carry two cannons sticking out from its starboard side, surrounded by doodads of unknown functions. The cannons seemed to dare any other flyer to get in their way.

Taryn leaned into the radio. "General Halfbald—come in."

The receiver crackled before a voice came through. The static must have been a byproduct of the ancient radio holding up the other end of the conversation. "What are you doing here?" said Halfbald. "You're supposed to be in the brig."

"Obviously, we escaped, and don't waste time asking how, because we'd sooner swallow arsenic than tell you. You might as well turn back. Your game is over. We've already told our superiors on Merlin the story of how the Mutineers destroyed Pitcairn's native civilization. They'll relay the message to the G.T.O. before the day is out."

Sheera was mystified. When had she contacted Merlin?

Taryn went on. "Your best option, now that the word is out, is to prove you're better than your ancestors. Show humane treatment to the remnant of intelligent aliens, and the G.T.O. might allow you to stay. If you fire on them, you'll only compound the crime."

Oh. A bluff.

Taryn muted the outgoing messages, making it impossible for the other ship's crew to hear her next words. "Jan, take us as far away as you can while keeping them in visual range. Just a precaution, in case he decides to use those cannons to take out his frustrations on us."

Jan ordered their computer to draw them back until the warship was a speck in the clouds. Taryn cancelled the mute function.

Halfbald's voice filled the passenger compartment. "Recommendation noted and rejected. You're nuts, Doctor, if you think I'm turning back now, when I'm about to fulfill my destiny. I was born to make this world safe for humans, and that's exactly what I intend to do. As soon as I destroy the last of those creatures, it ain't gonna matter, no more, whether you alien-lovers squeal to the G.T.O." A faint chortle sounded. "Tell the entire Galaxy every detail of my great achievement, for all I care."

"His mind has come unhinged," Taryn whispered, then raised her voice. "Have you thought this through, General? The G.T.O. will track you down as a war criminal."

Halfbald ranted. "You seem to be under the misimpression that I care what becomes of me. Those fools at the G.T.O. always take the side of aliens against humans, so they'll come gunning for my hide. Let 'em. Worst they can do is make me rot in some cold dungeon for the rest of my days. Small price to pay, as long as I give my people what they deserve: a new Pitcairn, where they won't be forced to share their world with an inferior species."

Jan punched the mute button and sighed. "No one is more dangerous than a maniac who's determined to become a martyr."

Taryn released the mute function and argued into the radio. "The people of Pitcairn will lose their world if the G.T.O. requires them to relocate because of your crime."

"That's where you're wrong," Halfbald shot back. "The G.T.O. will arrest me, but they won't uproot the entire population of Pitcairn. What would the alien-lovers have to gain by it? They can't hand the world back to a race that no longer exists. As long as one of those creatures remains alive, there'll be somebody to claim prior title to our land, but once the last of them is dead, we'll be safe."

"He's right," Davis said. "The human claim to the planet will be stronger, not weaker, with the winged aliens extinct, regardless of how they got that way."

Sheera shuddered. He sounded almost as if he was taking Halfbald's side.

Taryn spoke again, this time with desperation in her tone. "The Protectors have tolerated our association with your dictatorship thus far, but we won't cooperate with leaders who would resort to a slaughter of this magnitude. Our Headquarters on Merlin will transfer me from the planet and withdraw its support for the Clinic."

Laughter burst through the radio. "Are you trying to get your way by threatening to shut down your Clinic again? Won't work this time. Ain't nothing more important than making Pitcairn secure for humans. Nothing. This communication is over. Next time we talk, the winged aliens will no longer exist."

A click broke off the connection. "That didn't go well, did it?" Taryn said. "I estimate we're twice as fast as they are, so we might as well make use of the only advantage we have. We'd better get to the valley as soon as possible."

Jan leaned over the controls. "Computer, same coordinates as before, maximum speed."

Clouds sped past. "That could have solved everything," Jan said. "You were right to insist on coming along. Negotiation was worth a try."

"It was worth a try," Taryn agreed. "But I failed."

*   *   *

An hour later, the four Protectors and the major hovered over the saucer-like roof of Quixl's mountainside laboratory. "Is it safe to land?" Davis asked, eyeing the jagged cliffs above and below the niche where the brick building nestled, overlooking the village.

"Sure," Steven said. "If you have wings."

Jan gave a sharp look, as if to scold him with her eyes, and then answered Davis's question. "The ledge is wide enough to accommodate our flyer. Just watch your step getting out." She commanded the flyer to touch down, and it glided to a landing in the space between the laboratory and a hundred-meter drop.

Sheera took in the view of the village, wondering if there would be anything left of it by nightfall. She dreaded the discussion to follow. There seemed no good way to inform the two avians inside that attackers from her species were hellbent on rendering theirs extinct. Worse, that they had more than enough firepower to succeed.

Major Davis went ahead of the others, watching his feet as he baby-stepped. He stood before the door, poised his fist to rap, then hesitated. He looked back at his companions, exiting the flyer one at a time. "Do these creatures gain entry by knocking?" he asked.

Sheera held back, becoming last to join the group gathered at the door. "Quirip told me knocking is unnecessary. The custom is to barge in. But if that makes you uncomfortable, feel free to knock. The doctor will hear the noise and step out to investigate."

Davis thumped on the door. A minute later, the door swung open and Quixl appeared, wings fluttering as he balanced on three limbs. His skin turned up on both sides of his beak, in what Sheera took for a smile. She couldn't tell for certain on a face with two black dots for eyes and a beak for a mouth.

"I didn't expect you to return so soon," Quixl said, his wings beating a little faster. "I see you have brought two new friends, a male and a female, I believe."

Jan shoved her way to the front. "No time for introductions, Doctor. Is Quirip here? We have a message of extreme urgency to give you, and he needs to hear it too. Don't fret about his freedom. We're not here to arrest him."

Quixl turned around and warbled a few words in his own language.

Sheera, translating in her head, gathered he was complying with the request. Quirip strode to the entry on two legs, in human fashion, and stood beside Quixl.

Jan explained the nature of Halfbald's mission, speaking slowly and pronouncing every syllable distinctly. The two aliens listened in silence, either without emotion, or failing to display any emotion that would register with a human. "You won't be able to resist the attack," Jan concluded. "I suggest you fly to the village and warn the others. They'll need to find shelter outside the valley."

"The fools," Quixl croaked.

"You're right," Jan agreed. "General Halfbald, and the other humans who think like him—they're fools. I hope you realize they don't speak for the whole of our race."

"Not humans. I was referring to the fools of my own species. I told them, if we isolated ourselves from the newcomers to our world, except to kidnap and kill them, some day they would come after us with weapons we would be helpless to defend against. You are correct that we have no choice but to escape, if we can, though we have nowhere to go. How much time remains?"

"I don't know how your society measures increments of time," Jan said. "I can only tell you the attack will happen soon. Long before your sun begins to set. "

For the first time in her life, Sheera felt embarrassed to be human. "I'm sorry," she murmured, earning her a quizzical look from Steven.

Quixl and Quirip took to the air without a word, their wings beating hard against the air. Sheera followed their path with her eyes, and saw them land in the village, tiny figures in the distance. "Quirip is taking a terrible chance," she said. "He was afraid that if he went among his own kind again, he'd be taken into custody for having aided humans."

"The survival of his species is at stake," Jan responded. "I guess he's willing to put that above his own freedom."

Sheera nodded sadly. She could make out dozens of avians bustling among the houses, some on the ground and some fluttering just above it. Were they listening to the warning? Or making plans to seize Quirip as a criminal? "I pray our two friends won't be Cassandras," she whispered.

"The Trojan prophetess who made predictions of catastrophe that everyone ignored," Steven said. "Right?"

Taryn frowned at the two strikers. "You two can discuss Greek fables while a civilization perishes, if you wish. I'm getting back inside the flyer. The rest of you—stay here. There's a job I'll need to do alone."

Alone? That could mean only one thing, Sheera thought. The same thing she had been secretly plotting to do. She edged into the narrow gap between Taryn and the flyer, blocking the way. "The real reason you came with us had nothing to do with persuading Halfbald. You knew all along diplomacy wouldn't work with that loony. You wanted to commandeer the flyer to smack it into the warship. Didn't you?"

Taryn folded her arms across her chest. "The Precept obligated me to seek a peaceful resolution, so I tried one. But I never put much faith in Halfbald's ability to listen to reason. There's only one way to prevent the warship from obliterating the village. A way that requires me to take human lives, but justifiable under the *defense of others* exception to the Precept. The

Guidance Committee will approve, and even if it doesn't, it won't be able to punish me."

Sheera's face burned, as she realized why Taryn was confident her superiors couldn't punish her. "Don't talk in circles. Just say it. You're going to stop the massacre at the cost of your life. If that's how we're going to fight this battle, I ought to pilot the flyer. I'm the one who disappeared for so long, the people assumed the avians had killed me. That gave Halfbald the pretext he needed to instigate his attack. I've caused enough damage. Don't make me responsible for your death, too."

"If anybody uses our flyer as a battering ram, it should be me," Jan insisted. "The Precepts are clear that it's my responsibility as a ranger. Neither of you has combat training."

"Stop that crazy talk," Davis snapped. "All three of you. I admire your courage, but it's a silly idea that'll get one of you killed for no purpose. I know this flyer was built to smash through a building or a brick wall, but Halfbald's ship is designed to resist the most powerful hits. Not that you're likely to get anywhere near him. He'll blast you out of the sky like a clay pigeon."

Sheera was dimly aware Davis had entered the argument, but his words bounced off her. Her duty seemed logical. She should make amends for her mistake by absorbing the risk. It was as simple as that. "Who cares about combat training?" she said. "What training does it take to collide one machine against another?"

"More than you think," Jan answered. Her voice sounded condescending, a deliberate effort, perhaps, to remind Sheera which branch had the superior knowledge of battle tactics. "For one thing, all ships of that era had automatic force shields to guard against collisions. I know how to deactivate the shield. Do you?"

"I don't see why you're standing around," Steven said. "If you think we should kamikaze our flyer, there's an easy way for one of us to make sure he'll be the pilot." As Sheera was noticing that he had used the masculine pronoun, he added, "Just do it. Like this." He dashed to the flyer.

"Stop him," Sheera called, but Steven had already settled into the driver's seat. "Computer, take me into the sky. I don't care where."

Sheera's head tilted up. She watched the flyer rise until it became a speck, circling overhead. Behind her, Jan called into her communication jewel. "Contact S-T-E-V-E-N. What do you think you're doing up there, striker? Come back. That's an order."

Steven's voice boomed through the jewel. "Can't do that. But look on the bright side. If Halfbald shoots me down, you won't have to write me up for insubordination."

Sheera's lips nearly grazed Jan's ring. "You said yourself that we can't trust Quirip. The people need you alive, to protect them in case he turns hostile again. Let me take your place. I'm more expendable."

There was a silence, for so long Sheera feared communication had been cut off. Then Steven spoke, in a voice that was annoyingly calm compared to her own growing panic. "You don't seriously expect me to agree to your suggestion, do you? Uh-oh. I see a shape coming at me from the west. That Army ship must be swifter than we thought."

A shadow moved across the valley. Sheera looked to the sky. Halfbald's warship flew low, with nothing to fear from below. She stared at the two ships sharing the same airspace, almost side-by-side Pitting the smaller against the larger was like matching a sparrow against an eagle. "You don't stand a chance," she called. "That ship is thirty times your size. You won't even scratch the hull."

"I can't hear you. Must be atmospheric interference. If you'll excuse me, I have an atrocity to prevent."

"Wait." If she was going to lose him forever, Sheera thought, he might as well die knowing her secret. "I love you."

"Don't say that. The Precept forbids it."

The click at the other end sounded loud and final. She didn't blame him for throwing the Precept in her face in response to her declaration of love. She had done the same thing to him back on Pendragon. If she could give him another chance, perhaps next time he would give her an answer closer to what she hoped to hear. The odds looked slim that "next time" would ever come to pass.

Steven climbed, faded into a cloud, and reappeared seconds later, plummeting like a meteor into the warship's path. The hood of Steven's flyer struck a blow against the side of the other ship. The two vessels careened in opposite directions. Halfbald's warship zigzagged through the air for a minute, then set itself right. It sped onward, ignoring its attacker. Steven's flyer pursued, still in the air, but for how long?

Jan's eyes focused on the sky. "He did well for someone with limited experience. He struck the enemy's most vulnerable spot. That's the mark of a skilled pilot. Or else he had more luck than anybody had a right to expect."

Davis pointed to the warship. "Look closely. It has a wobble that wasn't there before the crash."

"Our man scored damage to his opponent," Jan said. Concern registered in her eyes. "But nowhere near as much as he must have inflicted on himself. If he keeps this up, there's no doubt the bigger ship can hold out longer."

Sheera looked away. Seconds later, she felt Taryn's arm wrap around her. She looked into Taryn's face, and saw her gaze upward. "If you can make yourself look, so can I," Sheera whispered.

The flyer smashed into the warship a second time, and again bounced away, still airborne.

"Two collisions." Jan said. "That's two more than he should have had any hope of surviving. He won't last through a third. Ah—Halfbald's aiming the cannons."

Spheres, engulfed in flames, shot through the air. Sheera understood the round fireballs were not what they had to worry about. The cannons belched globs of invisible zeta-energy, and the radiation exploded air molecules into scarlet bursts as it sped through the atmosphere. The burning molecules created the image of orbs bombarding their target, but the invisible energy that struck the flyer was the part that could destroy it.

Five fireballs soared harmlessly into space. Steven stretched the distance between the two vessels. The warship gave up firing and took off in pursuit, as if angling for a better shot. The flyer dipped, did a ninety-degree turn, and headed directly for the face of a cliff. The warship followed, spitting two more fireballs along the way.

"It won't work," Davis said. "I assume he intends to speed towards the mountain until he's centimeters away from catastrophe, then pull away. He's gambling the larger ship will be unable to brake or turn in time, and will crash. The flaw in his plan is, Halfbald's not that stupid. He'll maintain a prudent distance from the cliff."

Steven's flyer, as Davis had predicted, pulled straight up in time to avoid striking the cliff. But then it reversed course and traveled upside down over the warship's topside. It turned right side up again, and lowered its altitude until it was chasing the warship from directly behind. A second later, it rammed the warship from the rear. The force of the blow sent the larger ship careening forward, out of control. It swerved moments before it would have smashed nose-first into the cliff, scraping its edge against the mountainside in a shower of yellow sparks.

"Halfbald suffered punishment," Jan said. "But from the way Steven is slowing down, it looks like the latest collision damaged his engine. I doubt he'll be able to stay aloft for long."

"It's another trick," Sheera said. "He's deliberately slowing. It's some sort of strategy." But as she talked, she realized she was speaking from desperation, clinging to hope where, logically, she had no reason for it.

The warship closed the gap and fired a volley of zeta-ray blasts. A burst of radiation scored a hit. The flyer glowed a shade of crimson, so bright Sheera's eyes stung to watch it. She glanced away, as a rumble from above assaulted her ears. When the glow dissolved and the noise faded, nothing remained in the sky except the warship and a few puffs of smoke.

Sheera searched the sky, as if the flyer might reappear if she looked for it hard enough. She didn't look down until she heard Major Davis say, "That's the bravest thing I ever saw. The ultimate sacrifice."

Taryn chimed in. "The Bird People attacked him when he came to them in peace. Yet he gave his life trying to save them. Nathaniel would have been proud."

Weakness came over Sheera's body. She collapsed to the ground, her spine braced against Quixl's laboratory, and buried her face in her hands. "It should have been me," she said. She couldn't stop remembering she was the one who insisted they go on the mission that gave Halfbald his pretext to attack the valley.

"It wasn't the sacrifice you think it was," Jan said.

Sheera pulled her hands away from her eyes. How dare she say that? "Show respect. I'll make sure every Protector in the Galaxy learns how Steven gave his life for the Bird People. His legend will live in history, enshrined among the greatest heroes of the Community."

Jan shrugged. "Before you do that, you'd better make sure he's dead."

Had she gone mad? "Of course he's... he's... We all saw it happen."

A familiar voice burst through Jan's communication jewel. "That was exhilarating, but don't ask me to do it again."

"You're lucky Halfbald shot you down," Jan replied. "One more kamikaze attack, and your atoms would have been scattered across the valley."

"How is it possible for him to be talking with us?" Sheera asked, breaking into a smile, but not quite believing what she heard. "He dissolved into thin air."

The others nodded their puzzlement.

"You can thank Halfbald's error," Jan said. "If he'd allowed our flyer to collide with his ship one more time, Steven would have gone out in a burst of flame. Fortunately, Halfbald got tired of playing demolition derby, and took to his cannons. That gave our guy a grace period while the metal absorbed the zeta-energy from the single hit. It took an instant for the flier to dissolve. Only an instant, but that was enough." She smiled with her lips closed, then said, "Two seconds can be as useful as an hour to the person at the wrong end of the gun barrel, provided he knows how to use them. I figured that, unless I totally misjudged his prowess, he'd grab his opportunity. We had no chance of seeing him eject in the extreme brightness. For a moment, it was like looking into a sun—the same moment he left the exploding ship."

Sheera grabbed Jan's ring finger and called, "Where are you now?"

The answer came from overhead, through the air rather than the jewel. "Look up the side of the mountain, and you'll see." He was scaling down a cliff, grasping shrubs and jagged rocks as handholds, and bracing his feet in tiny crevices. Sheera gasped when his boot missed a toehold and scraped against the surface.

"Be careful," she called up.

"In this gravity? I couldn't be safer if I was a squirrel."

He leaped and landed beside Sheera. She fell into his arms in a way that was as automatic and natural as breathing. He held her while she buried her face against his chest, listening to his heart and giving thanks it was still beating.

"I've been thinking," he said. "About your words... you know... just before the first time I smacked into Halfbald's ship."

She pulled away. "Please don't. It would be better if you forget what I said."

His forehead crinkled. "Forget what you said? How'm I supposed to do that?"

She had no answer. She had revealed the secret that she loved him. Now there seemed no way out of talking about it, but hopefully later, at a better—and more private—time and place. To her relief, Major Davis steered the conversation in a different direction. "Surviving the explosion was one thing. How did you survive the fall?"

"Give Taryn credit for that. She nagged me to wear a thruster pack when I flew the aerobike, and I guess her advice finally sank in. I strapped on one of the packs that's standard equipment in Protector flyers, and programmed it to set me down on this ledge. It aimed me too high, but near enough." His eyes scanned the western sky, where the warship circled over the avian village. "I made a mess of things, didn't I? Blew up our only means of getting out of here, and failed to halt the genocide."

Jan frowned. "You damaged the warship, but it's limping along. And we just saw proof that its cannons still function."

"Any Bird People evacuated yet?"

"Not that we've seen," Davis said. He slumped, looking at the ground. "I guess they didn't believe the warning. Just like in the Greek fable you mentioned. Cassandra."

The cluster of humans huddled together to witness the annihilation of a species.

Sheera mused. "I wonder how far back their recorded history extends. Do they have literature? Music? Paintings and sculptures? A religion, with rituals more positive than human sacrifice? What a dunce I was! I should have gathered as much data as I could, while members of the species were alive to pass it on."

Davis straightened and his voice took on a new determination. "There must be ruins. Artifacts the Mutineers weren't able to destroy. We should do whatever we can to preserve their memory."

Taryn nodded. "I'll petition Headquarters to organize a team of archeologists to study this planet's pre-human past." She balled her hands into fists. "If Halfbald doesn't like it, let him try to stop us." Nobody mentioned the obvious shortcoming to her plan. It wasn't clear how they'd ever get to a location where they could petition Headquarters.

The warship halted in mid-flight, and hovered over the village. Both cannons loomed in the air, positioned to fire on the village below.

"Hey, look!" Steven cried. "Two of 'em are flying away. Three—four—a whole flock. It's about time."

Sheera traced the creatures' trajectory with her eyes. This was no evacuation. The Bird People were traveling on a course to intercept the ship. They soared skyward, like a swarm of locusts, surrounded the ship, then climbed above it. One by one, they swooped down and landed on the vehicle's topside. A cannon spit out fireballs, and a hovel on the ground vaporized. The assault seemed to inspire more aliens to join the group that clung to the warship's exterior. It faltered under the weight and sank, then recovered and bounced back to its former altitude. The cannon fired more blasts, and fireballs rained down.

Jan turned to Davis. "How much added weight can one of those models handle, Major, before it can't stay up in the air?"

"In peak condition, it could support several times the combined weight of those creatures, if that's what you're driving at. But this ship is badly damaged, so it's hard to say."

Steven grimaced. "If the ship crashes, the Bird People clinging to it will be killed. Most of them."

The spectacle went on for several minutes. The warship spit one fireball after another, as it swayed and pitched, lurching under the weight of the alien hoard.

The macabre sky dance brought to Sheera's mind an event that once took place on Earth, long before humans had ventured beyond their original solar system. "Could you tolerate one more reference to history?" she asked the group. She hoped someone would answer in the affirmative. She needed to distract herself by talking, or else go mad from the devastation unfolding in front of her.

Jan, Taryn, and Davis, absorbed by the events below them, paid her no attention. But Steven, his eyes riveted to the struggle in the sky, grabbed the bait. "Why not? I'm used to your metaphors."

Did he sense that talking would help her cope with the destruction? She felt a need to be physically near him. She edged to his side, until their bodies almost touched, and did her best to speak without choking. "Do you know what happened on September eleventh, twenty-oh-one?"

He looked at her. "That date sounds familiar. It had something to do with an attack on America. Was that when airplanes bombed Hawaii?"

Not bad. He was only off by sixty years. "No, you're thinking of December seventh, nineteen forty-one. I'm talking about the day terrorists seized planes for a purpose that was evil almost beyond belief. They deliberately crashed two planes into the tallest buildings in New York City, and one into the headquarters for the United States military. Did you know there was a fourth plane?"

A second wave of avians piled on the backs of the first group. The warship zigzagged, unable to shake off the intruders. It unleashed more zeta-radiation blasts, but they fell wide of any target that mattered. The vessel surrendered two-thirds of its altitude.

She had to keep talking. "Yes, a fourth plane. The skyjackers intended to destroy another site that morning, probably the United States Capitol, but they never reached their destination. A feat of incredible heroism by the passengers defeated them. The counter-attack began when a man yelled, 'Let's roll.' They overpowered the terrorists, and caused the plane to plunge into an empty field, killing everyone on board, but sparing the lives of innocent people in Washington. It appears the Bird People have a similar aim."

"Listen," Jan interrupted. "The ship is supposed to fly in silence, or at most with a tiny hum. But now..."

The noise of grinding engines, like metal scraping metal, screeched from the warship. It took a half-hearted hiccup upward, then gave up the struggle, and sank like a dead hulk. The hoard of winged aliens continued to cling to its topside. Below, a quarter of the village had disappeared from the face of the planet. Circles of charred soil pocked the settlement in places that once held clusters of homes. The warship smashed into the ground, bursting into a shower of sparks and flames.

Sheera found what consolation she could. At least the crash did no additional damage to the village, missing what was left of the population and structures. Winged aliens tumbled to the ground from the top of the wreckage. Had the flock deliberately pushed the warship beyond range of the village, or did it miss by chance? Would there be any survivors to someday ask? She also thought of the humans inside. Men and women, her age or a little older, following orders. They probably believed they were doing the right thing.

Steven and Sheera watched together from the ledge, standing a little apart from the others. She was less than an Earth-standard year out of the Scholar Novitiate, and already she had witnessed more devastation than she had expected to see over the course of her lifetime. How much more suffering would she watch if she devoted her life to the Community?

A pressure against Sheera's fingers made her aware she and Steven were holding hands. She wasn't sure when or how that had happened, but she didn't pull away. They were violating the Precept, or coming close to it, in front of two senior Protectors, and she didn't care. She needed the touch of Steven's hand, wrapped around hers, packed with enormous power yet gripping her gently.

There was a way. A way she could make sure she would never again have to see death on such a scale. A way she could be with the man she loved.

She squeezed his hand until her knuckles ached. "What's the worst they can do to us for violating the Precept that keeps us apart? Expel us from the Community? So what? With my qualifications, some prestigious university will grant me a full scholarship to its pre-med program, and any planet's security force will be eager to take you on as an officer. Then we can be together."

Steven stared straight ahead at the wreckage of the avian village. "That sounds tempting, except for one thing. I don't want to join some planet's security force. See those Bird People down there? Humans did this to them. They'll need the help of humans if they're going to rebuild. Where's that help going to come from? If we Protectors don't pitch in, nobody else will. I figure, I'll have to get off probation and stick with the program if I'm going to do my part to repair the damage."

Their hands dropped to their sides.

EPILOGUE

"Each scholar shall complete a thesis on Protector lore before advancing from the status of novice to striker."
—Non-Canonical Precept, added after
the death of D.F. Nathaniel

Pitcairn was the only topic I ever considered for my advancement thesis. I learned, when I was nine years old, that members of my branch must research some aspect of Protector history before we can advance from novice to striker. I knew, from the first moment I heard about this project, that, when my turn came, I would write about the Massacre of the Winged Aliens.

My own role in the saga inspired me to record the events that eventually led to the showdown in the sky, beginning with the death of the Warlord. In selecting the incidents that seemed worth recounting, I included the time Steven saved my life by rescuing me from the slab that was crushing my body. I didn't relate this mishap out of any exaggerated sense of my own importance, but because I really did make a necessary contribution to Steven's and Sheera's adventure. Had it not been for my blunder, he would not have impressed the Guidance Committee with his heroism in saving me, it might not have cleared him for duty on an outlying world, and the events I've recounted might never have taken place.

Source material was easy to come by. I consulted the reports Taryn and Jan filed with Headquarters after the warship's crash. But mostly, I relied on face-to-face interviews.

Steven and Sheera

Steven and Sheera, who by lucky chance were conducting business on Merlin, granted me hours of time for interviews. They openly discussed secrets they had kept hidden until now, and gave me permission to reveal them. Examples? I was the first person they ever told about their kiss in the Pendragon garden, and about Steven's vision of D.F. Nathaniel in the alien prison. They weren't worried about the Guidance Committee taking action against them after the passage of so much time. As Steven put it to me: "My superiors won't care today about an apparition that hasn't bothered me since I was a striker. They'll care even less that, ten years ago, I kissed a girl I had no business kissing."

A month after the Massacre, the Guidance Committee lifted Steven's probation on the strength of his willingness to risk his life to preserve an alien species. He and Sheera made Pitcairn their home for the next two Earth-standard years, helping the avians rebuild their town. They carried out the rebuilding project without ever again setting foot inside the Valley of Winged Aliens, not so much for their own safety, as for the safety of the avians who would have attacked them. An attack would have forced Steven to retaliate in ways that would have set inter-species relations back even further. The Community of Protectors funneled supplies through a cadre of avians, brought together by Dr. Quixl. This group rejected the notion, common among its species, that all us humans deserve to be beheaded on sight.

After Steven and Sheera finished their project on Pitcairn, they moved on to studies and assignments on other worlds, never facing discipline over the Precept that forbids romantic entanglements between members of the opposite branches. Taryn never reported the hand-holding incident, so that, too, remained secret until now. It didn't rise to the level of a violation anyway, according to the Precept lawyers I consulted.

Sheera earned a medical degree with a concentration in Psychiatry four years ago. She oversees a staff of mental health workers at a facility on Mars, and frequently travels to Earth for mentoring by Doctor Aloysius at the London Hospital. She's given notice she'll resign from the Community of Protectors at the end of her current term. Her resignation would dissolve the prohibition that keeps her and Steven apart, but she refuses to say whether that has anything to do with her decision to exit the Community.

The Escape from the Valley

I concluded my history of the Massacre with the five expedition members trapped in the Valley, within reach of aliens who would gladly have killed them, with their flyer destroyed, and vast stretches of territory standing between them and the nearest civilization. Not an enviable position. The official reports don't explain how they got back, but Sheera answered that question during our interview. Quirip carried her to the human settlement under cover of night, dropped her off within walking distance of Fort Wilkerson, then flew away. That was the last time any human ever laid eyes on the alien once known as the harpy.

General Carstens received her into the fort, then ordered Army mechanics to make one of the surviving warships flight-worthy. She dispatched it on a rescue mission to the valley.

How I Traveled to and from Pitcairn

I toured Pitcairn for three weeks, conducting interviews and doing research. Today, as ten years ago, the best way for a traveler to get there is by means of a spacesuit launched through a dwarf portal into the planet's stellar system. After finishing my research, I departed the planet on a freighter that was orbiting the planet during the same weeks. The freighter carried me to the portal's edge, where it shot me out of Pitcairn's system in the same manner I came into it. Another ship scooped me from open space on the opposite side. Alas, in the decade since Pitcairn announced the end of its isolation, astro-physicists have yet to discover a nearby portal large enough for a ship to squeeze through. I doubt they are looking very hard, since Pitcairn doesn't have much to offer the rest of the Galaxy.

What Happened to the Others

I learned the fates of others, human and alien, who figured in the events leading to the Massacre. GENERAL HALFBALD perished in the crash of the warship, along with his entire crew of eleven.

The crash also killed thirty-seven avians, by the most reliable count. Some of the heroes who piled onto the warship survived the crash, but the number is unclear. DOCTOR QUIXL says the number of survivors will never be determined. He jokes (yes, his species has a sense of humor) that, if every avian who claims to have helped bring down the warship was really there, there must have been two or three warships instead of one. The best estimate is that survivors numbered more than ten and less than thirty.

I interviewed PATRICIA after I returned to Merlin, through a video link with Earth, where she attends a university. She doubts she will return to her home world when her studies are over, as there is nothing for her there.

JAN battles space pirates in a corner of the Galaxy where video links are unavailable, travel is dangerous, and my opportunity to interview her was zero.

TARYN welcomed me as her houseguest during my stay on Pitcairn. She plans to live on that planet for the rest of her natural life. After she escaped the Valley of Winged Aliens, she analyzed the serum in her laboratory. A few minor modifications altered the serum's molecular structure so that it could cure humans without poisoning them. The need for the Clinic evaporated, once her medicine reduced Helium Rejection Syndrome to the status of minor annoyance, about as troublesome as the common cold and more easily curable. She dissolved the Clinic for lack of patients.

After Taryn tamed the planet's most deadly disease, and finished her work rebuilding the avians' village, she turned her brilliant intellect to the task of investigating a puzzle of aerodynamics: how do the avians fly with bodies too bulky for their wings to lift? She found the answer in the overload of helium that lurks in the planet's atmosphere. The avians have hollow bones that absorb helium as they breathe. They float as much as they fly, using their wings more for propulsion than lift. The combination of muscular wings, low body weight, feeble gravity, and a lighter-than-air gas permeating their bones provides about ninety percent of the explanation for how they get off the ground. Taryn is still searching for the elusive other ten percent.

Her aerodynamics research isn't a full-time job. It's more of a hobby. The rest of the time, she and Doctor Quixl co-administer a school for teaching avians and humans to understand the language and culture of the other.

GENERAL CARSTENS seldom stoops to talk with civilians other than Taryn, but she agreed to let me interview her as a favor to the Protectors. She inherited the job of Presiding General, and immediately relaxed the restriction on traffic with the rest of the Galaxy. Her next act was to reverse Halfbald's decision to keep Pitcairn out of the Data Base of Worlds. Now.

anybody can log onto a computer and learn all about the planet. Unfortunately, hardly anybody wants to.

I wish I could report that a stream of commerce propelled Pitcairn into the modern age. Maybe some day. Pitcairn has little to offer merchants, and less to offer tourists. It's too far off the trade routes to serve as a way-station between Someplace and Anyplace Else. But seven intrepid freighters, at last count, have made the long journey across surface space and docked there. The fourth freighter of the seven, by coincidence, transported both Patricia and NURSE GRETCHEN away from the planet. The freighter docked at an artificial satellite in interstellar space, where Patricia transferred to a ship bound for Earth, and Gretchen's trail disappeared. Patricia says she and Gretchen had nothing to say to each other during the voyage.

MAJOR DAVIS is still in the Army, bumped up a rank to Colonel. He told me he'd like to soften the military dictatorship with a system that allows more citizen input, leading eventually to free elections. General Carstens so far refuses to budge in that direction. In her case, opposing genocide doesn't translate to supporting democracy.

The Future of Pitcairn

A shadow hangs over Pitcairn. What is to be done with the descendants of the Mutineers, and can they remain on the planet? The issue is in litigation before the Galactic Treaty Organization. At the pace justice crawls in the courts of the G.T.O., it will probably remain there for years to come.

Quirip

Many residents of Pitcairn claim to have spotted Quirip soaring across the horizon. Every sighting so far has been explainable as a different flying creature, an overactive imagination, or an outright hoax. A warrant for his arrest, issued by General Carstens, gives him a good reason for avoiding contact with humans. If Doctor Quixl knows where the so-called harpy hides (and I suspect he does), he isn't chirping.

My Greatest Disappointment

I failed to arrange a meeting with my childhood companion and partner in mischief, Bobbi. I haven't seen or spoken to her since her final day on Merlin, when she boarded the shuttle to Pendragon, leaving me to cope without her. The lifestyle of a ranger novice places limits on contact with outsiders during her final year, and Bobbi's superiors turned down my petition for an exemption.

Last month I used my dorm room computer to peek into her record. I learned she is nearing the end of her novice training, and will soon advance to striker.

I plan to pump drugs into my veins, brave Pendragon's crushing gravity, and pay a call on Bobbi once she can receive visitors. It's easier for a scholar to secure permission to visit Pendragon after reaching striker status, which I'll achieve as once this thesis is approved. She can't help me with the project any longer, because I intend to turn it in as soon as I finish writing this page, but that's all right. I just want to see her again. And I'm eager to see Pendragon up-close, instead of only as an orb floating in the night sky.

My friends tease me by insisting that I be careful about re-uniting with Bobbi. They point out that, if our bond remains as firm as it was when we were small, I'll place myself at risk of committing the same Precept violation that nearly destroyed the careers of Steven and Sheera. I'm not concerned. My discipline will give me the power to avoid that pitfall.

Why shouldn't my discipline be strong enough? I'm a Protector.

ACKNOWLEGMENTS

This novel was possible only with the help of others. I'm indebted to my daughter, Cheryl Mahoney, and my sister, Dolores Roche, for reading the entire book and making excellent suggestions. I also thank the members of my critique group, Gini Grossenbacher, Paula Zaby, Robert Pascholik, and Daniel Babka for looking at my work chapter by chapter and giving me their valued comments. I owe additional thanks to martial arts expert Lisa Deines for her advice on the fight sequences. Finally, I acknowledge all the members of the California Writers Club for their encouragement.

ABOUT THE AUTHOR

Dennis Mahoney grew up in northern California. He had no sooner learned to read that he became hooked on comic books that portrayed the universe, not as it was, but as it ought to be: a place where heroes flitted from planet to planet, encountering aliens with wondrous heads. He thought, I'm going to tell that kind of story. Later, he graduated from the University of California at Berkeley, and served aboard a destroyer in the U.S. Navy. After he finished his military service, he earned a law degree from the University of Santa Clara, and went on to be an environmental attorney. He never got cured of the story-telling bug, however, and this novel is the result. He lives in Sacramento, California, with his wife, Diane, and has one daughter, Cheryl.

www.ingramcontent.com/pod-product-compliance
Lightning Source LLC
Chambersburg PA
CBHW061541170626
46811CB00001B/40